The Princes

COLLECTION

January 2020
Finding Her Prince

February 2020
An Heir for the Prince

March 2020
Her Exotic Prince

April 2020
Working for the Prince

May 2020
Deceiving Her Prince

June 2020
Seducing Her Prince

Her Exotic Prince

LIZ FIELDING

RACHAEL THOMAS

TESSA RADLEY

MILLS & BOON

HER EXOTIC PRINCE © 2020 Harlequin Books S.A.

Her Desert Dream © 2009 Liz Fielding
The Sheikh's Last Mistress © 2016 Rachael Thomas
One Dance with the Sheikh © 2012 Harlequin Books S.A.

Special thanks and acknowledgement to Tessa Radley for her contribution to the *Dynasties: The Kincaids* series.

ISBN: 978-0-263-28101-9

MIX
Paper from
responsible sources
FSC® C007454
FSC
www.fsc.org

HER DESERT DREAM

LIZ FIELDING

CHAPTER ONE

LYDIA YOUNG was a fake from the tip of her shoes to the saucy froth of feathers on her hat but, as she held centre stage at a reception in a swanky London hotel, she had the satisfaction of knowing that she was the best there was.

Her suit, an interpretation of a designer original, had been run up at home by her mother, but her mother had once been a seamstress at a couturier house. And while her shoes, bag and wristwatch were knock-offs, they were the finest knock-offs that money could buy. The kind that only someone intimate with the real thing would clock without a very close look. But they were no more than the window dressing.

She'd once heard an actress describe how she built a character from the feet up and she had taken that lesson to heart.

Lydia had studied her character's walk, her gestures, a certain tilt of the head. She'd worked on the voice until it was her own and the world famous smile—a slightly toned down version of the mile-wide one that came as naturally as breathing—was, even if she said it herself, a work of art.

Her reward was that when she walked into a room full of people who knew that she was a lookalike, hired by the hour to lend glamour to the opening of a club or a restaurant or to appear at the launch of a new product, there was absolutely nothing in her appearance or manner to jar the fantasy and, as a result, she was treated with the same deference as the real thing.

She was smiling now as she mixed and mingled, posing for photographs with guests at a product launch being held at the kind of hotel that in her real life she would only glimpse from a passing bus.

Would the photographs be framed? she wondered. Placed on mantels, so that their neighbours, friends would believe that they'd actually met 'England's Sweetheart'?

Someone spoke to her and she offered her hand, the smile, asked all the right questions, chatting as naturally as if to the stately home born.

A dozen more handshakes, a few more photographs as the managing director of the company handed her a blush-pink rose that was as much a part of her character's image as the smile and then it was over. Time to go back to her real world. A hospital appointment for her mother, then an evening shift at the 24/7 supermarket where she might even be shelving the new brand of tea that was being launched today.

There was a certain irony in that, she thought as she approached the vast marble entrance lobby, heading for the cloakroom to transform herself back into plain Lydia Young for the bus ride home. Anticipating the head-turning ripple of awareness as she passed.

People had been turning to look, calling out 'Rose' to her in the street since she was a teen. The likeness had been striking, much more than the colour of her hair, the even features, vivid blue eyes that were eerily like those of the sixteen-year-old Lady Rose. And she had played up to it, copying her hairstyle, begging her mother to make her a copy of the little black velvet jacket Lady Rose had been wearing in the picture that had appeared on the front page of every newspaper the day after her sixteenth birthday. Copying her 'look', just as her mother's generation had slavishly followed another young princess.

Who wouldn't want to look like an icon?

A photograph taken by the local paper had brought her to the attention of the nation's biggest 'lookalike' agency and overnight being 'Lady Rose' had not only given her wheel-chair-bound mother a new focus in life as she'd studied the clothes, hunted down fabrics to reproduce them, but had provided extra money to pay the bills, pay for her driving lessons. She'd even saved up enough to start looking for a car so that she could take her mum further than the local shops.

Lost in the joy of that thought, Lydia was halfway across the marble entrance before she realised that no one was looking at her. That someone else was the centre of attention.

Her stride faltered as that 'someone' turned and she came face to face with herself. Or, more accurately, the self she was pretending to be.

Lady Roseanne Napier.

England's Sweetheart.

In person.

From the tip of her mouth-wateringly elegant hat, to the toes of her matching to-die-for shoes.

And Lydia, whose heart had joined her legs in refusing to move, could do nothing but pray for the floor to open up and swallow her.

The angel in charge of rescuing fools from moments of supreme embarrassment clearly had something more pressing to attend to. The marble remained solid and it was Lady Rose, the corner of her mouth lifting in a wry little smile, who saved the day.

'I know the face,' she said, extending her hand, 'but I'm afraid the name escapes me.'

'Lydia, madam, Lydia Young' she stuttered as she grasped it, more for support than to shake hands.

Should she curtsy? Women frequently forgot themselves sufficiently to curtsy to her but she wasn't sure her knees, once down, would ever make it back up again and the situation was quite bad enough without turning it into a farce.

Then, realising that she was still clutching the slender hand much too tightly, she let go, stammered out an apology.

'I'm s-so sorry. I promise this wasn't planned. I had no idea you'd be here.'

'Please, it's not a problem,' Lady Rose replied sympathetically, kindness itself as she paused long enough to exchange a few words, ask her what she was doing at the hotel, put her at her ease. Then, on the point of rejoining the man waiting for her at the door—the one the newspapers were saying Lady Rose would marry—she looked back. 'As a matter of interest, Lydia, how much do you charge for being me? Just in case I ever decided to take a day off?'

'No charge for you, Lady Rose. Just give me a call. Any time.'

'I don't suppose you fancy three hours of Wagner this evening?' she asked, but before Lydia could reply, she shook her head. 'Just kidding. I wouldn't wish that on you.'

The smile was in place, the voice light with laughter, but for a moment her eyes betrayed her and Lydia saw beyond the fabulous clothes, the pearl choker at her throat. Lady Rose, she realised, was a woman in trouble and, taking a card from the small clutch bag she was holding, she offered it to her.

'I meant what I said. Call me,' Lydia urged. 'Any time.'

Three weeks later, when she answered her cellphone, a voice she knew as well as her own said, 'Did you mean it?'

Kalil al-Zaki stared down into the bare winter garden of his country's London Embassy, watching the Ambassador's children racing around in the care of their nanny.

He was only a couple of years younger than his cousin. By the time a man was in his thirties he should have a family, sons...

'I know how busy you are, but it's just for a week, Kal.'

'I don't understand the problem,' he said, clamping down on the bitterness, the anger that with every passing day came closer to spilling over, and turned from the children to their mother, his cousin's lovely wife, Princess Lucy al-Khatib. 'Nothing is going to happen to Lady Rose at Bab el Sama.'

As it was the personal holiday complex of the Ramal

Hamrahn royal family, security would, he was certain, be state-of-the-art.

'Of course it isn't,' Lucy agreed, 'but her grandfather came to see me yesterday. Apparently there has been a threat against her.'

He frowned. 'A threat? What kind of threat?'

'He refused to go into specifics.'

'Well, that was helpful.' Then, 'So why did he come to you rather than Hanif?'

'I was the one who offered her the use of our Bab el Sama cottage whenever she needed to get away from it all.' She barely lifted her shoulders, but it was unmistakably a shrug. 'The Duke's line is that he doesn't want to alarm her.'

Line?

'He thought the simplest solution would be if I made some excuse and withdrew the invitation.'

The one thing that Kal could do was read women—with a mother, two stepmothers and more sisters than he could count, he'd had a lot of practise—and he recognised an *as if* shrug when he saw one.

'You believe he's making a fuss about nothing.'

'He lost his son and daughter-in-law in the most brutal manner and it's understandable that he's protective of his granddaughter. She wasn't even allowed to go to school...'

'Lucy!' he snapped. This all round the houses approach was unlike her. And why on earth she should think he'd want to babysit some spoiled celebrity 'princess', he couldn't imagine. But Lucy was not the enemy. On the contrary. 'I'm sorry.'

'I've no doubt there's been something,' she said, dismissing his apology with an elegant gesture. 'Everyone in the public eye gets their share of crank mail, but...' there it was, the *but* word '...I doubt it's more than some delusional creature getting hot under the collar over rumours that she's about to announce her engagement to Rupert Devenish.'

'You're suggesting that it's no more than a convenient excuse to apply pressure on you, keep her under the paternal eye?' He didn't believe it. The woman wasn't a child; she had to be in her mid-twenties.

'Maybe I'm being unjust.' She sighed. 'I might believe that the man is obsessively controlling, but I have no doubt that Rose is very precious to him.'

'And not just him.' He might suspect the public image of purity and goodness was no more than a well-managed PR exercise, but it was one the media were happy to buy into, at least until they had something more salacious to print on their front pages. 'You do realise that if anything were to happen to Lady Roseanne Napier while she's in Ramal Hamrah, the British press would be merciless?' And he would be the one held to blame.

'Meanwhile, they'll happily invade her privacy on a daily basis in the hope of getting intimate pictures of her for no better reason than to boost the circulation of their grubby little rags.'

'They can only take pictures of what she does,' he pointed out.

'So she does nothing.'

'Nothing?' He frowned. 'Really? She really is as pure, as angelic as the media would have us believe?'

'It's not something to be sneered at, Kalil.' Her turn to snap. 'She's been in the public eye since she was dubbed the "people's angel" on her sixteenth birthday. She hasn't been able to move a finger for the last ten years without someone taking a photograph of her.'

'Then she has my sympathy.'

'She doesn't need your sympathy, Kal. What she's desperate for is some privacy. Time on her own to sort out where she's going from here.'

'I thought you said she was getting married.'

'I said there were rumours to that effect, fuelled, I have no doubt, by the Duke,' she added, this time making no attempt to hide her disapproval. 'There comes a point at which a virginal image stops being charming, special and instead becomes the butt of cruel humour. Marriage, babies will keep the story moving forward and His Grace has lined up an Earl in waiting to fill this bill.'

'An arranged marriage?' It was his turn to shrug. 'Is that so bad?' In his experience, it beat the ramshackle alternative of love hands down. 'What does Hanif say?'

'In his opinion, if there had been a genuine threat the Duke would have made a formal approach through the Foreign Office instead of attempting to bully me into withdrawing my invitation.'

With considerably more success, Kal thought.

'Even so,' he replied, 'it might be wiser to do everyone a favour and tell Lady Rose that the roof has fallen in at your holiday cottage.'

'In other words, knuckle under, make life easy for ourselves? What about Rose? They give her no peace, Kal.'

'She's never appeared to want it,' he pointed out. Barely a week went by without her appearance on the front pages of the newspapers or some gossip magazine.

'Would it make any difference if she did?' She shook her head, not expecting an answer. 'Will you go with her, Kal? While I don't believe Rose is in any actual danger, I daren't risk leaving her without someone to watch her back and if I have to ask your uncle to detail an Emiri guard, she'll simply be exchanging one prison for another.'

'Prison?'

'What would you call it?' She reached out, took his hand. 'I'm desperately worried about her. On the surface she's so serene, but underneath there's a desperation...' She shook her head. 'Distract her, Kal. Amuse her, make her laugh.'

'Do you want me to protect her or make love to her?' he asked, with just the slightest edge to his voice. He'd done his best to live down the playboy image that clung to the al-Zaki name, but he would always be the grandson of an exiled playboy prince, the son of a man whose pursuit of beautiful women had kept the gossip writers happily in business for forty years.

Building an international company from the floor up, supporting Princess Lucy's charities, didn't make the kind of stories that sold newspapers.

'Consider this as a diplomatic mission, Kal,' Lucy replied enigmatically, 'and a diplomat is a man who manages to give everyone what they want while serving the needs of his own country. You do want to serve your country?' she asked.

They both knew that he had no country, but clearly Lucy saw this as a way to promote his cause. The restoration of his family to their rightful place. His marriage to the precious daughter of one of the great Ramal Hamrahn families. And, most important of all, to take his dying grandfather home. For that, he would play nursemaid to an entire truckload of aristocratic virgins.

'Princess,' he responded with the slightest bow, 'rest assured that I will do everything in my power to ensure that Lady Roseanne Napier enjoys her visit to Ramal Hamrah.'

'Thank you, Kal. I can now assure the Duke that, since the Emir's nephew is to take personal care of her security, he can have no worries about her safety.'

Kal shook his head, smiling despite himself. 'You won't, I imagine, be telling him which nephew?'

'Of course I'll tell him,' she replied. 'How else will he be able to thank your uncle for the service you have rendered him?'

'You think he'll be grateful?'

'Honestly? I think he'll be chewing rocks, but he's not about to insult the Emir of Ramal Hamrah by casting doubt on the character of one of his family. Even one whose grandfather tried to start a revolution.'

'And how do you suppose His Highness will react?'

'He will have no choice but to ask his wife to pay a courtesy visit on their distinguished visitor,' she replied. 'The opportunity to meet your aunt is the best I can do for you, Kal. The rest is up to you.'

'Lucy...' He was for a moment lost for words. 'How can I...'

She simply raised a finger to her lips, then said, 'Just take care of Rose for me.'

'How on earth did you swing a week off just before Christmas, Lydie?'

'Pure charm,' she replied, easing her shoulder as she handed over her checkout at the end of her shift. That and a cross-her-heart promise to the manager that she'd use the time to think seriously about the management course he'd been nagging her to take for what seemed like forever. He'd been totally supportive of her lookalike career, allowing her to be flexible in her shifts, but he wanted her to start thinking about the future, a real career.

'Well, remember us poor souls chained to the checkout listening to *Jingle Bells* for the umpteenth time, while you're lying in the sun, won't you?'

'You've got to be kidding,' she replied, with the grin of a woman with a week in the sun ahead of her.

And it was true; this was going to be an unbelievable experience. Rose had offered her the chance of a dream holiday in the desert. An entire week of undiluted luxury in which she was going to be wearing designer clothes—not copies run up by her mother—and treated like a real princess. Not some fake dressed up to look like one.

The euphoria lasted until she reached her car.

She'd told her colleagues at work that she'd been invited to spend a week at a friend's holiday apartment, which was near enough to the truth, but she hadn't told a soul where she was really going, not even her mother, and that had been hard.

Widowed in the same accident that had left her confined to

a wheelchair, Lydia's 'Lady Rose' gigs were the highlight of her mother's life and normally they shared all the planning, all the fun, and her mother's friends all joined vicariously in the excitement.

But this was different. This wasn't a public gig. The slightest hint of what she was doing would ruin everything for Rose. She knew that her mother wouldn't be able to resist sharing such an incredible secret with her best friend who'd be staying with her while she was away. She might as well have posted a bulletin on the wall of her Facebook page.

Instead, she'd casually mentioned a woman at work who was looking for a fourth person to share a last-minute apartment deal in Cyprus—which was true—and left it to her mother to urge her to grab it.

Which of course she had.

'Why don't you go, love?' she'd said, right on cue. 'All the hours you work, you deserve a break. Jennie will stop with me while you're away.'

That the two of them would have a great time together, gossiping non-stop, did nothing to make Lydia feel better about the deception.

Kal had been given less than twenty-four hours to make arrangements for his absence, pack and visit the clinic where his grandfather was clinging to life to renew the promise he'd made that he should die in the place he still called home.

Now, as he stood at the steps of the jet bearing the Emir's personal insignia, he wondered what His Highness's reaction had been when he'd learned who would be aboard it today.

It wasn't his first trip to the country that his great-grandfather had once ruled. Like his grandfather and his father, Kalil was forbidden from using his title, using the name Khatib, but, unlike the old man, he was not an exile.

He'd bought a waterfront apartment in the capital, Rumaillah. His aircraft flew a regular freight service into Ramal Hamrah, despite the fact that they remained stubbornly empty. No one would dare offend the Emir by using Kalzak Air Services and he made no effort to break the embargo. He did not advertise his services locally, or compete for business. He kept his rates equal to, but not better than his competitors. Took the loss.

This was not about profit but establishing his right to be there.

He'd been prepared to be patient, sit it out, however long it took, while he'd quietly worked on the restoration of his family home at Umm al Sama. But he'd continued to remain invisible to the ruling family, his family, a stranger in his own country, and patience was no longer an option. Time was running out for his grandfather and nothing mattered but bringing him home to die.

He'd do anything. Even babysit a wimp of a woman who wasn't, apparently, allowed to cross the road without someone holding her hand.

He identified himself to Security, then to the cabin crew, who were putting the final touches to the kind of luxury few airline passengers would ever encounter.

His welcome was reserved, but no one reeled back in horror.

A steward took his bag, introduced him to Atiya Bishara, who would be taking care of Lady Rose during the flight, then gave him a full tour of the aircraft so that he could check for himself that everything was in order.

He was treated no differently from any anonymous security officer who'd been asked to escort Lady Rose on a flight that, historically, should have been his grandfather's to command. Which said pretty much everything he needed to know about how the rest of the week was likely to pan out.

His aunt might pay a courtesy visit to Lady Rose, but even if she acknowledged his presence it would be as a servant.

Lydia rapidly exchanged clothes with Rose in the private room that had been set aside for her as guest of honour at the Pink Ribbon Lunch.

Lady Rose had walked into the room; ten minutes later Lydia, heart pounding, mouth dry, had walked out in her place.

She held her breath as a dark-suited security man fell in behind her.

Would he really be fooled? Rose had assured her that he would be looking everywhere but at her, but even wearing Rose's crushed raspberry silk suit, a saucy matching hat with a wispy veil and the late Duchess of Oldfield's famous pearl choker, it seemed impossible that he wouldn't notice the difference.

But there was no challenge.

Smile, she reminded herself as she approached the hotel manager who was waiting to escort her to the door. It was just another job. And, holding that thought, she offered the man her hand, thanked him for doing such a good job for the Pink Ribbon Club, before stepping outside into the thin winter sunshine.

Rose had warned her what to expect but, since rumours of a wedding had started to circulate, media interest had spiralled out of control. Nothing could have prepared her for the noise, the flashes from dozens of cameras. And it wasn't just the paparazzi lined up on the footpath. There were dozens of ordinary people hoping for a glance of the 'people's angel', all of them taking pictures, video, with their cellphones. People who thought she was the real thing, deserved the real thing, and she had to remind herself not just to smile, but to breathe.

It was the photographers who saved her, calling out, 'Lady Rose! This way, Lady Rose! Love the hat, Lady Rose!'

The eye-catching little hat had been made specially for the occasion. Fashioned from a stiffened loop of the same material as the suit, it had a dark pink net veil scattered with tiny velvet ribbon loops that skimmed her face, breaking up the outline, blurring any slight differences that might be picked out by an eagle-eyed picture editor.

Breathe, smile…

'How was lunch, Lady Rose?' one of the photographers called out.

She swallowed down the nervous lump in her throat and said, 'It was a wonderful lunch for a great cause.' Then, when there was still no challenge, no one pointed a finger, shouted, *Fake!*, she added, 'The Pink Ribbon Club.' And, growing in confidence, she lifted her right hand so that the diamond and amethyst ring on her right hand flashed in the sunlight as she pointedly touched the little ribbon-shaped hat. 'Don't forget to mention it.'

'Are you looking forward to your holiday, Lady Rose?'

Growing in confidence—it was true, apparently, that people saw only what they expected to see—she picked out the photographer who'd asked the question and smiled directly at him.

'Very much,' she said.

'Will you be on your own?' he dared.

'Only if you all take the week off, too,' she replied, raising a laugh. Yes! She could do this! And, turning her back on the photographers, she walked down the steps and crossed to the real people, just as she had seen Lady Rose do a hundred times on news clips. Had done herself at promotional gigs.

She took the flowers they handed her, stopped to answer questions—she could have entered *Mastermind* with Lady Rose as her specialist subject—paused for photographs, overwhelmed by the genuine warmth with which people reached out to her. To Rose…

'Madam…' The security officer touched his watch, indicating that it was time to leave.

She gave the crowd a final wave and smile and turned back to the limousine, stepped inside. The door closed behind her and, within moments, she was gliding through London behind a liveried chauffeur.

At which point she bit back a giggle.

This wasn't like any other job. No way. At this point, if it had been an ordinary job, she'd be heading for the hotel cloakroom for a quick change before catching the bendy bus back to work. Instead, she was in a top-of-the-range Mercedes,

heading for an airfield used by people for whom the private jet
was the only way to travel. The final hurdle before she could
relax and enjoy being Lady Rose without the risk of someone
taking a second look and challenging her.

It was a thought to bring the giggle under control. Not the
fear of being challenged. The thought of getting in a plane.

Kal paced the VIP lounge, certain that he was wasting his time.

Lucy was wrong. Playing nanny to a woman known to the
world as 'England's Sweetheart', or 'angel' or even *virgin*,
for heaven's sake, wasn't going to make him any friends in the
Ramal Hamrahn court. Unless there really was an attempt on
her life and he saved her. Maybe he should arrange one…

He stopped fantasising and checked the time.

Another minute and she'd be late. No more than he'd
expected. She was probably still posing for photographs, being
feted by her fans.

He'd seen her on the news—she was impossible to avoid—a
pale, spun-sugar confection, all sweetness and light. He knew she
was a friend of Lucy's but, really, could anyone be that perfect?

He was about to pick up a newspaper, settle down to wait,
when a stir at the entrance alerted him to her arrival. That she
had arrived exactly on schedule should have been a point in her
favour. It only served to irritate him further.

Lydia could not believe the ease with which she moved through
airport formalities but when you were an A-list VIP, related to
the Queen, even if it was goodness knew how many times
removed, it seemed that the ordinary rules did not apply. Forget
the usual hassle with the luggage trolley. She hadn't even seen
the bags that Rose had packed for this trip.

And no one was going to make her line up at a check-in
desk. Clearly, people who flew in their own private jets did not
expect to queue for *anything*.

She didn't have to take off her jacket and shoes, surrender

the handbag and briefcase she was carrying to be X-rayed.
Instead, she was nodded through the formalities and escorted
to the departure lounge by Lady Rose's security officer.

Rose had explained that he would see her to the aircraft and
after that she'd be on her own, free from all risk of discovery.
And once she was in Ramal Hamrah, ensconced in the luxury
of Princess Lucy's holiday cottage at Bab el Sama, all she had
to do was put in the occasional appearance in the garden or on
the beach to ensure that the paparazzi were able to snatch
pictures of her while she lived like a princess for a week.

It was like some dream-come-true fairy tale. Checkout girl
to princess. Pure Cinderella.

All she needed was a pair of glass slippers and a fairy godmother to provide her with someone tall, dark and handsome
to play Prince Charming.

She wouldn't even have to flee when the clock struck
twelve. She had a whole week before she turned back into
Lydia Young, whose job as supermarket checkout girl was occasionally enlivened by a lookalike gig.

She automatically reached for the door to the VIP departure
lounge, but it opened as she approached; a 'Lady' with a capital
L did not open doors for herself. She was so intent on covering
her mistake by adjusting the veil on her hat that she missed the
fact that her escort had stopped at the door.

'Mr al-Zaki will take care of you from here, madam.'

Who?

She thought the word, but never voiced it.

All sound seemed to fade away as she looked up. She was
tall, but the knee-meltingly gorgeous man waiting to 'take
care' of her was half a head taller and as his eyes, dark and
intense, locked with hers, she felt the jolt of it to her knees. And
yes, no doubt about it, her knees melted as he lowered his head
briefly, said, 'Kalil al-Zaki, Lady Rose,' introducing himself
with the utmost formality. 'Princess Lucy has asked me to
ensure that your holiday is all that you wish.'

Graceful, beautiful, contained power rippling beneath exquisite tailoring, he was, she thought crazily, the embodiment of Bagheera, the bold, reckless panther from her childhood favourite, *The Jungle Book*. She'd made her father read over and over the description of his coat like watered silk, his voice as soft as wild honey dripping from a tree.

Her own, as she struggled for a suitable response, was non-existent.

Kalil al-Zaki might favour well-cut British tailoring over a fancy Ruritanian uniform but he was as close to her own Prince Charming fantasy as she was ever likely to come and she had to resist the temptation to look around for the old lady with wings and a wand who'd been listening in on her thoughts.

CHAPTER TWO

'YOU'RE coming with me to Bab el Sama?' she managed finally, knowing that she should be horrified by this turn of events. The frisson of excitement rippling through her suggested that she was anything but.

'There and back,' he confirmed. 'My instructions are to keep you safe from harm. I have a letter of introduction from Princess Lucy, but the aircraft is waiting and the pilot will not wish to miss his slot. If you're ready to board?'

Lydia just about managed a nod and the noise flooded back like a shock wave as, his hand curling possessively around her elbow, he walked her to the door, across the tarmac towards the plane. Where she received shock number two.

When Rose had explained that she'd be flying in a private jet, Lydia had anticipated one of those small executive jobs. The reality was a full-sized passenger aircraft bearing the royal livery.

She'd fantasized about being treated like a princess, but this was the real deal; all that was missing was the red carpet and a guard of honour.

If they found out she was a fake they were not going to be amused and, as Kalil al-Zaki's touch sizzled through her sleeve, Lydia had to concentrate very hard on marshalling her knees and putting one foot in front of the other.

This was anything but a fairy tale and if she fell flat on her face there would be no fairy godmother to rescue her with the wave of a wand.

Concentrate, concentrate…

She'd already had an encounter with one of Rose's security guards. He hadn't looked at her the way that Kalil al-Zaki had looked and he certainly hadn't touched. The closest he'd been was when he'd opened the car door and his eyes had not been on her, but the crowd.

No matter what he said about 'keeping her safe', it was clear that this man was not your standard bodyguard, so who on earth was he?

Should she have recognised his name?

Think…

He'd mentioned Princess Lucy. So far, so clear. She was the friend who'd lent Rose her holiday 'cottage' for the week. The wife of the Emir's youngest son, who was the Ramal Hamrahn Ambassador to London.

Rose had filled her in on all the important background details, a little of their history, the names and ages of their children, so that she wouldn't make a mistake if any of the staff at Bab el Sama mentioned her or her children.

But that was it.

This was supposed to be no more than a walk-on role with only servants and the occasional telephoto lens for company.

A few minutes performing for a bunch of journalists, and getting away with it, had given her a terrific buzz, but playing the part convincingly under the eyes of someone like Kalil al-Zaki for an entire week was a whole different ball game.

Hopefully, the letter of introduction would fill in the details, she thought as his hand fell away at the top of the steps and she was greeted by the waiting stewardess.

'Welcome aboard the royal flight, Lady Rose. I am Atiya Bishara and I will be taking care of you today.' Then, looking at the flowers she was clutching like a lifeline, 'Shall I put those in water?'

Lydia, back on more or less familiar territory, began to breathe again. This was the basic lookalike stuff she'd been doing since she was fifteen years old and she managed to go through the standard 'How d'you do?' routine as she surrendered the flowers and the dark pink leather briefcase that exactly matched her hat. The one Rose had used to conceal the cash she'd needed for her week away and which now contained Lydia's own essentials, including her own passport in the event that anything went wrong.

'Your luggage has been taken to your suite, Lady Rose. I'll take you through as soon as we're in the air,' Atiya said as she led her to an armchair-sized seat.

A suite?

Not *that* familiar, she thought, taking out her cellphone and sending a one word message to Rose to let her know that she'd got through security without any hiccups. Apart from Kalil al-Zaki, that was, and Rose couldn't do anything about that.

That done, she turned off the phone and looked around.

From the outside, apart from the royal livery, the aircraft might look much like any other. On the inside, however, it bore no similarity to the crammed-tight budget airlines that were a necessary evil to be endured whenever she wanted a week or two in the sun.

'Would you like something to drink before we take off?' Atiya asked.

Uh-oh.

Take and *off*, used in tandem, were her two least favourite words in the English language. Until now her head had been too busy concentrating on the role she was playing, enjoying the luxury of a chauffeur-driven limousine, free-wheeling around the unexpected appearance of Kalil al-Zaki, to confront that particular problem.

'Juice? A glass of water?'

'Water, thank you,' she replied, forcing herself to concentrate, doing her best not to look at the man who'd taken the seat across the aisle.

And failing.

His suit lay across his broad shoulders as if moulded to him and his glossy black hair, brushed back off a high forehead curled over his collar, softening features that could have been chiselled from marble. Apart from his mouth.

Marble could never do justice to the sensuous droop of a lower lip that evoked such an immediate, such a disturbing response in parts of her anatomy that had been dormant for so long that she'd forgotten how it felt.

As if sensing her gaze, Kalil al-Zaki turned and she blushed at being caught staring.

Nothing in his face suggested he had noticed. Instead, as the plane began to taxi towards the runway, he took an envelope from the inside pocket of his jacket and offered it to her.

'My introduction from Princess Lucy, Lady Rose.'

She accepted the square cream envelope, warm from his body, and although she formed the words, *Thank you*, no sound emerged. Praying that the dark pink net of her veil would camouflage the heat that had flooded into her cheeks, she ducked her head. It was embarrassment, she told herself as she flipped open the envelope and took out the note it contained.

Dear Rose,
I didn't get a chance to call yesterday and explain that Han's cousin, Kalil al-Zaki, will be accompanying you to Bab el Sama.

I know that you are desperate to be on your own, but you will need someone to drive you, accompany you to the beach, be generally at your beck and call while you're in Bab el Sama and at least he won't report every move you make to your grandfather.

The alternative would be one of the Emir's guards, good men every one but, as you can imagine, not the most relaxing of companions.

Kal will not intrude if you decide to simply lie by the

pool with a book, but you shouldn't miss out on a visit to
the souk—it's an absolute treasure of gold, silks, spices—
or a drive into the desert. The peace is indescribable.

Do give me a call if there is anything you need or you
just need someone to talk to but, most of all rest, relax,
recharge the batteries and don't, whatever you do, give
Rupert a single thought.

All my love,
Lucy

Which crushed her last desperate hope that he was simply escorting her on the flight. 'There and back', apparently, included the seven days in between.

And things had been going so well up until now, she thought as the stewardess returned with her water and she gratefully gulped down a mouthful.

Too well.

Rose's grandfather had apparently accepted that taking her own security people with her would be seen as an insult to her hosts. The entire Ramal Hamrahn ruling family had holiday 'cottages' at Bab el Sama and the Emir did not, she'd pointed out, take the safety of his family or their guests lightly.

The paparazzi were going to have to work really hard to get their photographs this week, although she'd do her best to make it easy for them.

There had been speculation that Rupert would join Rose on this pre-Christmas break and if she wasn't visible they might just get suspicious, think they'd been given the slip. Raise a hue and cry that would get everyone in a stew and blow her cover.

Her commission was to give them something to point their lenses at so that the Duke was reassured that she was safe and the world could see that she was where she was supposed to be.

Neither of them had bargained on her friend complicating matters.

Fortunately, Princess Lucy's note had made it clear that Rose hadn't met Kalil al-Zaki, which simplified things a little. The only question left was, faced with an unexpected—and unwanted—companion, what would Rose do now?

Actually, not something to unduly tax the mind. Rose would do what she always did. She'd smile, be charming, no matter what spanner had been thrown into her carefully arranged works.

Until now, protected by the aura of untouchability that seemed to encompass the Lady Rose image, Lydia had never had a problem doing the same.

But then spanners didn't usually come blessed with smooth olive skin moulded over bone structure that had been a gift from the gene fairies.

It should have made it easier to respond to his smile—if only with an idiotic, puppy-like grin. The reality was that she had to concentrate very hard to keep the drool in check, her hand from visibly trembling, her brain from turning to jelly. Speaking at the same time was asking rather a lot, but it certainly helped take her mind off the fact that the aircraft was taxiing slowly to the runway in preparation for the nasty business of launching her into thin air. She normally took something to calm her nerves before holiday flights but hadn't dared risk it today.

Fortunately, ten years of 'being' Lady Rose came to her rescue. The moves were so ingrained that they had become automatic and instinct kicked in and overrode the urge to leap into his lap and lick his face.

'It would seem that you've drawn the short straw, Mr al-Zaki,' she said, kicking the 'puppy' into touch and belatedly extending her hand across the aisle.

'The short straw?' he asked, taking it in his own firm grip with just the smallest hint of a frown.

'I imagine you have a dozen better things to do than…' she raised the letter an inch or two '…show me the sights.'

'On the contrary, madam,' he replied formally, 'I can assure you that I had to fight off the competition.'

He was so serious that for a moment he had her fooled. Unbelievable!

The man was flirting with her, or, rather, flirting with Lady Rose. What a nerve!

'It must have been a very gentlemanly affair,' she replied, matching his gravity, his formality.

One of his dark brows lifted the merest fraction and an entire squadron of butterflies took flight in her stomach. He was good. Really good. But any girl who'd worked for as long as she had on a supermarket checkout had not only heard it all, but had an arsenal of responses to put even the smoothest of operators in their place.

'No black eyes?' she prompted. 'No broken limbs?'

He wasn't quite quick enough to kill the surprise at the swiftness of her comeback and for a moment she thought she'd gone too far. He was the Ambassador's cousin, after all. One of the ruling class in a society where women were supposed to be neither seen nor heard.

Like that was going to happen…

But then the creases deepened in his cheeks, his mouth widened in a smile and something happened to the darkest, most intense eyes she'd ever seen. Almost, she thought, as if someone had lit a fire in their depths.

'I was the winner, madam,' he reminded her.

'I'm delighted you think so,' she replied, hanging on to her cool by the merest thread, despite the conflagration that threatened to ignite somewhere below her midriff.

There had never been anyone remotely like this standing at her supermarket checkout. She was going to have to be very, very careful.

Kal just about managed to bite back a laugh.

Lucy—with Hanif's unspoken blessing, he had no doubt—was placing him in front of the Emir, forcing his uncle to take note of his existence, acknowledge that he was doing something for his country. Offering him a chance to show himself to be someone worthy of trust, a credit to the name he was forbidden from using. And already he was flirting with the woman who had been entrusted to his care.

But then she wasn't the least bit what he'd expected.

He had seen a hundred photographs of Lady Rose on magazine covers and nothing in those images had enticed him to use her friendship with Princess Lucy to attempt a closer acquaintance.

The iconic blue eyes set in an oval face, yards of palest blonde hair, the slender figure were, no doubt, perfect. If you liked that kind of look, colouring, but she'd lacked the dark fire, a suggestion of dangerous passion, of mystery that he looked for in a woman.

The reality, he discovered, was something else.

As she'd walked into the VIP lounge it had seemed to come to life; as if, on a dull day, the sun had emerged from behind a cloud.

What he'd thought of as pallor was, in fact, light. A golden glow.

She was a lot more than a colourless clothes horse.

The famous eyes, secreted behind the wisp of veil that covered the upper half of her face, sparkled with an excitement, a vitality that didn't come through in any photograph he'd seen. But it was the impact of her unexpectedly full and enticingly kissable mouth, dark, sweet and luscious as the heart of a ripe fig, that grabbed and held his complete attention and had every red blood cell in his body bounding forward to take a closer look.

For the briefest moment her poise had wavered and she'd appeared as nonplussed as he was, but for a very different reason. It was obvious that Lucy hadn't managed to warn her that she was going to have company on this trip. She'd swiftly gathered herself, however, and he discovered that, along with all her other assets, she had a dry sense of humour.

Unexpected, it had slipped beneath his guard, and all his good intentions—to keep his distance, retain the necessary formality—had flown right out of the window.

And her cool response, 'I'm delighted you think so,' had

been so ambiguous that he hadn't the least idea whether she was amused by his familiarity or annoyed.

His life had involved one long succession of his father's wives and mistresses, a galaxy of sisters who ranged from nearly his own age to little girls. Without exception they were all, by turn, tempestuous, sphinxlike, teasing. He'd seen them in all their moods and it had been a very long time since he hadn't known exactly what a woman was thinking.

Now, while the only thought in his own head should be *danger, out of bounds,* what he really wanted was for her to lift that seductive little veil and, with that lovely mouth, invite him to be really bad…

Realising that he was still holding her hand, he made a determined effort to get a grip. 'You are as astute as you are lovely, madam,' he replied, matching her own cool formality, as he released it. 'I will be more circumspect in future.'

Her smile was a private thing. Not a muscle moved, only something in her eyes altered so subtly that he could not have described what happened. He'd felt rather than seen a change and yet he knew, deep down, that she was amused.

'Rose,' she said.

'I beg your pardon, madam?'

'According to her letter, Lucy thought you would make a more relaxing companion than one of the Emiri guard.'

'You have my word that I won't leap to attention whenever you speak to me,' he assured her.

'That is a relief, Mr al-Zaki.'

Lydia had to work a lot harder than usual to maintain the necessary regal poise.

She had no way of knowing on what scale Princess Lucy measured 'relaxing' but she must lead a very exciting life if spending time with Kalil al-Zaki fell into that category.

With his hot eyes turning her bones to putty, heating her skin from the inside out, *relaxed* was the last word she'd use to describe the way she was feeling right now.

'However, I don't find the prospect of an entire week being "madamed" much fun either. My name is…' she began confidently enough, but suddenly faltered. It was one thing acting out a role, it was quite another to look this man in the eye, meet his dark gaze and utter the lie. She didn't want to lie to him, to pretend… 'I would rather you called me Rose.'

'Rose,' he repeated softly. Wild honey…

'Can you manage your seat belt, Lady Rose?' the stewardess asked as she retrieved the glass. 'We're about to take off.'

'Oh…' Those words again. 'Yes, of course.'

She finally managed to tear her gaze away from her companion—wild honey was a dangerous temptation that could not be tasted without getting stung—and cast about her for the straps.

'Can I assist you, Rose?' he asked as her shaking hands fumbled with the buckle.

'No!' She shook her head as she finally managed to clip it into place. 'Thank you, Mr…'

'Kal,' he prompted. 'Most people call me Kal.' The lines bracketing his mouth deepened into a slow, sexy smile. 'When they're being relaxed,' he added.

She just about managed to stifle a hysterical giggle. She hadn't hesitated because she'd forgotten his name. He'd made an indelible impression…

No.

She'd been so busy worrying about whether he knew Rose personally, countering the effect of that seductive voice, that she'd overlooked the really important part of Princess Lucy's letter. The bit where she'd mentioned that Kalil al-Zaki was her husband's cousin. As she'd said the word 'Mr' it had suddenly occurred to her who he really was. Not just some minor diplomat who'd been given the task of ensuring a tricky visitor didn't get into trouble while she was at Bab el Sama.

Oh, dear me, no.

That wouldn't do for Lady Rose. Cousin of the Queen,

patron of dozens of charities as well as figurehead of the one
founded by her parents, she was an international figure and she
was being given the full red-carpet treatment. Right down to
her watchdog.

Kalil al-Zaki, the man who'd been roped in to guard their
precious guest, was the cousin of the Ambassador, Sheikh
Hanif al-Khatib. Which made him a nephew of the Emir
himself.

'Kal,' she squeaked, slamming her eyes closed and gripping
the arms of the chair as the plane rocketed down the runway
and the acceleration forced her back into the chair, for once in
her life grateful that she had her fear of take-off to distract her.

She was fine once she was in the air, flying straight and level
above the clouds with no horizon to remind her that she was
thirty thousand feet above the ground. Not that much different
from travelling on a bus, apart from the fact that you didn't have
to keep stopping so that people could get on and off.

Until now, what with one thing and another, she'd been
doing a better than average job of not thinking about this
moment, but not even the sudden realisation that Kalil al-Zaki
wasn't plain old *mister* anyone, but *Sheikh* Kalil al-Zaki, a
genuine, bona fide prince, could override her terror.

She'd have plenty of time to worry about how 'charming'
he'd prove to be if he discovered that she was a fake when they
were safely airborne.

But just when she'd reached the point where she forgot how
to breathe, long fingers closed reassuringly over hers and, surprised into sucking in air, she gasped and opened her eyes.

'I'm sorry,' Kal said as she turned to stare at him, 'but I've
never liked that bit much.'

What?

His expression was so grave that, for just a moment, she
wasn't sure whether or not he was serious. Then she swallowed.

Idiot.

Of course he wasn't serious. He was just being kind and, for once in her life, she wished she really was Lady Rose. Because then he'd be looking at her like that…

'You'll be all right now?' she managed, still breathless when, minutes later, the seat belt light pinged out. Doing her best to respond in kind, despite the fact that it was his steadying hand wrapped around hers. That she was the one who'd experienced a severe case of collywobbles. Wobbles that were still rippling through her, despite the fact that they had left the earth far beneath them.

'I believe so,' he replied gravely, but in no rush to break contact.

It was perhaps just as well that Atiya reappeared at that moment or they might have flown all the way to Ramal Hamrah with their hands intertwined.

Not that there would have been anything wrong with that…

'Shall I show you to your suite so that you can change before I serve afternoon tea, Lady Rose?'

'Thank you,' she said, using her traitorous hand to pull free the seat belt fastening so that she could follow Atiya. Straighten out her head.

Not easy when she discovered that the sumptuously fitted suite contained not only a bed, but its own bathroom with a shower that lent a whole new meaning to the words 'freshen up'.

'Would you like help changing?' Atiya offered, but Lydia assured her that she could manage and, once on her own, leaned back against the door, rubbing her palm over the hand Kal al-Zaki had held. Breathing slowly until her heart rate returned to normal. Or as near to normal as it was likely to be for the next week.

Kal watched Rose walk away from him.

His grandfather, a man who'd lost a throne, lost his country—but not the fortune that his father had hoped would compensate him for choosing his younger brother to succeed him—was a man without any purpose but to enjoy himself.

He'd become part of the jetset, a connoisseur of all things beautiful, including women.

Kalil's father had, as soon as he was old enough, taken the same path and Kalil too had come dangerously close to following in their footsteps.

His boyhood winters had been spent on the ski slopes of Gstaad and Aspen, his summers shared between an Italian palazzo and a villa in the South of France. He'd gone to school in England, university in Paris and Oxford, post-grad in America.

He had been brought up in an atmosphere of wealth and privilege, where nothing had been denied him. The female body held no mystery for him and hers, by his exacting standards, was too thin for true beauty.

So why did he find her finely boned ankles so enticing? What was it about the gentle sway of her hips that made his hand itch to reach out and trace the elegant curve from waist to knee? To undress her, slowly expose each inch of that almost translucent peaches and cream skin and then possess it.

Possess her.

'Can I fetch you anything, sir?' the stewardess asked as she returned.

Iced water. A cold shower…

He left it at the water but she returned empty-handed. 'Captain Jacobs sends his compliments and asked if you'd like to visit the flight deck, sir. I'll serve your water there,' she added, taking his acceptance for granted.

It was the very last thing he wanted to do, but it was a courtesy he could not refuse. And common sense told him that putting a little distance between himself and Rose while he cooled off would be wise.

He'd reached out instinctively when he'd seen her stiffen in fear as the plane had accelerated down the runway. It had been a mistake. Sitting beside her had been a mistake. His brief was to ensure her security and, despite Lucy's appeal to amuse her, distract her, make her laugh, that was it.

Holding her hand to distract her when she was rigid with fear didn't count, he told himself, but sitting here, waiting to see if he'd imagined his gut-deep reaction to her was not a good idea.

Especially when he already knew the answer.

Then the name registered. 'Jacobs? Would that be Mike Jacobs?'

'You are in so much trouble, Lydia Young.'

She hadn't underestimated the enormity of what she'd undertaken to do for Rose and they'd gone through every possible scenario, using a chat room to brainstorm any and all likely problems.

And every step of the way Rose had given her the opportunity to change her mind. Back out. Unfortunately, she was long past the *stop the plane, I want to get off* moment.

It had been too late from the moment she'd stepped out of that hotel room wearing Lady Rose's designer suit, her Jimmy Choos, the toes stuffed with tissue to stop them slipping.

Not that she would if she could, she realised.

She'd had ten years in which being 'Lady Rose' had provided all the little extras that helped make her mother's life easier. She *owed* Rose this. Was totally committed to seeing it through, but falling in lust at first sight with a man who had flirtation down to an art was, for sure, not going to make it any easier to ignore what Kalil al-Zaki's eyes, mouth, touch were doing to her.

'Come on, Lydie,' she said, giving herself a mental shake. 'You don't do this. You're immune, remember?'

Not since she'd got her fingers, and very nearly everything else, burnt by a stunningly good-looking actor who'd been paid to woo her into bed. She swallowed. She'd thought he was her Prince Charming, too.

It had been five years, but she still felt a cold shiver whenever she thought about it.

Pictures of the virginal 'Lady Rose' in bed with a man would have made millions for the people who'd set her up. Everyone would have run the pictures, whether they'd believed them or not. Covering themselves by the simple addition of a question mark to the 'Lady Rose in Sex Romp?' headline. The mere suggestion would have been enough to have people stampeding to the newsagents.

She, on the other hand, would have been ruined. No one would have believed she was an innocent dupe. If it had been anyone else, she wouldn't have believed it either.

She looked at the bed with longing, sorely tempted to just crawl beneath the covers and sleep away the next eight hours. No one would disturb her, expect anything from her.

But, since sleeping away the entire seven days was out of the question, she needed to snap out of it.

She'd been knocked off her feet by the heightened tension, that was all. Unsurprising under the circumstances. Anyone would be unsettled. Kal al-Zaki's presence had been unexpected, that was all. And she turned to the toilet case and overnight bag that had been placed on a stand.

The first was packed with everything a woman could ever need. The finest hairbrush that money could buy, the best skin care products, cosmetics, a selection of sumptuous scents; a perfect distraction for out of control hormones.

She opened one, sighed as she breathed in a subtle blend of sweet summer scents, then, as she sprayed it on her wrist, she caught an underlying note of something darker that tugged at forbidden desires. That echoed the heat in Kal al-Zaki's eyes.

Dropping it as if burned, she turned to the overnight bag. On the top, in suede drawstring bags, were the cases for the jewellery she was wearing, along with a selection of simpler pieces that Lady Rose wore while 'off duty'.

There was also a change of clothes for the long flight. A fine silk shirt the colour of champagne, wide-cut trousers in dark brown linen, a cashmere cardigan and a pair of butter-soft leather loafers in the right size. Supremely elegant but all wonderfully comfortable.

Rose had also packed a selection of the latest hardback bestsellers to while away the long flight. But then she hadn't expected that her stand-in would be provided with company.

Or not. According to Princess Lucy, it was up to her.

While she'd urged Rose to allow him to show her the sights, she'd made it clear that if she preferred to be alone then Kal would not intrude.

Not intrude?

What had the woman been *thinking*?

Hadn't she looked at him?

Anyone with half a brain could see that he wouldn't have to do a damn thing. One smile, one touch of his hand and he was already indelibly imprinted on her brain. In her head for ever more.

Intrusion squared.

In fact, if she didn't know better, she might be tempted to think that the Princess had planned a holiday romance as a little treat for her friend.

The idea was, of course, patently absurd.

Not that she didn't deserve a romance. A dark-eyed prince with a killer smile who'd sweep her off her feet.

No one deserved a little fun more than Rose, but anyone who knew her would understand just how impossible a casual, throwaway romance would be for her. And that was the essence of a holiday romance. Casual. Something out of time that had nothing to do with real life. That you left behind when you went home.

Anyone who truly cared for her would understand that.

Wouldn't they?

About to remove the pin that fastened the tiny hat to her chignon, she paused, sank onto the edge of the bed as a phrase in Lucy's letter came back to her.

Don't give Rupert a single thought...

She and Lucy were in total agreement on that one. Rose's

grandfather, the newspapers, even the masses out there who thought they knew her, might be clamouring for an engagement, but she'd seen the two of them together. There was absolutely no chemistry, no connection.

Rose had made a joke about it, but Lydia hadn't been fooled for a second. She'd seen the desperation in her face and anyone who truly cared for her would want to save her from sleepwalking into such a marriage simply because it suited so many people.

Could Princess Lucy have hoped that if she put Rose and Kalil together the sparks would fly of their own accord without any need to stoke the fire? No doubt about it, a week being flirted with by Kal al-Zaki would have been just the thing to bring the colour back into Rose's cheeks.

Or was it all less complicated than that?

Was Lucy simply relying on the ever-attendant paparazzi, seeing two young people alone in a perfect setting, to put one and one together and make it into a front page story that would make them a fortune?

Who cared whether it was true?

Excellent plan, Lucy, she thought, warming to the woman despite the problems she'd caused.

There was only one thing wrong with it. Lady Rose had taken matters into her own hands and was, even now—in borrowed clothes, a borrowed car—embarking on an adventure of her own, safe in the knowledge that no one realised she'd escaped. That she could do what she liked while the world watched her lookalike.

Of course there was nothing to stop her from making it happen, she thought as she finally removed the hat and jewellery she was wearing. Kicked off her shoes and slipped out of the suit.

All it would take would be a look. A touch. He wasn't averse to touching.

She began to pull pins from her hair, absently divesting herself of the Lady Rose persona, just as she did at the end of every gig.

And she wouldn't be the victim this time. She would be the one in control, watching as the biter was, for once, bit.

Then, as her hair tumbled down, bringing her out of a reverie in which Kal touched her hand, then her face, her neck, his lips following a trail blazed by his fingers she let slip a word that Rose had probably never heard, let alone used.

It had taken an age to put her hair up like that and, unlike Rose, she didn't have a maid to help.

Just what she deserved for letting her fantasy run away with her. There was no way she was going to do anything that would embarrass Rose. Her part was written and she'd stick to it.

She began to gather the pins, but then realised that just because Rose never appeared in photographs other than with her hair up, it didn't mean that when she shut the door on the world at the end of the day—or embarked on an eight-hour flight—she'd wouldn't wear it loose.

She was, after all, supposed to be on holiday. And who, after all, knew what she did, said, wore, when she was behind closed doors?

Not Kalil al-Zaki, that was for sure.

And that was the answer to the 'keeping up appearances' problem, she realised.

Instead of trying to remember that she was Lady Rose for the next seven days, she would just be herself. She'd already made a pretty good start with the kind of lippy responses that regulars on her checkout at the supermarket would recognise.

And being herself would help with the 'lust' problem, too.

For as long as she could remember, she'd been fending off the advances of first boys, then men who, when they looked at her, had seen only the 'virgin' princess and wanted to either worship or ravish her.

It had taken her a little while to work that one out but, once she had, she'd had no trouble keeping them at arm's length, apart from the near miss with the actor, but then he'd been paid to be convincing. And patient. It was a pity he'd only, in the end, had an audience of one because he'd put in an Oscar-winning performance.

Kal, despite the way he looked, was just another man flirting with Lady Rose. That was all she had to remember, she told herself as she shook out her hair, brushed it, before she freshened up and put on the clothes Rose had chosen for her.

So which would he be? Worshipper or ravisher?

Good question, she thought as she added a simple gold chain and stud earrings before checking her reflection in a full length mirror.

It wasn't quite her—she tended to favour jeans and funky tops. It wasn't quite Lady Rose either, but it was close enough for someone who'd never met either of them, she decided as she chose a book, faced the door and took a slow, calming breath before returning to the main cabin.

In her absence the seats had been turned around, the cabin reconfigured so that it now resembled a comfortable sitting room.

An empty sitting room.

CHAPTER THREE

HAVING screwed herself up to be 'relaxed', the empty cabin was something of a let-down, but a table had been laid with a lace cloth and, no sooner than she'd settled herself and opened her book, Atiya arrived to serve afternoon tea.

Finger sandwiches, warm scones, clotted cream, tiny cakes and tea served from a heavy silver pot.

'Is all this just for me?' she asked when she poured only one cup and Kal had still not reappeared.

She hadn't wanted his company, but now he'd disappeared she felt affronted on Lady Rose's behalf. He was supposed to be here, keeping her safe from harm.

'Captain Jacobs invited Mr al-Zaki to visit the crew on the flight deck,' Atiya said. 'Apparently they did their basic training together.'

'Training?' It took her a moment. 'He's a *pilot*?'

Okay. She hadn't for a minute believed that he was bothered by the take-off, but she hadn't seen *that* coming. A suitable career for a nephew of an Emir wasn't a subject that had ever crossed her mind, but working as a commercial airline pilot wouldn't have been on her list even if she had. Maybe it had been military training.

A stint in one of the military academies favoured by royals would fit.

'Shall I ask him to rejoin you?' Atiya asked.

'No,' she said quickly. She had wanted him to keep his distance and her fairy godmother was, apparently, still on the case. 'I won't spoil his fun.'

Besides, if he returned she'd have to share this scrumptious spread.

Too nervous to eat lunch, and with the terrifying take-off well behind her, she was suddenly ravenous and the temptation to scoff the lot was almost overwhelming. Instead, since overindulgence would involve sweating it all off later, she managed to restrain herself, act like the lady she was supposed to be and simply tasted a little of everything to show her appreciation, concentrating on each stunning mouthful so that it felt as if she was eating far more, before settling down with her book.

Kal paused at the door to the saloon.

Rose, her hair a pale gold shimmer that she'd let down to hang over her shoulder, feet tucked up beneath her, absorbed in a book, was so far removed from her iconic image that she looked like a completely different woman.

Softer. The girl next door rather than a princess, because that was what she'd be if she'd been born into his culture.

Was the effect diminished?

Not one bit. It just came at him from a different direction. Now she looked not only luscious but available.

Double trouble.

As he settled in the chair opposite her she raised her eyes from her book, regarding him from beneath long lashes.

'Did you enjoy your visit to the cockpit?'

An almost imperceptible edge to her voice belied the softer look.

'It was most informative. Thank you,' he responded, equally cool. A little chill was just the thing to douse the heat generated by that mouth. Maybe.

'Did your old friend offer you the controls?' she added, as if reading his mind, and suddenly it all became clear. It wasn't the fact that he'd left her side without permission that bothered her.

The stewardess must have told her that he was a pilot and she thought he'd been laughing at her fear of flying.

'I hoped you wouldn't notice that little bump back there,' he said, offering her the chance to laugh right back at him.

There was a flicker of something deep in her eyes and the suspicion of an appreciative dimple appeared just above the left hand corner of her mouth.

'That was you? I thought it was turbulence.'

'Did you?' She was lying outrageously—the flight had been rock steady since they'd reached cruising altitude—but he was enjoying her teasing too much to be offended. 'It's been a while since I've flown anything this big. I'm a little rusty.'

She was struggling not to laugh now. 'It's not something you do seriously, then?'

'No one in my family does anything seriously.' It was the standard response, the one that journalists expected, and if it didn't apply to him, who actually cared? But, seeing a frown buckle the smooth, wide space between her eyes, the question that was forming, he cut her short with, 'My father bought himself a plane,' he said. 'I wanted to be able to fly it so I took lessons.'

'Oh.' The frown remained. 'But you said "this big",' she said, with a gesture that indicated the aircraft around them.

'You start small,' he confirmed. 'It's addictive, though. You keep wanting more.'

'But you've managed to break the habit.'

'Not entirely. Maybe you'd like a tour of the flight deck?' he asked. She clearly had no idea who he was and that suited him. If she discovered that he was the CEO of a major corporation she'd want to know what he was doing playing bodyguard. 'It sometimes helps ease the fear if you understand exactly what's happening. How things work.'

She shook her head. 'Thanks, but I'll pass.' Then, perhaps thinking she'd been less than gracious, she said, 'I do understand that my fear is totally irrational. If I didn't, I'd never get on one of these things.' Her smile was self-deprecating. 'But while, for the convenience of air travel, I can steel myself to suffer thirty seconds or so of blind panic, I also know that taking a pilot's eye view, seeing for myself exactly how much nothing there is out there, will only make things worse.'

'It's really just the take-off that bothers you?' he asked.

'So far,' she warned. 'But any attempt to analyse my fear is likely to give me ideas. And, before you say it, I know that flying is safer than crossing the road. That I've more chance of being hurt going to work—' She caught herself, for a fraction of second floundered. 'So I've heard,' she added quickly, as if he might dispute that what she did involved effort.

While opening the new wing of a hospital, attending charity lunches, appearing at the occasional gala might seem like a fairy tale existence to the outsider, he'd seen the effort Lucy put into her own charity and knew the appearance of effortless grace was all illusion.

But there was something about the way she'd stopped herself from saying more that suggested... He didn't know what it suggested.

'You've done your research.'

'No need. People will insist on telling you these things,' she said pointedly.

Signalling that the exchange was, as far as she was concerned, at an end, she returned to her book.

'There's just one more thing...'

She lifted her head, waited.

'I'm sure that Lucy explained that once we arrive in Ramal Hamrah we'll be travelling on to Bab el Sama by helicopter but—'

'Helicopter?'

The word came out as little more than a squeak.

'—but if it's going to be a problem, I could organise alternative transport,' he finished.

Lydia had been doing a pretty good job of keeping her cool, all things considered. She'd kept her head down, her nose firmly in her book even when Kal had settled himself opposite her. Stretched out those long, long legs. Crossed his ankles.

He'd removed his jacket, loosened his tie, undone the top button of his shirt.

What was it about a man's throat that was so enticing? she wondered. Invited touch…

She swallowed.

This was so not like her. She could flirt with the best, but that was no more than a verbal game that she could control. It was easy when only the brain was engaged…

Concentrate!

Stick to the plan. Speak when spoken to, keep the answers brief, don't let slip giveaways like 'going to work', for heaven's sake!

She'd managed to cover it but, unless she kept a firm rein on her tongue, sooner or later she'd say something that couldn't be explained away.

Lady Rose was charming but reserved, she reminded herself.

Reserved.

She made a mental note of the word, underlined it for emphasis.

It was too late to recall the 'helicopter' squeak, however, and she experienced a hollow feeling that had nothing to do with hunger as Kal, suddenly thoughtful, said, 'You've never flown in one?'

She had never been in a helicopter, but it was perfectly possible that Lady Rose hopped about all over the place in one in order to fulfil her many engagements. Quite possibly with her good friend Princess Lucy.

She hadn't thought to ask. Why would she?

After what seemed like an eternity, when she was sure Kal was going to ask her what she'd done with the real Lady Rose, he said, 'So?'

'So?' she repeated hoarsely.

'Which is it to be?'

'Oh.' He was simply waiting for her to choose between an air-conditioned ride in leather-upholstered comfort, or a flight in a noisy machine that didn't even have proper wings. Her well-honed instinct for self-preservation was demanding she go for the four-wheeled comfort option.

Her mouth, taking no notice, said, 'I can live with the helicopter.'

And was rewarded with another of those smiles that bracketed his mouth, fanned around his eyes, as if he knew just how much it had cost her.

'It's certainly simpler,' he said, 'but if I get scared you will hold my hand, won't you?'

Lydia, jolted out of her determined reserve by his charm, laughed out loud. Then, when he didn't join in, she had the weirdest feeling that their entire conversation had been leading up to that question and it was her breath that momentarily caught in her throat.

'I don't believe you're scared of anything,' she said.

'Everyone is scared of something, Rose,' he said enigmatically as he stood up. 'I'll leave you to enjoy your book. If you need me for anything I'll be in the office.'

Showers, bedrooms, now an office…

'Please, don't let me keep you from your work,' she said.

'Work?'

He said the word lightly, as if it was something he'd never thought of, but a shadow, so brief that she might have missed it had she not been so intent on reading his thoughts, crossed his face and she felt horribly guilty at her lack of gratitude. No matter how inconvenient, this man, purely as a favour, had given up his own time to ensure she had the perfect holiday.

Or was he recalling her earlier slip?

'For the next seven days you are my first concern,' he assured her. 'I'm simply going to check the weather report.'

Whew…

His first concern.

Wow…

But then he thought that she was the real thing. And when he turned those midnight-dark eyes on her she so wanted to be real. Not pretending. Just for a week, she thought, as she watched him stride away across the cabin on long, long legs.

No, no, no!

This was no time to lose it over a gorgeous face and a buff body and, determined to put him out of her mind, she turned back to her book. She had to read the same paragraph four times before it made sense, but she persevered, scarcely wavering in her concentration even when Kal returned to his chair, this time armed with a book of his own.

She turned a page, taking the opportunity to raise her lashes just enough to see that it was a heavyweight political treatise. Not at all what she'd expect from a man with playboy looks who'd told her that he did nothing 'seriously'.

But then looks, as she knew better than most, could be deceptive.

Atiya appeared after a while with the dinner menu and to offer them a drink. They both stayed with water. Wasted no time in choosing something simple to eat.

But for the continuous drone of the aircraft engines, the cabin was quiet. Once she lifted her head, stretched her neck. Maybe the movement caught his eye because he looked up too, lifting a brow in silent query. She shook her head, leaned back against the thickly padded seat and looked down at a carpet of clouds silvered by moonlight.

Kal, watching her, saw the exact moment when her eyes closed, her body slackened and he caught her book as it began to slide from her hand. It was the autobiography of a woman who'd founded her own business empire. She'd personally inscribed this copy to Rose.

He closed it, put it on the table. Asked Atiya for a light

blanket, which he laid over her. Then, book forgotten, he sat and watched her sleep, wondering what dreams brought that tiny crease to her forehead.

'Sir,' Atiya said softly, 'I'll be serving dinner in ten minutes. Shall I wake Lady Rose?'

'I'll do it in a moment,' he said. Then, when she'd gone, he leaned forward. 'Rose,' he said softly. 'Rose…'

Lydia opened her eyes, for a moment not sure where she was. Then she saw Kal and it all came rushing back. It hadn't been a dream, then. She really was aboard a flying palace, one that wouldn't turn into a pumpkin at midnight. She had an entire week before she had to return to the checkout.

'What time is it?' she asked, sitting up, disentangling herself from the blanket that Atiya must have put over her.

'Seven minutes to eight in London, or to midnight in Ramal Hamrah if you want to set your watch to local time.'

She glanced at her wrist, touched the expensive watch, decided she'd rather do the maths than risk tampering with it.

'Atiya is ready to serve dinner.'

'Oh.' Her mouth was dry, a sure sign that she'd been sleeping with it open, which meant he'd been sitting there watching her drool.

Memo to self, she thought, wincing as she put her feet to the floor, searched with her toes for her shoes. Next time, use the bed.

'I apologise if I snored.'

His only response was a smile. She muffled a groan. She'd snored, drooled…

'Late night?' he asked, not helping.

'Very,' she admitted.

She'd had a late shift at the supermarket and, although her mother was determinedly independent, she always felt guilty about leaving her, even for a short time.

'I was double-checking to make sure that I hadn't left any loose ends trailing before taking off for a week,' she replied.

Everything clean and polished.

Fridge and freezer stocked so that Jennie wouldn't have to shop.

Enough of her mother's prescription meds to keep her going.

The list of contact numbers double-checked to make sure it was up to date.

While Rose wouldn't have been faced with that scenario, she'd doubtless had plenty of other stuff to keep her up late before she disappeared for a week.

And, like her, she would have been too wound up with nerves to sleep properly.

'I'd better go and freshen up,' she said but, before she could move, Kal was there to offer his hand, ease her effortlessly to her feet so that they were chest to chest, toe to toe, kissing close for a fraction of a second; long enough for her to breathe in the scent of freshly laundered linen, warm skin, some subtle scent that reminded her of a long ago walk in autumn woods. The crushed dry leaves and bracken underfoot.

Close enough to see the faint darkening of his chin and yearn to reach up, rub her hand over his jaw, feel the roughness against her palm.

She'd barely registered the thought before he released her hand, stepped back to let her move and she wasted no time putting some distance between them.

She looked a mess. Tousled, dishevelled, a red mark on her cheek where she'd slept with her head against the leather upholstery. She was going to have to duck her entire head under the cold tap to get it working properly, but she didn't have time for that. Instead, she splashed her face, repaired her lipstick, brushed the tangles out of her hair and then clasped it at the nape of her neck with a clip she found in the case that Rose had packed for her.

Then she ran through the pre-gig checklist in an attempt to jolt her brain back into the groove.

Smoothed a crease in the linen trousers.

Straightened the fine gold chain so that it lay in an orderly fashion about her neck.

Rehearsed her prompt list of appropriate questions so that there would never be a lull in the conversation.

Putting the situation in its proper context.

It was something she'd done hundreds of times, after all.

It was just another job!

Kal rose as she entered the main saloon and the *just another job* mantra went straight out of the window. Not that he *did* anything. Offer her his hand. Smile, even.

That was the problem. He didn't have to *do* anything, she thought as he stood aside so that she could lead the way to where Atiya was waiting beside a table that had been laid with white damask, heavy silver, crystal, then held a chair for her.

Like a force of nature, he just *was*.

Offered wine, she shook her head. Even if she'd been tempted, she needed to keep a clear head.

She took a fork, picked up a delicate morsel of fish and said, 'Lucy tells me that you're her husband's cousin. Are you a diplomat, too?'

Conventional, impersonal conversation. That was the ticket, she thought as she tasted the fish. Correction, ate the fish. She wasn't tasting a thing.

'No.' He shrugged. 'My branch of the family has been personae non gratae at the Ramal Hamrahn court for three generations.'

No, no, no!

That wasn't how it worked. She was supposed to ask a polite question. He was supposed to respond in kind. Like when you said, 'How are you?' and the only proper response was any variation on, 'Fine, thanks.'

'Personae non gratae at the Embassy, too,' he continued, 'until I became involved in one of Lucy's charitable missions.'

Better. Charity was Rose's life and, firmly quashing a desire to know more about the black sheep thing, what his family had done three generations ago that was so terrible—definitely off the polite questions list—Lydia concentrated on that.

'You help Lucy?'

'She hasn't mentioned what I do?' he countered.

'Maybe she thought I'd try and poach you.' Now that was *good*. 'What do you do for her?'

'Not much. She needed to ship aid to an earthquake zone. I offered her the use of an aircraft—we took it from there.'

Very impressively 'not much', she thought. She'd definitely mention him to Rose. Maybe they would hit it off.

She squashed down the little curl of something green that tried to escape her chest.

'That would be the one your father owns?' she asked. Again, she'd imagined a small executive jet. Clearly, where this family was concerned, she needed to start thinking bigger.

'Flying is like driving, Rose. When you get your licence, you don't want to borrow your father's old crate. You want a shiny new one of your own.'

'You do?'

A lot bigger, she thought. He came from a two-plane family. Something else occurred to her.

He'd said no one in his family did anything seriously, but that couldn't possibly be true. Not in his case, anyway. Obtaining a basic pilot's licence was not much different from getting a driving licence—apart from the cost—but stepping up to this level took more than money. It took brains, dedication, a great deal of hard work.

And, yes, a heck of a lot of money.

'You are such a fraud,' she said but, far from annoying her, it eased her qualms about her own pretence.

'Fraud?'

Kal paused with a fork halfway to his lips. It hadn't taken Lucy ten minutes to rumble him, demand to know what he expected from Hanif in return for his help, but she knew the family history and he hadn't expected his offer to be greeted with open arms.

He'd known the only response was to be absolutely honest with her. That had earned him first her sympathy and then, over the years, both her and Hanif's friendship.

Rose had acted as if she had never heard of him but, unless Lucy had told her, how did she—

'Not serious?' she prompted. 'Exactly how long did it take you to qualify to fly something like this?'

Oh, right. She was still talking about the flying. 'I do fun seriously,' he said.

'Fun?'

'Give me a chance and I'll show you,' he said. Teasing was, after all, a two-way street; the only difference between them was that she blushed. Then, realising how that might have sounded, he very nearly blushed himself. 'I didn't mean... Lucy suggested you might like to go fishing.'

'Fishing?' She pretended to consider. 'Let me see. Wet. Smelly. Maggots. That's your idea of fun?'

That was a challenge if ever he'd heard one. And one he was happy to accept. 'Wet, smelly and then you get to dry out, get warm while you barbecue the catch on the beach.'

'Wet, smelly, smoky and then we get sand in our food. Perfect,' she said, but a tiny twitch at the corner of her mouth suggested that she was hooked and, content, he let it lie.

Rose speared another forkful of fish.

'In her letter,' she said, 'Lucy suggested I'd enjoy a trip to the souk. Silk. Spices. Gold.'

'Heat, crowds, people with cellphones taking your photograph? I thought you wanted peace and privacy.'

'Even the paparazzi have children to feed and educate,' she said. 'And publicity oils the wheels of charity. The secret is not to give them something so sensational that they don't have to keep coming back for more.'

'That makes for a very dull life,' he replied gravely, playing along, despite the fact that it appeared to fly directly in the face of what Lucy had told him. 'But if you wore an *abbayah*, kept your eyes down, your hair covered, you might pass unnoticed.'

'A disguise?'

'More a cover-up. There's no reason to make it easy for them, although there's no hiding your height.'

'Don't worry about it.'

'It's what I'm here for.'

'Really?' And she was the one challenging him, as if she knew he had an agenda of his own. But she didn't wait for an answer. 'So what did you buy?' she asked.

He must have looked confused because she added, 'Car, not plane. I wouldn't know one plane from another. When you passed your test?' she prompted. 'A Ferrari? Porsche?'

'Far too obvious. I chose a Morgan.'

Her turn to look puzzled.

'It's a small sports car. A roadster,' he explained, surprised she didn't know that. 'The kind of thing that you see pilots driving in old World War Two movies? My father put my name on the waiting list on my twelfth birthday.'

'There's a waiting list?'

'A long one. They're hand-built,' he replied, smiling at her astonishment. 'I took delivery on my seventeenth birthday.'

'I'll add patient to serious,' she replied. 'What do you drive now?'

'I still have the Morgan.'

'The same one?'

'I'd have to wait a while for another one, so I've taken very good care of it.'

'I'm impressed.'

'Don't be. It stays in London while I'm constantly on the move, but for the record I drive a Renault in France, a Lancia in Italy and in New York…' he grinned '…I take a cab.'

'And in Ramal Hamrah?' she asked.

Suddenly the smile took real effort.

'There's an old Land Rover that does the job. What about you?' he asked, determined to shift the focus of their conversation to her. 'What do you drive for pleasure?'

She leaned forward, her lips parted on what he was sure would have been a protest that she wasn't finished with the question of Ramal Hamrah. Maybe something in his expression warned her that she was treading on dangerous ground and, after a moment, she sat back. Thought about it.

He assumed that was because her grandfather's garage offered so wide a choice. But then she said, 'It's...' she used her hands to describe a shape '...red.'

'Red?' Why was he surprised? 'Good choice.'

'I'm glad you approve.'

The exchange was, on the surface, perfectly serious and yet the air was suddenly bubbling with laughter.

'Do you really have homes in all those places?' she asked.

'Just a mews cottage in London. My mother, my father's first wife, was a French actress. She has a house in Nice and an apartment in Paris. His second wife, an English aristocrat, lives in Belgravia and Gloucestershire. His third was an American heiress. She has an apartment in the Dakota Building in New York and a house in the Hamptons.'

'An expensive hobby, getting married.' Then, when he made no comment, 'You stay with them? Even your ex-stepmothers?'

'Naturally. They're a big part of my life and I like to spend time with my brothers and sisters.'

'Oh, yes. I didn't think...' She seemed slightly flustered by his father's admittedly louche lifestyle. 'So where does Italy come in? The Lancia?' she prompted.

'My father bought a palazzo in Portofino when he was wooing a contessa. It didn't last—she quickly realised that he wasn't a man for the long haul—but he decided to keep the house. As he said, when a man has as many ex-wives and mistresses and children as he has, he needs a bolt-hole. Not true, of course. It's far too tempting a location. He's never alone.'

He expected her to laugh. Most people took what he said at face value, seeing only the glamour.

'From his history, I'd say he's never wanted to be,' Rose

said, her smile touched with compassion. 'It must have been difficult. Growing up.'

'Life was never dull,' he admitted with rather more flippancy than he felt. Without a country, a purpose, his grandfather had become rudderless, a glamorous playboy to whom women flocked, a lifestyle that his father had embraced without question. His family were his world but after one relationship that had kept the gossip magazines on their toes for eighteen months as they'd followed every date, every break up, every make up, he'd realised that he had no wish to live like that for the rest of his life.

'You didn't mention Ramal Hamrah,' she said, ignoring the opportunity he'd given her to talk about her own grandfather. Her own life.

Rare in a woman.

Rare in anyone.

Most people would rather talk about themselves.

'Do you have a home there?'

'There is a place that was once home,' he told her because the apartment overlooking the old harbour, bought off plan from a developer who had never heard of Kalil al-Zaki, could never be described as the home of his heart, his soul. 'A faded photograph that hangs upon my grandfather's wall. A place of stories of the raids, battles, celebrations that are the history of my family.'

Stories that had grown with the telling until they had become the stuff of legend.

It was an image that the old man looked at with longing. Where he wanted to breathe his last. Where he wanted to lie for eternity, at one with the land he'd fought for.

And Kalil would do anything to make that possible. Not that sitting here, sharing a meal with Lady Rose Napier was as tedious as he'd imagined it would be.

'No one has lived there for a long time,' he said.

For a moment he thought she was going to ask him to tell her more, but all she said was, 'I'm sorry.'

She was quiet for a moment, as if she understood the emptiness, the sense of loss and he began to see why people, even those who had never met her, instinctively loved her.

She had an innate sensitivity. A face that invited confidences. Another second and he would have told her everything but, at exactly the right moment, she said, 'Tell me about your brothers and sisters.'

'How long have you got?' he asked, not sure whether he was relieved or disappointed. 'I have one sister, a year younger than me. I have five half-sisters, three half-brothers and six, no seven, steps of both sexes and half a dozen who aren't actually related by blood but are still family.'

She counted them on her long, slender fingers.

'Sixteen?' she asked, looking at him in amazement. 'You've got sixteen brothers and sisters? Plus six.'

'At the last count. Sarah, she's the English ex, and her husband are about to have another baby.'

Lydia sat back in her chair, stunned. As an only child she had dreamed of brothers and sisters, but this was beyond imagining.

'Can you remember all their names?' she asked.

'Of course. They are my family.' Then, seeing her doubt, he held up his hand and began to list them. 'My sister is Adele. She's married to a doctor, Michel, and they have two children, Albert and Nicole. My mother has two other daughters by her second husband…'

As they ate, Kal talked about his family in France, in England and America. Their partners and children. The three youngest girls whose mothers his father had never actually got around to marrying but were all part of a huge extended family. All undoubtedly adored.

His family, but nothing about himself, she realised. Nothing about his personal life and she didn't press him. How a man talked about his family said a lot about him. She didn't need anyone to tell her that he was a loyal and caring son. That he loved his family. It was there in his smile as he told stories about his mother in full drama queen mode, about his sister. His pride in all their achievements.

If he'd had a wife or partner, children of his own, he would certainly have talked about them, too. With love and pride.

'You're so lucky having a big family,' she told him as they laughed at a story about one of the boys causing mayhem at a party.

'That's not the half of it,' he assured her. 'My grandfather set the standard. Five wives, ten children. Do you want their names, too? Or shall I save that for a rainy day?'

'Please tell me that it doesn't rain in Ramal Hamrah.'

'Not often,' he admitted.

Neither of them said anything while Atiya cleared the table, placed a tray of sweet things, tiny cakes, nuts, fruit, before them.

'Can I bring you coffee or tea?' Atiya asked.

'Try some traditional mint tea,' Kal suggested before she could reply. He spoke to Atiya in Arabic and, after a swift exchange, which apparently elicited the right answer, he said, 'Not made with a bag, it will be the real thing.'

'It sounds delicious.'

'It is.'

He indicated the tray, but she shook her head.

'It all looks wonderful but I can't eat another thing,' Lydia said. 'I hope there's a pool in Bab el Sama. If I keep eating like this I won't fit into any of my clothes when I get home.'

'I don't understand why women obsess about being thin,' he said.

'No? Have you never noticed the way celebrities who put on a few pounds are ridiculed? That would be women celebrities,' she added.

'I know. Adele went through a bad patch when she was a teenager.' He shook his head. Took a date, but made no attempt to push her to eat. Instead, he bestowed a lazy smile on her and said, 'Now you know my entire family. Your turn to tell me about yours.'

Lydia waited while Atiya served the mint tea.

Completely absorbed by his complex relationships, the little vignettes of each of his brothers and sisters that had made them all seem so real, she had totally forgotten the pretence and needed a moment to gather herself.

'Everyone knows my story, Kal.'

Kal wondered. While he'd been telling her about his family, she'd been by turns interested, astonished, amused. But the moment he'd mentioned hers, it was as if the lights had dimmed.

'I know what the press write about you,' he said. 'What Lucy has told me.'

That both her parents had been killed when she was six years old and she'd been raised by an obsessively controlling grandfather, the one who'd taken a newspaper headline literally and turned her into the 'people's angel'.

'What you see is what you get,' she replied, picking up the glass of tea.

Was it?

It was true that with her pale hair, porcelain skin and dazzling blue eyes she could have stepped out of a Renaissance painting.

But then there was that mouth. The full sultry lips that clung for a moment to the small glass as she tasted the tea.

A tiny piece of the crushed leaf clung to her lower lip and, as she gathered it in with the tip of her tongue, savouring the taste, he discovered that he couldn't breathe.

'It's sweet,' she said.

'Is that a problem?'

She shook her head. 'I don't usually put sugar in mint tea, but it's good.' She finished the tea, then caught at a yawn that, had she been anyone else, he would have sworn was fake. That she was simply making an excuse to get away. 'If you'll excuse me, Kal, it's been a long day and I'd like to try and get a couple of hours' sleep before we land.'

'Of course,' he said, easing her chair back so that she could stand up and walking with her to the door of her suite, unable to quite shake the feeling that she was bolting from the risk that he might expect the exposure of her own family in return for his unaccustomed openness.

Much as he adored them, he rarely talked about his family to outsiders. He'd learned very early how even the most innocent remark to a friend would be passed on to their parents and, in a very short time, would appear in print, twisted out of recognition by people who made a living out of celebrity gossip.

Rose, though, had that rare gift for asking the right question, then listening to the answer in a way that made a man feel that it was the most important thing she'd ever heard.

But then, at the door, she confounded him, turning to face him and, for a moment, locked in that small, still bubble that enclosed two people who'd spent an evening together, all the more intimate because of their isolation as they flew high above the earth in their own small time capsule, neither of them moved and he knew that if she'd been any other woman, if he'd been any other man, he would have kissed her. That she would have kissed him back. Maybe done a lot more than kiss.

She was a warm, quick-witted, complex woman and there had, undoubtedly, been a connection between them, a spark that in another world might have been fanned into a flame.

But she was Lady Roseanne Napier, the 'people's angel'. And he had made a promise to his grandfather that nothing, no one, would divert him from keeping.

'Thank you for your company, Rose,' he said, taking her hand and lifting it to his lips, but his throat was unexpectedly constricted as he took a step back. He added, 'Sleep well.'

It was going to be a very long week.

CHAPTER FOUR

TIRED as she was, Lydia didn't sleep. Eyes closed, eyes open, it made no difference.

The hand Kal had kissed lay on the cover at her side and she had to press it down hard to keep it from flying to her mouth so that she could taste it.

Taste him.

His mouth had barely made contact and yet the back of her fingers throbbed as if burned, her body as fired up as if she'd had a faint electric shock.

In desperation she flung herself off the bed, tore off her clothes and threw herself beneath the shower, soaping herself with a gel that smelled faintly of lemons. Warm at first, then cooler until she was shivering. But still her skin burned and when Lydia lifted her hand to her face, breathed in, it was not the scent of lemons that filled her head.

It was nothing as simple as scent, but a distillation of every look, every word, the food they'd eaten, the mint tea they'd drunk. It had stirred the air as he'd bent over her hand, leaving her faint with the intensity of pure sensation that had rippled through her body. Familiar and yet utterly unknown. Fire and ice. Remembered pleasure and the certainty of pain.

Distraction.

She needed a distraction, she thought desperately as she wrapped herself in a fluffy gown, combed out her damp hair, applied a little of some unbelievably expensive moisturiser in an attempt to counteract the drying effects of pressured air.

She could usually lose herself in a book—she'd managed it earlier, even dozed off—but she'd left her book in the main cabin and nothing on earth would tempt her back out there until she had restored some semblance of calm order to her racketing hormones.

She chose another book from the selection Rose had packed for her and settled back against the pillows. All she had to do now was concentrate. It shouldn't be hard, the book was by a favourite author, but the words refused to stay still.

Instead they kept merging into the shape of Kal's mouth, the sensuous curve of his lower lip.

'Get a grip, Lydie!' she moaned, abandoning the book and sliding down to the floor where she sat cross-legged, hoping that yoga breathing would instil a modicum of calm, bring her down from what had to be some kind of high induced by an excess of pheromones leaking into the closed atmosphere of the aircraft.

Combined with the adrenalin charge of confronting the newsmen, tension at the prospect of facing airport security with Rose's passport, then the shock of Kalil al-Zaki arriving to mess up all their carefully laid plans, it was scarcely any wonder that the words wouldn't stay still.

That he was astoundingly attractive, took his duty of care to extraordinary lengths, had flirted outrageously with her hadn't helped.

When they'd sat down to their dinner party in the sky, she'd been determined to keep conversation on the impersonal level she employed at cocktail parties, launches.

Kal had blown that one right out of the water with his reply to her first question and she'd forgotten all about the 'plan' as he'd in turn amused, shocked, delighted her with tales of his family life.

And made her envious at the obvious warmth and affection they shared. His might be a somewhat chaotic and infinitely extendable family but, as an only child with scarcely any close relations, she'd been drawn in by the charm of having so many people who were connected to you. To care for and who cared back. Who would not want to be part of that?

And that was only half the story, she realised. Sheikh Hanif was his cousin and there must be a vast Ramal Hamrahn family that he hadn't even mentioned, other than to tell her that he and his family were personae non gratae at the Ramal Hamrahn court.

More, she suspected, than he told most people. But then Rose had that effect on people. Drew them out.

Instead, he had turned the spotlight on her, which was when she'd decided to play safe and retire.

There was a tap on the door. 'Madam? We'll be landing in fifteen minutes.'

'Thank you, Atiya.'

She reapplied a light coating of make-up. Rose might want her picture in the paper, but not looking as if she'd just rolled out of bed. Brushed out her hair. Dressed. Putting herself back together so that she was fit to be seen in public.

The seat belt sign pinged as she returned to the cabin and she shook her head as Kal half rose, waved him back to his seat and sat down, fastening her seat belt without incident before placing her hands out of reach in her lap. Not looking at him, but instead peering out at the skein of lights skirting the coast, shimmering in the water below them.

'Landing holds no terrors for you?' Kal asked and she turned to glance at him. A mistake. Groomed to perfection he was unforgettable, but after eight hours in the air, minus his tie, in need of a shave, he was everything a woman would hope to wake up to. Sexily rumpled, with eyes that weren't so much come to bed, as let's stay here for the rest of the day.

As if she'd know…

Quickly turning back to the window as they sank lower and the capital, Rumaillah, resolved from a mass of lights into individual streets, buildings, her attention was caught by a vast complex dominated by floodlit domes, protected by high walls, spread across the highest point of the city.

'What is that?' she asked.

Kal put a hand on the arm of her chair and leaned across so that he could see out of her window, but he must have dialled down the pheromone count, or maybe, like her, he was tired because, even this close, there was no whoosh of heat.

'It's the Emiri Palace,' he told her.

'But it's huge.'

'It's not like Buckingham Palace,' he said, 'with everything under one roof. The Emir's palace is not just one building. There are gardens, palaces for his wives, his children and their families. The Emiri offices are there too, and his Majlis where his people can go and see him, talk to him, ask for his help, or to intercede in disputes.'

'I like the sound of that. The man at the top being approachable.'

'I doubt it's quite as basic as it was in the old days,' he replied. There was an edge to his voice that made her forget about the exotic hilltop palace and look more closely at him. 'We've come a long way from a tent in the desert.'

We.

He might be excluded but he still thought of himself as one of them. She resisted the urge to ask him. If he wanted her to know he would tell her.

But, fascinated, she pressed, 'In theory, anyone can approach him?'

'In theory.'

There was something in his voice, a tension, anger, that stopped her from saying more.

'And you said "wives". How many has he got?'

'The Emir? Just one. The tradition of taking more than one wife began when a man would take the widows, children of brothers slain in battle into his family. Then it became a sign of wealth. It's rare these days.' Then, with a curl of his lip that could have been mistaken for a smile if you hadn't seen the real thing, 'My family are not typical.'

'And even they take only one at a time,' she replied, lifting her voice a little so that it was gently teasing.

'Legally,' he agreed. 'In practice there tends to be some overlap.'

'And you, Kal?'

'How many wives do I have?' And this time the smile was a little less forced. 'None, but then I'm a late starter.'

That she doubted, but suddenly the runway lights were whizzing past and then they were down with barely a bump.

Before she left the aircraft she visited the cockpit—now that it was safely on the ground—to thank the crew for a wonderful flight and, by the time she stepped outside into the warm moist air of the Gulf, her luggage had already been transferred to the waiting helicopter.

'Ready?' Kal asked.

She swallowed, nodded.

She'd been bold enough when the reality of committing her safety to what seemed to be a very small, fragile thing beside the bulk of the jet had been a distant eight hours away.

Now she was afraid that if she opened her mouth her teeth would start chattering like a pair of castanets.

Apparently she wasn't fooling Kal because he said, 'That ready? It's not too late to change your mind.'

She refused to be so pathetic and, shaking her head once in a *let's get this over with* gesture, she took a determined step forward. His hand at her back helped keep her moving when she faltered. Got her through the door and into her seat.

He said something to the pilot as he followed her—what, she couldn't hear above the noise of the engine.

He didn't bother to ask if she needed help with the straps, but took them from her and deftly fastened them as if it was something he'd been doing all his life. Maybe he had.

Then he gently lowered the earphones that would keep out

the noise and allow the pilot to talk to them onto her head, settling them into place against her ears.

'Okay?' he said, not that she could hear, but she'd been sent on a lip-reading and signing course by the supermarket and had no problem understanding him.

She nodded and he swiftly dealt with his own straps and headset before turning in his seat so that he was facing her.

'Hands,' he said, and when she lifted them to look at them, not knowing what she was supposed to do with them, he took them in his and held them as the rotor speed built up.

She tried to smile but this was far worse than in a passenger aircraft. Everything—the tarmac, the controls, the reality of what was happening—was so close, so immediate, so in your face.

There was no possibility of pretence here.

No way you could tell yourself that you were on the number seven bus going to work and, as the helicopter lifted from the ground, leaving her stomach behind, she tightened her grip of his hands but, before the scream bubbling up in her throat could escape, Kal leaned forward and said, 'Trust me, Rose.'

And then he kissed her.

It wasn't a gentle kiss. It was powerful, strong, demanding her total attention and the soaring lift as they rose into the air, leaving the earth far behind them, was echoed by a rush of pure exhilaration that flooded through her.

This was flying. This was living. And, without a thought for what would follow, she kissed him back.

Kal had seen Rose's momentary loss of courage as she'd looked across the tarmac from the top of the aircraft steps to the waiting helicopter, followed by the lift of her chin, an unexpectedly stubborn look that no photographer had ever managed to capture, as she'd refused to back down, switch to the car.

It didn't quite go with the picture Lucy had painted of the gentle, biddable girl—woman—who'd lovingly bowed to the dictates of her grandfather. Who was desperate for some quiet time while she fathomed out her future.

That was a chin that took no prisoners and, certain that once she was airborne she'd be fine, he hadn't argued. Even so, her steps had faltered as they'd neared the helicopter and as they'd boarded he'd told the pilot to get a move on before she had time for second thoughts.

This was not a moment for the usual round of 'Lady Rose' politeness, handshakes, introductions. All that could wait until they arrived at Bab el Sama.

And he'd done his best to keep her distracted, busy, her eyes on him rather than the tarmac.

But as the engine note changed in the moment prior to take-off, her hands had gripped his so hard that her nails had dug into his palms and he thought that he'd completely misjudged the situation, that she was going to lose it.

Hysterics required more than a reassuring hand or smile, they needed direct action and there were just two options—a slap or a kiss.

No contest.

Apart from the fact that the idea of hitting anyone, let alone a frightened woman, was totally abhorrent to him, letting go of her hands wasn't an option.

His 'Trust me' had been a waste of breath—she couldn't hear him—but it had made him feel better as he went in for the kiss, hard and fast. This wasn't seduction, this was survival and he wanted her total attention, every emotion, fixed on him, even if that emotion was outrage.

He didn't get outrage.

For a moment there was nothing. Only a stunned stillness. Then something like an imperceptible sigh breathed against his mouth as her eyes closed, the tension left her body and her lips softened, yielded and clung to his for a moment, warm and sweet as a girl's first kiss. Then parted, hot as a fallen angel tempting him to sin.

At which point the only one in danger of losing anything was him.

How long was a kiss? A heartbeat, minutes, a lifetime?

It seemed like all three as his hands, no longer captive, moved to her waist, her back, drawing her closer. A heartbeat while he breathed in the clean, fresh scent of her skin; minutes as the kiss deepened and something darker, more compelling stirred his senses; a lifetime while his hormones stampeded to fling themselves into the unknown without as much as a thought for the consequences.

Exactly like his grandfather. Exactly like his father.

Men without a purpose, without a compass, who'd put their own selfish desires above everything.

That thought, like a pitcher of cold water, was enough to jar him back to reality, remind him why he was here, and he drew back.

Rose took a gasping, thready little breath as he broke the connection. Sat unmoving for long moments before her lids slowly rose, almost as if the long, silky lashes were too heavy to lift.

Her lips parted as if she was going to speak but she closed them again without saying a word, instead concentrating on her breathing, slowing it down using some technique that she'd probably learned long ago to manage nerves.

When she raised her lashes again, she was sufficiently in control to speak.

He couldn't hear what she was saying, but she mouthed the words so carefully that he could lip-read enough to get the gist, which was, as near as damn it, 'If you were that scared, Kal, you should have told me. We could have taken the car.'

It was the response of a woman who, with ten years of inter-action with the public behind her, knew exactly how to rescue an awkward moment, who could put anyone at ease with a word.

It put a kiss that had spiralled out of hand into perspective, allowing them both to move on, forget it.

Well, what had he expected?

That she'd fall apart simply because he'd kissed her?

She might—or might not—be a virgin princess, but she'd already proved, with her dry and ready wit, that she was no shrinking violet.

He knew he should be grateful that his rescue mission had been recognised for what it was. Received with her legendary good humour, charm.

But he wasn't grateful. Didn't want to forget.

He wanted to pull her close, kiss her again until that classy English cool sizzled away to nothing, her 'charm' shattered in a pyrotechnic blaze that would light up the night sky and this tender Rose, nurtured under glass, broke out and ran wild.

It wasn't going to happen.

Even if had been an appropriate time or place, their destinies were written. Even if she rejected the Earl in waiting her grandfather had lined up to walk her down the aisle and chose someone for herself, it was never going to be the scion of a disgraced and dispossessed exile.

And when he took a bride, it would not be in response to carnal attraction, the sexual chemistry that masqueraded as love, stealing your senses, stealing your life. His marriage would be an affair of state that would cement an alliance with one of the great Ramal Hamrahn families—the Kassimi, the Attiyah or the Darwish. The surrender of one of their precious daughters an affirmation that he had restored his family to their rightful place.

Had brought his grandfather home.

But time was running out. He had been infinitely patient and he no longer had years. His grandfather was already on borrowed time, stubbornly refusing to accept the death sentence that had been passed on him until he saw his grandson married as a Khatib should be married. Could die in peace in the place where he'd been born.

An affair that would cause scandalised headlines worldwide would do nothing to help his cause. He had to keep himself focused on what was important, he reminded himself, even while he held Rose, could feel her corn silk hair tumbling over his hands, her soft breath upon his cheek.

Fight, as he'd always fought, the demanding, selfish little gene he'd inherited, the one telling him to go for it and hang the consequences. The knowledge that she wanted it as much as he did. The pretence that it would just be a holiday romance, wouldn't hurt anyone.

That wasn't true. You could not give that much and walk away without losing something of yourself, taking something of the other with you. Already, in the closeness of the hours they had spent together, he had given more than he should. Had taken more. He concentrated on the clean, vast infinity of the night sky—diamonds against black velvet—until it filled his head, obliterating everything else.

Lydia wanted to curl up and die with embarrassment. Not because Kal had kissed her. That had been no more than straightforward shock tactics, designed to prevent her from doing something stupid.

And it had worked.

She hadn't screamed, hadn't tried to grab the pilot and make him stop.

Why would she when the minute his lower lip had touched hers, she'd forgotten all about the fact that they were rising from the ground in a tiny glass bubble?

Forgotten her fear.

Forgotten everything as the warmth of his mouth had first heated her lips, then curled through every part of her body, touching the frozen core that had remained walled up, out of reach for so long. As it felt the warmth, whimpered to be set free, he'd drawn her close and the kiss had ceased to be shock tactics and had become real, intense.

A lover's kiss, and as her arms had wrapped themselves around his neck she hadn't cared who he thought she was. He was kissing her as if he wanted her and that was all that mattered, because she wanted him right back.

She hadn't cared that he thought it was Rose who'd reacted so wantonly. Who'd wanted more. Who would still be kissing him as if the world was about to end if he hadn't backed off.

He was still holding her, still close enough that she could feel him breathing. Close enough that when she was finally brave enough to open her eyes she could see the *what-the-hell-happened-there?* look in his eyes. She wanted to explain that it was okay. That she wasn't Rose, just some dumb idiot girl who was having a very strange day.

That he could forget all about it. Forget about her.

But that was impossible.

She had to put things right, restore Rose's reputation. Instead, she closed her eyes again and concentrated on her breathing. Slowing it down. And, as her mind cleared, she realised that the answer was simple. Fear.

She could put it all down to her fear. Or his, she thought, remembering how he'd pretended to be the one who was scared as they'd lifted off.

If she could make him laugh it would be all right. They would be able to move on, pretend it had never happened.

But he hadn't laughed; there was no reaction at all and she realised that just because she could lip-read didn't mean that he could, too. He hadn't a clue what she was saying.

She took her hands from his shoulders, tried to concentrate on what he was saying as he looked up, beyond her. Shook her head to indicate that it hadn't got through.

He turned, looked straight at her as he repeated himself. 'And miss this?'

What?

She didn't want to take her eyes from him. While she was looking at him, while he was still holding her, she could forget that there was nothing but a thin wall of perspex between her and the sky.

But he lifted one of his dark brows a fraction of a millimetre, challenging her to be brave, and she finally tore her gaze from him, turned her head.

In the bubble of the helicopter they had an all round view of the sky which, away from the light pollution of the airport, the city, she could see as it was meant to be seen, with the constellations diamond-bright, the spangled shawl of the Milky Way spread across the heavens.

It was an awe-inspiring, terrifying sight. A reminder of how small they were. How vulnerable. And yet how spectacularly amazing and she didn't look away. But, although she wanted to reach back, share the moment with Kal, she remembered who she was supposed to be.

Not the woman on the checkout who anyone could—and did—flirt with. Not Lydia Young, who had a real problem with leaving the ground, but Lady Rose Napier, who could handle an unexpected kiss with the same natural charm as any other minor wobble in her day.

Instead, she concentrated on this unexpected gift he'd given her, searching for constellations that she recognised until she had to blink rather hard because her eyes were watering. At the beauty of the sky. That was all…

Kal must have said something. She didn't hear him, just felt his breath against her cheek, then, as he pointed down, she saw a scatter of lights below, the navigation lights of boats riding at anchor as they crossed a wide creek.

As they dropped lower, circling to land on the far bank, Lydia caught tantalising glimpses of the domes, arches of half a dozen or more exotic, beautiful beach houses. There was a private dock, boats, a long curve of white sand. And, behind it all, the dramatic, sharply rising background of jagged mountains, black against a sky fading to pre-dawn purple.

While she had not been fooled by the word 'cottage', had anticipated the kind of luxury that few people would ever experience, this was far beyond anything she could have imagined.

It reminded her of pictures she'd seen of the fantasy village of Portmeirion, more like a film set, or something out of a dream than anything real, and by the time the helicopter landed and she'd thanked the pilot, her heart was pounding with excitement, anticipation.

She'd been so determined to keep her reaction low-key, wanting to appear as if this was what she was used to, but that wasn't, in the end, a problem. As Kal took her hand and helped her down, she didn't have to fight to contain a *wow*. The reality was simply beyond words.

There was an open Jeep waiting for them, but she didn't rush to climb in. Instead, she walked to the edge of the landing pad so that she could look out over the creek. Eager to feel solid earth beneath her feet. To breathe in real air laden with the salty scent of the sea, wet sand, something else, sweet and heavy, that she did not recognise.

It was still quite dark, but all the way down to the beach lights threaded through huge old trees, shone in the water.

'I don't think I've ever seen anything so beautiful,' she said as Kal joined her. 'I expected sand, desert, not all this green.'

'The creek is in a valley and has a microclimate of its own,' he said. 'And Sheikh Jamal's father began an intensive tree planting programme when he took the throne fifty years ago.'

'Well, good for him.'

'Not everyone is happy. People complain that it rains more these days.'

'It rains more everywhere,' she replied, looking around for the source of the sweet, heady fragrance filling the air. 'What is that scent?' she asked.

'Jasmine.' He crossed to a shrub, broke off a piece and offered it to her with the slightest of bows. 'Welcome to Bab el Sama, Lady Rose,' he said.

CHAPTER FIVE

LYDIA, holding the spray of tiny white flowers, didn't miss the fact that he'd put the 'Lady' back in front of her name. That his voice had taken on a more formal tone.

That was good, she told herself. Perfect, in fact.

One kiss could be overlooked, especially when it was purely medicinal, but it wouldn't do to let him think that Lady Rose encouraged such liberties.

'The luggage is loaded.'

He might as well have been done with it and added *madam*.

'The pilot won't take off until we're clear of the pad. If you are ready?'

It was right there in his tone of voice. It was the one he'd used before he'd started flirting. Before she'd started encouraging him.

She turned to look at the Jeep, where a white-robed servant was waiting to drive them to the cottage. She'd been sitting for hours and, now she was on her feet, wasn't eager to sit again unless she had to.

'Is it far?' she asked. 'I'd like to stretch my legs.'

He spoke to the driver, who answered with a shake of his head, a wave of the hand to indicate a path through the trees.

Lydia watched the exchange, then frowned.

Kal wasn't telling the man that they'd walk, she realised, but asking the way. He'd seemed so familiar with everything that she'd assumed he had been here before, but clearly this was his first time, too.

She hadn't taken much notice when he'd said his family were personae non gratae at the Ramal Hamrahn court.

Court, for heaven's sake. Nobody talked like that any more. But now she wondered why, for three generations, his family had lived in Europe.

What past crime was so terrible that he and his siblings had never been invited to share this idyllic summer playground with their cousins? It wasn't as if they'd be cramped for space. Even if they all turned up at the same time.

'There's a path through the gardens,' he said. Then, 'Will you be warm enough?'

'You're kidding?'

Rose had warned her that it wouldn't be hot at this time of year and maybe it wasn't for this part of the world. Compared with London in December, however, the air felt soft and balmy.

Then, as a frown creased Kal's brows, she realised that her response had been pure Lydia. Not quite on a scale with Eliza Doolittle's blooper at the races, but near enough.

She was tired and forgetting to keep up the Lady Rose act. Or maybe it was her subconscious fighting it. Wanting to say to him *Look at me, see who I really am...*

'The temperature is quite perfect,' she added. And mentally groaned. She'd be doing the whole, *How kind of you to let me come* routine if she didn't get a grip.

Didn't put some distance between them.

In a determined attempt to start as she had meant to go on— before he'd taken her hand, made her laugh—she said, 'You don't have to come with me, Kal. Just point me in the right direction and I can find my own way.'

'No doubt. However, I'd rather not have to explain to Lucy why I had to send out a search party for you.'

'Why would she ever know?'

'You're kidding?'

She ignored the wobble somewhere beneath her midriff as he repeated her words back to her as if he was mocking her, almost as if he knew. 'Actually, I'm not,' she said, knowing that it was only her guilty conscience making her think that way.

'No? Then let me explain how it would happen. At the first hint of trouble the alarm would be raised,' he explained. 'The Chief of Security would be alerted. The Emir's office would be informed, your Ambassador would be summoned—'

'Okay, okay,' she said, holding up her hands in surrender, laughing despite everything. 'I get it. If I go missing, you'll be hauled up before the Emir and asked to explain what the heck you were doing letting me wander around by myself.'

There was a momentary pause, as if he was considering the matter. Then he shrugged. 'Something like that, but all you need to worry about is the fact that Lucy would know what had happened within five minutes.'

Not something she would want to happen and, while she didn't think for one moment she'd get lost, she said, 'Point taken. Lead the way, Mr al-Zaki.'

The steps were illuminated by concealed lighting and perfectly safe, as was the path, but he took her arm, presumably in case she stumbled.

Rose wouldn't make a fuss, she told herself. No doubt someone had been holding her hand, taking her arm, keeping her safe all her life. It was what she'd wanted to escape. The constant surveillance. The cotton wool.

As he tucked her arm beneath his, she told herself that she could live with it for a week. And, as she leaned on him a little, that he would expect nothing else.

The path wound through trees and shrubs. Herbs had been planted along the edges, spilling over so that as they brushed past lavender, sage, marjoram and other, less familiar, scents filled the air.

Neither of them spoke. The only sound was the trickle of

water running, the splash of something, a fish or a frog, in a dark pool. She caught glimpses of mysterious arches, an ornate summer house, hidden among the trees. And above them the domes and towers she'd seen from the air.

'It's magical,' she said at last as, entranced, she stored up the scents, sounds, images for some day, far in the future, when she would tell her children, grandchildren about this *Arabian Nights* adventure. Always assuming she ever got to the point where she could trust a man sufficiently to get beyond arm's length flirting.

Meet someone who would look at her and see Lydia Young instead of her famous alter ego.

The thought leached the pleasure from the moment.

She'd been featured in the local newspaper when she'd first appeared as Lady Rose, had even been invited to turn up as Rose and switch on the Christmas lights one year when the local council were on a cost cutting drive and couldn't afford a real celebrity.

Even at work, wearing an unflattering uniform and with her name badge clearly visible, the customers had taken to calling her 'Rose' and she couldn't deny that she'd loved it. It had made her feel special.

Here, now, standing in her heroine's shoes, she discovered that being someone else was not enough.

That, instead of looking at Lydia and seeing Rose, she wanted someone, or maybe just Kalil al-Zaki, to look at Rose and see Lydia.

Because that was who she'd been with him.

It was Lydia who'd been afraid of taking off, whose hand he had held. Lydia he'd kissed.

But he'd never know that. And she could never tell him.

He was silent too and once she risked a glance, but the floor level lighting only threw his features into dark, unreadable shadows.

Then, as they turned a corner, the view opened up to reveal

that while behind them, above the darker bulk of the mountains, the stars still blazed, on the far side of the creek a pale edge of mauve was seeping into the pre-dawn purple.

'It's nearly dawn,' she said, surprised out of her momentary descent into self-pity. It still felt like the middle of the night, but she'd flown east, was four hours closer to the day than her mother, fast asleep in London.

She was on another continent at sunrise and, to witness it, all she had to do was stand here and wait.

Kal didn't even ask what she wanted to do. He knew.

'There's a summer house over there,' he said, urging her in the direction of another intricately decorated domed and col-onnaded structure perfectly situated to enjoy the view. 'You can watch in comfort.'

'No…'

It was open at the front and there were huge cane chairs piled with cushions. Total luxury. A place to bring a book, be alone, forget everything. Maybe later. Not now.

'I don't want anything between me and the sky,' she said, walking closer to the edge of the paved terrace where the drop was guarded by a stone balustrade. 'I want to be outside where I can feel it.'

He let her go, didn't follow her and she tried not to mind.

Minding was a waste of time. Worse. It was a stupid con-tradiction. Distance was what she had wanted and the old lady with the wand was, it seemed, still on the job, granting wishes as if they were going out of fashion.

She should be pleased.

It wasn't as if she'd expected or needed to be diverted, amused. She had a pile of great books to amuse her, occupy her mind, and exploring the garden, wandering along the shore should be diversion enough for anyone. If the forbidden delights of Kal al-Zaki's diversionary tactics hadn't been such a potent reminder of everything she was missing. The life that she might have had if she hadn't looked like Lady Rose.

But then, as the mauve band at the edge of the sky widened, became suffused with pink, she heard a step behind her and, as she half turned, Kal settled something soft around her.

For a moment his hands lingered on her shoulders, tense and knotted from sitting for too long, and without thinking she leaned into his touch, seeking ease from his long fingers. For a moment she thought he was going to respond, but then he stepped back, putting clear air between them.

'You will get cold standing out here,' he said with a brusqueness that suggested he had, after all, been affected by their closeness. That he, too, was aware that it would be inappropriate to take it further.

'And you don't want to explain to Lucy how I caught a chill on your watch?' Light, cool, she told herself.

'That wouldn't bother me.' He joined her at the balustrade, but kept his eyes on the horizon. 'I'd simply explain that you stubbornly, wilfully insisted on standing outside in the chill of dawn, that short of carrying you inside there was nothing I could do about it. I have no doubt that she'd agree with me.'

'She would?' The idea of Rose being wilful or stubborn was so slanderous that she had to take a breath, remind herself that he was judging Rose on her behaviour, before she nodded and said, 'She would.' And vow to try a little harder—a lot harder—to be like the real thing.

'His Highness, the Emir, on the other hand,' Kal continued, 'would be certain to think that I'd personally arranged for you to go down with pneumonia in order to cause him maximum embarrassment.'

He spoke lightly enough, inviting amusement, but she didn't laugh, sensing the underlying darkness behind his words.

'Why on earth would he think that?' she asked, but more questions crowded into her head. Without waiting for him to answer, she added, 'And why do you always refer to him as His Highness or the Emir?' She made little quote marks with her fingers, something else she realised Rose would never do, and let her hands drop. 'Sheikh Jamal is your uncle, isn't he, Kal?' she prompted when he didn't answer.

'Yes,' he said shortly. Then, before she could say another word, 'Someone will bring tea in a moment.'

'This is your first visit here, too,' she said, ignoring the abrupt change of subject. 'Why is that?'

'Watch the sunrise, for heaven's sake,' he practically growled at her.

In other words, Lydia, mind your own business, she thought, unsure whether she was pleased or sorry that she'd managed to rattle him out of his good manners.

Here was a mystery. A secret.

That she wasn't the only one hiding something made her feel less guilty about the secret she was keeping for Rose, although no better about lying to him, and without another word she did as she was told.

Neither of them spoke or moved again while the darkness rolled back and the sun, still below the horizon, lit up bubbles of cloud in a blaze of colour that was reflected in the creek, the sea beyond, turning them first carmine, then pink, then liquid gold. As it grew light, the dark shapes against the water resolved themselves into traditional dhows moored amongst modern craft and beyond, sprawling over the steep bank on the far side of the creek, she could see a small town with a harbour and market which were already coming to life.

'Wow,' she said at last. 'Double wow.'

She caught a movement as Kal turned to look at her and she shrugged.

'Well, what other word is there?' she asked.

'Bab el Sama.' He said the words softly. 'The Gate of Heaven.'

She swallowed at the poetry of the name and said, 'You win.'

He shook his head and said, 'Are you done?'

'Yes. Thank you for being so patient.'

'I wouldn't have missed it,' he assured her as they turned and walked back towards the summer house—such an ordinary word for something that looked as if it had been conjured up by Aladdin's djinn—where a manservant was laying out the contents of a large tray.

The man bowed and, eyes down, said, '*Assalam alaykum, sitti. Marhaba.*'

She turned to Kal for a translation. 'He said, "Peace be upon you, Lady. Welcome."'

'What should I say in return?'

'*Shukran. Alaykum assalam,*' Kal said. 'Thank you. And upon you peace.'

The man smiled, bowed again, when she repeated it, savouring the words on her tongue, locking them away in her memory, along with Bab el Sama. He left them to enjoy their breakfast in private.

As she chose a high-backed cane chair and sank into the vivid silk cushions, Kal unwrapped a napkin nestled in a basket to reveal warm pastries.

'Hungry?'

'I seem to have done nothing but eat since I left London,' she said. 'I'll have to swim the creek once a day if I'm going to keep indulging myself this way.'

Maybe it was the thought of all that effort, but right now all she wanted to do was close her eyes and go to sleep. Tea would help, she told herself, just about managing to control a yawn.

'Is that a yes or a no?' he asked, offering her the basket.

'Breakfast *is* the most important meal of the day,' she said, succumbing to the enticing buttery smell. 'I suppose it is breakfast time?'

'It's whatever time you care to make it,' he assured her as he poured tea into two unbelievably thin china cups. 'Milk, lemon?'

'Just a touch of milk,' she said. Then, 'Should you be doing this?' He glanced at her. 'Waiting on me?'

Kal frowned, unable, for a moment, to imagine what she meant.

'Won't it ruin your image?'

'Image?'

He hadn't been brought up like his grandfather, his father, to believe he was a prince, above the mundane realities of the world. Nor, despite his Mediterranean childhood, was he one of those men who expected to live at home, waited on by a doting mother until he transferred that honour to a wife. Even if he had been so inclined, his mother had far more interesting things to do.

As had he.

His image was not about macho posturing. He had never needed to work, never would, but once he'd fallen in love with flying he had worked hard. He'd wanted to own aircraft but there was no fun in having them sit on the tarmac. He'd started Kalzak Air Services as a courier service. Now he flew freight worldwide. And he employed men and women—hundreds of them—on their qualifications and personal qualities first, last and everything in between.

'Hanif nursed his first wife, nursed Lucy, too, when she was injured,' he said.

'He did?'

'Lucy has not told you?'

'Only that he loved her.'

'He loved his first wife, too.' The girl who had been chosen for him. A traditional arranged marriage. 'He has been twice blessed.'

'Maybe he is a man who knows how to love,' she said.

Was that the answer?

It was not a concept he was comfortable with and, remembering what Lucy had said about Rose not being able to lift a finger without someone taking a photograph of her, he carried his own cup towards the edge of the promontory and leaned against the parapet. A man enjoying the view. It was what anyone would do in such a place.

The sun was in the wrong direction to reflect off a lens that would betray a paparazzo lying in wait to snatch a photograph. Not that he imagined they would ever be that careless. The only obvious activity was on the dhows as their crews prepared to head out to sea for a day's fishing.

As he scanned the wider panorama, the distant shore, he saw only a peaceful, contented community waking to a new day, going about its business. He let the scene sink into his bones the way parched earth sucked up rain.

As a boy, his grandfather would have stood in this same spot, looking at the creek, the town, the desert beyond it, certain in the knowledge that every drop of water, every grain of sand would, *insh'Allah,* one day be his.

Except that Allah had not willed it. His grandfather had followed his heart instead of his head and, as a result, had been judged unworthy. A lesson he had learned well.

He drained his cup, took one last look, then returned to the summer house.

Sparrows, pecking at a piece of pastry, flew up at his approach and a single look was enough to tell him that Rose had fallen asleep, tea untouched, croissant untasted.

And, now that the sun had risen high enough to banish the shadows from the summer house and illuminate her clear, fair skin, he could see the faint violet smudges beneath her eyes.

Clearly sleep had eluded her aboard the plane and a long day, a long flight, had finally caught up with her. This was no light doze and he did not attempt to wake her, but as he bent and caught her beneath the knees she sighed.

'Shh,' he said, easing her arm over his shoulder, around his neck. 'Hold on.'

On some level of consciousness she must have heard him because, as he lifted her out of the chair, she curled her hand around his neck and tucked her head into the hollow of his shoulder.

She wasn't anywhere near as light, as ethereal as she looked, he discovered as he carried her along the path to Lucy and Han's seaside retreat. Not an angel, but a real, solid woman and he was glad that the huge doors stood wide to welcome her.

He walked straight in, picking up a little group of women who, clucking anxiously, rushed ahead to open doors, circled round them tutting with disapproval and finally stood in his way when he reached her bedroom.

'Move,' he said, 'or I'll drop her.'

They scattered with little squeals of outrage, then, as he laid her on the bed, clicked his fingers for a cover in a manner that would have made his grandfather proud—and he would have protested was utterly alien to him—they rushed to do his bidding.

He removed her shoes but, about to reach for the button at her waist to make her more comfortable, he became aware of a silence, a collectively held breath.

He turned to look at the women clustered behind him, their shocked faces. And, remembering himself, took a step back.

That he could have undressed her in a completely detached manner had the occasion demanded it was not in question. But this was not London, or New York, or Paris. This was a world where a man did not undress a woman unless he was married to her. He should not even be in her room.

'Make her comfortable,' he said with a gesture that would have done his grandfather proud. Maybe it was the place calling to his genes, he thought as he closed the door behind him, leaving the women to their task.

Then, to an old woman who'd settled herself, cross-legged, in front of the door like a palace guard, 'When she wakes she should have a massage.'

'It will be done, sidi.'

Lord…

'Don't call me that,' he said, straightening, easing his own aching limbs.

'You don't want to be given your title, Sheikh?' she asked, clearly not in the slightest bit in awe of him. 'Your grandfather wanted to be the Emir.'

About to walk away, he stopped, turned slowly back to face her.

'You knew him?'

'When he was a boy. A young man. Before he was foolish.'

She was the first person he'd met in Ramal Hamrah who was prepared to admit that. He sat before her, crossing his legs so that the soles of his feet were tucked out of sight.

'Here? You knew him here?'

'Here. In Rumaillah. At Umm al Sama. He was the wild one. Headstrong.' She shook her head. 'And he was stubborn, like his father. Once he'd said a thing, that was it.' She brushed her palms together in a gesture he'd seen many times. It signalled an end to discussion. That the subject was closed. 'They were two rocks.' She tilted her head in a birdlike gesture, examining him closely. 'You look like him,' she said after a while. 'Apart from the beard. A man should have a beard.'

He rubbed his hand self-consciously over his bare chin. He had grown a beard, aware that to be clean-shaven was the western way; it would be something else the Emir could hold against him.

'My grandfather doesn't have a beard these days,' he told her. The chemo baldness hadn't bothered him nearly as much as the loss of this symbol of his manhood and Kal had taken a razor to his own beard in an act of solidarity. It had felt odd for a while, but he'd got used to it.

'They say that he is dying,' she said. He did not ask who had said. Gossip flowed through the harem like water down the Nile.

'But still stubborn,' he replied. 'He refuses to die anywhere but in the place he still calls home.'

She nodded, 'You are stubborn, too,' she said, reaching up to pat his hand. 'You will bring him home, *insh'Allah*. It is your destiny.'

'Who are you?' he asked, with a sudden sinking feeling, the certainty that he had just made a complete fool of himself.

'I am Dena. I was found, out there,' she said with the wave of an elegant hand, the rattle of gold on her skinny wrists. 'Your great-grandmother took me into her house. Made me her daughter.'

Oh, terrific. This woman was the adopted child of the Khatib and he'd spoken to her as if she were a servant. But from the way she'd settled herself in front of Rose's bedroom door…

He'd been brought up on his grandfather's stories, had studied his family, this country, clung to a language that his father had all but forgotten, but he still had so much to learn.

He uncurled himself, got to his feet. 'My apologies, *sitti*,' he said with a formal bow.

'You have his charm, too,' she said. 'When you speak to him tell him that his sister Dena remembers him with fondness.' Then, 'Go.' She waved him away. 'Go. I will watch over your lady while you sleep.'

His lady…

Dena's words echoed in his mind as he stood beneath the shower, igniting again the memory of Rose's lips, warm, vital as they'd softened beneath him, parted for him. His mouth burned but as he sucked his lower lip into his mouth, ran a tongue over it, he tasted Rose and, instead of cooling it down, the heat surged like a contagion through his body.

Do you want me to protect her or make love to her…?

Lucy had not answered his question, but it would have made no difference either way. He was not free. He flipped the shower to cold and, lifting his face to the water, stood beneath it until he was chilled to the bone.

And still he burned.

CHAPTER SIX

LYDIA woke in slow gentle ripples of consciousness. Blissful comfort was the first stage. The pleasure of smooth, sweet-smelling sheets, the perfect pillow and, unwilling to surrender the pleasure, she turned over and fell back into its embrace.

The jewelled light filtering through ornate wooden shutters, colours dancing on white walls, seeping through her eyelids, came next.

She opened her eyes and saw an ornate band of tiny blue and green tiles shimmering like the early morning creek. She turned onto her back, looked up at a high raftered cedar wood ceiling.

It was true then. Not a dream.

'Bab el Sama.' She said the name out loud, savouring the feel of it in her mouth. The Gate of Heaven. '*Marhaba...*' Welcome. 'Kalil al-Zaki...' Trouble.

'You are awake, *sitti?*'

What?

She sat up abruptly. There was a woman, her head, body swathed in an enfolding black garment, sitting cross-legged in front of a pair of tall carved doors, as if guarding the entrance.

She rose with extraordinary grace and bowed her head. 'I am Dena, *sitti*. Princess Lucy called me, asked me to take care of you.'

'She seems to have called everyone,' Lydia said.

So much for being alone!

She threw off the covers, then immediately grabbed them back, clutching them to her chest, as she realised that she was naked.

Realised that she had no memory of getting that way. Only of the sunrise with Kal, soft cushions, the scent of buttery pastry. Of closing her eyes.

'Bin Zaki carried you here, *sitti*. We made you comfortable.'

Lydia swallowed, not quite sure how she felt about that. Whether it was worse that an unknown 'we' had undressed her sleeping body or Kal.

The woman, Dena, picked up a robe, held it out so that she could turn and slip her arms through the sleeves, wrap it around her, preserve a little of her modesty before sliding out of the bed.

It clung to her, soft and light as the touch of a butterfly wing, leaving her feeling almost as exposed as if she was wearing nothing at all. The kind of thing a pampered concubine might have worn. With a sudden quickening of something almost like fear, laced through with excitement, she said, 'Where is Kal?'

'He went to the stables.' The woman's eyes, as she handed her the glass of juice she'd poured from a flask, saw the flush that heated her skin and smiled knowingly. 'He took a horse,' she said. Then, 'I will bathe you and then you will have a massage.'

What?

'That won't be necessary,' she said.

'Bin Zaki ordered it so. Princess Lucy always needs a massage when she comes home.'

'Really?'

But the woman had opened a door that led into a bathroom that was out of a fantasy. A deep sunken tub. A huge shower with side jets. A seat big enough for two.

'Which?' Dena asked.

'The shower,' Lydia said, dismissing the disturbing image of sinking into the huge tub, sharing it with Kal.

She really, really needed something to clear her head, wake her up.

Dena turned it on, adjusted the temperature, apparently oblivious of the fact that her floor length black dress was getting wet. Apparently waiting for her to shed the robe and step into the shower so that she could wash her.

No, no, no…

Lydia swallowed, said, 'I can manage. Really.'

She nodded. 'Come into the next room when you are ready and I will ease the ache in your shoulder.'

Lydia stared after her. Raised her left hand to her right shoulder, the one that ached when it was cold or damp. After a long shift on the checkout. The legacy of years of lifting other people's groceries across a scanner.

How did she know? What had given her away?

She shook her head.

Nothing. Dena couldn't know that she was a fake. If she did, the whole house of cards would be tumbling around her ears by now, she told herself as she slipped out of the wrap, stepped under the warm water.

If she was a trained masseuse she would be observant, that was all, would notice the slightest imbalance. It didn't mean anything.

She might have slept awkwardly on the plane or strained it in a hundred ways.

She turned up the heat and let the water pound her body, easing an ache which, until that moment, she'd been scarcely aware of herself.

Lathered herself in rich soap.

Washed her hair.

Putting off, for as long as possible, the moment when, wrapped in a towel that covered her from breast to ankle, her hair wrapped in a smaller one, she would have to submit herself to the ministrations of the slightly scary Dena.

But as she lay down and Dena's hands found the knots in her muscles, soothed away the tension of the last twenty-four hours, all the stress floated away and she surrendered to total pampering.

Wrapped tenderly in a robe, seated in a chair that tilted back, her hair was released and unseen hands massaged her scalp, gently combed out her hair, while a young girl did miraculous things to her feet, her hands.

Painted her nails, drew patterns with henna.

By the time they were finished, she was so utterly relaxed that when one of the girls held out a pair of exquisite French knickers she stepped into them without a flicker of embarrassment.

Slipped into a matching lace bra and left it for someone else to fasten.

Held up her arms as Dena slipped a loose silk kaftan over her head that had certainly not been part of the wardrobe packed by Rose.

It floated over her, a mist of blue, then settled over her shoulders, her arms, falling to the floor before nimble fingers fastened the dozen or more silk-covered buttons that held it together at her breast.

Then she stepped into a pair of soft thong sandals that were placed in front of her.

A week of this and she'd be ruined for real life, she thought, pulling her lips back against her teeth so that she wouldn't grin out loud.

Wow! Wow! Wow!

Thank you, Rose! I hope you're enjoying every second of your freedom. Having the most wonderful time.

And, with that thought, reality rushed back as she looked around for the clutch bag she'd been carrying.

A word and it was in her hand and she took out her mobile phone to send the agreed 'arrived safely' message, followed by another more detailed message to her mother. Not just to let her know that she'd got to her destination without mishap, but that the apartment was great and she was having a great time.

So far, so true. Unless… Did kissing Kal count as a mishap?

She looked at the message doubtfully, then, with a rueful smile, hit 'send', grateful that her mother had insisted that overseas mobile calls were too expensive, that the occasional text was all she expected. She would never be able to bluff her way through an entire week of this, not with her mother. With Kal…

She looked up and realised that everyone was waiting to hear what she wanted to do next.

She slipped the phone into a pocket in the seam of the kaftan and said, 'May I look around?'

Dena led the way, down a series of steps to a lower level entrance lobby with a two-storey domed ceiling richly decorated in floral designs with tiny ceramic tiles, her helpers following, all anxious to see her reaction. Clearly wanting her to love this place they called home.

They waited patiently while she stopped, turned slowly, looking up in awe at the workmanship.

'This is a holiday cottage?' she asked in amazement. 'It's so beautiful!'

Dena was unreadable, but the two younger women were clearly delighted.

The tour took in a formal dining room where ornate carved doors had been folded back to reveal a terrace and, below it, set in a private walled garden, a swimming pool.

More steps and then Dena said, 'This is the room the family use when they are here.'

Furnished with richly coloured sofas and jewel-bright oriental rugs that softened the polished wooden floor, Lydia might have been totally overwhelmed by its sheer size, but then she spotted a fluffy yellow toy duck half hidden amongst the cushions.

It was a reminder that this was someone's holiday home, a place where children ran and played. She picked it up and held it for a moment and when she looked up she saw that Dena was smiling.

'It is Jamal's,' she said. 'He left it there to keep his place while he was away.'

'Bless,' she said, carefully tucking it back where she'd found

it and, looking around, saw the touches that made this unbelievably grand room a home.

The box filled with toys. A pile of books that suggested
Lucy's favourite holiday activity was reading. A child's
drawing of the creek, framed as lovingly as an old master.
Children's books in English and Arabic.

'You like children?' Dena asked as she picked up an
alphabet colouring book similar to one she'd had as a child.
Except that the alphabet was Arabic.

She nodded. 'Even the little monsters…'

Even the little monsters who whined and nagged their
stressed mothers for sweets at the checkout. Their soft little
mouths, big eyes that could be coaxed so quickly from tears to
a smile with a little attention.

She was so relaxed that she'd completely forgotten to guard
her tongue but, while Dena regarded her thoughtfully, the
younger women giggled, repeating 'little monsters' as if they
knew only too well what she meant.

She managed a shrug and Dena, making no comment,
folded back doors similar to the ones in the dining room,
opening up one side of the room to the garden so that Lydia
could step out onto a wide terrace that overlooked the creek.

'All children love Bab el Sama,' she said. 'You will bring
your children here.'

It sounded more like a statement than a question and
Lydia swallowed.

She had two careers and no time for romance, even if she
could ever trust a man again sufficiently to let him get that
close.

Maybe Kal was the answer. He, at least, wouldn't be pretending…

She, on the other hand, would be.

Since the one thing she demanded of a man was total
honesty, to kiss with a lie on her lips was not something she
could live with, no matter how alluring the temptation.

'I'm sure they have a wonderful time,' she said, responding to her first comment, ignoring the second as she walked quickly to the edge of the terrace as if to take a closer look at the beach.

They were much lower here than on the bluff where she'd watched the sunrise, not more than twenty feet above the beach. And, looking around, she thought that the adults must love it too.

There were pots overflowing with geraniums, still flowering in December, the rustle and clack of palm fronds in the light breeze, a snatch of unfamiliar music carrying across the glittering water.

It was peaceful, beautiful, with a delicious warmth that seeped into the bones and invited her to lift her face to the sun and smile as if she were a sunflower.

Even as she did that, a movement caught her eye and below, on the beach, she saw a horseman galloping along the edge of the surf, robes streaming out behind him.

The horse, its hooves a blur in the spray, seemed to be almost flying, elemental, a force of nature. Lydia's breath caught in her throat and she took a step closer, her hand lifting towards him as if reaching to catch hold, be lifted up to fly with him.

'It is Bin Zaki,' Dena said, but Lydia knew that.

He might have shed his designer suit, donned a robe, hidden his dark curls beneath a *keffiyeh,* but his chiselled face, the fierce hawkish nose were imprinted on her memory and, as he flashed by in a swirl of cloth, hooves, spray, the profile was unmistakable.

'He is chasing his demons. So like his grandfather.'

For a moment she didn't respond, scarcely registered what the woman had said, but Kal had gone, lost from sight as the beach curved around massive rocks, the final fling of the mountain range behind them. And already the sea was smoothing away the hoof prints, rubbing out all trace of his passing.

She turned to discover that Dena was watching her and, suddenly coming back to reality, she dropped her hand self-consciously.

'Demons? What demons?'

'He will tell you in his own good time. Do you need anything, *sitti?*'

Only to be held, enfolded, caressed, but not by some anonymous, faceless figure. All the longings and desires that haunted her had become focused on one man and she turned back to the empty beach as if his spirit was still there for her to reach out and touch.

'I think I'll take a walk,' she said, suddenly self-conscious, certain that Dena knew exactly what she was thinking. 'Explore a little. Is there anywhere I shouldn't go?'

'Bab el Sama is yours, *sitti.*'

Dena left her alone to explore and she skirted the terrace, noticing how cleverly it was shielded from the creek by the trees so that no one from below would be able to see the royal family at play.

Taking a path, she found steps that led invitingly downwards in the direction of the beach but, conscious of the silk kaftan flowing around her ankles, she turned instead along a path that led upward through the garden.

After the crash that had killed her father and left her mother in a wheelchair, she and her mother had moved from their small house with a garden into a ground floor flat that had been adapted for a wheelchair user.

She'd missed the garden but, ten years old, she'd understood the necessity and knew better than to say anything that would hurt her mother. It was the hand that life had dealt but even then she'd used her pocket money to buy flowering pot plants from the market. Had grown herbs on the windowsill.

This garden was like a dream. Little streams ran down through the trees, fell over rocks to feed pools where carp rose at her appearance.

There were exquisite summer houses tucked away. Some were for children, with garden toys. Some, with comfortable chairs, were placed to catch a stunning view.

One, with a copper roof turned green with verdigris, was laid with rich carpets on which cushions had been piled, and looked like a lovers' hideaway. She could imagine lying there with Kal, his lips pressed against her throat as he unfastened the buttons...

She lifted her hand to her breast, shook her head, trying to rid herself of an image that was so powerful that she could feel his hands, his mouth on her body.

As she backed away there was a scuffle near her feet as a lizard disappeared in a flurry of emerald tail. For a moment she stared at the spot, not sure whether she'd imagined it. Then she looked up and saw Kal standing just a few feet away.

The *keffiyeh* had fallen from his head and lay gathered about his neck. His robes were made of some loosely woven cream material and the hem was heavy with sea water and sand. As they stood there, silent, still, a trickle of sweat ran from his temple into the dust on his cheek.

After what seemed like an age he finally moved, lifting his elbow to wipe his face on his sleeve.

'I've been riding,' he said wearily.

'I saw you. You looked as if you were flying,' she said.

'That's me,' he said, the corner of his mouth lifting in a self-mocking smile. 'Addicted to the air.' He took a step forward but Lydia, almost dizzy with the scent of leather, of the sea clinging to his clothes, of tangy fresh sweat that her body was responding to like an aphrodisiac, didn't move.

Hot, sweaty he exuded a raw sexual potency and she wanted to touch his face. Kiss the space between his thumb and palm, taste the leather; lean into him and bury her face in his robes, breathe him in. Wanted to feel those long, powerful hands that had so easily controlled half a ton of muscle and bone in full flight, on her own body.

She cooled her burning lip with the tip of her tongue, then, realising how that must look, said, 'Maybe my problem with flying is that I didn't start in the right place.'

He frowned. 'You don't ride?'

'No.' Having studied every aspect of her alter ego's life, she knew that while most little girls of her class would have been confidently astride her first pony by the time she was three, Rose was not one of them. 'But, if I had to choose, I think I'd prefer it to fishing.'

His smile was a lazy thing that began in the depths of his eyes, barely noticeable if you weren't locked in to every tiny response. No more than a tiny spark that might so easily have been mistaken for a shaft of sunlight finding a space between the leaves to warm the darkness. Then the creases that fanned out around them deepened a little, the skin over his cheekbones tightened and lifted. Only then did his mouth join in with a slightly lopsided *gotcha* grin.

'Here's the deal,' he said. 'You let me take you fishing and I'll teach you to ride.'

His voice, his words seemed to caress her so that it sounded more like a sexual proposition than a simple choice between this or that outdoor activity. Standing there in the dappled sunlight, every nerve-ending at attention, sensitized by desire, she knew that if he reached out, touched her, she would buckle, dissolve and if he carried her into the summer house and laid her amongst the cushions, nothing could save her.

That she wouldn't want to be saved.

This powerful, instant attraction had nothing to do with who they were. Or weren't. It was pure chemistry. Names, titles meant nothing.

She lowered her lids, scarcely able to breathe. 'Is that your final offer?'

His voice soft, dangerously seductive, he said, 'How about if I offered to bait your hook for you?'

Baited, hooked, landed…

She swallowed, cooled her burning lower lip with her tongue. 'How could I resist such an inducement?'

A step brought him alongside her and he took her chin in

his hand, ran the pad of his thumb over her mouth in an explora-
tory sweep as if to test its heat.

'It is a date, Rose.'

He was so close that she could see the grains of sand thrown
up by the flying hooves which clung to his face and, as she
closed her eyes to breathe in the pure essence of the man, his
mouth touched hers, his tongue lightly tracing her lower lip,
imitating the route her own had taken seconds before, as if
tasting her.

Before she could react, clutch at him to stop herself from
collapsing at his feet, it was over.

'You will fish with me this afternoon. I will ride with you
at dawn.'

'Perfect,' she managed through a throat that felt as if it was
stuffed with cotton wool. Through lips that felt twice their
normal size.

Then, as she opened her eyes, he stepped back and said,
'You might want to wear something a little less…distracting.'

Before she could respond, he strode away in a swirl of robes
and she did not move until she was quite alone.

Only when the path was quite empty, the only sound—apart
from the pounding of her heart—was the rattle of palm fronds
high above her, did she finally look down, see for herself how
the light breeze was moulding the thin blue silk to her body so
that it outlined every contour. Her thighs, the gentle curve of
her belly. The hard, betraying, touch-me peaks of her breasts.

CHAPTER SEVEN

KAL stood beneath the pounding icy shower. He did not need hot water; the heat coming off him was turning the water to steam.

He closed his eyes but it didn't help. Without visual distraction, the image of Rose Napier, silk clinging to every curve, filled his head, obliterating everything from his mind but her.

If he had ever doubted her innocence, he was now utterly convinced of it. No woman who had a scintilla of experience would have let a man see such naked desire shining out of her eyes, been so unconscious of the *come-and-take-me* signals her body was semaphoring in response to his nearness. Given him such power over her.

But maybe they were both out of their depth.

Preoccupied with his own concerns and apparently immune to this pale beauty that the entire world appeared to be in love with, his guard had been down.

Knocked sideways from his first sight of her and, knowing that he wouldn't sleep, he'd gone to the stables, determined to blow away the demands of his body in hard physical activity.

But as hard as he'd ridden he could not shake loose the image of those blue eyes. One moment *keep-your-distance* cool, the next sparkling with life, excitement. A touch of mischief.

Almost, he thought, as if she were two women.

The adored, empathetic public figure—as flawless and beautiful as a Bernini marble, as out of reach as the stars.

And this private, flesh and blood woman whose eyes appealed for his touch, for him to take her, bring her to life.

Living with those eyes, those seductive lips that drew him to her, would not make for a comfortable week. And he'd just made it a thousand times worse.

He'd ridden off the sexual energy that had built over their long flight. Had been totally in control, with the self-discipline to keep his hands off her.

All he'd had to do was keep his distance, leave it to her to initiate any outings. He had his own agenda and it certainly didn't include getting involved with a woman, especially one who was a national icon.

Until he'd taken a turn in the path and saw her standing before him, her hair hanging like silk around her shoulders. Wearing an embroidered silk kaftan that exactly matched eyes shining like a woman on her wedding night.

And he'd been the one insisting that the two of them should spend time alone together on a boat.

Offering to teach her to ride.

Unable to resist touching her lip with his thumb, his tongue, wanting to test the heat, knowing that it was for him.

It had taken every ounce of self-discipline to stop himself from carrying her into the pavilion hidden in the trees behind her. Making her his.

To force himself to step back, walk away.

He flipped off the water, stepped from the shower, grabbed a towel and wrapped it round him.

His clothes had been pressed and hung up but someone, Dena, probably, had added an array of casual and formal robes for his use while he was at Bab el Sama.

The kind of clothes that Hanif would wear. A sheikh, relaxing in the privacy of his own home, with his children around him.

It was Dena, undoubtedly, who'd dressed Rose in that silk dress, had painted her hands with henna. He frowned, wondering what she thought she was doing.

He shook his head. Rose was on holiday in an exotic location and no doubt Lucy had ordered that her friend be totally pampered.

She certainly looked a great deal more rested. Unlike him. He lifted his shoulders, easing them, then reached for his cell-phone and called his grandfather at the clinic.

After he'd asked how he was, as if he didn't know—in desperate pain but stubbornly refusing palliative care until he was permitted to return home to die—and getting the same answer, he said, 'I met someone today who knew you.'

'And is prepared to admit it?'

'She said that you were stubborn, *Jaddi*. But charming—'

There was a short harsh laugh, then, 'She?'

'She said, "Tell him that his sister Dena remembers him with fondness."'

'Dena?' There was a rare catch in the old man's voice. 'She is well?'

'She is well,' he confirmed. 'She said it was time you were home.'

'Tell her… Tell her I will be there, *insh'Allah*. Tell her that I will not die until I have kissed her.'

'It will be so, *Jaddi'l habeeb*,' Kal said softly. 'I swear it.'

He put down the phone, spent a moment reminding himself why he was here, gathering himself.

Then he pulled out the jeans he'd brought with him, chose a loose long-sleeved white shirt from the wardrobe and pulled it over his head and stepped into thong sandals that seemed more suitable than any of the shoes he'd brought with him.

As he picked up the phone to stow it in his pocket, it rang. Caller ID warned him that it was Lucy and he said, 'Checking up on me, Princess?'

She laughed. 'Why? What are you up to?' Then, not waiting for an answer, 'I just wanted to be sure that Rose arrived safely.'

'So why not call her?'

'She wants to cut herself off from everyone while she's

away. She wants to think about the future without anyone else offering their opinions, clouding the picture.'

'Instead, she got me,' he said. 'Tell me, was there a single word of truth in what you told me?'

'Absolutely. Cross my heart,' she swore. 'Why do you think her grandfather was so desperate to stop her? He doesn't want her doing anything as dangerous as thinking for herself, not without someone on hand to guide her thoughts in the right direction.'

'And that would be in the direction of the marriage he's arranged?' he asked casually enough, despite the fact that the thought of another man touching her sent a shaft of possessive heat driving deep into his groin.

'She's longing for a family, children of her own, Kal, and I think she's very nearly desperate enough to marry Rupert Devenish to get them.'

'What other reason is there for a woman to marry?' he asked.

Or a man, for that matter.

Far better to have people who had known you all your life, who understood your strengths and weaknesses, to seek a bride whose temperament, expectations matched your own, than rely on unbridled passion that, no matter how intense the heat, would soon become ashes. He'd seen it happen. His grandfather, his father…

'Oh, pish-posh,' Lucy said with the impatience of a woman who'd found a rare love and thought he should be making an effort to do the same. 'How is she?'

'Rose? She slept for a while, but now she's exploring the garden.'

'On her own?'

'I have no doubt that your Dena has someone within call.' Someone who would have seen him kissing her? 'She's safe enough,' he said abruptly. 'And we're about to have lunch.'

'Maybe when you've eaten you'll be in a better mood. Perhaps I should call you then?'

'No. Really. I've just spoken to my grandfather. And, as for your Rose, well, she isn't quite what I expected. I imagined un-ruffled serenity.'

'Oh? In what way is she not serene?'

In the quick blush that warmed her pale skin, in her eyes, a mouth, a body that gave away too much.

'Well,' he said, pushing away the disturbing images, 'I would have welcomed a warning that she's a nervous flyer.'

'Rose? I never knew that. How did she cope with the heli-copter?' Her concern was genuine enough, Kal decided, giving her the benefit of the doubt.

'I managed to keep her distracted.' Before she could ask him how, he added, 'I was surprised to discover that she doesn't ride.'

'I think a pony bolted with her when she was little.' He could see the tiny frown as she tried to remember. 'Something like that.'

'Well, she appears to be willing to give it another go.'

'You're going to take her riding?'

'Amuse and entertain her, that was the brief.'

'Absolutely. I'm glad you're taking it so seriously. But the reason for my call is to give you advance warning that Rose should be getting a courtesy visit from Princess Sabirah later in the week. The household will be warned of her arrival, but I thought you might welcome a little extra time to prepare yourself.'

'Thank you, Lucy. If I haven't sufficiently expressed my grat—'

'It's little enough in return for everything you've done for my charity, Kal. Just do me one favour. Don't tell Rose that I was checking up on her.'

'I won't. Lucy…'

He hesitated. He knew his doubts were foolish. Lady Rose Napier had been hand delivered to him by her security guard…

'Yes?' she prompted.

'Nothing. Take care.'

He disconnected, pushed the phone into his back pocket and, bearing in mind that it was his duty to keep her safe, he went to find Rose.

Lydia resisted the urge to fling herself into the nearest pool to cool herself down. Instead, she walked the winding paths, swiftly at first, outrunning feelings she could not control, until her breath was coming in short gasps and she almost collapsed into a seat that seemed to have been placed precisely for that purpose.

She sat there for an age while her breathing returned to normal and the heat gradually faded from her skin, attempting to make sense of what had happened.

She might as well try to catch mist in her hand.

There *was* no sense in it. Love—or just plain lust—as she knew to her cost, made fools of everyone.

'Get a grip, Lydie,' she said intently, startling a bird from the tree above her. 'Rose is depending on you. This madness will go away.' Then, after a long time, 'It will go away.'

By the time she returned to the terrace her flush might easily have been put down to nothing more than a brisk walk on a sunny day.

Just as well, because one of the girls who'd taken care of her was sitting cross-legged in the shade, embroidering a piece of silk.

'You will eat, *sitti?*' she asked, rising gracefully to her feet.

Food was the last thing on her mind, but it had been a long time since the croissant that she'd barely tasted and eating was a proven distraction for heartache.

'Thank you… I'm sorry, I don't know your name.'

'It is Yatimah, *sitti.*'

'Yatimah,' she repeated, rolling the word around her mouth, tasting the strangeness of it. 'Thank you, Yatimah. Your English is very good.'

'Princess Lucy has taught me. She speaks Arabic as if she

was born here, but her mother comes sometimes. From New Zealand. And her friends from England.'

'And they do not,' Lydia said.

'A few words,' she said with a smile.

'Will you teach me?'

'*Nam,*' she said. And giggled. 'That means yes.'

'*Nam,*' she repeated. Then, remembering the word Kal had taught her, she said, '*Shukran.* Thank you.' And received a delighted clap. Encouraged, she asked, 'What is "good morning"?'

'Good morning is *sabah alkhair* and the reply is *sabah alnur.*'

Lydia tried it and got the response from Yatimah who, an eager teacher, then said, 'Good afternoon is *masa alkhair* and the reply *masa alnur.* And goodnight is—'

'*Leila sa'eeda.*'

Startled by Kal's voice from the doorway, Yatimah scuttled away, leaving Lydia alone with him.

The last time he'd kissed her, she'd managed to dismiss it as if it was nothing. They both knew that wasn't going to happen this time and for a moment neither of them moved, spoke.

'Lucy called,' he said at last, stepping onto the terrace.

He'd showered and changed into a loose white collarless shirt that hung to his hips. Soft faded jeans. Strong, bare feet pushed into thong sandals. The clothes were unremarkable but with that thin high-bridged nose, polished olive skin, dark hair curling onto his neck, he looked very different from the man in the suit who'd met her at the airport. More like some desert lord surveying his world.

'She wanted to be sure you'd arrived safely.'

'Then why didn't she call me?' Lydia asked, brave in the knowledge that if she'd rung Rose, by the magic of the cellphone, she'd have got Rose, wherever she was. Except, of course, that Rose didn't know anything about Kal. She'd need to send a message, she thought, her hand going to the phone in her pocket, warn her...

'My own reaction,' he replied, 'but she seemed to be under

the impression that you'd rather not talk to anyone from home. That you did not want to be disturbed.'

...or maybe not.

He turned to her in expectation of polite denial.

Being a lookalike was an acting role, stepping into the shoes of another person, copying the moves, the gestures, the facial expressions. Practising the voice until it became her own. But nothing that Rose had ever done had prepared her for this.

In a situation like this, all she had to fall back on was the supermarket checkout girl with the fast mouth.

And that girl wouldn't let him off with a polite anything. That girl would look him in the eye, lift an eyebrow and say, 'She should have thought about that before she invited you to my party.'

Just like that.

If she'd hoped to raise a smile, she would have been sadly disappointed.

Apart from the slightest contraction of a muscle at the corner of his mouth—as if she needed any encouragement to look at it—his expression didn't alter for so long that, but for that tiny giveaway, she might have wondered if he'd actually heard her.

Then, with the merest movement of his head, he acknowledged the hit and said, 'No doubt that's why she asked me not to tell you she'd called.'

'So why did you?' she demanded, refusing to back down, play the lady. She might not know what Rose would do under these circumstances, but she jolly well knew what she should do after that very close encounter in the garden.

That had gone far beyond simple flirting. Far beyond what had happened in the helicopter, where his kiss had been simple enough. It had been her own reaction that had turned into something much more complex; fear, strangeness, the need to cling to something safe would do that and it was easy enough to dismiss as an aberration.

But what had happened in the garden was different.

He'd touched her mouth as if marking her as his, taken her lower lip into his mouth as intimately as a lover, certain of his welcome.

And she had welcomed him.

That moment had been an acknowledgement of the intense attraction that had been bubbling beneath the surface from the moment she had walked into the airport and found him waiting for her.

It was a dance where they circled one another, getting closer and closer. Touching briefly. Moving apart as they fought it but, like two moths being drawn closer and closer to a candle, totally unable to resist the fatal attraction, even though they both knew they would go down in flames.

Except that she had no choice. She had to withstand the temptation or tell him the truth, because she knew how it felt to be made love to by someone who was acting. Knew how betrayed she'd felt.

And she couldn't tell him the truth. Couldn't betray Rose for her own selfish desires. Not that he'd want her if she did. He was not a man to accept a fake. A copy. If he knew the truth he'd lose interest, turn away.

And if he didn't…

'Kal…'

'You are hungry?'

Her life seemed to be happening in slow motion, Lydia thought. Neither of them moved or made a move to answer Dena's query for what seemed like forever.

It did not matter. Apparently oblivious to the tension between them, she bustled across the terrace to a table set beneath the trees, issuing orders to the staff that trailed after her.

A cloth was laid, food was set out.

'Come, eat,' she said, waving them towards the table.

Kal moved first, held out a chair for her, and she managed to unstick her feet from the flagstones and join him at the table.

'This looks wonderful, Dena,' she said, trying very hard to ignore his hands grasping the back of her chair, the beautiful bones of his wrists, the dark hair exposed where he'd folded back the sleeves of his shirt, the woody scent of soap and shampoo as she sat down and he bent over her to ease the chair forward.

It was like living inside a kaleidoscope of the senses. Everything was heightened. The food glowed, gleamed with colour, enticed with spices. The arm of her chair, worn smooth by many hands. The starchy smell, the feel of the damask cloth against her legs. A silence so intense that she could almost feel it.

Then a bird fluttered down, anticipating crumbs, and gradually everything began to move again and she realised that Dena was speaking. That both she and Kal were looking at her.

'What?' she asked.

Dena excused herself, leaving Kal to pass on the message, but he shook his head as if it was nothing important and instead took her on a culinary tour of the table.

Rice cooked with saffron and studded with pine nuts and sultanas. Locally caught fish. Chicken. Jewelled salads. Small cheeses made from goats' milk.

'It's a feast,' she said with every appearance of pleasure, even though alarm bells were going off in her head, certain that she'd missed something. That somehow they knew… 'I just hope Dena does not expect me to eat it all. I usually have a sandwich for lunch.'

'And here I was thinking that you spent every day at a lavish lunch, raising money for charity.'

His words were accompanied by a wry smile and the bells quietened a little, the tension seeping away beneath the honeyed warmth of his voice, his eyes.

'Not more than once a week,' she assured him. Then, managing a smile of her own, 'Maybe twice. But I only taste the food.'

'A taste will satisfy Dena. None of the food will be wasted.' He took her plate. 'Rice?'

'A spoonful,' she replied, repeating the same word each

time he offered her a new dish. He put no more than a morsel of each on her plate but, by the time he had finished, it was still an awful lot of food to eat in the middle of the day and she regarded it doubtfully.

'It will be a long time until dinner, Rose. We eat late. And you're going to need plenty of energy before then.' She looked up. 'We're going fishing, remember?'

'Is it hard work? I thought you just sat with a rod and waited for the fish to bite.' She picked up a fork. 'Was that what you were arranging with Dena?'

He hesitated for a moment, as if he had some unpleasant news to impart, and the bells began jangling again.

'Kal?'

He shook his head. 'It was nothing to do with this afternoon. She's had a message from Rumaillah. It seems that the Emir's wife has decided to pay you a courtesy call.'

The fork in Lydia's hand shook and the waiting sparrows dived on the scattered grains of rice.

'The Emir's wife?'

'I know that you hoped to be totally private here, Rose, but I'm sure you understand that Princess Sabirah could not ignore your presence in her country.'

Lydia felt the colour drain from her face.

When Rose had asked her to do this it had all seemed so simple. Once she was out of the country there would be nothing to do but indulge herself in one of those perfectly selfish holidays that everyone dreamed about occasionally. The kind where you could read all day and all night if you wanted to. Swim. Take a walk on the beach. Do what you wanted without having to think about another person.

And, like Rose, do some serious thinking about the future.

She'd had ten good years as Rose's lookalike and had no doubt that she could go on for ten more, but now she'd met Kal and the only person she wanted to be was herself.

No pretence.

No lies.

Not that she was kidding herself. She knew that if, in the unlikely event that he'd ever met her as 'herself', he wouldn't have even noticed her.

Everything about him was the real deal, from his designer suit to the Rolex on his wrist—no knock-offs for this man. Including women.

The pain of that was a wake-up call far louder, the argument for reality more cogent than any that her boss at the supermarket could make, even using the in-store announcement system.

She had been coasting through her own life, putting all her energies into someone else's, and she would never move on, meet someone who wanted her, the real Lydia Young, unless she started building a life of her own.

'When?' she asked, ungluing her tongue. 'What time?'

Maybe she could throw a sickie, she thought a touch desperately, but instantly rejected the idea as she realised what kind of fuss *that* would cause. This wasn't some anonymous hotel where you could take to your bed and no one would give a damn. And she wasn't some anonymous tourist.

If Lady Rose took to her bed, panic would ensue, doctors would be summoned—probably by helicopter from the capital. And Kal or Dena, probably both, would call Lucy, the Duke of Oldfield and then the game would be up.

No, no, no…

She could do this. She had to do it.

'Relax. She won't be here for a day or two and she won't stay long,' Kal said, not looking at her, but concentrating on serving himself. 'Just for coffee, cake. Dena will arrange everything,' he added, that tiny muscle in his jaw tightening again.

What was that? Tension?

What was his problem?

'Does she speak English? What will we talk about?'

'I believe her English is excellent and I imagine she'll want to talk about your work.'

'Really?' Lydia had a flash image of herself politely explaining the finer points of the checkout scanner to Her Highness over a cup of coffee and had to fight down a hysterical giggle as the world began to unravel around her.

'Play nice,' he said, 'and you'll get a generous donation for one of your good causes.'

Kal's flippancy brought her crashing back to reality. This was not in the least bit funny and her expression must have warned him that she was no more amused by his remark than Rose, whose parents had been killed on a charity mission, would have been.

'I'm sorry, Rose,' he said immediately. 'That was unforgivable.' He shook his head and she realised that for some reason he was as on edge as she was. 'I'm sure she'll just want to talk about Lucy and her grandchildren. It's a while since she's seen them.'

As if that was better!

She'd assumed that being at Bab el Sama would be like staying in a hotel. Great service but everything at a distance. She hadn't anticipated having to live with the pretence of being Rose in this way. This minute by minute deception.

She'd come dangerously, selfishly close to confessing everything to Kal before Dena had interrupted her but she could not, no matter how desperately she wanted to, break Rose's confidence.

She had made this offer with a free heart and couldn't, wouldn't let her down just because that heart wanted to jump ship and fling itself at someone else.

'I appear to have spoiled your appetite,' Kal said, and she took a little heart from the fact that he didn't seem particularly comfortable to hear of their unexpected visitor either.

'I'm good,' she said, picking up her fork and spearing a piece of chicken so succulent that, despite her dry mouth, she had no trouble swallowing it. 'So tell me what, exactly, is your problem, Kal?'

CHAPTER EIGHT

EXACTLY? Kal took a piece of bread, tore it in two.

'Why would you think I have a problem?' he asked, playing for time in the face of Rose's unexpected challenge.

'There's a muscle just by the corner of your mouth that you'd probably be wise to cover when you play poker,' she replied.

She reached out and touched a spot just below the right hand corner of his mouth.

'Just there.'

As their eyes locked, he kept perfectly still, knowing that if he moved an inch he would be tasting those long, slender fingers, sliding his tongue along the length of each one, and food would be the furthest thing from his mind. That the only thing he'd be eating would be her.

As if sensing the danger, she curled them back into her palm, let her hand drop.

'Should I ever be tempted to gamble, I'll bear that in mind,' he said. Took a mouthful of bread before he blurted out the real reason he had been foisted on her by Lucy and she sent him packing.

Rose made no move to eat, but continued to regard him. 'Well?' she prompted, refusing to let the matter drop. 'I recall that you mentioned your family were personae non gratae at court and presumably, as a royal residence, Bab el Sama is an extension of that. Will Princess Sabirah's visit be awkward for you?'

The breath stopped in his throat. Not suspicion, concern. She was anxious for him…

'This was originally the site of the Khatib tribe's summer camp,' he told her, not sure where exactly he was going with this, but wanting her to understand who, what he was. 'The mountains provided not only water, grazing for the animals, but a fortress at their back in troubled times.' He looked up at the barren peaks towering above them. 'They are impassable.'

'So is that a yes or a no?' she asked, refusing to be diverted by history.

'Good question.'

And the answer was that, far from awkward, Lucy was using court etiquette for his benefit, putting him in a place where his aunt could not, without causing offence to an honoured guest, ignore him.

In London, in her elegant drawing room, it had all seemed so simple. Before he'd met Rose. Now nothing was simple and if this had been for him alone he would have stepped back, taken himself out of the picture for the morning. But this was for his grandfather.

'Maybe you'd better tell me what happened, Kal,' she said when he didn't offer an answer. 'Just enough to stop me from putting my foot in it.'

'Your foot?'

'I'm sorry. You speak such perfect English that I forget that it isn't your first language.' She frowned. 'I'm not even sure what your first language is. Arabic, French…?'

'Take your pick,' he said. 'I grew up speaking both. And quickly added English when my father married for the second time. I know what "putting your foot in it" means. But, to answer your question, the court is wherever the Emir happens to be, so I'm safe enough unless he decides to accompany his wife.'

'And if he does?'

He couldn't get that lucky. Could he? Or was the Emir, like

everyone else, fascinated by this English 'Rose' who'd been orphaned so tragically as a little girl. Who, from the age of sixteen, had taken up her parents' cause, devoted her whole life to the charity they'd founded, adding dozens of other good causes over the years.

'I'm wherever you happen to be, Rose. And you are an honoured guest in his country. Who knows,' he said with a wry smile, 'he might be sufficiently charmed by you to acknowledge my existence.'

'Whoa, whoa…' She put down her fork, sat back. 'Back up, buster. I need to know what I'm getting into here.'

'"Back up, buster"?' he repeated, startled out of his own concerns. 'Where on earth did Lady Rose Napier pick up an expression like that?'

She blinked, appeared to gather herself, physically put the cool façade back in place. 'I meet all kinds of people in my work,' she said. Even her voice had changed slightly, had taken on a hint of steel, as if she was drawing back from him, and he recalled his earlier feeling that she was two separate people. The formal, untouchable, unreadable 'Lady'. And this other woman whose voice was huskier, whose lush mouth was softer, whose eyes seemed to shine a brighter blue. Who used unexpectedly colloquial expressions.

The one he couldn't seem to keep his hands off.

The selfish gene, the one he'd been fighting all his life, urged him to reach out, grasp her hand, stop that Rose from slipping away.

Instead, like her, he took a moment to gather himself, take a step back before, control restored, he said, 'What happened is no secret. Google my family and you'll find enough gossip to fill a book.'

'I'd rather save that for when I've run out of fiction,' she replied crisply. 'The edited highlights will do.'

'I wish it was fiction,' he said. 'My grandfather was hardly a credit to his family.'

He reached for a pitcher of water, offered it to her and, when she nodded, he filled both their glasses.

'Kalil al-Khatib, my grandfather, was the oldest son of the Emir and, although a ruler is free to name his successor, no one ever doubted that it would be him.'

'You have the same name as your grandfather?' she asked.

'It is the tradition. My first son will be named Zaki for my father.' If he achieved recognition, a traditional marriage, a place in the society that had rejected his family.

'That must become rather confusing.'

'Why?'

'Well, if a man has two or three sons, won't all their first-born sons have the same name?' Then, 'Oh, wait. That's why Dena calls you "bin Zaki". That's "son of", isn't it?'

He couldn't stop the smile that betrayed his pleasure. She was so quick, so intelligent, eager to learn.

The curl of desire as, equally pleased with herself for 'getting it', she smiled back.

Then her forehead puckered in a frown as she quickly picked up on what else he'd told her. 'But I don't understand. Why do you call yourself al-Zaki and not al-Khatib?'

'It's a long story,' he said, forcing himself to concentrate on that, rather than the curve of her cheek, the line of her neck. The hollows in her throat that were made for a man's tongue.

'I have all afternoon.'

He sought for a beginning, something that would make sense of tribal history, the harshness of the life, the need for a strong leader.

'My grandfather was his father's favourite. They both loved to ride, hunt in the desert with their falcons. They were, people said, more like twins than father and son. They were both utterly fearless, both much respected. Loved.'

He thought of Dena. She'd called herself his sister, but she was not related to him by blood. Had she loved him, too?

Then, realising that Rose was waiting, 'He was everything that was required of a ruler in those simpler times.'

'Everything?'

'Strong enough to hold off his enemies, to protect the summer grazing, the oases. Keep his people and their stock safe.'

'That would be before the oil?'

He nodded. 'They were still the qualities admired, necessary even in a charismatic leader, but it is true that once the oil started flowing and money began to pour into the country, the role needed a greater vision. Something beyond the warrior, the great hunter, the trusted arbitrator. A man to take the international stage.'

'And your grandfather couldn't adapt?'

'Oh, he adapted,' Kal said wryly. 'Just not in the right way. He was a big man with big appetites and wealth gave him the entire world in which to indulge them. He spent a fortune on a string of racehorses, enjoyed the gaming tables, never lacked some beauty to decorate his arm and, as the heir apparent to one of the new oil rich states, his excesses inevitably attracted media attention. None of it favourable.'

'I bet that went down well at home,' she said with a wry look and he caught again a glimpse of the inner Rose. The one she tried so hard to keep suppressed.

'Like a lead balloon?' he offered.

She laughed, then clapped her hand to her mouth.

'That is the correct expression?' he asked.

'You know it is, Kal.' She shook her head. 'I'm sorry. It's not funny.'

'It all happened a long time ago. My grandfather has long since accepted that he has no one but himself to blame for what happened.'

'So what did happen?' she asked, concentrating on her food rather than looking at him, as if she understood how difficult this was for him. He, on the other hand, watched as she successfully negotiated a second forkful of rice and knew that he could sit here and watch her eat all day.

Instead, he followed her example, picking up a piece of fish, forcing himself to concentrate on the story.

'In an attempt to remind Kalil of his duty,' he went on, 'encourage him to return home and settle down, his family arranged his marriage to the daughter of one of the most powerful tribal elders.'

'Arranged?' He caught the slightly disparaging lift of her eyebrows, the sideways glance.

'It is how it is done, Rose. To be accepted as the husband of a precious daughter is to be honoured. And an alliance, ties of kinship between families, adds strength in times of trouble.'

'Very useful when it comes to hanging on to land, I imagine. Especially when it lies over a vast oilfield. Does the girl get a say at all?'

'Of course,' he said.

'But who would refuse the man who was going to be Emir?'

'Marriage binds tribal societies together, Rose. I'm not saying that ours is an infallible system, but everyone has a stake in the partnership succeeding. No one wants to match two young people who will be unhappy.'

'Yours?'

She sounded sceptical. He could see why she might be. He was the second generation to be born and live his entire life in Europe. But at heart…

'There's no place for love?'

'That would be the happy-ever-after fairy tale perpetrated by Hollywood?' he responded irritably.

He'd hoped that she would understand. Then, remembering Lucy's concern that she was being guided towards marriage not of her own choice, he realised that she probably did understand rather more than most. And found himself wondering just how much choice a girl really had in a society where being married to a powerful man was the ideal. When her family's fortune might rise or fall on her decision.

'Hollywood came rather late in the story, Kal. Ever heard

of Shakespeare? "Love is not love, Which alters when it altera-
tion finds, Or bends with the remover to remove: Oh, no! it is
an ever-fixéd mark, That looks on tempests and is never shaken;
It is the star to every wandering bark…"'

She said the words with such passion, such belief, that a stab
of longing pierced him and for a moment he couldn't breathe.
Wanted to believe that out of an entire world it was possible
for two people to find one another. Reach out and with the
touch of a hand make a commitment that would last a lifetime.

Knowing it for nonsense, that anyone who believed in it was
going to get hurt, he shook his head.

'It's the same story for the same gullible audience,' he
replied. That kind of attraction is no more than sexual chemistry. Powerful, undoubtedly, but short-lived. 'I've lived with
the aftermath of "love" all my life, Rose. The hurt, the disillu-
sion. The confused children.'

She reached out, laid her hand over his. 'I'm sorry.' Then,
as swiftly she removed it. 'I didn't think.'

He shrugged. 'I admit that my family is an extreme case,'
he said, but how could he ever put his trust in such here today,
gone tomorrow feelings? He'd much rather leave the matter to
wiser heads. 'Not that it was a problem in my grandfather's
case. His response to the summons home for the formal be-
trothal was a front page appearance on every newspaper with
his new bride, a glamorous British starlet who was, he swore,
the love of his life.'

'Ouch!' she said. Then, her face softening, 'But how romantic.'

'The romance was, without doubt, intense…' 'Like a
rocket', was the way his grandfather had described it. Hot,
fast, spectacular and gone as quickly as the coloured stars
faded from the sky. 'But the reason for the swift marriage was
rather more prosaic. She was pregnant.'

'Oh.'

'He knew his father would be angry, his chosen bride's
family outraged, but, universally popular and always a favour-

ite, he was confident that the birth of a son would bring him forgiveness.'

'I take it he was mistaken.'

'When a favoured son falls from grace it's a very long drop, Rose.'

'So his father disinherited him.'

'Not immediately. He was told his new bride was not welcome in Ramal Hamrah, but that when he was prepared to settle down he could come home. My grandfather wasn't a man to abandon his bride and return like a dog with his tail between his legs.'

'I like him for that.'

'Everyone likes him, Rose. That was part of the problem.'

'And you,' she said gently. 'You love him.'

'He is my *jaddi'l habeeb*,' he told her. 'My beloved grandfather. While my own father was following in his father's footsteps, *Jaddi* taught me to speak Arabic, the stories of my people. Their history.'

'And he gave it all up for love.'

'While his studious, dutiful younger brother soothed outraged sensibilities and rescued his father's tattered pride by marrying the girl chosen for the heir. Within a year he had a son with blood that could be traced back a thousand years and was visibly putting all this new found wealth to work for his father's people.'

'A new man for a new age.'

'Smarter than my grandfather, certainly. When his father had a stroke *Jaddi* raced home, but he was too late. The Emir had slipped into a coma and was beyond extending the hand of forgiveness. There was to be no feast for the prodigal.'

'Poor man.'

He glanced at her, uncertain who she was referring to.

'I wonder if there was a moment when he knew it was too late. The Emir. Wished he had acted differently? You think that you have all the time in world to say the words. When my father was killed I wanted to tell him…'

She broke off, unable to continue, and it was his turn to reach out for her hand, curl his fingers around it, hold tight as she remembered the family that had been torn from her.

After a moment she shook her head. 'I'm fine, Kal.'

Was she? He'd never lost anyone close to him. Rose had only her grandfather and he wished he could share his many grandparents, parents, siblings with her.

'What did you want to tell him, Rose?' he pressed, wanting to know about her. How she felt. What her life had been like.

'That I loved him,' she said. And for a moment her eyes were noticeably brighter. 'He used to take me for walks in the wood on Sunday mornings. Show me things. The names of trees, flowers, birds.'

'Your mother didn't go with you?'

She shook her head. 'She stayed at home and cooked lunch but we'd always look for something special to take home for her. A big shiny conker or a bird's feather or a pretty stone.'

The Marchioness slaving over a hot stove? An unlikely image, but Rose's mother hadn't been born to the purple. She'd qualified as a doctor despite the odds, had met her polo playing Marquess in A&E when he'd taken a tumble from his horse.

Such ordinary domesticity must evoke a genuine yearning in the breast of a young woman who'd been brought up by a starchy old aristocrat who probably didn't even know where the kitchen was.

'I should have told him every day how much I loved him. That's all there is in the end, Kal. Love. Nothing else matters.'

'It's tragic that you had so little time to get to know him. Be with him. With both of them,' he said. 'To lose a mother so young… What do you remember about her?'

She started, as if brought back from some distant place, then said, 'Her bravery, determination. How much she loved my father.'

She looked at her hand, clasped in his, reclaimed it.

'Go on with your story, Kal,' she urged.

He didn't want to talk about his family. He wanted to know more about her. His six-year-old memories of his mother were of stories, treats, hugs. Were Rose's most abiding memories really of her mother's bravery? Or was that the result of years of media brainwashing?

'What happened after your great-grandfather died?' she pressed.

There was definitely something wrong here, he could sense it, but Rose Napier was no more than a means to an end, he reminded himself. She was not his concern.

'When *Jaddi* learned that his father had named his younger brother as Emir his heart broke, not just with grief,' he told her, refocusing himself on what was important, 'but with guilt, too. For a while he was crazy.'

He stared at the plate in front of him. Somehow, he'd managed to clear it, although he hadn't tasted a thing.

'What happened?' she pressed. 'What did he do?'

'He refused to swear allegiance to his younger brother, raised disaffected tribes in the north, attacked the citadel. He thought that the people would rise to him, but he'd been away for a long time. While they'd once adored the dashing young sheikh, in his absence they had grown to admire and respect his brother.'

'Was anyone hurt?'

He shook his head. 'When it was obvious that he lacked popular support, his allies were quick to make their peace with the man holding the purse strings.'

'It's like something out of a Shakespearean tragedy,' she said.

'I suppose it is. But it was of his own making. Even then, if he'd been prepared to acknowledge his brother as ruler, publicly bow the knee, he would have been allowed to stay. Play his part. When he refused to humiliate himself in that way, his brother exiled him from the tribe, stripped him of his name, title, banished him. All he was left with was the financial settlement that his father had hoped would compensate him for being supplanted by his younger brother.'

'And your father? Was he included in this punishment?'

'Banishment was for *Jaddi* alone, but the rest followed. If a father does not bear the name of his tribe, the title owed to him by birth…'

'So you are al-Zaki.'

'A name without history,' he said. Without honour. 'My father and I are free to come and go, as is my sister. I have an office, an apartment in Rumaillah but, without a family, I remain invisible.' His letters returned unanswered. Barred from his place in the *majlis*. Forbidden any way of appealing for mercy for a dying man. Reduced to using this woman.

'What do you think will happen when Princess Sabirah comes here? Will she "see" you?' she asked.

'Don't worry about it,' he said, angry with himself, angry with the Emir, angry with her for making him feel guilty. 'Her Highness won't do anything to embarrass her distinguished guest.'

That was what Lucy was relying on, anyway. If she acknowledged him, he would beg her to intercede with the Emir for his grandfather. That was all that was left, he thought bitterly. A chance to plead with the woman who shared the Emir's pillow to show pity on a dying man.

Lydia felt the emptiness in Kal's words, the loss, an underlying anger too, but to say that she was sorry would be meaningless and so she said nothing—she'd already said far too much, come close to blowing the whole deal.

The silence drifted back, broken only by the clink of dishes when Yatimah appeared to clear the table, loading everything on to the tray.

Having come—in a moment of high emotion—perilously close to letting slip the truth about her own father's death, she took the chance to gather herself before turning to Yatimah to thank her for the meal.

'*La shokr ala wageb, sitti.* No thanks are due for duty.'

'Will you say that again?' Lydia begged, grabbing the

chance to move away from dangerous territory. Listening carefully and repeating it after her self-appointed teacher.

'I will bring coffee?'

'*Nam. Shukran.*'

When she'd gone, Kal said, 'You listen well, Rose.'

'I try to pick up a few words of the local language when I'm on holiday. Even if it's only hello and thank you.' The truth, and how good that felt, but before he could ask where she usually went on holiday, 'So, what time are we going fishing?'

'Maybe we should give that a miss today,' he said. 'Wait until you're really bored.'

She tried not to look too happy about that.

'You might have a long wait. I've got the most beautiful garden to explore, a swimming pool to lie beside and a stack of good books to read. In fact, as soon as we've had coffee I'll decide which to do first.'

'*Qahwa.* The Arabic for coffee is *qahwa.* You make the q sound in the back of your throat.'

'*Ga howa?*'

'Perfect.' Then, with one of those slow smiles that sent a dangerous finger of heat funnelling through her, 'Maybe we should add Arabic lessons to the schedule.'

Doing her best to ignore it, she said, 'You do know that I had planned to simply lie in the sun for a week?'

'You can listen, speak lying down, can't you?'

Lydia tried to block out the image of Kal, stretched out on a lounger beside her at the pool she'd glimpsed from the dining room, his skin glistening in the sun while he attempted to teach her the rudiments of a language he clearly loved.

Did he really believe that she would be able to concentrate?

'Lying in the sun resting,' she elaborated swiftly, all the emphasis on *resting.* 'You seem determined to keep me permanently occupied. Rushing around, doing stuff.'

'It won't be hard work, I promise you.'

His low honeyed voice promised her all kinds of things,

none of them arduous, and as he picked up her hand the heat intensified.

'We can begin with something simple.' And, never taking his eyes from her face, he touched his lips to the tip of her little finger. '*Wahid.*'

'*Wahid?*'

'One.'

'*Ithnan.*' His lips moved on to her ring finger, lingered while she attempted to hold her wits together and repeat the word.

'*Ithnan.* Two.'

'*Thalatha.*'

Something inside her was melting and it took her so long to respond that he began to nibble on the tip of her middle finger.

'*Thalatha!*'

'*Arba'a.*' And he drove home the message with four tiny kisses on the tip, the first joint, the second joint, the knuckle of her forefinger.

'*Arba'a.*' It was her bones that were the problem, she decided. Her bones were melting. That was why she couldn't move. Pull free. 'Four.'

'*Khamsa.*' He looked for a moment at her thumb, then took the length of it in his mouth before slowly pulling back to the tip. 'Five.'

He was right. This was a language lesson she was never going to forget. She mindlessly held out her other hand so that he could teach her the numbers six to ten, already anticipating the continuation of a lesson involving every part of her body.

He did not take it and, catching her breath as she came back to earth, she used it to sweep her hair behind her ear, managing a very creditable, '*Shukran,* Kal.'

Yatimah placed a tray containing a small brass coffee pot and tiny cups on the table beside her.

Feeling ridiculously light-headed as she realised that he must have seen her coming, that he had not rejected her but chosen discretion, she said, 'Truly, that was a huge improvement on Mrs Latimer's Year Six French class.'

'Mrs Latimer?' Lucy had been saying something about Rose not being allowed to go to school when he'd interrupted her. He wished now he'd been less impatient…

For a moment Lydia's mind froze.

'A t-tutor,' she stuttered as Kal continued to look at her, a frown creasing that wide forehead.

She longed to tell him everything. Tell him about her brave mother who'd lost her husband and her mobility in one tragic moment on an icy road. Tell him about school, how she'd left when she was sixteen because what was the point of staying on when she would never have left her mother to go away to university? Tell him everything…

She was rescued from his obvious suspicion by the beep of a text arriving on her mobile phone.

'Excuse me,' she said, retrieving it from her pocket. 'It might be…' She swallowed, unable to say the word *grandfather,* turned away to check it, assuming that it was simply a 'have fun' response from her mother to her own text.

But it wasn't from her mother. It was from Rose.

Vtl you b on frnt pge am!

Vital you be on the front page tomorrow morning…

Lydia swallowed. Had she been recognised? Clearly she had to convince someone that she really was in Bab el Sama.

She quickly keyed in *OK* and hit 'send', returning the phone to her pocket. Realised that Kal was watching her intently.

'Is there a problem?' he asked as Yatimah offered them each a cup, then filled them with a thin straw-coloured aromatic liquid that was nothing like any coffee she'd ever seen.

'Good heavens, no!' she said with a nervous laugh which, even to her own ears, rang about as true as a cracked bell.

Only him.

Only her guilt that she was lying to a man who made her feel things that needed total honesty. And she couldn't be

honest. The text was a timely reminder just how deeply she was
embedded in this pretence. She was doing this for Rose and
right now only she mattered…

They were four hours ahead of London, plenty of time to make
the morning papers, but to accomplish that she had to get into the
open in daylight. On her own. Wearing as little as possible.

She and Rose both knew that what the paparazzi were really
hoping for was a picture of her in a private 'love nest' scenario
with Rupert Devenish.

That was never going to happen, so in order to keep them
focused, they'd planned a slow striptease to keep those lenses
on her for the entire week.

First up would be a walk along the beach in shorts with a
shirt open over a bathing suit.

After that she was going to discard the shirt to reveal a
bathing suit top beneath it. Rare enough to excite interest, but
nothing particularly sensational—it was a very demure bathing
suit. Finally she'd strip down to the swimsuit. That should be
enough to keep the photographers on their toes, but there was
a bikini in reserve in case of unforeseen emergencies.

Rose's text suggested they were in the 'unforeseen emergency' category. What she didn't, couldn't know was that her
good friend Lucy al-Khatib had provided her with a 'protec-
tor'. Kal was relaxed about letting her wander, unseen by the
outside world, in the shelter of the gardens, but she very much
doubted that he'd sit back and let her take a walk along the
beach without her minder.

While it was true that his presence would absolutely guarantee a front page spot, she also recognised that the presence
of some unknown man in close attendance would cause more
problems than it solved.

She was going to have to evade her watchdog and get down to
the beach and she had less than an hour in which to manage it.

Kal watched Rose sip gingerly at the scalding coffee.
Clearly, whatever had been in the text had not been good news.

The colour had drained from her face and a man didn't have to be fluent in body language to see that she was positively twitching to get away.

Which begged the question, why didn't she just say, *Great lunch, see you later…* and walk away? Or tell him that something had come up that she had to deal with?

Why was she sitting there like a cat on hot bricks, doing her best to pretend that nothing was wrong?

A gentleman would make it easy for her. Make an excuse himself and leave her to get on with whatever it was she wanted to do.

A man who'd been charged with her safety, in the face of some unspecified threat, would be rather less obliging. Lucy might have disparaged the Duke's concerns, but she hadn't dismissed them entirely.

She hadn't elaborated on them, either. Could it be that she was more worried about what Rose might do than what some imaginary assailant had in mind?

Maybe he should give her a call right now. Except that would leave Rose on her own, which didn't seem like a great idea.

'This is desert coffee,' he said conversationally. 'The beans are not ground but boiled whole with cardamom seeds. For the digestion.'

'Really? It's different. Very good,' she said, although he doubted she had even tasted it.

As she put the cup down, clearly eager to be away, he said, 'Traditionally, politeness requires that you drink two cups.'

'Two?'

She scarcely managed to hide her dismay and his concern deepened. What on earth had been in that text?

'They're very small. If you hold out the cup, like this,' he said, holding out his own cup, 'Yatimah will refill it for you.'

Obediently she held out the cup. Drank it as quickly as she could without scalding her mouth, handed the cup back to the girl.

And it was refilled a third time.

'She'll refill it as often as you hold it out like that,' he explained. 'When you've had enough you have to shake the cup from side to side to indicate that you have had enough.'

'Oh. Right.' She swallowed it down, shook the cup the way he told her, thanked Yatimah who, at a look from him, quickly disappeared. Rose, looking as if she wanted to bolt after her, said, 'If you'll excuse me, Kal, I'll go and get my book. Find somewhere quiet to read. You don't have to stand guard over me while I do that, do you?'

'Not if you stay within the garden,' he said, rising to his feet, easing back her chair.

'What about the beach?' she asked, so casually that he knew that was where she would be heading the minute he took his eyes off her. 'That's private, isn't it?'

'It's private in that no one will come ashore and have a picnic. Local people respect the privacy of the Emir and his guests, but the creek is busy.' He glanced across the water. 'There are plenty of boats where a photographer hoping to catch a candid shot of you could hide out.' He turned back to her. 'Lucy said you found the intrusion stressful but if you want to risk a walk along the shore, I'll be happy to accompany you.'

'Lady Rose Napier plus unknown man on a beach? Now, that really would make their day.' Her laughter lacked any real suggestion of amusement. 'I'll stick to the garden, thanks.' Then, 'Why don't you take yourself off on that fishing trip you're so keen on? Give me a break from the maggots.'

Give her a break? Where on earth had the secluded Lady Rose picked up these expressions?

'The maggots will be disappointed,' he said, coming up with a smile. 'I'll see you at dinner?'

'Of course.'

Her relief was palpable at the prospect of an entire afternoon free of him. He would have been offended but, from the way she'd responded to his kisses, he knew it wasn't personal.

'Although I'd better put in a few laps at the pool, too, or at this rate none of the clothes I brought with me will fit.'

'There's an upside to everything,' he replied.

His reward was a hot blush before she lifted her hand in a small, oddly awkward, see-you-later gesture and walked quickly towards the cottage.

Kal, getting the message loud and clear, didn't move until she was out of sight.

CHAPTER NINE

LYDIA'S luggage had been unpacked and put away and she quickly hunted through drawers, doing her best not to linger and drool over silk, cashmere, finest linen, as she searched for a swimsuit.

She had refused to accept a penny from Rose for this assignment. This was a labour of love, gratitude, respect and she'd insisted on taking a week of her paid holiday entitlement. But Rose had found a way to reward her anyway. She'd raided her wardrobe for more clothes than she could possibly wear in a week at the beach. Clothes she had never worn. Insisting that Lydia keep them.

The half a dozen swimsuits that she'd packed, each bearing the name of a world famous designer, were uniformly gorgeous. Each, inevitably, had the 'pink rose' theme and Lydia chose a striking black one-piece costume with a single long-stemmed rose embroidered across the front from the right hip, with stem and leaves curling diagonally across the stomach, so that the bud bloomed above her heart.

It was clearly a one-off that had been made especially for her and, with luck, the delighted designer would call the gossip pages and claim whatever PR was going. Which would help to establish that it could be no one but Rose on the Bab el Sama beach.

It fitted her like a glove, holding, lifting in all the right places. She didn't waste any time admiring her reflection, however, but threw the kaftan over it, ran a brush through her hair, freshened her lipstick and grabbed a book.

All she had to do now was find her way down to the beach unobserved and, avoiding the exit through the garden room to the terrace where Kal might still be lingering, she slipped out through the dining room.

Kal stood in the dark shadows at the top of a rocky outcrop, sweeping the water with a pair of powerful glasses, hoping to pick up anything out of place. Anyone who didn't have business on the water.

It was as peaceful a scene as a bodyguard could hope for. Fishermen, traders, local people pottering on their boats.

He glanced at his watch, wondering how much longer Rose would be. Because she'd come. He'd put money on it. But why?

He took out his BlackBerry and put Rose's name into the search engine. There was a picture of her leaving the lunch yesterday, '…radiant…' as she left for a week in Bab el Sama. Raising the question of whether she'd be alone.

There were other photographs. One of her with Rupert Devenish a couple of weeks earlier. Not looking radiant.

Maybe she had just been tired. Or perhaps the hollows in her cheeks, around her eyes were the result of a cold or a headache. Perhaps the camera angle was unflattering. Whatever it was, she had none of the glow that had reached out, grabbed him by the throat and refused to let go.

In fact she looked like a pale imitation of his Rose. He continued his search for answers until the soft slap of leather thongs against the stone steps warned him that she was on her way. He could have told her that to be silent she would need to remove her shoes. But then she hadn't expected him to be there.

She paused in a deep patch of shade at the bottom of the steps that led from the garden, a book in one hand, presumably

an alibi in case he hadn't done as she'd suggested and conve-
niently removed himself from the scene, but instead taken his
promise to Lucy seriously enough to stick around and keep an
eye on her.

He kept very still as she looked around, checking that the
beach was empty. Even if she had looked up, he was well
hidden from the casual glance, but she was only concerned that
the beach was empty and, having made certain the coast was
clear, she put the book on the step. Then she took the mobile
phone from her pocket and placed it on top.

No…

The word stilled on his lips as she reached back and pulled
the kaftan over her head to reveal a simple one-piece black
swimsuit that displayed every curve, every line of her body to
perfection. A slender neck, circled with a fine gold chain on
which hung a rosebud pendant. Wide, elegant shoulders, an
inviting cleavage that hadn't appeared on the photograph of her
in the evening gown. A proper waist, gently flared hips and then
those endless legs, perfect ankles, long slender feet.

For a moment she stood there, as if summoning up the
courage to carry on.

Don't…

The thought of his Rose appearing on the front page of
tomorrow's papers in a swimsuit, her body being leered at by
millions of men, was utterly abhorrent to him and he knew that
the rush of protectiveness he felt had nothing whatever to do
with the charge that Lucy had laid on him.

He'd spent much of his life on beaches, around swimming
pools with women who would have raised their sophisticated
eyebrows at such a puritan reaction and he knew his response
was the very worst kind of double standard.

By modern standards, the costume she was wearing was
modest.

Before he could move, do anything, she draped the kaftan
over a low branch and she stepped into the sun. Shoulders

back, head high, she walked towards the water, where she paused to scan the creek.

The light breeze caught her hair, lifting tiny strands that caught the light, lending her an ethereal quality.

Dear God, she was beautiful.

As cool and mysterious as a princess in some *Arabian Nights* story, escaped from some desperate danger and washed up on an unknown shore, waiting for Sinbad to rescue her, restore her to her prince.

'That's enough,' he whispered. 'Turn back now. Come back to me.'

She glanced round, looking up, as if she'd heard him, but it was a bird quartering the air that had caught her attention and, having watched it for a moment, she turned, then took a step…

'No!'

…bent to pick up something from the sand. It was a piece of sand-polished glass and, as she held it up to the light, he caught an echo of the flash out on the creek.

He lifted the glasses, scanned the water and this time found the telltale glint as the sunlight dancing on the water was reflected off a lens hidden beneath a tarpaulin on an anonymous-looking motor launch. It was anchored amongst half a dozen or so boats on the far side of the creek, its name obscured, deliberately, he had no doubt, and he had to fight the urge to race after Rose, drag her back.

But the one thing they were in complete agreement about was that she must not be photographed with him.

It would provoke a feeding frenzy among the press and it wouldn't take them five minutes to uncover his identity. His entire history would be rehashed in the press, along with the playboy lifestyle of both his grandfather and father, to fuel innuendo-laden speculation about why he was in Bab el Sama with Rose.

And no one was going to believe that the millionaire CEO of an international air freight business had accompanied Lady Rose Napier to Bab el Sama as her bodyguard. The millionaire grandson of an exiled sheikh, son of an international playboy, he hadn't been exactly short of media coverage himself before he'd stopped the drift. Found a purpose in life.

The fallout from that would cause a lot more embarrassment than even the most revealing photograph.

Worse, her grandfather, the Duke, would be apoplectic and blame Lucy for embroiling her in such a mess. Not to mention the fact that the Emir would be so angry that Kalil could kiss goodbye forever to any chance of *Jaddi*'s banishment being lifted so that he could die in peace at Umm al Sama.

His sole remit was to protect Lady Rose from danger. Shooting her with a camera didn't count, especially when she was going out of her way to make it easy for whoever was laid up in that boat.

He watched her as, apparently oblivious to scrutiny from both sea and shore, she wandered along the shoreline, stopping now and then to pick up a shell or a pebble. Lifting a hand to push back her hair. It was a classic image, one he knew that picture editors around the world would lap up, putting their own spin on it in a dozen headlines, most of them including the word *alone*.

So who had sent the message that had her scurrying to expose herself to the world's press?

He looked down at the shady step where she'd left her phone.

Lydia stood for a moment at the edge of the water, lifting her face to the sun, the gorgeous feeling of wet sand seeping between her toes taking her back to childhood holidays when her father had been alive, memories of her mother laughing as the waves caught her.

She remembered one holiday when she'd collected a whole bucket full of shells. By the end of their stay, they had smelled so bad that her father had refused to put them in the car. To stop her tears at the loss of her treasures, her mother had washed the most special one, given her a heart-shaped box to keep it in.

She still had her memory box. It contained a picture of

her father, laughing as she splashed him with a hosepipe. Her mother with the world famous couturier she'd worked for before the accident. The newspaper picture of her in the very first 'Lady Rose' outfit her mother had made when she was fifteen.

There had been a rush of additions in that brief spell when she'd thought she was in love. All but one of those had been tossed away with many more tears than the shells when she'd realised the truth. She'd kept just one thing, a theatre programme, because all memories were important. Even the bad ones. If you didn't remember, you didn't learn...

After that the memories had nearly all involved her looka-like gigs. Her life as someone else.

Looking around, she saw the edge of an oyster shell sticking out of sand washed clean by the receding tide.

She bent to ease it out, rinsed it off in the water, turned it over to reveal the pink and blue iridescence of mother-of-pearl. A keepsake to remind her of this moment, this beach, Kal al-Zaki kissing her fingers as he taught her Arabic numbers. A memory to bring out when she was old and all this would seem like a dream that had happened to someone else.

The last one she'd ever put in that old box, she vowed. She was never going to do this again, be Rose. It was time to start living her own life, making her own memories. No more pretence.

She stood for a moment, holding the shell, uncertain which way to go. Then, choosing to have the wind in her face, she turned right, towards the sea, wishing that Kal was walking with her to point out the landmarks, tell her the story behind a crumbling tower on the highest point on the far bank. To hold her hand as she turned through the curve that had taken Kal out of sight that morning.

Until now Kal had been able to dismiss the turmoil induced by his charge as nothing more than the natural response of a healthy male for a woman who had hit all the right buttons.

He was thirty-three, had been surrounded by beautiful women all his life and was familiar with desire in all its guises, but as he'd got older, become more certain what he wanted, he'd found it easy to stay uninvolved.

That he'd been knocked so unexpectedly sideways by Lady Rose Napier was, he'd been convinced, no more than the heightened allure of the unobtainable.

All that went out of the window in the moment she stepped out of his sight.

Lydia continued for as long as she dared, scanning the creek, hoping for some sign that there was someone out there.

Then, because she doubted it would be long before someone realised that she wasn't where she was meant to be and start looking for her, she turned back, relieved to be picking her way across the soft sand to the shade, the anonymity of the giant rock formation near the foot of the steps.

She'd half expected to find Yatimah standing guard over her book, her phone, her expression disapproving, but her escapade had gone unobserved. Relieved, she pushed her feet into the leather thong sandals, then turned to carefully lift the kaftan from the branch.

It wasn't there and she looked down to see if it had fallen.

Took a step into the shadows behind the rocks, assuming that it had been caught by a gust of wind and blown there.

And another.

Without warning, she was seized from behind around the waist, lifted clear of the sand, her body held tight against the hard frame of a man.

As she struggled to get free, she pounded at the arm holding her, using the edge of the shell as a weapon, opened her mouth to scream.

A hand cut off the sound.

'Looking for something, Lady Rose?'

She stilled. Kal…

She'd known it even before he'd spoken. Knew that woody scent. Would always know it…

As soon as she stopped struggling he dropped his hand and, knowing he was going to be mad at her, she got in first with, 'I thought you were going fishing.'

'And I thought you were going to curl up by the pool with a good book.'

He set her down and, with the utmost reluctance, she turned to face him.

'I am.' Head up. And Lady Rose, the Duke's granddaughter at her most aristocratic, she added, 'I decided to take a detour.'

'And give one of your paparazzi army tomorrow's front page picture?'

She instinctively glanced at the phone lying defenceless on top of her book. 'Have you been reading my messages?' she demanded.

'No need. You've just told me everything I need to know.'

'No…'

'What is it, Rose?' he asked. 'Are you a publicity junkie? Can't you bear to see an entire week go by without your picture on the front page?'

She opened her mouth to protest. Closed it again.

His anger was suppressed, but there was no doubting how he felt at being deceived, made a fool of, and who could blame him? Except, of course, he hadn't. He'd been ahead of her every step of the way. Instead, she shook her head, held up her hands.

'You've got me, Kal. Bang to rights.' She took a step back. 'Can I have my dress back now?'

As he reached up, lifted the kaftan down from the place he'd hidden it, she saw the blood oozing from his arm where she'd slashed at him with the shell she was still clutching.

She dropped it as if it burned, reached out to him, drew back without touching him. She'd lied to him and he knew it.

'I hurt you,' she said helplessly.

He glanced at the wound she'd made, shrugged. 'Nothing that I didn't ask for.'

'Maybe, but it still needs cleaning.' Ignoring the dress he was holding out to her, she began to run up the steps. 'Sea shells have all kinds of horrible things in them,' she said. 'You can get septicaemia.'

'Is that right?'

Realising that he hadn't followed her, she stopped, looked back. 'Truly.' Then, realising that perhaps that wasn't the best choice of word, 'I've been on a first aid course.' She offered her hand but, when he didn't take it, said, 'Please, Kal.'

Relenting, he slung the dress over his shoulder, stooped to pick up the book and phone she'd abandoned in her rush to heal, adding the number of his mobile phone to her contact list. Adding hers to his as he followed her up to the house, the bedroom where he'd left her sleeping a few hours earlier, into the huge, luxurious bathroom beyond.

'I've put my number in your phone,' he said, putting them on a table. 'In case you should ever need it.'

She rolled her eyes. 'Sit there!'

He obediently settled himself on a wide upholstered bench while she took a small first aid box from a large cupboard that was filled with the cosmetics and toiletries she'd brought with her and searched through it for sachets containing antiseptic wipes.

'Why did you do it?' He addressed the top of her head as she bent over him, cleaning up the scratches she'd made.

'This is nothing,' she said. 'I did a self-defence course and you're really lucky I wasn't wearing high heels.'

'I wasn't referring to your attempt to chop my arm off. Why did you strip off for that photographer?'

'I didn't strip off!' she declared, so flustered by the accusation that for a moment she forgot what she was doing. Then, getting a grip, 'I took a walk on the beach in a swimsuit. A very modest swimsuit.'

Modest by today's standards, maybe, but this close, clinging like a second skin, revealing perhaps more than she realised, as she bent over him—suggesting more—the effect was far more enticing than an entire beach filled with topless lovelies.

She looked up. 'Did you say "photographer"?'

'I did.'

She straightened abruptly as she saw exactly where his eyes were focused.

'You saw him?'

'He was in a launch out on the creek and well camouflaged from above. He forgot about the sun reflecting off the water.'

The tension went out of her shoulders, her neck. Relief, he thought. That was sheer relief.

'So why did you do it?' he persisted.

'I thought we'd established that,' she said, concentrating once more on his arm.

The speed with which she'd grabbed at the insulting explanation he'd offered suggested desperation to hide the real reason for her exhibitionism. While he had his own suspicions, he was beginning to wish he'd overcome his squeamishness about plundering her phone for the answer.

'Maybe you'd better run it by me again.'

Apparently satisfied with the clean up job on his arm, or maybe just wanting to put a little distance between them, she gathered up the used wipes, dropped them in a bin.

'It's a game, Kal,' she said, busying herself, filling a marble basin with warm water. Looking anywhere but at him. 'We need each other. Celebrities need headlines, the media have an insatiable appetite for stories. The trick is to give them what they want and then hope they'll leave you alone.'

She plunged her hands in the water, then looked around for soap.

He took a piece from a crystal bowl but did not hand it to her. Instead, he put his arms around her, trapping her as he leaned into her back, his chin against her hair as he dipped his hands into the water and began to soap her fingers.

'Kal!' she protested, but feebly. They both knew she wasn't going anywhere until she'd told him what was going on.

'What, exactly, do they want from you?' he asked.

'Right now?' The words came out as a squeak and he waited while she took a breath. 'Right now,' she repeated, 'they'd give their eye teeth for a picture of me here, in flagrante with Rupert Devenish.' She tried a laugh, attempting to ignore the way his thumb was circling her palm. The way she was relaxing against him. 'He's—'

'I read the newspapers,' he said, not wanting to hear the words on her lips. Or that it was Lucy who'd filled him in on the marriage mania in the gossip columns. 'But that isn't going to happen, is it?'

Unless he'd got it totally wrong and the text had been from Devenish announcing his imminent arrival, urging Rose to convince the paparazzi that she was alone before he joined her.

In which case her eager response to him, the way she had softened in the circle of his arms, surrendered her hands for him to do with what he would, was going to take a little—make that a lot of—explaining.

'It's not going to happen,' she confirmed. 'I'm afraid they're going to have to make do with the clichéd Lady Rose, alone on a beach, how sad, picture.'

And it was his turn to feel the tension slide away from his shoulders.

But only halfway.

According to Lucy, Rose was falling apart because of the constant intrusion into her life. Ten years without being able to lift a finger unobserved, she'd said.

He wasn't getting that impression from Rose. Far from it. She seemed totally relaxed about what could only be construed as a unwarranted intrusion into her private life.

'And if they aren't?' he asked.

A tiny tremor rippled through her and he knew that there was a lot more to this than she was telling him.

'Trust me, Rose,' he said. 'The picture will be a sensation.' He reached for a towel, taking her hands, drying them one finger at a time. Then, because he was still angry with her, 'And if I'm wrong you can always go for the topless option tomorrow.'

'Tomorrow will be too late...'

She caught herself, no doubt realising that she should have objected to the 'topless', not the 'tomorrow'. But he had the answer to at least one of his questions.

For some reason she wanted a picture of herself on the front page and for some reason it had to be tomorrow. And he went straight back to that mysterious threat.

Was this what it was all about? Give me a photograph or... Or what?

What on earth could anyone have over the universally loved and admired 'people's angel'?

Except, of course, that the woman in his arms was not Rose Napier.

On some subconscious level he'd known that from the moment she'd walked into the VIP lounge at the airport. Right from the beginning, he'd sensed the split personality, the separation between the woman playing a role—and occasionally slipping—and the woman who shone through the disguise, lighting him up not just like a rocket, but the whole damn fourth of July scenario. Whoosh, bang, the sky filled with coloured stars.

He didn't trust it, knew it was a temporary aberration, nothing but chemistry, but he finally understood why his grandfather had lost his head, lost his country over a woman.

He was here on a one-off last-chance mission and from the moment she'd appeared on the scene this woman had attacked all his systems like a virus taking over a computer memory, supplanting herself in place of everything that was vital, important, real.

Lucy had obviously told him a pack of lies—he was only here to inveigle his way into a meeting with Princess Sabirah, so why would he be bothered with something as important as the truth?

Presumably the real Rose was holed up in some private love nest with Rupert while this woman, this lovely woman who was superficially so like her, was nothing but a plant to keep the press focused on Bab el Sama.

So what had gone wrong? Had someone found out? Threatened to expose the switch? Directing his own personal photo shoot by text?

In which case he had no doubt that the topless scenario would be the next demand. Because, even if she was a fake, that picture would be worth millions to the photographer who delivered it to a picture agency.

'You've got nothing to worry about,' he said, tossing the towel aside, not sure who he was most angry with, Lucy or this woman, whoever she was, for putting at risk his own mission.

No, that was wrong. Lucy had used the situation to give him a chance. This woman had lit him up, responding to his kisses as if he was the last man on earth. Lies, lies, lies…

'I guarantee you that there won't be a picture editor in London who won't grab that picture of you for their front page tomorrow.'

Her all too obvious relief flipped something in his brain and he stroked the pad of his thumb over the exquisite rose that curved invitingly across her breast in an insultingly intimate gesture, opened his mouth over her all too obvious response as the bud beneath the costume leapt to his touch.

Her throat moved as she swallowed, doing her best to ignore the intimacy of his touch, but the tiny shiver that rippled through her betrayed pleasure, desire, need and her response was not to pull away but buckle against him.

Too late, he discovered that he was the one caught in a lie, because it didn't matter who she was, he desired her as he had never desired any other woman. Not just with his body, but with his heart, his soul and simply holding her was not enough.

Nothing could disguise from her how very much it wasn't enough but, as the wildfire of desire swept through him, he was not alone. Her seeking lips found his neck, trailed moist kisses across his chin, touched his lips, her need as desperate as his.

'Whoever you are,' he murmured, looking down at her, 'you can trust me on that…'

For a moment she looked at him, her mouth soft, her lids heavy with desire and the slow-burning fuse, lit in the moment their eyes had first met, of that unfinished kiss, lay between them.

The air was heavy with the desire of two people for whom the need to touch, to explore, to be one, blotted out memory, bypassed hard-learned lessons, destroyed reason.

Lydia heard him, understood what he was saying, but wrapped in the powerful arms of a man she desired beyond sense, this was not a time for questions, answers. Time was suspended. There was no past, no future. This was for now. Only the senses survived—scent, taste, touch—and she reached out and with her fingertips traced the perfection of Kal's profile.

His wide forehead, the high-bridged nose, lingering to trace the outline of those beautifully carved lips.

The thin clothing pressed between them did nothing to disguise the urgent response of his body and she was seized by a surge of power, of certainty that this was her moment and, leaning into him so that her lips touched his, she whispered, 'Please…'

As her fingers, her lips touched his, took possession of his mouth, Kalil al-Zaki, a man known for his ice-cold self-control, consigned his reputation to oblivion.

His arms were already about her and for a moment he allowed himself to be swept away. To feel instead of think.

Drink deep of the honeyed sweetness of a woman who was clever, funny, heartbreakingly lovely. Everything a man could ever want or desire.

Forget, just for a while, who he was. Why he was here.

Her mouth was like silk, her body eager, desperate even, but it wasn't enough and, lost to all sense as he breathed in the scent of her skin, the hollows of her neck, her shoulders, he slowly peeled away the swimsuit to taste the true rosebuds it concealed.

Her response was eager, as urgent as his own, and yet, even as she offered him everything, he could not let go, forget the lies…

How she'd played the virgin, acted the seductress. Was this just another lie to buy his silence?

She whimpered into his mouth as he broke free, determined to regain control of his senses, yet unable to let go as she melted against him.

'Who are you?' he demanded helplessly. 'Why are you here?' When she didn't answer he leaned back, needing to look her in the face, wanting her to see his. But her eyes were closed, as if by not seeing, she would be deaf to his words. 'What do you want from me?'

'Nothing!' Then, more gently, 'I'm sorry.' And, without looking at him, she slowly disentangled herself and, shivering, clutched her costume to her and said, 'You can g-go fishing now, Kal. I promise I'll g-go and sit by the pool like the well behaved young woman I'm supposed to be.'

Torn between wanting her to behave and wanting her to be very, very bad indeed, he reassembled the shattered pieces of his cast-iron self-control, picked up his shirt and, taking her hands, fed them into the sleeves, buttoning it around her as if she were a child.

'I'm going nowhere until you tell me the truth,' he said. Then, with a muttered oath, 'You're shivering.' She couldn't be cold… 'What can I get you?'

'A proper cup of tea?' She sniffed and he lifted her chin, wiped a tear from beneath her eye.

Shivering, tears… He wanted to shake her, hold her, yell at her, make love to her…

'Tea?' he said, trying to get a grip.

'Made in a mug with a tea bag, milk from a cow and two heaped spoons of sugar.' She managed a rueful smile. 'Stirred, not shaken.'

'I'm glad your sense of humour survived intact,' he said.

'My sense of humour and everything else.' She lifted her

shoulders in a simple up and down shrug. 'I've only come that close to losing my virginity once before, Kal. I'm beginning to think I'm destined to be an old maid and the really bad news is that I'm allergic to cats.'

Better make that two cups of hot, sweet tea, he thought, picking up the phone.

CHAPTER TEN

'WHO are you?'

Lydia, her hands around the mug of tea he'd rustled up for her, was sitting in the shuttered balcony of her room, bars of sunlight slanting through into a very private space and shimmering off Kal's naked shoulders.

'What are you?'

'Lydia. Lydia Young. I've been a professional lookalike pretty much from the moment that Lady Rose made her first appearance.'

'Lydia.' He repeated her name carefully, as if memorising it. 'How old were you?'

'Fifteen. I'm a few months younger than Rose.' She sipped at the hot tea, shuddering at the sweetness. 'How did you know?' Then, because it was somehow more important, 'When did you know?'

'I think that on some level I always knew you weren't Rose.' He glanced at her. 'I sensed a dual personality. Two people in the same body. And you have an unusual turn of phrase for a young woman with your supposedly sheltered upbringing. Then there was the Marchioness slaving over Sunday lunch. And Mrs Latimer.'

'Year Six French.' She took another sip of tea. 'I knew you'd picked up on that. I hoped I'd covered it.'

'You might have got away with it but once that text arrived

you were in bits. It wasn't difficult to work out that you'd be heading for the beach as soon as you'd got rid of me so, while I waited for you to show up, I took a look at the Internet, hoping to pick up some clue about what the hell was going on.'

'What was the clincher?' she asked. Not a Lady Rose word, but she wasn't pretending any more.

'You made the front page in that cute little hat you were wearing. The caption suggested that after recent concerns about your health you appeared to be full of life. Positively glowing, in fact. Fortunately for you, they put it down to true love.'

She groaned.

'I should have done more with my make-up, but we were sure the veil would be enough. And it was all going so well that I might just have got a bit lippy with the photographers. What an idiot!'

'Calm down. There was nothing in the stories to suggest that you were a fake,' he assured her. 'Just a recent photograph of Rose with Rupert and some salacious speculation about what you'd be doing here.'

'But if you had no trouble spotting the difference—'

'Only because I've become intimately acquainted with your face, your figure,' he said. 'I don't pay a lot of attention to celebrity photographs, but the "people's angel" is hard to miss and I expected someone less vivid. Not quite so…' He seemed lost for an appropriate adjective.

'Lippy?' she offered helpfully.

'I was going to say lively,' he said, his eyes apparently riveted to her mouth. 'But lippy will do. One look at the real thing and I knew you were someone else.' Then, turning abruptly, he said, 'So what's going on? Where is Rose Napier? With Rupert Devenish?'

'Good grief, I hope not.'

'Strike two for Rupert. Lucy isn't a fan either. I take it you've met him?'

'I've seen him with her. He's an old style aristocrat. Her grandfather,' she explained, 'but thirty years younger.'

'Controlling.'

She thought about it for a moment, then nodded. 'Rose and I met by chance one day. I'd been booked for a lookalike gig, a product launch at a swanky hotel. I had no idea Rose was going to be a guest at a lunch there or I'd have turned it down, but as I was leaving we came face to face. It could have been my worst nightmare but she was so sweet. She really is everything they say she is, you know.'

'That's another reason I saw through you.' He reached out, wiped the pad of his thumb across her mouth. 'You're no angel, Lydia Young.'

She took another quick sip of her tea.

'How is it?'

'Just what the doctor ordered. Too hot, too sweet. Perfect, in fact.'

'I'll remember the formula.'

She looked at him. Remember? There was a future?

Realising just how stupid that was, she turned away. Just more shocks, she decided, and concentrated on getting through her story.

'Rose spent a little too long chatting with me for Rupert's liking and when he summoned her to heel she asked me how much I charged. In case she ever wanted an evening off.'

'How much do you charge?' he asked pointedly.

'This one is on the house, Kal. I owe Rose. My father was killed in a car accident when I was ten years old. My mother was badly injured—'

'Your brave, determined mother.'

'She lost the man she loved, the use of her legs, her career in the blink of an eye, Kal.'

'I'm sorry.'

She shook her head. It was a long time since she'd cried for the loss and when he reached out as if to take her hand, offer comfort, she moved it out of reach. Right now, comfort would undo her completely and she was in enough trouble without that.

'Is this what you do? I mean, is it a full-time job?'

'Hardly. Two or three gigs a month at the most. The day job is on the checkout at a supermarket. The manager is very good about me swapping shifts.' She was going to tell him that he wanted her to take a management course. As if that would make any difference... 'The money I earn as Rose's lookalike has made a real difference to my mother's life.'

The electric wheelchair. The hand-operated sewing machine. The car she'd saved up for. And the endless driving lessons before she'd eventually passed her test.

'So, like Rose, you have no other family?'

She shook her head.

'And, like her, no lover? You are a beautiful, vivid woman, Lydia. I find that hard to believe.'

'Yes, well, I live a rather peculiar life. My day job is in a supermarket, where staff and customers alike call me Rose despite the fact that I wear a badge with my real name on it. Where most of them can't quite decide whether I'm fish or fowl. The rest of the time I'm pretending to be someone else.'

'And taking care of your mother. I imagine that takes a chunk out of your time, too. Who is with her while you're here?'

'A friend stays with her sometimes so that I can take a holiday. And I'm not totally pathetic. I do get asked out. Of course I do. But I'm never sure exactly who they think they're with.'

'Someone must have got through. If we... If I... If that was the second time.'

She nodded. 'He said he was a law student. He always came to my checkout at the supermarket. Chatted. Brought me tiny gifts. Wooed me with sweet words and posies, flattery and patience. Endless patience. It was weeks before he asked me out.'

Months before he'd suggested more than a kiss. So long that she'd been burning up with frustration. Ready to go off like a fire-cracker.

'It was the patience that did it,' she said. 'The understanding.

How many men are prepared to put up with the missed dates, always coming second to my mother, the job, the gigs? To wait?'

'A man will wait for what is precious,' Kal said.

'And who could resist that?' Not her. She'd fallen like a ton of bricks. 'It was that flash, bang, wallop love thing that you so distrust, Kal. In this case with good reason because when I say precious, I do mean precious. My worth, it seems, was above rubies.'

She could have made a lot of money selling the story to the newspapers but she'd never told anyone what had happened. Not her mother. Not her friends. Not even the agency that employed her. But, sitting here in this quiet space above a beautiful garden carved out of the desert, nothing but the truth would do. She had lied to Kal, hidden who she was, and if she was to win his trust now, win him over so that she could fulfil her promise to Rose, she had to strip herself bare, tell him everything.

'When he asked me to go away for the weekend I felt like the sun was shining just for me. He made it so special, booked the honeymoon suite in a gorgeous hotel in the Cotswolds. I suppose I should have wondered how a student could afford it, but I was in love. Not thinking at all.'

'So what went wrong?'

'Nothing, fortunately. The "Lady Rose" effect saved me.'

He frowned. Well, why wouldn't he? Unless you'd lived it, how would anyone know?

'An elderly chambermaid—a woman who'd seen just about everything in a long career making beds—thought I was Rose and she waylaid me in the corridor to warn me, told me where to find the hidden cameras.'

She swallowed. Even now the memory of it chilled her.

'When I confronted my "student" he confessed that he was an actor who'd been hired to seduce me by a photographer who intended to make a fortune selling pictures of "Lady Rose" losing her virginity with some good-looking stud. Someone who worked in the hotel was in on it, of course. He even offered me a cut of the proceeds if I'd go ahead with it since, as he so eloquently put it, "I was gagging for it anyway". I declined and since then…' she shrugged '…let's say I've been cautious.'

'And yet you still believe in love?'

'I've seen it, Kal. My parents were in love. They lit up around each other and my mother still has a dreamy look whenever she talks about my dad. I won't settle for less than that.' She looked at him. 'I hope that Rose won't either. That this week away from everyone, being anonymous, will help her decide. Will you let her have that?'

'She's safe?' Kal asked, reserving judgement.

'She's been wrapped in cotton wool all her life. I've loaned her my car and right now she's as safe as any anonymous woman taking a few days to do something as simple as shopping without ending up like the Pied Piper of Hamelin, or appearing on the front page of next day's newspaper eating a hot dog.'

'So what was the panic this morning?'

'I think someone must have said something that panicked her. She's not as used to people commenting on the fact that she looks like Lady Rose as I am.' She used her free hand to make little quotes, put on a quavery voice. '"Has anyone ever told you look a bit like Lady Rose, dear?"'

Kal smiled, but wondered what it must be like to always be told you look like someone else. Whether she sometimes longed for someone to say that Lady Rose looked like her.

'I'll bet that gets old. How do you cope?'

'It depends. If some old biddy whispers it to me in the supermarket, I whisper back that I really am Lady Rose and I'm doing undercover research into working conditions. Warn her not to tell a soul, that she's spotted me. Then wait to see how long it takes before she points me out to someone.'

'That's really bad.'

'You said it, Kal. I'm no angel.'

And for a moment he thought only about the touch of her

lips beneath his fingers, the taste of them beneath his mouth. Then forced himself to remember that she had deceived him. Put his own mission in jeopardy. If the Emir, the Princess ever discovered the truth...

'Sometimes I do a flustered "good heavens, do you really think so, no one has ever said that before" routine,' she said, distracting him with the whole surprised expression, fluttery hand to chest routine.

'I like that one,' he said, which brought that light-up-the-day smile bubbling to her face.

'My favourite is the one where I put on a slightly puzzled smile...' she did a perfect version of the world famous luminous smile that was about a hundred watts less bright than her natural one '...and say "Only a bit?" and wait for the penny to drop.'

'You're a bit of a clown on the quiet, aren't you, Lydia Young?'

'Quiet?' she repeated.

He'd caught glimpses of this lively woman beneath the Rose mantle, but in full flood she was irresistible. Now that she'd stepped out of the shadows, was wholly herself, he knew that it was the lippy woman desperate to break out of the restraints of being Lady Rose that he desired, liked more and more. Her laughter lit him up, her smile warmed him. Even when he was furious with her he wanted to kiss her, wrap her up in his arms and keep her safe, love her...

'Maybe that wasn't the most appropriate word,' he said quickly. 'Did you never consider a career as an actress?'

'No.'

One minute they were laughing, the next they weren't.

'No more,' she said. 'I can't do this any more, Kal. I shouldn't be here. Rose shouldn't be hiding and I shouldn't be living a pretend life.'

'No.' Then, 'You've stopped shivering.'

'Nothing like tea for shock,' she said.

'I'm sorry if I frightened you.'

'Only for about a millisecond. Then I knew it was you.'

'I was angry,' he said.

Lydia swallowed, nodded. Of course he was angry. He'd been charged with protecting her—protecting Rose—and she had sneaked off the minute his back was turned.

'You had every right,' she said. 'But you stuck around to look out for me, even when you knew I wasn't Rose.'

Long after her momentary fear had been forgotten, she'd still feel his strong, protective arm as he'd held her against him. She recalled the warm scent of his skin.

She wouldn't need a shell or anything else to remember that. Remember him.

'So,' she said, sensing the weight of unspoken words between them and, recalling his earlier tension, she repeated the question she'd asked him then, 'what's your problem, Kal? What aren't you telling me?'

'Not just lovely, not just cool under pressure and a loyal friend, but smart, too,' he said, not looking at her. 'You're right, of course. I have a confession to make.'

'You got me at lovely,' she said. Then, because when a man needed to confess, it was never going to be good news, she summoned up all the flippancy at her command and said, 'Don't tell me. You're married.'

No one would have guessed that, in the time it took him to answer, her heart had skipped a beat. Two. Maybe he was right. She should take up acting.

'No, Lydia, I'm not married.'

'Engaged?' This time the pause was longer, but he shook his head.

'That wasn't totally convincing,' she said.

'I am not in a relationship of any kind.'

Better, but there was something he wasn't telling her. Maybe if she shut up and let him get on with his 'confession' in his own way it would all become clear.

It took another half a dozen heartbeats before he said, 'I want you to understand that Lucy was truly concerned for

Rose. Her grandfather tried to talk her into withdrawing the invitation, said there had been a threat of some kind.'

'A threat? What kind of threat?' she asked, alarmed.

'Lucy was certain there was nothing, that it was just a ploy to keep her under his control, but she had to do something to pacify the Duke so she told him that the Emir's nephew would be in charge of his granddaughter's security.'

'That would be you. And he was happy with that?'

'No, but he couldn't object without offending the Emir.'

'And what about the Emir? Wasn't Lucy afraid of offending her father-in-law?'

'She saved Hanif. She can get away with things that no one else would dare to. Even be my friend. My grandfather is dying, Lydia. He lives only to return to Ramal Hamrah to die in the house where he was born.'

Her hand found his and she squeezed it, knowing how much he loved the old man.

'Lucy knew that Princess Sabirah would want to pay her respects to Rose and she seized the chance to put me where I could make a personal appeal to her, beg her to intercede with her husband.'

'And?'

'That first. Above everything…'

'But, once he has been allowed home, you hope the rest will follow. That you can become a Khatib again. With everything that entails.' His name, his title…

'It is as if I have been cut off from half my life. I have the language, I have property here, can study the culture, the history, but without my family…'

The metaphorical clock struck twelve. Time for the coach to turn back into a pumpkin, for Cinderella to go back to the checkout and check out the alternatives to getting a cat. Maybe a rabbit or a guinea pig, she thought. Or half a dozen white mice. Just in case the fairy godmother ever dropped in again.

'Not just your name, your title, but you want the ultimate prize of an arranged marriage to one of the precious daughters of a powerful Ramal Hamrahn family.'

His silence was all the answer she needed.

'That was why you stopped.' She swallowed. 'Would not make love with me.'

'Honour would not allow it,' he agreed.

Honour. What a rare word, but this man who'd been raised in the west was steeped in the culture that had excluded him.

'Absolutely,' she agreed. The kitchen telegraph would be humming to news of an affair before they disturbed the sheets. Princess Sabirah would suddenly find herself too busy to call and all Kal's hopes and dreams would fly right out of the window. 'Good call.'

Lydia stood up, pushed open one of the shutters, looked out over the garden, needing a little space to recover, put the smile back on.

'I'm glad that we were able to be honest with one another, Kal.'

Honest.

This was honest?

This was honour?

Lydia was pretending to be someone she was not, while he was about to collude with her deception, not just of the world's press but the Emir of Ramal Hamrah.

She turned to him.

'Will you take me to the souk tomorrow? I'd like to buy a gift for my mother.'

The request was simple enough, but that wasn't the question she was asking. They both knew it and when, after the briefest pause, he responded in the affirmative with a slight but formal bow, he was confirming that there would be a tomorrow for 'Lady Rose' at Bab el Sama.

What choice did he have?

He had been prepared to be patient, wait for those precious things he wanted for himself, no matter how long it took. But for his grandfather time was running out, leaving him with no choice but to seize the chance Lucy had given him.

She wasn't sure that honour had much to do with it, but love was there in abundance.

'You should believe in love, Kal,' she said. 'You are living proof of its existence. Your love of your family shines through when you talk of them. You yearn with all your heart for this country, for everything that you have lost here and yet you would risk it all on this chance to bring your grandfather home. That's love at its finest. Unselfish, pure, the real thing.'

'I am asking a great deal of you, Lydia. I would understand if you said you could not go through with it.'

'We both have debts, Kal, and to pay them we need each other.' Then, 'You'll excuse me if I ask you to leave now? I need to change.'

Kal watched her wrap herself in the figurative mantel of Lady Rose Napier. Stand a little taller, inject the crispness back into her voice as she distanced herself from him. And where he had been warmed by her smile, her presence, a touch as she'd reached out without thinking, there was now an icy chill.

'Will you come to the stables in the morning?' he asked.

He saw her neck move as she swallowed, glimpsed a momentary longing for the closeness that would give them as he lifted her to the saddle, fitted her feet in the stirrups, placed her hands just so on the reins.

Then she shook her head just once and said, 'Lady Rose is afraid of horses.'

'And Lydia?'

'It's safer to stick to Rose, don't you think?'

He wasn't thinking. That was the problem. He'd set out on a quest that he'd believed nothing in the world could distract him from. How wrong could one man be?

He leaned forward, kissed her cheek. 'I'll send Yatimah to you.'

* * *

When Yatimah arrived, Lydia was filling the huge sunken bath.

'*Sitti!*' she declared. 'I must do that for you.' Then, 'Bin Zaki says that you are going to the souk tomorrow. I will bring you an *abbayah* to keep the dust from your clothes,' she said as she ladled something into the bath that foamed magically, filling the air with an exotic, spicy fragrance. 'Would you like me to wash your hair?'

'Not tonight. I'm really tired so I'll just take a bath and then go to bed.'

She closed the bathroom door, locked it. Leaned back against it. Lifted her hand to her cheek.

Flash, bang, wallop…

Kal walked along the shore that she had walked, but went much further before sitting on a rock and calling his grandfather in London. He didn't ask how he was feeling. He knew he would be in pain because he refused to slide into the morphine induced coma that would lead to death.

Instead, he described the scene before him. The lights along the far shore, the boats riding on the water, the moon rising, dripping, from the ocean so that he could, in his heart, be here with him.

He called his mother, who'd complained of a cold the last time they'd spoken, listened to her news, her happiness at becoming a grandmother again. She demanded to know when he was going to settle down and add to her joy.

Talked to a brother who was struggling at university. Made a promise to go and see him soon.

This was what Lydia called love, he thought. Joint memories that needed only a word to bubble to the surface. Shared connections, history. To know that you could reach out and there would be a hand waiting.

Without that, how would you ever know how to see beyond the fireworks and make a marriage?

How could you ever know for sure?

He was still holding the phone and he scrolled through his contact list until he found 'Rose'.

'Kal?'

Was that it? When just the sound of her voice made your heart sing?

'Where are you, Kal?'

'On the beach, watching the moon rise. I called my grandfather so that he could share it.'

'And now you're sharing it with me?' she asked, still distant, still 'Rose'.

'I'm making a memory, Lydia.' One that, for the rest of their lives, whenever either of them looked at the rising moon would bring back this moment. 'Go onto your balcony and you will see it rise above the trees.'

He heard her move. A door opening. A tiny breath that was not quite a gasp, not quite a sigh. 'It's there,' she said. 'I can just see the top of it.'

'Be patient…'

Was it when you could sit miles apart watching the same spectacle and words weren't necessary?

'Thank you, Kal,' she said, minutes later when it was high enough to have cleared the trees around Bab el Sama. Her voice softer. Pure Lydia.

'*Afwan ya habibati, hada mussdur sa'adati,*' he replied. Then, when she'd broken the connection, 'It is the source of my pleasure, beloved.'

Lydia stood on the terrace at dawn, sipping the orange juice that Dena had brought her, staying to watch Kal ride along the beach.

'He is faster this morning,' Dena said enigmatically. 'The demons must be getting closer.'

'Yes,' she replied without thinking. 'They are.'

She'd scarcely slept—at this rate she would soon look

exactly like Rose—and had watched the sky grow light, barely able to stop herself from going to the stables, just to be near him.

'Come, *sitti,* I will prepare you.'

Two hours later, resolved to keep her distance and wearing a feather-light black silk wrap, she and Kal crossed the creek to visit the souk.

It started well enough. They'd kept a clear foot between them and the conversation safely on topics such as the weather, Arabic vocabulary, followed by a whole lot of incoherent babbling as she'd seen the amazing array of colourful spices that came in dustbin-sized containers instead of tiny little glass jars.

Neither of them had mentioned the full moon they'd watched rising from the far ends of Bab el Sama. Apart and yet more intensely together than if they had been in each other's arms.

'Would you like the full tour?' he asked, 'or shall we go straight for the good stuff?'

She gave him a 'Lady Rose' look and said, 'The full tour. I want to see everything.'

Maybe that was the wrong answer. The area where the blacksmiths worked was noisy, hot and sparks flew everywhere. There were tinsmiths hammering away too and carpenters repairing furniture.

Once they turned into an area where tailors were waiting to run her up a dress in an hour or two things improved. There were tiny shops containing all kinds of strange and wonderful foods that weren't on the shelves of the supermarket that was her second home. She tasted Turkish delight flavoured with cardamom, a glass of tea from a man wandering about with an urn, little sticky cakes from a stall.

It was a different world and she sucked up every experience, her guard dropping long before they reached the stalls piled high with gorgeous silks.

Once there, she realised that she was not alone in wearing western clothes beneath the *abbayyeh*. There were plenty of woman who, when they leaned forward to look at the goods on display, revealed business suits, trousers, simple dresses beneath them. And although her pale hair and blue eyes made her an obvious foreigner, no one took much notice.

'They're used to Lucy and her friends,' Kal said. 'And another cousin, Zahir, is married to an English woman, too. A redhead in his case.'

'I read about it,' she said. 'It caused quite a sensation but I had no idea he was your cousin. Do you know him?'

'Our paths have crossed,' he said. 'We're in the same business.' He shrugged. 'My planes carry freight. His carry passengers.'

'Air freight? When you said you'd hadn't quite broken the habit of acquiring planes, you weren't joking, were you?'

'I ran out of room, so I had to keep some of them in the air,' he said. Joking, obviously. He had to be joking. 'Have you decided what you want?' he asked.

'It's impossible, but I've narrowed it down to three,' she said.

'I thought you were looking at this one?' He lifted the edge of a rich, heavy cream silk that would be perfect for a wedding dress.

'It's lovely,' she said, 'but I have no use for it.'

'Why do you have to have a use for something?' With a gesture that took in all four fabrics, he spoke briefly to the stall-holder. Moved on.

'Kal,' she protested. 'I haven't paid. I haven't told him how much I want. And what about my parcels?'

'He'll deliver them. And Dena will settle with him. Unless you want to haggle?'

Giving it up as a lost cause, she said, 'No, thanks. I'd rather hear more about this air freight business of yours. Does it have a name?'

'Kalzak Air Services.'

'Kalzak? That's your company?' Even she'd heard of them. Everybody had heard of them. 'I…um…hadn't made the connection. It's not exactly a hobby, then?'

'No,' he admitted. 'It's not a hobby. But I wasn't interested in the family business.'

She frowned. He hadn't mentioned a family business but there must be one or how else had they supported all those wives, children?

'Exiled playboy?' he prompted.

'I'm sorry—'

He stopped her fumbling apology with a touch to the elbow. 'It's okay. My grandfather lost his throne, but his father made a generous financial settlement—probably out of guilt.'

'And his brother didn't take that away?'

'He couldn't have, even if he'd wanted to, but I imagine he thought he was less dangerous playing with his racehorses and women than taking to the hills and fermenting more trouble.'

'You said he was the clever one.'

She thought that Kal was a lot more like his great-uncle, with his work ethic and philanthropy, than the grandfather he adored.

'Well, you and your cousin have something in common. Isn't that a starting place?'

'I help Lucy out when she needs to move disaster relief supplies. Zahir al-Khatib suggested I was taking advantage of her and offered to carry anything she needed so that she wouldn't have to turn to me for help.'

'Oh…'

And then, just when she was feeling desperately sorry for him, he gave her one of those slow smiles calculated to send her hormones into a dizzy spin.

'She probably shouldn't have told him that I had more aircraft, fewer family commitments. That I could afford to bear the cost more easily. His airline is very new,' he explained. 'But she wanted him to understand that my participation wasn't a matter for discussion.'

'Honestly,' she declared, 'I was just about to open up my heart and bleed for you.'

'I know.' And he touched the spot just by her mouth where she had pointed out his own giveaway muscle. 'You probably shouldn't ever play poker unless you're wearing a full face mask, Lydia,' he said softly. Then, as if nothing had happened, 'Gold next, I think.'

She followed him on rubbery legs to the glittering gold souk where the metal shone out of tiny shop windows and the air itself seemed to take on a golden glow.

It was a stunning spectacle and she could have spent hours there, but she quickly chose a pair of earrings, a waterfall of gold and seed pearls for her mother—who wore her hair up and adored dangly earrings—and a brooch set with turquoise for Jennie for looking after her.

'You will not choose something for yourself?'

He lifted the heavy rose pendant she was wearing at her throat. 'I imagine you'll have to give this back?'

'You imagine right.' But she could read him too, and she shook her head. 'Don't!' Then, 'Please, don't even think it…' she said, and walked quickly away in the direction of the harbour and the launch that had brought them across the creek, knowing that he had no choice but follow.

But later that afternoon four bolts of cloth were delivered to her room. And when she asked about paying for them Dena simply shrugged and suggest that she ask 'bin Zaki.'

Lydia didn't know much about the protocol in these things, but she was fairly certain that a man on the lookout for a bride was not supposed to buy another woman anything, let alone something as personal as cloth she would wear next to her skin.

Easy to see, in retrospect, that the spark that flared between them had been lit in the first moment they had set eyes on one another and for a moment it had burned so intense that, even while he was single-mindedly focused on his future, he had still come close to losing control.

There could be nothing 'little' between them and she was holding herself together with nothing but willpower.

CHAPTER ELEVEN

LYDIA wanted this over. Was desperate for Princess Sabirah to pay her call and the week to be over so that she could just stop pretending and go home.

Stop pretending to be Rose. Stop pretending that she felt nothing for Kalil. Not that that worked. He'd only had to call in the darkness. She only had to hear his voice. If she hadn't cared she would have hung up, not stood there with her phone pressed to her ear, imagining she could hear him breathe while that huge moon rose above them.

Why had he done that?

He was the one who'd stepped back from the brink, broken the most intense, the most intimate connection there could ever be between a man and a woman even when it was obvious he'd wanted her as much as she'd wanted him.

Trapped, like her, committed to a course from which there was no escape but unable to stop himself from touching her. Calling her. Making love to her with words.

Breaking her heart.

She had taken lunch alone, keeping her nose firmly in a book until the words all ran together in a smeary blur, swam fifty lengths of the pool just to stop herself from thinking about him.

Except that when she emerged, slightly dizzy with the effort, he was waiting to wrap a towel around her.

'You shouldn't be here,' she said.

'I am your bodyguard. It is my duty.'

'I'm not in any danger.'

Only from falling in love with a man who didn't believe in love. Who thought marriage was no more than a convenient contract arranged by two families for their advantage. Maybe the girls did have some say, but the pressure had to be intense to make a 'good' marriage. Scarcely any different from the way that medieval barons gave their daughters to men whose land marched with theirs, or who could bring them closer to the King.

'Please…' She grabbed the towel and ran from the poolside to her room. Sat with it pressed to her face.

'Be strong, Lydie. You have to be strong…'

But, no matter how she ignored him, Kal's presence permeated the house.

Everywhere she went, she was sure he'd been there a second before. She couldn't escape the woody scent that clung to him, the swish of freshly laundered robes, the gentle flapping sound of leather thongs against marble floors.

The thrumming beat of hooves against sand.

It was all in her head, she knew, but she retreated to her room, allowing Yatimah to pamper her with facials, massage the tension out of her shoulders, paint more ornate patterns on her hands and feet with henna.

She caught sight of them as she reached for the phone, hoped they would wear off before she went back to work or they'd cause a few comments from the regulars as she swished their weekly shop over the scanner.

She checked the caller ID and, when she saw it was Kal, considered not answering. But then he'd come looking for her.

She took a deep breath, composed herself.

'Kal?' she queried, ice-cool.

'Just checking. I haven't seen you all day. Are you hiding from me?'

Reckless, bold, dangerous Bagheera, whose skin shimmered like watered silk, whose mouth tasted like wild honey—only a fool wouldn't hide.

'Just putting my feet up, taking it easy while I plan my future,' she said.

'Oh? What did you have in mind?'

'Well,' she said, her fingers lingering on the bolt of cream silk on the table beside her, 'now I'm giving up the lookalike business I thought I might set myself up in the rag trade,' she said. 'Costing is tricky, though. I need to know how much to budget for material.'

'Oh, I see. This is about the silk…'

'I can't wear it all myself,' she pointed out. Not unless she made a wedding dress with a thirty foot train. 'I need to know how much it cost.'

'You must ask Dena. She dealt with the merchant.'

'She told me to ask you.'

'Then it's a mystery,' he said with an infuriating hint of laughter in his voice that undid all her good intentions, all her cool.

'Kal!' she exploded. 'I just wanted a few metres for a suit or dress. I can't take all that home with me.'

'No problem.' Now he was enjoying himself. 'I'll deliver.'

'Deliver them to your bride,' she snapped. 'Yatimah was telling me that's what a groom is supposed to do. Send jewels, cloth, carpets, the biggest flat screen television you can afford.'

'Yatimah has altogether too much to say for herself,' he snapped back and she rejoiced in having rattled him out of his teasing. He had no right to tease her. No right to call her and make her want him… For a moment neither of them spoke and the only sound was of raised breathing. Then, after a moment, his voice expressionless, his manner formal, Kal said, 'Lucy phoned to check up on how well I've been looking after you, *sitti*.'

'Tell her what you like,' Lydia replied, not even trying for cool. 'I won't tell tales. And cut out the *sitti*.' It was one thing having Dena or Yatimah calling her 'lady', quite another from Kal.

'I can't tempt you to come on a picnic?'

Oh, the man knew how to tempt.

She refused without having to think twice. Well, maybe twice, but she knew the attraction between them was too great to risk another close encounter. And that even while he was paying lip service to honour, his frustrated libido was refusing to quit.

'Sorry, Kal, but I'm planning a walk on the beach this afternoon and, unlike you, I'm happy with my own company,' she said, knowing how much that would infuriate him. But she was angry with him for putting her through this, with herself for aching for something so far out of reach. For bringing tears stinging to her eyes. 'But you're welcome to stand and watch if you like. Just remember how handy I am with a shell.'

She didn't wait for him to command her not to do it, but hung up. Then had to hold herself together. Physically wrap her arms around herself, holding her breath, just to stop herself from falling apart.

Kal took himself to the stables in the foulest, blackest mood.

He was behaving like a man who didn't know his own mind. Who had lost control of his senses.

It wasn't true. When he could have taken Lydia, he had known it was wrong. That, without commitment, honour, such an act was beneath him, could only hurt her.

He'd hurt her anyway.

She could hide nothing from him and he'd seen her eyes in the moment she had realised why he had refused the greatest gift a woman could bestow on any man. Had seen her pain in the way she'd moved as she'd taken herself away from him in the souk, when all he'd wanted to do was shower her with gold, pearls. Put diamonds in her ears, on every one of the fingers he had taken to his lips. When, seeing that in his face, she had begged him not even to think it.

He was furious because, even as he weakened, unable to stay

away, she grew stronger, keeping him at arm's length when he needed them around her.

A nagging, desperate need that came from somewhere deep inside, from a place he hadn't, until that moment, known existed. All he knew was that he was ready to consign common sense, five years of patient planning along with everything he had learned about the fleeting nature of 'love' from his grandfather, his father, to the deep blue sea.

And still she had turned him down. Not because she didn't want to go. He was attuned to every nuance in her voice, every hesitation and he'd heard the unspoken longing in a whisper of a sigh before she had said no to his picnic.

But, even when he was losing control, she was strong enough to save him from himself.

Lydia Young might not be a princess, but she had all the attributes of one. Courage, dignity that would become a queen. A spirit that was all her own. He wanted her with a desperation that was driving every other thought from his head.

At home he would have taken up the small biplane he used for stunting, shaken off his mood in a series of barrel rolls, loops. Here, the closest he could get to a release in the rush of power was on one of Hanif's fine stallions but, as he tightened the girth, the horse skipped edgily away from him, sensing his frustration.

But it wasn't simply his out of control libido, the sense of being too big for his skin. This was a need that went much deeper, challenging everything he believed in.

He'd spent the last five years planning the perfect life but Lydia was forcing him to face the fact that life wasn't something that you could plan. It happened. Some of it good, some of it bad, none of it 'safe'.

He had arrogantly assumed that his grandfather, his father had wasted their lives but, while their families were scarcely conventional, their quivers were full of the children of their youth and they were, he realised with a shock, happy men.

That, wherever his grandfather died, he would be surrounded by his children, grandchildren, people who loved him.

He lay his hand on the neck of the horse, gentling him with soft words, even while he yearned for the sound of Lydia's voice. The sweet scent that clung to her, as if she had been brushing her hands over jasmine. The touch of her hands against his skin.

Wanted to see her face, her eyes lighting up, her mouth softening, her hands describing what her lips were saying. Her quickness with a tender touch to show that she understood. Her laugh. The swiftness with which she melted to his kisses.

While he kept the world at bay, carefully avoiding the risk, the pain that was an inevitable part of what Lydia called 'love', she held nothing back.

She had answered every question he had asked of her with not just her body, but her heart and her soul and he wanted to shower her with gifts, buy her every bolt of cloth in the market, heap up gold, pearls, gems in a dower that she could not ignore.

Except, of course, she could and would. She had told him so. Her price was above rubies. Only his heart, freely given in an avowal of love, without negotiations, conditions, guarantees would win her acceptance.

She would not settle for less and neither, he knew now, would he. Because the nearest a man could come to perfection was to take every single moment and live it to the full. With love. And she was right. He was not a stranger to the emotion. Love for his family was part of who he was.

But this was new. This love for a woman who, from the first moment he had set eyes on her, had made the lights shine more brightly.

He'd lost the perfect moment, had hurt her. Now, to show her how he felt, he had to give her not just his heart but his world. Everything that made him who he was. And there was only one way he could do that, could win her trust.

The horse snorted impatiently, eager to be off, but he left the groom circling the yard as he made the calls that would change his life.

Lydia stepped onto the beach, kicking off her sandals. It was cooler today and she was wearing cotton trousers, a white shirt, a cashmere sweater knotted at her waist.

There were clouds gathering offshore and the wind coming off the sea was sharper, whipping up little white horses on the creek and, as she strode along the beach, hanging onto her temper by a thread, she glowered at the photographer's launch, bobbing on the waves, hoping that he was seasick.

She doubted that. There hadn't been pictures in the papers for a day or two. A sighting of Rupert Devenish at a business meeting in the States had downgraded interest in Bab el Sama and he would have packed up his telephoto lenses and gone in search of more lucrative prey.

It hadn't been a great week for anyone, she thought, her hand tightening around the note from Princess Sabirah's secretary that Dena had delivered to her as she'd left for her walk.

It was brief and to the point, informing her, regretfully, that the Princess had a cold and was unable to travel this week. Wishing her a pleasant stay and the Princess's sincere hope that they would meet soon in London.

Somewhere where there was no chance that Kal al-Zaki would pop out of the woodwork, presumably.

That the illness was diplomatic, she had no doubt, and she let out a very unladylike roar of outrage that all Kal's hopes and dreams had been crushed without even a chance to put in a plea for his grandfather.

What on earth was the matter with these people? It had all happened fifty years ago, for heaven's sake.

'Get over it!' she shouted to the sky, the seabirds whirling overhead.

He had to know. She would have to tell him and the sooner the better. Maybe there was still something he could do. She could do...

If she really had been Rose, she could have gone to Rumaillah by herself, taken some flowers to the 'sick' Princess. On her own, she would have been admitted. Could have pleaded for him.

She stopped, stood for a moment staring at the phone in her hand as she realised something else. That with his mission dead he would turn to her for comfort, would be free to love her...

She stopped the thought dead, ashamed even to have given it room in her head, and quickly scrolled down the contact list and hit 'dial'. Unexpectedly, it went straight to voicemail...

'Kal,' she began uncertainly, hating to be the bearer of such bad news. Then, as she hesitated, above the buffeting of the wind she heard another sound. The pounding of hooves. She swung round and saw him riding towards her astride a huge black horse, robes flying behind him, hand outstretched. Before she could think, move, there was a jolt as he swooped low, caught her round the waist, lifted her to his saddle.

It was the dream, she thought crazily as she clung to him, her face pressed against his pounding heart.

She'd reached out to him as she'd watched him from above, wanting to be lifted to the stars.

There were no stars and she knew that at any moment he would slow down, berate her for taking unnecessary risks.

But he didn't stop, didn't slow down until Bab el Sama was far below them, the horse rearing as he brought it to a halt, turned, slid to the ground with her.

'Did your English heart beat to be swept onto my horse, *ya habibati?*' He smiled as he curved his hand around her face. 'Did you feel mine, beloved?' He took her hand and placed it against his chest. 'Feel it now. It beats for you, Lydia Young.'

Beloved...

He had called her his beloved and as his lips came down on hers she was lost.

* * *

'This is kidnapping,' she said when he carried her to a waiting four-by-four. 'Where are you taking me?'

'You will see,' he said as he fastened the seat belt and climbed in beside her. 'Then I will ask you if you wish me to take you back.'

'But what about…?'

He silenced her protest with a kiss.

'The groom will take him back,' he said and she realised that this had not been a spur of the moment escapade but was a carefully arranged assault on her defences by a man who when he offered a treat refused to take no for an answer. No doubt there would be a picnic waiting for her at the side of the river, or some archaeological treasure.

But when he stopped there was nothing but a distant view.

'There,' he said. 'Do you see it?'

She could see something shimmering through the dust haze like a mirage. A tower, a shimmer of green above high walls, and she knew without doubt that she was looking at Umm al Sama.

'I see it,' she said. Then, turning to him, 'I see you, Kalil bin Zaki.'

'Will you go there with me?'

He had brought her to the place where his grandfather had been born. The place he called home. Not home as in the place where he lived, like the apartments in Rumaillah, London, New York, but the home of his heart. The place that an exile, generations on, still carried deep in the memory, in his soul.

That he would keep for a woman who meant more than a brief affair. This was the home he had been preparing not just for the return of his grandfather, but for the bride he would one day bring here and, even though he knew who she was, Lydia Young, he was offering it to her.

Words for a moment failed her, then a phrase came into her head, something from long ago Sunday School…

'Whither thou goest, I will go; and where thou lodgest, I will lodge…'

Kal knew this was a perfect moment. He had offered the woman he loved all that he was and she had replied with words that touched his soul and as he reached for her, embraced her, sealed their future with a kiss, he knew he owned the world.

Kal led her through Umm al Sama by the hand, through gardens that had run wild, but were being tamed. Beside pools that had been cleaned and reflected the blue of a sky that had magically cleared above them. Through arched colonnades decorated with cool blue and green tiles.

Showed her a wind tower that funnelled the air down to a deep cooling pool below ground. Buildings that had been beautiful once and would be beautiful again when he had finished restoring them.

One building, smaller than the rest, was finished. Kal watched her from the doorway as she walked around an exquisite sitting room touching fine tables, running a finger over the smooth curves of fine porcelain.

'This is so beautiful, Kal. So special.' She looked at him. 'What was this?'

Kal had not touched Lydia since they'd arrived at Umm al Sama. Outside, in the garden, where they might be seen, he'd kept a discreet distance between them. Showing her respect. He had not brought her here to make love to her, but to give her his heart. To give her this.

'My great-grandfather's wife lived here before they moved to the new palace at Rumaillah.'

'Leaving it to the heir apparent?'

'No one has lived here since my grandfather was banished. If you go upstairs, there should be something to eat on the balcony.'

'All this and food too?'

'I invited you on a picnic,' he reminded her, leading the way to a wide covered balcony with carved shade screens that ran the length of the building.

She stared for a moment at the distant view of the mountains, then pushed open a door to reveal the private apartment of a princess.

The polished floor was covered with rare carpets, the walls hung with vivid gauzy silk, as was the great bed at its heart.

Lydia looked back at him. 'Are you expecting Scheherazade?'

'Only you. Come, *ya habibati,*' he said, extending his hand to her. 'You must be hungry.'

'I'm starving, Kal.' As she raised her hand to meet his, she came into his arms, lifted her lips to his. 'Feed me.'

As she breathed the words into his mouth he shattered. The man who had been Kalil al-Zaki no longer existed. As he shed his clothes, fed Lydia Young, the wife of his heart, with his touch, his mouth, his body, she rebuilt him with her surprise, her delight, tiny cries of pleasure at each new intimacy and finally with her tears as they learned from each other and finally became one.

'I have to go back to Bab el Sama, Kal,' she protested the following morning as she lay in bed while he fed her pomegranate seeds and dates for breakfast. 'I have no clothes here.'

He kissed her shoulder. 'Why do you need clothes?'

'Because otherwise I can't leave this room.'

He nudged the edge of the sheet, taking the kiss lower. 'I repeat, why do you need clothes, *ya rohi, ya hahati?*'

He'd showered her with words she did not understand as he'd made love to her, but she refused to be distracted.

'Dena will be concerned.'

'Dena knows that you are with your bodyguard. Am I not guarding your body?' And his smile, his touch, made everything else go away.

Thoroughly and completely distracted, it was gone noon

when she stirred again. She was alone in the great bed they'd shared and, wrapping the sheet around her, she went to the balcony, expecting to find him there waiting for her to wake.

The balcony was deserted but her clothes, freshly laundered, were waiting for her on a dresser with a note from Kal.

> *Ask for whatever you want. Umm al Sama is yours. I will back soon.*

She held it to her breast, smiling. Obviously he'd gone to fetch her clothes, explain their absence, and she bathed, washed her hair, dressed. The note from the princess's secretary, forgotten in the wild excitement of her abduction, of Umm al Sama, of Kal, was at the bottom of the pile. That had been ironed, too.

She should have told him about that. As she put on Rose's watch she wondered what time he'd left. How long it would be before he returned.

Maybe he'd rung. She checked her messages but there was nothing. Tried his number but it went straight to voicemail but this wasn't news she could dump on him that way. And leaving a *When will you be back?* message seemed so needy...

A servant brought her food. She picked at it. Took a walk in the garden.

Checked her phone again. With nothing to read, no one to talk to, she switched to the Net and caught the urgent flash of a breaking news story and her blood ran cold.

Lady Rose kidnapped...

Rose...

But it wasn't Rose.

Of course it wasn't. It was her in the picture.

Make that a whole series of pictures.

Alone on the beach. Kal riding her down. Lifting her to his saddle. Disappearing into the distance.

The photographer hadn't gone anywhere, she realised. Or had he been tipped off because he'd had all the time in the world to get the whole story in pictures…?

No question by whom.

There was only one person at Bab al Sama who wanted to be visible.

Well, two. She had wanted to be visible and maybe she'd given Kal the idea. Because when he'd realised that the princess wasn't coming—Dena had no doubt had her own note from the palace and would certainly have told him—he must have been desperate.

Not for himself. Whatever happened, he'd thrown away his own hopes and dreams the minute he'd picked her up from the beach. The family name, the title, the bride. Five years of quiet diplomacy, of being invisible.

He'd done this solely out of love for his grandfather.

For love, she reminded herself as she stared at the pictures for one last moment.

One thing was certain—with the world's press on the case, he was no longer invisible. The Emir could no longer pretend he did not exist. On the contrary, he had probably sent his guard to arrest him, lock him up. That would explain his lengthy absence. Why his phone was switched off.

And only she could save him.

She resisted the temptation to leave him to cool his heels for a night in the cells and went to find someone to take her to Rumaillah.

All he'd planned was a photo opportunity followed by a picnic. She was the one who'd got completely the wrong end of the stick, responding to his polite invitation to visit his family home with a declaration of eternity. Led all the way with her desperate *'I'm starving…feed me'*. What on earth was a man to do faced with that? Say no, thanks—again?

Once she was on her way—and had stopped blushing long enough to think straight—she called Rose. She couldn't have

picked up the story yet, or she'd have been on the phone herself.
She growled with frustration as her call went straight to voicemail and she left a reassuring message.

Then she called her mother, not because she'd be worried,
but because she really, really needed to hear her voice.

Kal left his beautiful Lydia sleeping. He could have asked
for her things to be sent to Umm al Sama, but he wanted to
visit the souk.

While she had clearly understood the significance of his
taking her to Umm al Sama, that no one but his bride would
ever sleep in that bed, he wanted to buy her at least one of the
diamonds that he would shower on her.

He left Yatimah to pack their bags while he crossed the
creek in search of a perfect solitaire. A stone that would say
the things that words could never say. A pledge. A promise of
forever.

Then he called his grandfather to tell him that he must not
be in such a hurry to die. That, if he was patient, he would see
not only a wedding at Umm al Sama but a great-grandson born
there, too.

It was after lunch before he arrived home to be told that the
sitti had insisted on being taken to Rumaillah. To the palace.

Rumaillah…

Had there been a call? A summons from the Princess? No.
She would not have made a formal visit wearing a pair of
cotton trousers and a shirt. This was something else. He took
the stairs two at a time as he raced to the room where they had
spent the night in blissful discovery of each other, certain that
she must have left a message.

There was nothing.

Only the message he had left for her.

And a note from the palace with Princess Sabirah's
regrets…

Dena had told him that she'd been unwell; it was why she

hadn't come earlier. This must have been in Lydia's pocket when he'd taken her from the beach. It couldn't have anything to do with her racing off to Rumaillah.

Unless…

He flipped to the Net, saw the breaking news story. And swore long and inventively in several languages. He'd had the photographer warned off but he'd either come back or this was another one. It made no difference.

He knew exactly what Lydia must be thinking.

She'd assume that he'd known that the Princess was not coming and that he had used her to force the Emir to notice him.

That she'd trusted him with all that she was, given him her most precious gift, and he had betrayed her.

Lydia stood at the door to the *majlis*. She'd borrowed an *abbayeh* from one of the women at Umm al Sama but she was the only woman in the group of people who had arrived to petition the Emir. She was aware of a rumbling of disapproval, a certain amount of jostling, but she stood tall, refused to turn tail and run, and waited her turn.

The room was vast. At one end the Emir sat with his advisors. Along each wall men, drinking coffee from tiny cups, sat on rows of sofas.

As she kicked off her sandals, stepped forward, the *abbayeh* caught—or maybe someone was standing on it—and slipped from her hair and every sound died away.

The Emir rose, extended a hand in welcome and said, 'Lady Rose. We were concerned for your safety. Please…'

He gestured her forward.

She walked the length of the room. Bowed. Said, 'Thank you, Excellency, but as you see I am safe and well. If you have seized Kalil al-Zaki, have him locked in your cells, I must ask you to release him.'

There was a buzz, silenced by a look from the Emir.

'Who is Kalil al-Zaki?' he asked.

She gasped, snapped, 'Who is he? I don't believe you people! It's been fifty years since his grandfather was exiled. Was stripped of everything he cared about. Your nephew has an apartment in this city, yet you treat him as if he did not exist.'

Now there was silence. Pin drop silence, but she was too angry to care that she was flouting royal protocol. Even an Emir needed to hear the truth once in a while.

'Kalil al-Zaki is a man of honour, a man who cares for his family, who has built up an international business that would grace any nation. He wants nothing from you but to bring his grandfather home to die. You would grant that to a dog!' Then, in the ringing silence that followed this outburst, 'And, by the way, my name is Lydia Young. Lady Rose has taken a holiday in a place where she won't be photographed twenty-four hours a day!'

Then, because there was nothing left for her, she sank to her knees before him.

'The son of your great-grandfather is dying, Excellency. Will you not let him come home?'

Kal was too late to stop her. He was blocked at the doorway by the Emiri guard, forced to watch as she berated the Emir.

But, in the deathly silence that followed her appeal for mercy, even they were too stunned to stop him and he pushed the man aside, lifted her to her feet, then touched his head, his heart and bowed to her.

'*Ya malekat galbi, ya rohi, ya hahati*. You are beautiful, my soul, my life. Ahebbak, ya tao'am rohi. The owner of my heart. *Amoot feeki*. There is no life without you.' Then, 'I did not know, Lydia. Please believe me, I did not use you. I did not know.'

She would have spoken, but the Emir stepped forward. 'I have listened to your appeal, Lydia Young.'

That she was dismissed, neither of them were in any doubt, but as he turned to leave with her, caring only that she should believe him, the Emir said, 'I have not heard from you, Kalil al-Zaki.'

She touched his hand, said, 'Stay.'

'No…'

'For heaven's sake, Kal. This is what you wanted. Your chance. Don't blow it now.'

Then she turned and walked away.

Lydia had been taken to the Princess's quarters. She'd been fed and given a change of clothes and then, having asked to be allowed to go straight home, the British Consul had been summoned to provide her with temporary papers since her passport was with her belongings and only Kal knew were they were.

She arrived home to a dozen messages from newspapers wanting her story and one from a famous publicist who warned her to sign nothing until she'd talked to him. And reporters knee-deep on the footpath outside her mother's flat.

Her mother didn't say a word. Just hugged her.

Numb until then, she finally broke down and cried.

Rose called to make sure she was really all right. To apologise for the publicity. To thank her.

'You've changed my life, Lydia. Words cannot express my gratitude. You should sell your story, make a mint.'

'There is no story, Rose.' Then, 'Is there any chance of getting my car back soon? I'm due back at work the day after tomorrow.'

'That's a bit of a bad news, good news story, I'm afraid. The bad news is that I had a little bit of an accident,' she confessed.

'Oh.' The car had been her pride and joy. It had taken her forever to save up for it… 'Is it in the garage?'

'Er…a little bit more of an accident than that,' she admitted. 'It's nothing but a cube of metal in a scrapyard, but the good news is that George has arranged a replacement for you. A rather jolly red Beetle. I'll make sure it's delivered tomorrow.'

'Thank you. And Rose. Congratulations. I hope you will be really happy.'

'I'll send you and your mother an invitation to the wedding.'

There was nothing from Kal and, since she didn't want to

hear from the reporters, the newspapers or the publicist, she un-
plugged the phone and turned off her mobile.

She sent an email to the lookalike agency, informing them
that she would no longer be available and asking them to take
her off their books.

Deleted dozens from newsmen offering interviews, and
weirdos who just wanted to be weird.

She didn't open the door to the manager of the local garage
who came to deliver a brand-new red VW Beetle, which she
knew cost about three times what she'd paid for her car, until
he put a note through the door explaining who he was.

There was no missing the black and gold livery of the
Kalzak Air Services courier who pulled up outside and delivered her luggage. All those lovely clothes, the cosmetics, the
scent, the four bolts of silk.

She gave her mother and Jennie their gifts.

And then, in the privacy of her room, she cried again all over
the cream silk.

The Emir had given Kal a hard time. Made him wait while he
consulted his brothers, his sons, his nephews. Hanif had supported him and so, unexpectedly, had Zahir and all the time he
had been berating himself for letting Lydia walk away. Fly away.

She had thought he was in trouble and had come to help.
Had begged for him.

Only her 'stay' had kept him here while members of a family
he did not know video-conferenced from all over the world,
deciding the fate of his grandfather, eventually deciding that
compassion required that he should be allowed to return to
Umm al Sama. And that, after his death, his family could use
the name Khatib.

Kal told the Emir that he would bring his grandfather home
but under those terms they could keep their name. He didn't
want it. Lydia deserved better from him than acceptance of such
a mealy-mouthed offer.

And the Emir smiled. 'I remember him. You are just like him.'

'You honour me, Excellency.'

At which point His Excellency had thrown up his hands and said, 'Let the old man have his name and his title.'

'Will you permit Dena to return to London with me to fetch him, travel back with him and his nurses?'

'If she is agreeable.' Then, with heavy irony, 'Is there anything else you want, Kalil bin Zaki al-Khatib? One of my granddaughters as a bride, perhaps, now that you are a sheikh?'

'I am very conscious of the honour you bestow, Excellency,' he replied, 'but, like my grandfather, I have chosen my own bride. You have had the honour of meeting her.'

And this time the Emir laughed appreciatively.

'She is all fire, that one. You will have your hands full.' He did not appear to believe that this was a bad thing.

Since there was no other way to get rid of them, Lydia finally faced the newsmen, standing on the pavement outside her home giving an impromptu press conference, answering their questions.

'Who was the horseman?'

'A bodyguard rescuing me from intrusive photographers.'

Laughter.

'Lady Rose has cut her hair. Will you do that?'

'No.'

'When did you meet?'

'Will you be seeing her?'

'Have you met her fiancé?'

No. No. No.

She kept a smile pinned to her face, didn't lose her temper, even at the most intrusive questions, and eventually they ran out of things to ask.

And since she wasn't Lady Rose, it didn't take long for the madness to die down. One moment the pavement in front of their flat had been mobbed, the next there was no one.

The agency was still pleading with her to reconsider her

decision. They'd been inundated with requests for appearances since Rose had announced her engagement. But the publicist, who'd been so keen to negotiate a contract for her to 'write' the story of her career as Rose's lookalike—with the titillating promise to reveal who had really swept her away on that black stallion and what had happened afterwards—finally accepted that she meant it when she said 'no'.

With the excitement of Rose's engagement to occupy the gossip pages, she quickly became old news.

The story about the exiled Sheikh who had been pardoned by the Emir and allowed to return home to die probably wouldn't have made the news at all, except that Ramal Hamrah was where that very odd incident had taken place, when everyone thought Lady Rose had been kidnapped.

She had heard nothing from Kalil.

No doubt he had his hands full taking care of his grandfather, transferring him to Umm al Sama. Getting to know a whole new family.

She winced as *White Christmas* began to play for the fiftieth time that week on the seasonal tape. Turned to smile at yet another harassed mother doing her Christmas shop. Reached for yet another turkey.

Kal quietly joined the checkout queue.

All his duties done, he had come straight from the airport to find Lydia. Had gone to her home. He'd met her mother and, with her blessing, he had come to claim his love publicly, in her real world. Wanted her to know that there was no misunderstanding between them. That he knew who she was. That it was not some icon he had fallen in love with but Lydia Young.

Not the aristocrat in the designer suit, but the ordinary girl on the supermarket checkout wearing an overall and a ridiculous hat.

She looked exhausted. There were dark shadows beneath her eyes, her cheeks were hollow and had lost their glow, but the smile never faltered.

She greeted regular customers as friends. Asked what they were doing for the holiday and, as she listened with every appearance of interest, they lost a little of their tension as she swiftly dealt with their purchases. He watched her pack the shopping for one old lady whose hands were crippled with arthritis, helped her count out the money.

He made an instinctive move forward to help as she heaved a heavy bag of potatoes over the scanner, got a glare from the woman in front who was fiddling with a mobile phone. She was trying to take a picture of Lydia, he realised, and he leaned forward and said very quietly, 'Don't do that.'

About to tell him to mind his own business, she thought better of it and, muttering something about forgetting something, melted away.

Next in line was a woman with a toddler and a small baby who was grizzling with exhaustion.

Lydia whizzed the goods through, packed the bags, then took the baby, put it to her shoulder as the woman searched helplessly for her wallet. Reassuring the woman, patting the baby. The baby fell asleep, the wallet was found.

'Can I take you home with me?' the woman asked as she retrieved her baby.

He'd seen her dressed in designer clothes, every inch the Lady with a capital L.

He'd seen her sweetness with Yatimah, her eyes hot with passion, soft with desire. Seen her berate the Emir in a room filled with hostile men. Seen her on her knees begging for him…

Beauty was a lot more than skin-deep and with each revelation he'd fallen deeper in love with Lydia. And as he watched her kindness, her compassion, her cheerful smile even though she was exhausted, he fell in love with her all over again.

She lifted her hands to her face and rubbed it, turned as someone came alongside her. 'Your shift is nearly up. Just this last one and then I'll take over.'

His cue to place the basket he was carrying on the shelf, take out the single item it contained and place it on the conveyer.

He saw her gather herself for one last effort. Put the smile back in place, turn to wait for the goods to reach her. Saw the smile falter, the frown pucker her brow as she watched the tiny dark blue velvet-covered box move slowly towards her. The diamond solitaire at its heart sparking a rainbow of light.

Confused, she looked up. Saw him standing at the far end of the conveyer as, behind him, half a dozen shoppers stared open-mouthed. Rose slowly to her feet.

'Kal…'

'The ring was in my pocket when I returned to Umm al Sama, Lydia. I was sure that you knew, understood that the only woman I would take there would be my bride. But I wanted to give you a tangible token of my love. Something more than a dream.'

'I am not what you wanted.'

'Until I met you I didn't know what I wanted, but love is the star to every wandering bark, Lydia. You taught me that. I had been wandering all my life, without a star to guide me…' He sank to his knees. '*Ahebbak,* Lydia. I love you. I am begging you to marry me, to be my princess, my wife, my lover, the mother of my children, my soul, my life.'

The growing crowd of onlookers broke out into a spontaneous round of applause but it was Lydia who mattered.

'How is he?' she asked. 'Your grandfather?'

'Happy to be home. Thanks to you.'

'Then you have everything.'

'Everything but you.' He stood up, took the ring from the box, held it up, then touched it to each finger of her left hand, counting slowly in Arabic… '*Wahid, ithnan, thelatha, arba'a, khamsa…*'

'*Ithnan, ya habibi*—my beloved,' she said. '*Ahebbak,* Kalil. I love you.'

He slipped the ring onto the ring finger of her left hand, then walked around the checkout, took her in his arms and kissed her.

By this time they had brought the entire row of checkouts to a standstill. And the entire store was clapping.

'Maybe we had better leave, my love,' he said. 'These good people need to finish their shopping. And we have a wedding to arrange.'

Daily Chronicle, 2nd March 2010

LADY ROSE LOOKALIKE MARRIES HER LORD

Lydia Young, who for ten years made regular appearances as a Lady Rose lookalike, was married today at Umm al Sama in Ramal Hamrah to Sheikh Kalil bin Zaki al-Khatib, nephew of the Emir.

Sheikh Kalil, who founded the international air freight company Kalzak Air Services, met Miss Young before Christmas and proposed after a whirlwind romance.

The bride's mother Mrs Glenys Young, who was formerly a seamstress for a London couturier, made her daughter's wedding dress from a bolt of cream silk that was a gift from the groom.

Four of the groom's sisters were attendants and his brother was best man. Family members and guests flew in from all over the world to be present at the ceremony, amongst them Lady Rose Napier and her fiancé billionaire businessman George Saxon. The groom's grandfather, who is gravely ill, rallied sufficiently to make a short speech at the reception.

The couple will spend their time between homes in London, Paris, New York and Ramal Hamrah.

THE SHEIKH'S LAST MISTRESS

RACHAEL THOMAS

For James, Marian and David.

CHAPTER ONE

ZAFIR AL ASMARI WAS SCEPTICAL as he drove towards the old red-brick house, which was a stark contrast to the immaculate penthouse he'd just left in London. Was it possible the woman he was seeking really worked here? This riding school, nestled in the countryside beyond London, certainly looked as if it had seen better days—not at all where he had imagined finding Destiny Richards. Her reputation with difficult horses had made him travel from Kezoban personally to seek her out.

He parked his black sports car and got out, unsure if he should even continue with this madness. He must have been misinformed. Destiny Richards wouldn't be working somewhere so ordinary. Nothing about the old house or tired-looking sheds gave any hint of being professional stables. He was on the point of leaving when movement inside the shed beyond the house caught his eye.

Zafir walked forward, his shoes crunching on the grit of the driveway, and, unable to contain his curiosity, looked into the building being used as the riding school. Through an open door, he could see a tall, slim young woman lunging a chestnut horse around her. Intrigued, he walked down the side of the house, intent on seeing exactly who this woman was. If she was Destiny Richards, he could settle his unease and confirm he'd done the right thing by hiring her before coming to meet her personally.

'Ah, you have arrived.' A sharp female voice behind him dragged his attention from the young woman and horse. He stopped, turning abruptly to an older and somewhat overenthusiastic woman. 'Are you here for the Sheikh? To see Destiny work her magic?'

Zafir narrowed his eyes. Instinct warned him of this woman's insincerity. Her overzealous attitude jarred his nerves, but if she thought he was here for the Sheikh instead of actually being the Sheikh, then so much the better. He could ascertain if Destiny Richards did indeed possess the gift of horse whispering, something he very much hoped was true, but right now, given the surroundings, he was inclined to think he'd been misled.

'I am and I don't have time to waste. Where is Ms Richards?'

'My daughter is in the school. This way.' She gestured with a smile which didn't reach her eyes, backing up his first impression. It didn't bode well that Destiny Richards was this woman's daughter. First impressions counted for a lot in his culture and he was far from impressed, but had to remember this might be Majeed's last chance.

Without another word, he made his way to the school, aware the woman was following. Quietly he entered, stood against the wooden interior wall and watched. For a while the young woman he now knew was Destiny Richards had no idea he was there and he couldn't help his gaze sweeping over her, appreciating her tall and shapely figure and how the tight-fitting jodhpurs and T-shirt clung, in a way only a hot-blooded male could, just as he'd always done before duty had brought him to heel.

Her dark hair was pulled up high on her head into a ponytail, which swayed like a dancer to an unheard tune with each move she made. She was distracting and not at all what he'd expected, especially after having just met her mother.

The horse slowed to a walk, then stopped at her calm command. Destiny waited for the horse to walk to her and, as she touched its face, Zafir could hear the sound of soothing words, seeing the obvious connection of trust the horse had with her. Then she turned round, her eyes meeting his instantly.

Despite the distance something passed between them, jolting him with its intensity. She was beautiful and, for the first time since he'd inherited the title of Sheikh of Kezoban, he felt his interest stirring, awakening everything he'd turned his back on. He pushed that thought aside. Now was not the time to be distracted by a woman, not when Royal protocol dictated he had to select a bride. As the last remaining member of his family, providing his country with an heir was paramount.

'Destiny, this man is here for the Sheikh. You know, the one we told you about.' The older woman's voice held a hint of warning, despite her smile, and the sudden tension in the air between mother and daughter was palpable, like storm clouds about to break over a hot city.

He crossed the sandy surface towards Destiny as her mother continued to talk. He was sure he saw a flash of defiance rush across Destiny's beautiful face as she glanced briefly at her mother before looking at him once more. Her fine brows arched in disbelief and her lips set into a firm line of disapproval. He couldn't help wondering what kissing away that disapproval would be like, confident it would be as intense as the attraction he felt for her.

'I remember.' Her voice was soft and gentle, but he didn't miss the underlying note of determination. She stepped towards him, the horse moving with her, staying loyally at her side as she offered her hand in a Western handshake and smiled at him. 'Destiny Richards. How can I help you?'

A smile pulled at the corners of his lips. He liked the feisty spirit she was working hard to conceal, reminding him of a young horse that would rather run free with the wind across the desert sands than be confined and controlled. He'd had to put such ideas to one side after his father had died six years ago, his days of being the wild playboy Sheikh his father despaired of abruptly curtailed. For the first time since that day he wished he was free; the attraction for this woman was so intense all he could do was imagine taking her in his arms and kissing away her defiance.

He took her hand and the jolt of something new and exciting sizzled through him. The deep brown of her eyes, which reminded him of polished mahogany, mirrored the attraction. 'Forgive me for the intrusion. Your ability to work with horses that have been traumatised has come to the attention of the Sheikh of Kezoban. He has made an arrangement with the owners here for you to travel to Kezoban to work with his prized Arabian stallion, but he sent me to personally meet you before my return.'

The deceit slipped easily from him. He was preserving his sanity by omitting the truth, sure that her mother would make matters far worse for him and probably Destiny if she knew his true identity.

'I see. And if I don't wish to travel to Kezoban?' That firm edge in her voice was more pronounced now.

'Then we will have a problem. It is all arranged—subject to my confirmation that you are as gifted with horses as the Sheikh has been led to believe.' Zafir pressed his lips firmly together as Destiny's spirit shone through. Would she have spoken to him in such an honest and open way if she'd known he was the Sheikh, the man who'd made the deal for her presence in Kezoban?

'I have to see the horse first before I commit or agree to anything.' Was that a challenge he saw glittering in those dark eyes? He liked a challenge. He raised his brows in a silent answer.

'Destiny! What are you doing?' Her mother's shock was obvious. So too was his. He'd almost forgotten she was there. For a few brief moments as he and Destiny had spoken, it had just been the two of them. Nothing else had existed. The exclusive contact between him and a woman was not a sensation he was accustomed to at all.

'You may leave us.' The command in his voice was brittle as he turned his attention to the older woman, but it worked. She bowed her head very slightly in deference to him and backed away. So Destiny hadn't inherited her spirit from her mother.

'If you will excuse me, I need to deal with this horse.' Destiny didn't wait for his consent, but walked away. He stood and watched her go, slightly unnerved

by the fight for control he was experiencing, a totally
new concept for him.

Determined to settle the agreement, Zafir followed
at a distance as Destiny led the chestnut horse out of
the school. Usually he was more than able to appreciate
good horse stock, but right now his attention was riveted to the very alluring woman leading the horse. Her
strong will and defiance stirred something deep inside
him, something he had shut out of his life years ago.

Desire.

Why this woman? She was beautiful, but not in the
glamorous way he'd liked his women before his days
as Kezoban's ruler. She had an earthy innocence about
her and was far from compliant if the last minutes were
anything to go by, but there was something which had
connected to a forgotten and neglected part of him the
second their eyes had met.

She walked the horse into a stable, shutting the door,
making it clear he was to stay outside. He leant his
arms on the top of the stable door, watching as she
untacked the horse and brushed it down, her gently
rhythmic movements appreciated by the animal as it
pulled hay from the rack, munching noisily.

'So, have I passed the test?' She paused and looked
at him over the back of the horse, directly into his eyes.
Again he had the distinct impression a challenge was
being laid down—and he never refused a challenge.

'Yes. I have seen enough.'

'But you have not passed my test.' She angled her
head slightly, her ponytail swinging gently. 'I want to
know exactly what is expected of me.'

Zafir could only admire her courage. Nobody challenged him. Ever. Would she have been so unguarded

if she knew who he was? Briefly he was tempted to tell her, but he was enjoying this sparring so he decided to allow her to continue under the misapprehension of his identity that her mother had started. He had no wish to set her right just yet.

'You will travel to Kezoban where you will work with Majeed, the Sheikh's prized stallion.'

She looked at him, her brown eyes regarding him warily as she resumed brushing the horse. Zafir didn't appreciate the look of mistrust in those deliciously dark eyes, but he had no option other than to wait patiently for her response—and waiting was something he was not used to.

'What is the problem with the stallion?' She glanced briefly at him as she finished with the horse and came to the stable door.

Zafir stood back to allow her out, shocked that already her question was dragging up the past. He knew that would have to happen if he ever stood a chance of soothing Majeed's tortured spirit, but he hadn't expected it to be so soon. Neither had he envisaged being under her scrutiny.

'The stallion was involved in a tragic accident which claimed the life of the Sheikh's sister.' He was strangely detached as he spoke of his sister, referring to that night as if it hadn't really happened. Despite this temporary reprieve from guilt, he knew it didn't lessen the blame he'd set firmly at his own feet. He was the one Tabinah had been running from, the one who had made her unhappy. The knowledge of that would never leave him.

Destiny looked at the handsome man who seemed somehow unsuited to the jeans which hugged his long legs and the light blue shirt, open at the neck, giving her a tantalising view of dark hair against olive skin. She already knew him to be a man of the desert and, despite his casual clothes, she could just imagine him in white robes. He had a raw essence of power about him and was handsome enough to melt her vulnerable heart. But from the upright stance of his body and the regal tilt of his chin, she knew he was also very much used to giving orders—and having them obeyed.

Well, she wasn't about to be ordered around by anyone. She'd had enough of being the one who always had to give in to the demands of others. Her stepmother had gone too far this time, accepting the job before she'd even spoken to her. Everything was about money for her, never the person and least of all the horse involved.

Her stepmother was as cold as her father and equally controlling, which only reinforced Destiny's need to escape them. She couldn't stay here any longer. The stables might be entwined with precious childhood memories of her mother and the few short years of happiness before her death, but she had to leave. Just as her younger sister, Milly, had done. And she had to do it before her stepmother completely obliterated those happy memories.

'I'm very sorry about the situation the Sheikh is in, but I cannot help.' She kept her gaze locked with his, trying to meet his aura of power with determination, wanting to convey the message that she would not be controlled—not any more.

His eyes, as black as onyx, narrowed with irritation and his jaw clenched beneath the dark trimmed beard, so precise it was barely more than stubble. 'That is not the arrangement I have come to with Mrs Richards. She assured me you would be available to travel to Kezoban immediately.'

The words fired out at her but she stood her ground, adamant she would not to be ordered around be either this superior man or her stepmother.

'Firstly, I am her stepdaughter and, secondly, she had no right to make any such arrangement without consulting me. Not even with a wealthy Sheikh. So I suggest you look elsewhere for the help you require.'

She moved towards him, intending to walk past him and away, wanting only to turn her back on this man who exuded a potent mix of masculinity and sexuality which terrified yet enthralled her. His eyes, full of fiery intensity, met hers as she came level with him, but it was the enticing aura of this powerful man as she came close—too close—that made her step falter. It became impossible to do anything other than stand and look directly into his handsome face.

Her stomach somersaulted and, like a teenager in the throes of a first love, her heart skipped a beat. Not that she knew anything about first love, having shied away from all that, using horses as her shield. She was angry with her stepmother and not at all affected by this exotic man. She reminded herself of that fact, but struggled as his gaze continued to hold hers.

'The deal is agreed, Miss Richards. You will travel to Kezoban in two days.' The control in his voice, the hardened words and the command he exuded made anything other than looking up at him impossible, even though she wanted to get as far away from the effect he was having on her as possible. The anger glittering in the blackness of his eyes reminded her of the night sky, full of stars.

For the last sixteen years, since her stepmother had become a permanent feature in her and her younger sister's lives, she'd done her stepmother's and father's bidding, putting aside all of her dreams and aspirations. She'd wanted to be there for Milly as she grew up but more recently it had become all about helping Milly set herself up in London and escape their father's oppressive control. Now that Milly was settled and happy it was time she did the same.

Milly had left home earlier in the year and there was no one to protect now, no one to look out for but herself. She was free to do what she wanted. Now this man, with his high-handed attitude, thought he could waltz in and more or less demand she go to a desert country because it was what his Sheikh wanted. Surely the Sheikh had enough money to hire the top professionals in the field.

Could this man, this bizarre offer to travel to a desert kingdom she knew nothing about, be her opportunity of escape?

Her love of horses had been all-consuming as she'd grown up, leaving no room for any other kind of love and giving her the perfect excuse to escape from reality. Could she use her ability to connect with horses as her means of escape?

'I don't care what deal you have made. I will not go.' The words flew from her lips as the oppression of living under her father's strict rule surfaced. Going to an unknown country at the request of another equally controlling man was not something she'd planned for herself. All she wanted was to get away and as tempting as this offer was, it wasn't what she needed. She would find another way to gain her financial independence and ultimately her freedom.

'Majeed is a majestic creature. He wants only to please.' His words cut through her thoughts, tugging at those emotional heartstrings she always had for an animal. 'It is as if he knows the woman who rode him into the desert and fell from his back was the Sheikh's sister, as if he blames himself.'

Destiny looked up at him, her interest captured as she imagined the horse, but she couldn't be drawn into this man's problems. She had her own to solve.

'She died.' The words were hard and short, the pain within them tugging at her sentimental heart. He must genuinely love the horse and want to serve his master.

'I'm sorry for the Sheikh's loss, but really I cannot help.' Still she clung firmly to her refusal.

'The horse is living in torment. He is unapproachable, almost impossible to handle and a danger to himself and others. It has been a year since the accident. Many have tried to calm his troubled spirit. You are the Sheikh's last hope and if you cannot help Majeed there is only one other option.'

She drew in a sharp breath as the implications of his words hit her. He could stand there all day and argue about the deal he'd made with her stepmother and she wouldn't care, wouldn't back down. But as soon as he'd talked of the stallion, the compassion in his voice showing he at least cared about the horse and its fate, she knew she would go. But she wasn't about to let this man know that yet, not when she had her own deal to strike, one that would finally set her free from a life she would never have chosen for herself.

'What are the terms of the agreement you have

made?' She continued to stand glaring up him, the in-
justice of her situation filling her with the kind of courage which had evaded her for many years.

'The arrangement is that you will travel to Kezoban
for a minimum of two months, to work with the stallion. A substantial amount of money has already been
agreed.' His tone remained as commanding as ever,
but something in his expression softened slightly. Was
it possible a hard man such as this could soften? No,
she must be mistaken. He was as dominating and controlling as her father. She might be about to use him
as a chance to escape her father's iron rule, but she
was under no illusions: this man was the epitome of
supremacy. Her terms needed to be laid firmly down.

'This substantial amount of money has been agreed
with my stepmother, no doubt.' Destiny tried to keep
the icy coldness from her voice as she thought of the
woman who had replaced her mother. She knew now
that her father had never been happy and loving, as
she'd thought when she was a young child. That had
all been pretence. The day her mother had died, everything changed. He'd stopped pretending. He'd become
cold and mercenary, finally meeting his match in his
new wife. Now he was allowing her stepmother to use
his daughter's gift to extract money from the Sheikh
of a far-off desert kingdom.

'It has, yes. To cover your absence here. You are
a valued member of her team.' The man's words remained gentle and coaxing, maybe because he sensed
her impending agreement. But his chosen words made
her want to laugh out loud. Her stepmother did not
value her, always reminding her she was nothing, just

a stable girl. It was the money such a deal would generate she valued.

But Destiny couldn't let him know that his Sheikh's offer was going to be her way out, her chance to finally to do what she wanted in life and travel. If she could help the Sheikh's stallion in the process, all the better. It was, after all, something she was good at.

'I will, of course, have expenses to cover.' She knew she would never see any form of payment from her stepmother or the business; creating her own expenses was the only way to enable her to return to England and start a new life with money of her own. 'Double the original payment should be sufficient—and paid to me.'

'Naturally.' Was that a hint of sarcasm in his deep voice? His dark eyes narrowed slightly in suspicion and she thought she'd gone too far.

'I would need to see the horse first.' She kept her tone brisk, her gaze fixed on his handsome face, hardly able to believe he was accepting the conditions she was attaching to the agreement.

'In that case, my private jet will be at your disposal to fly you to Kezoban as soon as you are ready.' A smile of satisfaction touched his lips and those intensely dark eyes held hers, sending that spark rushing through her again, but she pushed the sensation aside, wanting only to ignore it.

'Your private jet?' Surely an aide to a Sheikh wouldn't have his own private jet? He must have meant the Sheikh's jet, but such details were insignificant now. Her much longed for escape from the ties of her father's rule were on the horizon and excitement fizzed inside her so much that she couldn't help but smile up at this strikingly handsome stranger who'd somehow turned her world upside down.

Zafir was on the verge of confessing that he was the Sheikh, that he'd allowed her to continue with her assumption that he was merely an aide sent to ascertain her ability, but, despite the brightness of her smile, the suspicion in her voice as she'd questioned his last words held him back. He couldn't risk her turning down his offer, not when his most precious horse still lived the nightmare of the night his sister had died. Everything in his life had spiralled out of control after that night and it was beyond time to put it right.

The marriage he'd known for years he'd have to make was looming, but Tabinah's death last year had put even more pressure on him to do his duty. And he would, once Majeed was healed. Only then could he put the nightmare of his sister's unhappiness at the marriage he'd arranged for her aside and fulfil his duty to make his own arranged marriage.

'My apology—the Sheikh's private jet.' His words were sharp but, lost in her own thoughts, she didn't notice. 'Do we have a deal, Miss Richards?'

He pushed down the guilt and shame of the night his sister had fled the palace. He would do anything to turn back the clock to the day he'd all but ordered Tabinah to do her duty and marry the man he'd selected for her. He hadn't been a brother to his younger sister, hadn't known how desperately unhappy she was. He'd just been the ruler of Kezoban, unaware she'd hated him, wanting only to shut him out of her life. The guilt that he'd made her so unhappy would always remain with him, even as he tried to piece his life together again, but soothing the tortured spirit of his stallion Majeed would help him finally put that night in the past.

He looked at Destiny, her soft brown eyes full of compassion, despite her bravado in standing up to him. Not only was he sure she possessed the gift to heal Majeed, he was certain she had the kindness in her heart the horse needed, unlike the others who had tried and failed.

'Yes, we do. I can be ready to leave in two days.'

Zafir offered his hand, wanting to seal the deal and return to his homeland. The dark-haired woman who'd captured his attention in more ways than one took his hand and the warmth from hers spread through him. It was as if their spirits were joining, recognising one another on an as yet undiscovered level. She looked up at him and the same confusion which consumed him blazed in her eyes.

Did she feel the pull of attraction too? Did she feel the connection, as if they knew one another, knew that they were fated to cross paths?

He pushed the thought aside. He didn't have the luxury of choosing his path through life, and this woman, whilst the kind of distraction he would have sought once, was not what he needed now—or ever again.

She intrigued him in a way no woman had ever done and, after the tragedy of the last twelve months, he liked the way she made him feel as her eyes met his. She was as spirited as a stallion and yet as nervous as a young filly foal. Today she'd been bold and fearless addressing him, but what would she be like once in Kezoban? Would she still have that feisty spark when she knew *he* was the Sheikh?

'Very well. I will return and prepare for your arrival.'

'And if I feel that I am unable to help the stallion?' Her hesitation lingered in the air. 'Can I leave?'

'You will not be a prisoner, Miss Richards. You will be the Sheikh's honoured guest and may leave whenever you wish.'

CHAPTER TWO

DESTINY LOOKED DOWN at the arid landscape below as the jet prepared for landing. The old town, seemingly carved from the desert, rose up around a rocky hill and next to a river; on the other side was a building of such splendour it could only be the Sheikh of Kezoban's palace. Around it, newer and more prosperous-looking buildings nestled, as if for safety, and beyond that lay an expanse of desert. Everything intrigued her and she wished she'd had more time for researching the place before she'd left England.

As the sumptuous jet touched down her excitement grew. This was to be her home for the next two months and, if she was really honest with herself, she was somewhat naively looking forward to seeing the Sheikh's aide again. It was only after he'd left the stables she'd realised she had been so intent on taking charge of her life she had no idea of his name. It had been his job, she'd reassured herself, to be controlling and demanding. Then there had been the moment he'd taken her hand, the memory of it still tugging at her unfulfilled romantic dreams.

There had been something about him, other than his undeniable good looks, and she'd been drawn to him with an attraction she'd never indulged in before. Despite the control he exuded, she'd briefly seen a different man as he'd spoken of the Sheikh's stallion. Then the hard exterior had slipped back into place, shielding the real man from her scrutiny.

This thought still played out in her mind as she left the cool air-conditioned interior of the jet and stepped out into the desert of Kezoban. Instantly a wall of heat almost pressed her back into the jet but, as a black SUV pulled up alongside the steps of the jet, she descended, hoping to see at least one familiar face.

She was alarmed, not just at her disappointment but that the man who'd come to the stables wasn't there. To hide it, she pulled the fine cream scarf she'd chosen to use as a headscarf a little tighter against her face and got into the SUV as the door was opened for her by a man in desert robes who seemed completely indifferent to her. If this was her welcome, what would the Sheikh be like when they finally met?

The drive from the airfield was short and she tried to glimpse the scenery as they passed from the dry desert land to the town. The streets were busy with people going about their daily lives and she longed to be among them—the anonymity, exploring the vibrant market. Soon the imposing walls of the palace loomed ahead of them and her stomach flipped over with nerves.

She was ushered from the SUV up cool marble steps and into the palace, where she was swept along by an entourage that made taking in anything more than a glimpse of the intricate and ornate design of the palace impossible. Her anxiety level rose as two large doors were swept open before them and all but two members of her escort left.

She just had time to glance around the high-ceilinged room, admire the blue and gold designs and the view into what must be the palace gardens before another set of doors opposite her opened.

The relief she felt at seeing the Sheikh's aide almost made her sigh, but that relief quickly changed to confusion as those around him bowed their heads and stepped back, leaving them alone but for the two men standing like guards by the door she'd entered.

She looked at the handsome face, framed by the white headdress he wore which served only to heighten his handsome features. His midnight black eyes looked directly into hers and she couldn't say anything as he walked towards her. His robes suited him far more than the jeans and shirt she'd first seen him in. With fine gold cloth over the robes, he looked positively regal.

'Allow me to introduce myself.' He spoke with a calm accented voice that had the velvety edge to it she remembered from that afternoon at the stables. 'I am Sheikh Zafir Al Asmari of Kezoban.'

Destiny fought against confusion, her words almost faltering. 'The Sheikh's aide?'

'No. The Sheikh.'

He had never told her his name, but he had definitely allowed her to believe he was the Sheikh's aide. Had he been testing her?

'It would have been nice to have known exactly who I was speaking to when you visited the stables.'

She should probably have spoken with more respect and, judging by his expression, he had expected her to. He took another step towards her and she tried to quell the tremor of attraction she felt for him, just as she had done that day at the stables. Even when she'd believed he was just the Sheikh's aide she'd known he would never notice someone like her, but that hadn't stopped the romantic in her dreaming of being swept away to his kingdom instead of being ordered there. Now she knew exactly who he was those romantic notions were about as likely as getting drenched from a storm cloud bursting above her head right now.

Everything about him suggested power and control; she just hadn't wanted to admit it—not when it put him in the same league as her father. Now it was worse. He wasn't just an aide to the Sheikh; he *was* the Sheikh. A leader. A man who should have power, and she despised controlling men. So why did her stomach flutter as his dark eyes locked with hers before his gaze slid down her body? She stood tall beneath his scrutiny, glad she'd opted to dress in keeping with the country's culture.

'It was your assumption that I visited on behalf of the Sheikh of Kezoban. I did not intend to mislead you and for that I apologise. Your stepmother made the assumption and I allowed it to continue.' He moved closer but she remained where she was, determined not to be intimidated by him. 'I trust we can move forward from the misunderstanding.'

His accented words were faultless English, his ability to use the language impressive, but it only added to his aura of command, the same command that had been absent as he'd talked of the Sheikh's sister—his sister. She'd assumed he'd been thinking about the stallion as emotion and pain had filled his words in England. He'd seen through her stepmother, making him seem more human, more feeling, and that was something this man, who stood regally watching her, could never be.

'I am here to work with your stallion, not pass judgement on you.' She lifted her chin and tried to ignore the sizzle racing around her body as his gaze locked with hers once more.

As she'd accepted the contract to work for this man she'd thought it was like stepping out of the shadow of her father's iron will and into the furnace of a much greater force. How right that had been. His ability to allow her to believe he was merely an aide to the Sheikh reinforced that, but working for the Sheikh was a gateway through which she must travel in order to start her new and independent life. It was the chance she'd been seeking and one she would take, no matter what.

When Destiny had been shown into his office Zafir had been overwhelmed to see her dressed modestly with respect for his culture. It should have stopped the hot thud of attraction which had surged through him from the moment he'd first seen her in England, but it didn't; it only served to intensify it. That day at the stables something had ignited between them and, if he wasn't mistaken, she was as reluctant to admit its presence as he was. Which only fuelled his ardour and intensified his curiosity to sample the forbidden.

'You have had a long journey. Tomorrow you will meet Majeed and begin your work. Tonight, as my guest, you will dine with me.' It was customary for him to dine with visitors but, from the look on her face, it was the last thing she'd expected.

She regarded him suspiciously and he fought the

need to smile. This was the first time he'd encountered a woman's reluctance to dine with him, but then he'd never invited a woman from another culture into his palace. Prior to inheriting the title of Sheikh of Kezoban he'd always kept his affairs confined to either London or New York.

'Thank you, but I am sure you have far more important things to do than entertain me.' Again the spark of fire leapt to life within him as her soft voice all but caressed his senses. He must have been living with the weight of duty for too long because he'd almost forgotten what such a sizzle of attraction could do to him. But never had it been so insistent.

'I always entertain my guests, Miss Richards. You will not be an exception.'

'Is it absolutely necessary?' The question was accompanied by the lift of her delicate eyebrows, but the courage of it didn't go unnoticed. Nobody would dare to address him like that, question his orders. He should be angry, should be making her error known, but he didn't want to. She wasn't speaking to him as Zafir the Sheikh but Zafir the man. Since he'd taken on the role of Sheikh of Kezoban after his father's death, no man or woman had treated him as anything other than that.

'It is.' He moved a little closer to her so that he could inhale her light floral scent and wished he'd dismissed everyone from the room. Right now all he wanted was to kiss her, taste the sweetness of those full lips.

He stepped back. What was he thinking? He was a desert ruler, a man of power with a duty to uphold. Kissing this woman, however much he wanted to, was not something he could ever do, especially when she was here in his palace as his guest.

'Then I look forward to it.'

'As will I.' It was the truth; he wanted to spend the evening in her company. 'We have much to discuss about your intended work with Majeed.'

He walked back to his large and ornate desk, where he turned and faced her once more. Distance was most definitely needed between him and this beautiful Western woman who had stirred the emotions and wild desires of the man he used to be.

'I appreciate it will be painful for you, but I will need to know all about what happened that night and how the stallion was before the accident.'

'And you shall.' But only what he absolutely had to say. He could never confess to anyone that he'd been guilty of neglecting his young sister so terribly. That the marriage he'd insisted she make had forced her to take such drastic steps. No, he could never allow anyone to know that. For the last year he'd been in the grip of that guilt and the way this woman was making him feel intensified it. He had no right to desire any woman when he was about to make an arranged marriage, not after insisting Tabinah did the same.

Destiny's nerves fluttered as she followed her escort through the cool interior of the palace to join the man she now had to keep reminding herself was the Sheikh of Kezoban. A man who had concealed his true identity, but she couldn't yet understand what he had to gain from that—apart from control.

She should have been able to relax in the luxury of her suite, with its views over the stunning palace gardens, but the thought of spending the evening with a man who intrigued and excited her as much as he irritated her with his need for control meant she was far from relaxed.

Darkness was falling and the palace was lit with lanterns at each of the ornate archways she passed through, giving everything a dreamlike quality. Then her escort stepped aside and gestured her through an arched doorway and along a vast walkway to another part of the palace gardens. She could see what resembled tents, draped almost completely in pale gold chiffon; lanterns glowed inside. It looked far too intimate for a formal dinner with the man who was effectively her boss for the next two months.

Then she saw him, his headdress discarded, giving him a more relaxed look, and her pulse leapt. Since when did the sight of a man do that to her?

'Good evening. I trust you are rested from your journey.' His deep sensual voice matched the mood created by his chosen venue for their meal and a brief skitter of panic raced over her before she dismissed it. As if this powerful Sheikh would be remotely interested in her. He probably had a harem of beautiful women.

'With such a gorgeous suite, how could I not be?' She couldn't look directly at him as heat infused her cheeks.

When she did glance his way, it was to see his lips lifting upwards in a smile, one that sent a spark of amusement to his dark eyes. It was the first time she'd seen anything other than a severe or commanding expression on his face. It was also a smile that would melt hearts, hers included if the heady beat of her pulse was anything to go by.

'I appreciate the effort you made today.' She frowned at him, not sure what he was referring to. 'You dressed to fit in with my culture and so this evening I wanted to show you a sample of life in the desert.'

'Thank you.' She forced the words out, totally taken aback by his thoughtfulness. Not at all what she would have expected from the man who had all but demanded she come to his country or the man who'd stood in his office just hours ago, an aura of power surrounding him.

'I only regret I could not have shown you the real desert.'

'This is lovely,' she said as she walked into the tent. The warm night air played with the pale gold curtains and candles glowed within ornate lanterns, lending a romantic ambience to the setting.

Should she be worried by this gesture? She glanced anxiously at the man she knew very little about—she had placed herself at his mercy, thousands of miles from home. Who was she trying to fool? This was a desert king. A man whose life was so different from hers he would never think inappropriately of someone like her and the sooner she got that idea fixed in her head the better.

'Does it not please you?' A hint of a feral growl sounded in his voice and she realised her silence had cast doubt on her appreciation of all he'd done.

'It's perfect. Utterly beautiful.'

Zafir watched as Destiny, wearing loose-fitting white trousers and a long top, looked around. The pale pink scarf she wore on her head made her appear as delicate as a bloom in his prized gardens. She took in every detail and he found himself wishing they were in the middle of the desert, far away from anyone and, even more importantly, his duty. Not that family duty and honour were a trait she understood if the tension between her and her stepmother were anything to go by. She was here under duress and she'd clearly stated her terms, but that didn't stop the sizzle of desire which flowed through him like the river his city was built around.

He wanted to tell her she was more beautiful than anything around them, but he hadn't brought her here to seduce her. This was his palace, his home and he'd never entertained any woman here, even throughout his wild playboy days. He also needed to remind himself of the marriage he had to make. This was a woman he couldn't afford to be distracted by for so many reasons.

'I'm pleased you approve.' He kept his voice as neutral as possible in an attempt to hide the effect she was having on him.

'I'm also looking forward to seeing your stallion tomorrow.' She glanced at him and he saw the apprehension on her face before she spoke again. 'I do need to know more of the incident.'

'By "incident" you mean the night my sister rode him out into the desert and met with her untimely death?' This was the last thing he wanted to talk about. All the guilt from that night rushed back at him. He would have to share a certain amount of information with Destiny, but he wasn't ready yet to reveal everything.

'If I am to help the horse then I am afraid I need to know.'

The sympathy on her face only made his guilt worse. She must think he was so heartbroken after the loss of his sister that he couldn't talk about it. Nothing could be further from the truth and nothing would make him admit the guilt he harboured.

'First we eat,' he said as his servants arrived with their meal. He gestured to the table, set with his colours, the same bright purple and gold that would adorn his private tent when he spent time in the desert, something he did several times a year.

She smiled at him and he could see his brusque tone had unsettled her, but it was necessary. Duty meant he could never let his emotions influence any decision he made. Duty also meant he could never have needs himself. It was always at the forefront of everything he did, just as it had been when he'd arranged Tabinah's marriage, resisting her pleas for him to reconsider.

'This is not what I expected to be doing this evening,' she said as she settled herself on the cushions around the low table. The excitement on her face made her skin glow and her eyes sparkle. She was even more beautiful than he remembered. Just as when he'd first met her, she appeared totally unaware of her beauty, almost as if she was intent on hiding or remaining out of the spotlight.

'What did you expect? That I would banish you to your room and lock you up unless you were working with Majeed?' Although it was meant in jest, he was shocked to see her cheeks flush with colour.

'No, not that,' she said softly, a hint of nerves in her voice. 'I just didn't expect such special treatment or the effort you've gone to.'

'You are here as my guest, Destiny.' It was the first time he'd used her name in conversation and it all but sizzled on his tongue and a spark of lust hurtled through him. 'I like to show all my guests what my kingdom and its people can offer.'

He had to add that, had to try and refocus his attention away from the way she was making him feel as she sat opposite him, her partially visible dark hair gleaming in the light from the lanterns and looking so soft he wanted to touch it, to feel its silkiness and slide it through his fingers as his lips claimed hers.

What was he thinking? He should not be entertaining such thoughts. Not just because she was here to do a job, or even because she was a woman from a different culture. He could never think about any woman that way, not even the woman he was soon to select as his bride.

'I am here to do a job.' Her words were stronger, confidence filling them as they had done the first time he'd met her. 'And to do that I need to know about certain events.'

He waited whilst his servants cleared the table and watched her face fill with delight and disbelief as an array of desserts were placed between them. As the servants quietly withdrew he wished Destiny was here as his guest, wished that he didn't have to reveal anything about the night Tabinah died. Inexplicably, it mattered what this woman thought of him.

'Tabinah was unhappy with the man I had chosen for her to marry. It was a marriage of duty on both sides, uniting two wealthy and powerful families. Unfortunately, Tabinah didn't share my view on duty. She wanted nothing but her freedom.'

'Her freedom?' Destiny's brows drew together as she tried to process the information, confusion clear on her face.

'She claimed to be in love with another man, one totally unsuitable for the sister of the Sheikh of Kezoban.' His words were dry and monotone. It was the first time he'd told anyone that his young sister had declared her love for a man other than the one she was engaged to. He knew it was talked of within the palace. He was no fool. He'd heard the whispered speculations. He'd just never admitted it to anyone before.

'I'm sorry.' She lowered her lashes, obviously embarrassed to look at him.

'It is of no consequence. Many arranged marriages do not contain any love at all,' he stated flatly as he wiped his fingers and signalled for the remains of their meal to be cleared.

'It is sad.' She looked directly at him and he had the distinct impression she was challenging him. How, he wasn't yet sure. 'Everybody needs love.'

'Have you ever been in love, Destiny?' He narrowed his eyes as anger simmered beneath his cool composure. So she believed in love and probably believed in fairy tales where everyone lived happily ever after. He, however, believed in real life.

'I have love in my life, yes.' The defensive tone of her voice goaded him to prod for more.

'As do I. Love for my people, my country and my family honour, but that is not what I asked. Have you ever believed you were in love?' Suddenly it mattered that she had the same foolish notions as Tabinah, that she was filling her head with romantic dreams of happiness.

'No.' Destiny fired the answer back at him, not liking the way his dark eyes were watching every move she made, every expression which crossed her face. She'd seen love in her mother's diary, felt it as she read the pages, but the fact that her father had remarried so soon after her mother had died told her all she needed to know. Her mother had loved, but had never been loved. Something she would never allow to happen to her. She would only give her heart to a man who loved her completely.

'And you have not married,' he said. It wasn't a question and silently she watched him. His expression was stern.

'My work has kept me busy.'

She followed his lead and stood up from the table, but when he approached her she couldn't ignore the sudden racing of her heart. She wanted to back away, give herself space, but his dark gaze held hers, mesmerising her.

'You shouldn't hide behind your work.' His voice was deep and sensuous and that little tremor she'd felt when she'd first seen him slipped down her spine again.

'I don't.' She couldn't help how defensive her voice sounded. 'I love my work. It's more than just work and that's why I'm here. I came here for your horse, not because my stepmother arranged it or because you demanded it, but to help your horse.'

For a moment she thought she'd gone too far, crossed that invisible line of protocol which she had realised surrounded this man within minutes of her arrival in Kezoban. But what she'd said was true; she was here primarily because he'd implied that she was the stallion's only hope.

The sound of insects from the darkness of the garden and the heady scents of the exotic flowers wrapped around her, making everything, from the man before her to the setting in which she'd just enjoyed the most delicious meal, even more romantic. She was tired from travelling yet her body fizzed with a new and strange fiery need.

'For that I am indebted to you. Tomorrow you will begin your work with Majeed and I am sure a spirited yet sympathetic woman such as you can help him.'

He moved towards her, his handsome face set in a firm mask of control, his dark eyes almost piercing hers. Was he teasing her? No, of course not. He was a powerful man, a ruler and used to getting what he wanted at all times.

'I'm looking forward to seeing the stallion. It will be an honour to work with such a majestic animal.' She tried to keep the conversation on the job, the reason she was here instead of allowing her mind to imagine he was looking at her with desire in his eyes.

'It will, no doubt, be a challenge.'

'I'm ready for a challenge.'

The smile which pulled at the corners of his lips did something to her, making her stomach flip as butterflies took flight. 'I shall walk you to your suite. This way.'

He gestured a path through the flora of the exquisite garden where small lights twinkled, giving it a magical appearance. She pushed aside her hesitancy and walked side by side with him, aware of his tall and strong body next to hers, just as she had been when they'd stood talking at the stables.

'Your gardens are so beautiful. I would never have expected it in the desert.' Again she talked to draw her attention away from the way he made her feel.

'I have spent many years researching irrigation in desert regions and now own a successful company doing just that.' The pride in his voice was clear and she looked at his profile, but when he turned to her she blushed, looking quickly away. 'Bringing water and better lives to my people is my passion.'

'Very impressive and interesting.'

'That pleases me.' His tone was more regal than she'd heard yet, reminding her just who this man was.

He opened a gate set beneath an arch of a white wall inlaid with intricate designs and stepped back to allow her through. 'These are the public palace gardens. You may walk in them whenever you wish.'

She walked beside him, more aware of him than she had ever been. He unsettled her with his raw masculinity and his overwhelming power, but more unnerving was the fact that she found him incredibly attractive.

She recognised the terraced area outside her suite but before she could say another word he stopped. 'I will bid you goodnight.'

She looked up at him, the intensity in his eyes sending a tremor of awareness surging through her. 'Thank you. For this evening.'

'The pleasure was all mine.'

A heavy silence fell over them, shrouding them in something profoundly powerful until she could hardly breathe. For one bizarre moment she thought he was going to kiss her and her body instinctively swayed towards his. Just in time she caught herself and stepped back. 'Goodnight.'

CHAPTER THREE

DESTINY DIDN'T SLEEP much that night. Her dreams were disturbed by the image of the man she'd spent the evening with. Zafir had infiltrated her mind, filling her thoughts with images of them together. She'd never behaved like this over a man before and, angry at her reaction, she got up early, going to sit on her private terrace, watching the sky turn from a dark orange to a bright and cloudless blue, bringing the warmth of a new day.

All she wanted was to begin her work with the Sheikh's stallion, but she would have to wait until she was escorted to the stables—or anywhere else within the palace. That much had been made clear to her on her arrival, making her feel more like a prisoner than a guest.

When a young boy knocked on her door and informed her he was to escort her to the stables it only reinforced that thought. She followed him through the bright white corridors of the palace, glimpsing the public part of the garden through the archways as she went, feeling the rising heat of the desert battle with the cool air within the palace.

Finally she reached the stables and the young boy

introduced her to the man in charge, but nothing could have prepared her for what she saw as she walked through another archway adorned with intricate metalwork. Beyond it she could see an almost endless row of stables on each side, all so elaborate it was hard to believe horses actually lived in them and a far cry from the stables her mother had started, which were now sadly neglected by her father. She used to think it was because he'd loved her mother so much that he couldn't face doing anything to them, but then she'd stumbled across her mother's diary and that myth had been shattered.

'Sheikh Al Asmari's stallion is stabled at the end,' the man said in almost perfect English, dragging her thoughts back from home. His plain white robes flared slightly as he walked towards the end of the long passageway, his feet almost silent on the sandy-coloured mosaic floor. He stopped and turned to her, caution and warning in his voice as he continued. 'The stallion will not leave the palace walls. Fear is in his eyes and mistrust in his soul. Many have tried to reach him, but none have succeeded.'

'He has not been outside these walls for almost a year?' Destiny knew a moment of panic as she realised this was a more serious problem than she'd been led to believe.

'Not since the Sheikh's young sister rode him out the night she died.'

'Then I have much work to do. I will need to spend time with him before I do anything else.' She was anxious to get started, wanting to see the horse for herself, needing to gain his trust. Only then could she begin to work with him and determine how long it would take, but already she wondered if the two months the Sheikh had stated would be adequate.

'This way.'

She followed the man to the end stable and couldn't help a gasp of admiration escape her. The stallion's black coat gleamed. He was as regal as his owner and easily had as much power and command surrounding him.

'I will groom him first.'

The man inclined his head in acknowledgement and a few moments later handed her several brushes. 'The bridle is hanging here.'

'Thank you.' She looked at the fine leather bridle adorned with bright coloured tassels, not sure any horse she'd worked with recently would tolerate such things on their bridles. Maybe Majeed wasn't so bad after all.

As the man walked away she entered the stable and stood, waiting for the stallion to accept her presence. His ears twitched as he inspected her from the corner of his stable, his head high and regal, his eyes wary.

'You're very handsome,' she said softly as she stood and waited for the stallion to relax. 'Almost as handsome as your master.'

Zafir's face came to mind in an image so clear it shocked her. She'd only seen him three times and already every last detail of those dark, attractive features was imprinted in her memory. If that wasn't a warning sign she was letting her imagination run wild, dragging her in too deep, she didn't know what was. The last thing she needed was the added complication of being attracted to the Sheikh.

* * *

Zafir had wanted to escort Destiny to the stables but had had to bow to protocol. She was here as his guest, a British woman employed to do a job and, as such, it wouldn't be right to be seen offering her extra favours. Especially now, when he was finally accepting his duty to marry and produce a future generation to rule Kezoban.

He entered the stables just in time to see Destiny go into Majeed's stable, apparently about to groom him. Not at all how others had approached the task. He frowned, then dismissed his doubts. He'd sought her out because of recommendation and he would have to accept her way of doing things—for now at least.

Silently he walked towards the stable and couldn't stem the satisfied smile as she spoke to the horse, complimenting both Majeed and him. It pleased him to know she was not as immune to him as she had led him to believe last night. It also notched up the simmering desire just being near her provoked.

As he'd walked her through the garden last night he'd known that if they were anywhere else but his palace he would have taken his attraction for her further. He would have kissed her. For the first time since he'd taken an oath to serve his people he wished such duties didn't exist, that he was free to explore whatever it was between them. As she'd looked up at him, her lovely face in partial darkness, he'd wanted to take her in his arms and savour her kiss, to hold her against him and become intoxicated by her sweet scent.

Had she known that? Had she wanted it too? Was that why she'd suddenly bolted last night as they'd stood by the terrace of her suite? He watched her now as she put out her hand, allowing Majeed to smell her. She didn't move, but the curious horse came to her. She touched his muzzle, then gently took hold of his head collar.

'Do you need any help?' He decided it would be best to make his presence known before he gave her and the horse a fright.

'How long have you been there?' She blushed and he knew she was worrying if he'd heard her earlier compliments to him and the horse.

'I have just arrived.'

She relaxed a little, then turned her attention to the horse. 'I will brush him for a while so that I can touch him all over, ensure he isn't unnerved by me. Then I will begin my work with him.'

Zafir found his thoughts wandering to how it would feel to be touched all over by her and for the first time in his life he was jealous of a horse. This woman seemed to bring out a magnitude of new emotions within him. What would be next?

He watched as she turned her back on him and began to brush Majeed's shiny black coat. She wore the traditional Western jodhpurs he'd seen her in when he'd called at the stables in England but, unlike then, she now wore a long shirt which covered her arms and the sexy bottom he'd studied briefly as he'd first watched her. She was bowing to his country's dress codes as much as her job would allow. For that he was grateful, but he couldn't help wondering what she'd look like in the silks women in his country wore. The thought intrigued him and he decided it would be something he would discover before she returned to England. He would give her a gift of the finest *abayas* and silks to wear.

'Very well, I will wait.'

She turned to look at him, her hand resting on Majeed's shoulder. 'For what?'

For a moment he couldn't speak. Nobody ever talked to him in that tone of voice. 'To see you work?' His tone was sharp with shock but the challenge in her eyes made him clench his jaw against further words.

'I don't work with an audience.'

'I am hardly an audience. I am the owner of this horse and, as the Sheikh of Kezoban, I expect to get what I want.' The audacity of the woman! How could she not know he would get just what he wanted and when he wanted it?

'Then we have a problem.'

'A problem?' Briefly he floundered, like a man stumbling down a large sand dune, his balance disrupted. 'I am not about to allow anyone to work with my horse without my knowledge of what is happening.'

She moved away from the horse, put down the brush and came to the door. 'Then it seems we have wasted one another's time.'

Had the world tipped on its axis? Had everything been turned upside down? He gave orders, not took them. He made demands, not met them.

She looked directly into his eyes, the shyness she'd displayed last night gone and in its place fierce determination.

'Can you help this horse?' He snapped the question out, his patience tested to the full and not just by her impertinence but by the way his body craved hers.

'Yes, I can, although it appears his master is in need

of some help too.' Her words were spoken in a low tone with smooth flowing syllables, but the unrelenting strength in them was unmistakable. Was it possible she knew how long he'd tortured himself with the guilt of not being there for Tabinah, of not hearing her pleas or understanding her unhappiness?

'You are not here to analyse me.' Maybe his presence here *would* affect the outcome. Was it possible Majeed sensed his guilt? This was all too deep for him. He didn't explore emotions—ever.

'When I work with a horse, I also invariably work with the owner as well.' The slight rise of her delicate brows gave her a superiority he found strangely attractive. Something else he didn't want to look too deeply into. It was time to retreat. Time to gather his strength.

'Very well. I will meet you in my office this afternoon and I expect your verdict on what Majeed needs.'

'Thank you.' She didn't smile and he couldn't. She had got the better of him, caught him totally off guard, a sensation which both unsettled and excited him.

Later that afternoon Destiny waited to see Zafir. She'd spent several hours with Majeed, wanting only to gain his trust, because she could see beneath his fear. She needed much more information about what had happened to change him so much. She sensed he was a gentle creature who only wanted to please, which was all the more reason to take things slowly.

The big problem now was how his master would react to having the death of his sister all but investigated by her.

'The Sheikh will see you now.' Zafir's aide approached and she followed him through the tall doors she'd first entered on her arrival. Was that really only yesterday?

As she stood before him, his gaze slid down her in an imperious way that sent a shimmer of awareness all over her as if he'd actually touched her and she was glad of her continued choice of clothes which fitted in with his culture and, more importantly, covered as much of her as possible.

'You may leave us.' He spoke to his aide but kept his gaze firmly fixed on her and she blushed, wishing somebody would stay. He gestured to a large chair in front of his desk. 'Please, sit.'

She did as he bid her and sat on the gilded chair. The room was so large, with arches opening out onto yet more ornate gardens, but she couldn't focus on any of that now. Zafir took all her attention. She needed to keep her mind focused and to quash the heady feeling that rushed around her just from being in the same room as him. Was that why she'd been so adamant that he couldn't stay this morning? Because of the way he made her feel? Or was it the need to test his authority, to push his control back and gain some for herself?

'Now that you have had time with Majeed, what is your professional opinion?' His voice was deep with a firm edge to it that highlighted his accent. It also did things to her she had never known possible, like a tingle rushing down her spine and a heavy sensation deep within her.

'Majeed needs time and he needs to build his confidence by facing his fears. As he has not left the palace walls since the accident I suggest I work towards that ultimate goal.'

Zafir nodded as he sat in his large and very regal

chair. She had to keep her nerve, keep her mind from thinking of his dark skin, the trimmed beard that made him so incredibly attractive. But it was his eyes which unsettled her most. Their dark intensity reached within her, bringing out a woman she'd never wanted to be, one who desired a man, wanted him in a way that was as impossible as her being in his kingdom in the first place.

'I had anticipated that you would say that. Tomorrow morning we will ride out. I will take you to where Tabinah was found and endeavour to impart as much of the events as possible.' His tone was courteous, his words firm and distinct and she wondered if she'd just imagined the last few moments when something like attraction had sparked between them.

'That will be good. I understand it must be painful for you, but it is something...'

'Painful?' He cut her words off before she could finish the remainder of the sentence. 'Why would it be painful?'

'It must be hard after losing your sister because of the need to follow tradition.'

He stood up abruptly, his eyes eagle-sharp, almost pinning her to the spot. 'I had thought because of the way you have been dressing that you were acquainted with my culture.'

Destiny frowned, unsure what she'd said to have changed things so drastically, but she wouldn't allow him to intimidate her. She was here of her own free will and would leave if necessary. She stood up as quickly as he had, her chin defiantly lifted even though inside she was trembling. 'I'm sorry if my sympathy offends.'

'It does not offend. It is misplaced.' He tempered his

tone and walked around the desk towards her slowly as if he feared she might bolt through the archway at any moment and into the gardens.

'Misplaced?' The question came out as a cracked whisper and she could hardly stand, her limbs were so weak. Still he moved towards her, coming so close she could smell the desert on him and the heady, raw masculine scent of power.

'It was to have been a marriage of convenience. Love was not involved. Just as it will not be when I take a wife.' He looked down at her and she refused to break eye contact, watching him even though just being this close weakened her knees and made her pulse leap wildly. 'Marriage is a contract, nothing more.'

'But what about love?' She couldn't help the question slipping from her lips and as she spoke his gaze flicked lower, as if watching her lips move, and she had to fight hard against the urge to bite down on her bottom lip. What was this man doing to her?

'Love is a concept I have not allowed in my life. Desire, however, is.' She could see it in his eyes, feel it with every pore of her skin. At that moment he desired her. Light-headed and shocked, she backed away from him, bumping into the chair she'd just leapt from.

'That is not something I know.' Why did her voice sound so husky?

'You have not desired something?' He was playing with her; she was sure of that. Was it punishment for speaking out of turn?

'Yes, of course I've desired things.' She let out a long breath. For a moment she'd thought he meant a man.

'Someone?'

She looked at him, knowing that right now she desired him. What had he done to her? He was a powerful Sheikh, a man used to getting what he wanted and probably had a harem of women tucked away in his palace somewhere. She had to stop this. She was getting in way too deep. If she wasn't careful, she would go down the same sorry road as her mother, falling for a man who could never love her.

'No. I have never desired anyone and neither do I intend to.'

'So if I touched your face with my fingertips you wouldn't tremble with desire and need for me.'

He reached out his hand and before he could touch her she knocked his arm away, glaring angrily at him. 'I am not here to become one of your harem. I am here to work with your stallion. Nothing more.'

He narrowed his eyes and she knew she'd insulted him. Was it because she'd touched him or because she hadn't fallen into a heap at his feet, begging him to make love to her?

'I do not have a harem of any size and I will be faithful to my wife from the day we are married. No woman has come close to threatening that ideal before today.' He turned on his heel, his robes flowing out wildly, and went to stand by the archway, the sunlight of the afternoon framing him.

He looked vulnerable and she swallowed down hard, finally able to breathe properly now that he'd stepped away. Last night she'd believed she'd been mistaken when she'd thought he'd been about to kiss her; now she wasn't sure. Was she doing something wrong? Giving him the wrong message? She was a naive virgin who'd barely shared a kiss with a man and this particular man was so overwhelmingly powerful she couldn't understand, let alone control, the way he made her feel.

'You should leave.' He didn't look at her and the rigid set of his back made his disapproval all too evident but she wasn't about to argue with him again.

She needed to get away, to calm herself and work out what was going on between them. Every time they met it became more intense, harder to ignore. Whatever *it* was.

She turned and walked to the door, about to reach for the large gold handle when she heard his voice again. Deep and soft.

'Destiny.'

She turned to him, not liking the way her heart lurched at the sight of him. Even across the vastness of his cool marbled office, she could feel his vulnerability, as if every barrier he'd ever used as a weapon was briefly down, exposing the real man.

'Yes?' she said stiffly, not willing to be fooled by his soft tone.

He frowned and regarded her suspiciously. 'Be ready by dawn.'

'Ready?' Her heart went into freefall. Ready for what?

'To ride out. We leave before the sun rises too high.'

His eyes locked with hers across the room and she couldn't break the contact, couldn't look away. Instead she nodded, her breath coming hard and fast. Finally she dropped her gaze and turned to pull open the door quickly, her haste to escape whatever spell he was casting on her making her clumsy.

How could she want a man such as this hard and dominating Sheikh? She couldn't answer that, but she did know she would have to keep her emotions much more firmly under control. He was too much like the man who'd broken her mother's heart and dominated her life ever since. So why did she yearn for his touch, his kiss?

CHAPTER FOUR

ZAFIR HAD BEEN up long before the first tendrils of dawn had shown themselves in the sky and now he waited impatiently at the stables. He'd wished he could simply go to Destiny's suite and escort her himself, but if he wanted to avoid scandal and protect her reputation, protocol had to be followed. He was the Sheikh and she was an unmarried woman. Their dinner on her first night had pushed those boundaries—and he'd always pushed boundaries—but with his staff waiting on them he'd considered them enough of a chaperone.

Yesterday he'd impulsively banished all his staff from his office, probably giving rise to speculation about why Destiny was here in Kezoban. He knew well enough how the tongues of gossip could spread rumours through his palace, yet now he was about to ride out into the desert alone with her because he didn't want her to hear the more elaborate tales connected with his sister's death. The only way to ensure that was to take her into the desert himself, tell her only what she needed to know. But still he questioned if he'd lost all sense of reason.

In a way he was not yet able to understand, Destiny scrambled his usual cool and rational thoughts.

He had a business to oversee as well as a kingdom to rule, duties and expectations to meet, and none of them involved the brown-eyed woman who had haunted his sleep, making him want things he could no longer have from the first moment he'd seen her working the chestnut mare in England.

He strode to the stables, knowing that soon he would be able to escape the confines of the palace—for a short while at least. Riding across the desert sands, following the edge of the river that was the lifeblood of his kingdom was the only time he ever felt truly free to be himself.

He'd never allowed anyone to accompany him before. Did it signify something deeper that he wanted Destiny to share such an intimate moment with him? Could it be more than attraction which kept pulling them ever closer to each other? He had to push aside the temptation to make it something more, even though he wanted to explore it until it fizzled out, as desire always did.

Movement behind him made him turn as he reached the ornate archway to the stables. Destiny was being escorted towards him and, as he watched her gracefully walk, he couldn't drag his gaze from her. She was beautiful and mesmerising.

A whispered curse slipped from his lips. What was he? A youth who'd never touched a woman before? It was so far from the truth, but right now he could be exactly that.

'Good morning.' She smiled at him as he dismissed her escort. 'I'm looking forward to this. Riding in the desert, I mean.'

Satisfaction slipped over him as she blushed, her

last words all but highlighting that she'd been looking forward not just to riding in the desert, but being with him. Again thoughts of a dalliance with this English woman rushed through his mind. He'd been committed to his duty from the first day he'd become the ruler of Kezoban, working hard and leaving behind a life of playing, one which had been filled with many beautiful women. He'd been faithful and true to his people, just as he would be to his new bride. But as yet he had not selected a bride from those chosen for him, and neither did he want to when all he could think of was Destiny Richards.

'As am I.' He looked down at her as colour stained her pale skin. 'It will be an honour to show you some of my country. The horses are ready.'

He turned and walked briskly to the end of the row of stables, where the tall arched doors were already wide open, as were those in the palace walls, showing the gold of the desert sand beyond. As always, pride swelled in his chest to think this was his country and that the people in it looked to him for leadership.

'I will need to see where the incident with Majeed and your sister happened.' Her voice was hesitant as she spoke of Tabinah.

'We shall go there first and after we can relax and enjoy the ride. I want you to experience my country at its best before the heat becomes too fierce for your fair skin.' As he spoke her eyes met and held his, their warm brown reminding him not for the first time of deeply polished mahogany.

He wanted to kiss her, to taste her on his lips and feel her against his body. He hadn't wanted a woman like this for many years—ever.

'We should go.' The cracked whisper of her voice was almost his undoing and he had to ignore the burning need rushing through him more fiercely than a desert storm.

'Yes.' He snapped the word out, opening the stable door of his finest grey Arab mare. 'This is Halima. Her name means "gentle" and I have selected her for her kind nature entwined with a courageous spirit.'

He wanted to add that was how he saw her and that maybe her name meant she had been fated to come into his life, but her obvious pleasure in the mare stemmed the words.

She reached out her hand to the mare, which sniffed curiously at the long slender fingers and Zafir couldn't drag his gaze from them. 'You are beautiful.' Her voice was soft and full of wonder as she spoke, sending a rush of heat hurtling through him.

'A beautiful horse for a beautiful woman.' The words were out before he could stop himself. Was it so wrong to express his thoughts? The expression on her face warned that now was not the time.

'You shouldn't say that.' Destiny's face heated as he continued to watch her with those midnight black eyes while she tightened her large scarf around her head. She didn't want her stomach to flip with anticipation, or her pulse to race with something close to desire for this man. She didn't want to find such a dominating and controlling man attractive. She hadn't hidden away from men's attention only to fall under this man's spell. How could she when she'd lived all her life under her father's iron rule?

'But I have and now I cannot take it back.'

Suddenly he moved to the next stable, leaving her holding the reins of her mare as he walked out a stunning grey stallion whose coat was flecked with brown and looked almost as commanding as Zafir.

She didn't say anything but led out her horse and mounted, a thrill of excitement rushing through her at the new experience of riding in the desert. Or was it simply the thrill of riding out with Zafir which excited her? That was a question she couldn't even think about.

When she looked at him, mounted on the stallion, which was restlessly all but dancing on the spot, her breath caught in her throat. Nothing could have prepared her for the image he created—one of power and command. He was devastatingly attractive and, for her sins, she wished he really had noticed her, that his compliment had been real, that he felt every spark too.

Enough, she reprimanded herself. She wasn't here to fall for a man, let alone one as commanding as Sheikh Zafir Al Asmari. She was here to work, to secure her new life, her future. 'Shall we?'

A smile twitched at the corners of his lips, then he pushed his mount on and she nudged her mare forward, following him into the outer region of the palace. The large cream stone walls loomed ahead of them and already the sun was warm.

As they approached the imposing and fortified doors in the walls, another rider came to join them and Zafir turned in the saddle, the fast flow of Arabic words sounding strange as he addressed the other man, who she recognised as one of his aides. Their words seemed heated and as her mare shifted excitedly on the spot she couldn't mistake the anger emanating from Zafir as his aide returned to the stables.

Before she could gather her thoughts Zafir turned to her. 'Come.' Seconds later, in a cloud of dusty sand, Zafir and the stallion were surging forward into the desert, her mare so eager for a gallop she could hardly hold her back.

It was exhilarating. Hooves thundered on the ground and the wind was warm on her face. Just ahead of her Zafir began to slow his pace and gradually the horses dropped back to a walk. Had he been so angry after speaking with his aide he'd needed to take off as if the devil were after him or did he always push his horses so hard?

'What was wrong just now?' she asked tentatively, wondering if she'd done something wrong by riding out with him. But it had been his idea.

'My aide is aggrieved we are out unchaperoned.' The harsh tone of his voice told her he did not share that view.

'Is my presence a problem for you?' She stroked the silky neck of the mare, guessing that her presence in Kezoban was probably creating some difficulties for him, even if he was the Sheikh.

'For me no, but for you, yes.' His profile was regal and stern as she glanced over at him. His back was tall and straight as he sat on the horse and she knew it was something he'd done since he was young. He was a natural horseman.

'For me? Why?'

'I am unmarried. As are you. Being alone with you goes against my culture. My aide reminded me of my duty to marry before the end of this year.'

She tried to stem the flow of disappointment his words brought. Of course she was a problem and of course they shouldn't be alone together. 'So being here *is* a problem for you?'

'No.' He turned to her, his dark eyes fierce as his horse stood level with hers, giving her little escape from the intensity in his eyes. 'It is not a problem for me. I want you here. You are what Majeed needs—and you are what I need.'

She couldn't say anything for a moment as the horses walked side by side and his eyes remained locked with hers. Something arced between them, more powerful than the sun's rays bouncing off the nearby water, lending the whole conversation a different meaning. Shock raced like lightning down her spine because right now she wanted to be the person he needed.

'I would like to talk more on this, but first we should deal with your request to know about the night Tabinah rode Majeed out here and met her death.' The strong determination in his voice couldn't conceal his pain at the loss of his sister so tragically.

Zafir halted his horse and dismounted and she followed suit, but as she did so she found herself falling into his waiting arms. He didn't let her go, pulling her close against him, and being held like that sent a spark hurtling through her. What was she thinking? This was where his sister had died. She shouldn't be wanting more when just being here would be painful for him. Quickly she moved free of his hold and for a moment thought she saw a flash of pain and guilt rush across his face, but as it disappeared behind his mask of control she wondered if she'd imagined it.

'This is where it is believed Tabinah began to make her way towards the rocky path over the mountains.' He paused for a moment and she didn't say anything, aware of just how difficult this must be for him. 'Her destination was on the other side.'

'So you knew where she was going?' He said nothing, but nodded his acknowledgement. She wanted to ask why Tabinah had planned to go over the mountains, but something kept the question a silent thought. She recalled him telling her that Tabinah had loved another man, one he didn't consider suitable. Her heart lurched for him. Maybe this proud and powerful man was able to feel grief. He just kept it deeply hidden. 'Do you know what happened?'

'There are many venomous snakes lurking in the shade of the rocks—they shelter beneath them at nightfall. We believe Majeed disturbed one, reared and Tabinah fell. The bite of the snake killed her, not the fall.'

'Majeed must feel so guilty.' She spoke in a soft whisper, more to herself than Zafir.

'Is it possible for a horse to feel guilty?'

'That is why he will not venture out beyond the palace walls. He is carrying guilt and fear over what happened. From what I have seen so far, he only wants to please and he knows he has displeased so won't come here again for fear of retribution.'

'I'm not sure I agree,' he said as he agilely flung himself back on his horse, thankfully putting more distance between them, giving her racing heart a chance to slow. 'Now you have the information you need, we ride.'

Destiny mounted her mare again and followed Zafir as his stallion began to trot away from the mountains that his sister had been trying to reach and back towards the sand of the desert. Thankfully, the mood lightened as the pace became fast and she couldn't help but laugh with delight when the wind snatched at her scarf, pulling it from her head and allowing her hair to be blown back behind her.

Zafir turned and glanced at her, but didn't slow as she thought he would. Instead he pushed the stallion on, increasing the pace and her exhilaration.

Finally Destiny saw Zafir slow his pace and eased her willing mare back. As she slowed she was able to look about her, seeing nothing but sand. It was strangely beautiful, shades of gold sculpted by the winds, and it felt right being here. Even the sun's ever increasing height didn't worry her. It would be hot very soon, of that she was sure, but she trusted Zafir; he wouldn't bring them here if they couldn't make it back before the sun scorched everything.

'This is where I ride to every morning.' His heavily accented words filtered through her thoughts. She looked about her. The sun was climbing ever higher and the wind was warm and very dry. As far as she could see was sand. Not another soul, just the two of them, and it felt strangely intimate. Exciting.

'It's beautiful,' she breathed as the horses walked on, slowly climbing before reaching the top of a dune. She looked out across a sea of sand and in the distance saw the range of mountains. 'It's more than beautiful—it's utterly gorgeous.'

'As are you.' His words were firm, but huskiness accentuated his accent, making her heart skip a beat.

Destiny looked across at him, the grey stallion prancing on the spot, but still Zafir kept his gaze fixed on her. He looked so regal in his desert robes, the wind blowing the headdress which concealed his dark hair.

Heat which had nothing to do with the sun sizzled down her spine.

In a total abandonment she'd never experienced before, she knew she wanted to be kissed by him, to be held in his strong arms. Her body was on fire for him. She wanted to be claimed by this man, wanted him to make her completely his. She wanted him and, more importantly, he wanted her. She should have seen it all along. The attraction which had sparked to life the first time they'd met was too strong to be ignored. No amount of professionalism or contrived distance could deny it.

This was a man fate had sent her way. A man so wild and exotic he could have been conjured up by her imagination. She had never hungered after passion and certainly not with a man such as Zafir but now that she had met him she knew it would only ever be him she'd want.

'I want you, Zafir.' She could scarcely believe she'd said the words. Her heart was pounding so fast in her chest, but she'd had to say it, had to tell him. Here, away from the palace, he seemed different, more relaxed, more like the man she'd thought had been about to kiss her that very first night. She too felt different out here, as if she'd uncovered a hidden part of her as they'd galloped across the sands, then discarded her usual caution, losing it to the warm winds, making her a different woman.

Zafir's horse whipped round, pawing the sand, eager to be off, but he soothed the agitation with words she didn't understand, words that sounded like poetry to her.

'I can't offer you what you're looking for, Destiny,'

he said, his voice almost harsh as he struggled with the prancing stallion.

Destiny's mare instantly picked up the excited vibes from the stallion and turned, leaving her facing Zafir, able to look into the dark swirling depths of his eyes.

'What am I looking for, Zafir?' she asked as the mare spun round again. Destiny held the reins firm, her body moving with each excited step the mare took and waited for his answer.

'I can't give you forever. I can't even promise you happiness, but I can promise you a night like no other.'

Deep down she'd known that all along, known that he was so far removed from her world that they would never have any kind of future together. But that hadn't stopped her wanting him from that very first moment she'd seen him at her stables—even if she hadn't rec- ognised it then.

Happy-ever-after would be nice. A dream come true. But dreams didn't come true—her mother was testa- ment to that—and before her now was a man offer- ing her a taste of such a dream. A taste she intended to sample to the full. She wanted to know what pas- sion and desire felt like before she returned to a fresh start in England.

'I hope you keep your promises, Your Highness,' she teased, feeling a recklessness she'd never known around a man before, and launched the mare into a gal- lop. Behind her she heard Zafir's mount as it whinnied with excitement, then the thundering of its hooves as the distance closed between them.

She laughed out loud, the wind snatching the sound away. She was totally free. The glint of passion she'd glimpsed in Zafir's eyes before she'd raced off hummed inside her as excitement and anticipation grew. She would be brave and sample the dream of happiness and forever, even if it was only for one night.

Zafir was relieved and angered as he saw his palace coming into view. The horses were hot and tired but still he wished he could have stayed out in the desert with Destiny all day. She made him feel alive, made him long to be carefree and wild, something he hadn't felt for many years, but once back within the confines of the palace he'd have to school his emotions, behave in the manner of the ruler he was.

His promise of one night would be all he could give her. She was not of his world and soon, too soon, he was going to have to select a bride—to provide the heirs his position demanded. His wife needed to be a woman able to deal with the harshness of not only desert life, but life married to the ruler of Kezoban. She needed to be someone his people could relate to, someone they could take to their hearts.

Destiny's dark hair was flowing behind her, the scarf she'd worn blowing in the wind. He deliberately held his mount back, enabling him to watch her, his eyes drawn to the firmness of her thighs as she pushed her mare on and the tantalising outline of her bottom as she leant forward in the saddle. She was gorgeous, beautiful and so full of life—exactly the kind of woman he wished he could have if his position as ruler of Kezoban didn't demand otherwise.

Excitement fizzed through him, making him ache with unquenched passion as he recalled her words. She wanted him, seeming to accept they had little or no future, even teasing him as she'd headed back across the sand. In that moment he knew he had to have her, had to make her his. She might be off limits but she would be his for one night.

Stable boys greeted them as they made their way back within the safety of palace walls. He couldn't resist another look at Destiny. Her cheeks were flushed from exertion, her eyes bright and alive. He wanted her so badly that if he was to avoid carrying her off to his bed right this minute he'd have to throw himself into his work.

'Thank you,' she breathed after dismounting, suddenly close to him. Too close.

'For what?' he asked, suspicion furrowing his brow, unaware he had done anything that required her thanks.

'For just now—it was wonderful. I haven't enjoyed a good gallop since Ellie was sold.'

'Who is Ellie?' He watched as she looked down at her hands as if trying to hide her emotions.

'My horse. Or she was until my father forced me to sell her. He couldn't accept the time I spent with Ellie.'

He sensed there was more, knew that, like him, she was hiding a part of herself. 'I'm sorry, but you may, of course, ride the mare any time.'

Around him Zafir was aware of the bustle of activity as the horses were led away. Destiny placed her hand on his arm as soon as they were alone. 'Thank you, for that and...' She paused, as if wondering if she should give voice to her thoughts.

Out there in the desert she'd been completely honest with him and, going against his better judgement, he'd been honest with her.

'For bringing me here and enabling me to have the chance of making a new start when I return home.' She looked up at him as she continued, directly into his eyes, and he saw a conflict of emotions racing across them before she lowered her lashes, shutting him out.

'I am honoured to have you here.' His voice was a cracked whisper as he closed the distance between them so that they were almost touching. His heart began to thump harder as he slowly and very gently held her face, his thumbs caressing her cheekbones. Very slowly, so slowly it was almost painful, he lowered his head until his lips brushed hers.

Heat skittered around Destiny's body with alarming speed, a soft sigh escaping her lips, only to be caught by his kiss. His stubble grazed her skin and her senses whirled as she inhaled his scent—bergamot, fresh and clean but with a hint of the desert.

Everything about the kiss felt so right, as did being this close to the heated hardness of his body. She ached to pull him closer, to wind her arms around his neck and slide her fingers into his hair. She wasn't sure how she even knew what to do. She was simply following her body's instinct.

'You smell good,' he whispered against her lips and her stomach flipped over, making her knees so weak she wondered if they'd be able to keep her upright. 'It is a change to find a woman who is happy not to be permanently doused in perfume, living life to the full.'

Destiny pulled back and looked sceptically up into his face. 'I'm not sure the last bit is a compliment or not,' she teased.

'Your sweet scent, so distinctly you, cannot be doused even as it mixes with leather and horse,' he said with a hint of a smile on his lips. Those heady words said by any other man would have sounded strange, but from Zafir, the man she desired with increasing need, they were like dynamite. The explosion of desire within her sealed her fate. She was already his.

'And that is good?' she teased him, emboldened by the fact that he had even noticed such details.

'Oh, it's good.' He feathered a kiss across her brow. 'I admire a woman who doesn't feel she has to be dressed in finery and decked in jewels. You're so different from any woman I've met before.'

Destiny couldn't help the image of what his past lovers must have been like coming into her head. Had any of them been the kind of woman he loved? Or was he referring to his sister? Maybe if she knew more of Tabinah she could not only help Majeed but satisfy her curiosity.

Finally that curiosity got the better of her and the words slipped from her lips before she could think of the consequences. 'What was Tabinah like?'

Zafir's body went cold and rigid against her instantly and she regretted her impetuous words. Surely there had been another way of asking the question. His arms dropped away from her and he stepped back.

'What Tabinah was like has no relevance to you or your work here.' The words snapped angrily from him and she cursed her stupid timing, but felt angered by his inability to open up to her, to allow her in. 'You have seen where the incident took place, where my sister was found. You do not need to know any more.'

'That is where you are wrong.' She said the words a little too quickly and moved farther away from him. If distance was what he craved, distance he'd get. 'I need to know so much more than you are willing to tell if you want me to help Majeed.'

'You do not, I repeat, do not need to know about my sister or my relationship with her.'

His eyes glittered as if the sun were shining on thousands of tiny diamonds. It should have served as a warning to her but she didn't see it, didn't want to see it.

'I'm making a connection with Majeed. He's letting me close, giving me his trust and it's a shame his master can't do the same.'

Before he could answer she marched from the stables and back towards the courtyard and the long wide corridor which led to the palace, not bothering to wait for her escort. Anger boiled inside her. How could he bring her here to help a horse he had no intention of helping himself?

Once inside her room she shut the door, leant her back against it and only then allowed her nerves full rein. Her body shook as if she was cold, her legs so weak she couldn't stand any longer and she slid down the door. It was not the way she'd spoken to the Sheikh, the ruler, or even the fact that he'd held her so tenderly, kissing her gently yet with barely concealed passion. It was the way she'd responded. From that first teasing moment in the desert when she'd all but begged him to make her his lover, to the way she'd allowed his mouth to claim hers.

She was doing exactly what she knew she shouldn't, what could only bring heartache and trouble. But she couldn't stop herself, couldn't help the fire that burned deep within her just thinking of him.

She was falling for the Sheikh, the devil of the desert.

CHAPTER FIVE

For the last two weeks Zafir had adhered to all the rules he'd mentioned at the beginning of their ride that morning in the desert, although that day they had both briefly thrown those rules to the wind as the horses had raced homeward. Destiny could still feel his lips on hers, still wanted so much more, but, just as he obviously didn't wish to, she wouldn't give into the attraction. Since their ride he'd been the perfect gentleman when they'd met and had ensured they had company at all times.

Zafir had allocated her a maid and she was certain it was to ensure they didn't find themselves alone again. Although the older woman had seemed initially in awe of her, she had found a good friend in Mina. Soon after had come the generous gifts of gorgeous silk *abayas* and other garments worn by the women of Zafir's kingdom and she kept telling herself he just wanted her to feel comfortable, to fit in and be part of life in the palace.

Each time she'd met with Zafir in his office to report on her progress with Majeed, he'd had at least one of his aides present, making it clear he'd inadvertently crossed boundaries and had spent the last two weeks erecting higher barriers between them.

In the thrill of the moment that morning, flirtation had taken over and she'd recklessly agreed to just one night. She'd agonised over how she would tell him she'd never spent one moment intimately with a man, let alone a night. But that now appeared a needless worry. Not once had he done anything to make her think he was still serious about spending a night with her.

For the last few hours Destiny had been at the stables with Majeed and she was shocked at the dishevelled state in her reflection as she passed the ornate gilt mirror in her suite. Her hair was wild, looking as if she hadn't been near a hairdresser for years, not weeks. Her face was streaked with dust after working with Majeed in the school; the long white blouse she'd worn for modesty was now grimy and dirty.

She'd looked as dishevelled the morning she and Zafir had returned from their ride, but he had seen past that then. She'd really believed he'd seen her for who she really was, that he'd wanted her in the way she'd wanted him. Doubts assailed her as she unbuttoned her blouse, dropping it to the marble floor and heading for the shower. She turned on the jets of warm water, discarded the remainder of her clothes and stepped under the soothing warmth of the water.

As she was dressing in one of the cool outfits Zafir had provided for her to wear when she wasn't working, Mina knocked and entered. The big smile on the woman's face showed nothing but approval for her choice of pale blue silks adorned with gold. 'His Highness has requested that you join him for an outing to the town.'

Destiny's heart jolted before hammering out a

steady beat. Zafir wanted to take her out. It would be a welcome change from working each day and, feeling like an excited child, she clasped her hands together in front of her chest in a way that had a lot more to do with the man who was taking her out rather than the outing itself.

'Do I need to change?' she asked Mina, wondering where they were going and if what she now wore was suitable.

'You have chosen well. I will be happy to be seen with you,' Mina said as she moved forward and fussed with the vibrant blue silk.

'Be seen with me?' she queried, the rush of anticipation at spending time with Zafir becoming clouded.

'It wouldn't be good for His Highness to be seen alone with you.' Mina stood back to survey her efforts, unaware of the confusion that ran riot inside Destiny's head. 'Now, if you are ready, we shall go.'

She followed Mina along the cool corridors, trying all the while to hide her disappointment that she and Zafir were to be accompanied. She wondered if this chaperone was intended for her sake or his. Then all her thoughts jumbled as they entered a large room where Zafir, deep in conversation with his aide, was dressed in robes befitting a king. The white robes, layered with a fine gold cloak, accentuated his potent masculinity and undoubted power, making her stomach knot and a heavy throb of desire pulse deep inside her.

She couldn't take her eyes from him. And from the fire within his, the question of their one night together still lingered tantalisingly between them. Had he kept his distance purposefully in an attempt to make her want him more?

Mina stepped into the background, as did his aide, and suddenly it was just the two of them again. His steady gaze held hers, forcing her heart rate to accelerate wildly. She'd never known such an attraction before and the hot desire in his midnight black eyes was almost too much.

A smile pulled at the corners of his mouth, as if he'd read her thoughts, heard her secret appraisal of him. 'I thought you would like to sample life in our city,' he said as he moved farther away from the other man, coming to join her. His gaze slid down her body and she tingled all over as if he'd actually touched her, a ragged breath escaping her as she tried to speak.

'Thank you, Your Highness.' She managed to sound demure even though her rampaging emotions were making her want things she shouldn't. If they were to be chaperoned she'd better conform to the expected etiquette when addressing him in public. 'It will be nice to see more of your country before I return to England.'

He quirked a heavy dark brow at her words, his gaze holding hers for just a little too long, causing his aide to cough politely behind him. 'I shall be honoured to show you.' Then he bowed his head quickly and turned, his white robe swirling around him, the gold cloak shimmering in the light.

It all felt surreal and Destiny wondered if she was dreaming as they were ushered out into the heat of the day and into a waiting car. She looked around as the door closed them inside the luxury of his car. She and Zafir were alone. No aide and no chaperone.

'They will follow in the car behind,' he offered as if he'd read her thoughts.

She drank in the image he created as he sat tall and proud, even though he couldn't be seen through the tinted windows. Her body ached for him, craved his touch, his kiss. The weeks since that snatched moment in the stables had done little to quell the throb of desire whenever he was near. The memory of his kiss still burned in her mind and on her lips.

He leant closer and for one moment she thought he was going to kiss her again. Instead he said softly and so quietly only she could hear, 'Do you remember what we spoke of the morning we rode out?'

She'd thought of nothing else. It was what she wanted. Did this mean it was a serious proposition instead of fun flirtation?

When she didn't respond to his question he leant a little closer. 'Do you still want me, Destiny?'

'Yes.' The cracked whisper which came from her sounded unreal and so unnatural.

He smiled a satisfied and very sexy smile, sending her senses into overdrive, but how their one night was ever going to happen, when either his aide or Mina was present each time they met, she didn't know.

He reached out and stroked the back of his fingers down her cheek, forcing her lashes to close and a soft sigh to escape her lips. He was speaking, she realised, but in Arabic, which served only to highlight how different their lives were. She pulled back and for a moment their gazes locked, the challenge and desire in his clear.

'Will Royal protocol be happy with us travelling together?' she couldn't resist teasing as she sat back, feigning indifference to him.

* * *

'It is only a short drive.' Zafir's gaze wandered over her as she looked out of the window, anywhere but at him, it would seem. The heat created moments ago by her whispered admission that she wanted him was only intensified by her apparent lack of interest in him. She was aloof, so superior and a far cry from the passionate woman he'd held far too briefly in his arms two weeks ago. Since then he hadn't been able to stop thinking of her, wanting so much more than a kiss. 'And we do have a driver, although he does not understand English.'

'So why the escort? Why any of this?' She turned and faced him and he fought hard to remain straight and upright in his seat, resisting the urge to reach for her and pull her close. He wanted to feel her body against his, touch her, taste her and kiss her in a way he'd never done with any woman before.

'I thought you'd want to see more than just the palace. Having an escort is not only what my people would expect, but also for your own good. I do not wish to tarnish your reputation in any way.' Zafir felt her gaze travel over him, leaving a trail of fire that set light to the desire he'd tried to deny since he'd first seen her working the horse at the stables in England.

'Oh,' she whispered, as if aware of how she was affecting him. 'I'm sorry if I've caused you a problem.'

The only problem she'd caused him was awakening his long ignored libido, leaving him unfulfilled and as ravenous as a man breaking a fast. And this was a problem he intended to redress fully once the hours of darkness had fallen. He'd tried to dismiss whatever it was between them but he couldn't ignore her or his need for her any longer.

Tonight she would be his.

He knew he shouldn't want her, but he couldn't resist her any longer. In a matter of weeks he would be expected to announce his engagement, but still he hadn't made any final decision, despite being urged by his aides to do so. He pushed the unsavoury thought of marriage aside, his senses clamouring for the satisfaction he knew only Destiny could give.

'It is not a problem, just our way.' He watched as she looked down at her hands clasped tightly in her lap, something he'd seen her do on that first night at the palace. It made her appear vulnerable, a trait he had no intention of looking for in his future wife, but one he found himself drawn to in Destiny. He wanted to look after her, protect her from hurt and even, he conceded, protect her from himself—and right now that was what she needed most.

The car stopped at the hotel he'd planned on and as the door opened he couldn't help but find pleasure in her smile. The noisy bustle of the streets filled the car and he watched as she got out carefully, mindful of her new garments.

'Come,' he ordered. 'We shall walk to the market before taking some light refreshment.'

'You actually walk in the street?' The incredulity in her voice forced him to stem his laughter.

'How else am I to show you my city?'

'But I hadn't thought… I mean…' She floundered and he wanted to touch her, to ease her discomfort. But in public, protocol *had* to be followed. No matter what.

'That I wouldn't do such a thing? They are my people and I am privileged to walk among them. It is expected.'

As they walked on, her attention was captured, or so she'd have him believe, by the hustle of the town as they made their way through the busy streets. He smiled as she looked from side to side, desperate not to miss anything. Spending a few hours with her would be enjoyable, even if they did have the constant shadow of Mina over them. It would also heighten the anticipation of the night he had every intention of spending with her.

Negotiating the busy streets proved to be somewhat of a distraction, but Zafir had the constant urge to keep Destiny safe, to maintain contact. The need to touch her was so great it was driving him crazy and with his hand almost permanently moving to the small of her back before being quickly withdrawn, he showed her the wonders of his city while they mingled with the crowds.

'This is such a wonderful place.' She turned her face up to his and smiled—a wide carefree smile that he'd not witnessed on her lips until that moment. 'The colours, the smells, the noise. It's just wonderful.'

He looked down at her face; excitement was sparkling in her eyes. She was so beautiful, so vibrant that she cast everything around her into shadow. Did she have any idea what she did to him? He wanted her so badly, but what if he hurt her, made her unhappy or, worse, let her down as he'd let Tabinah down? What if by being with him, even now, here in the market, she would be exposing herself to future unhappiness?

'Zafir?' she queried. 'What's the matter? You look like you've seen a ghost.'

Perhaps I have. The thought ploughed into him like

a runaway horse. *Perhaps I'm seeing the ghost of the man I could have been if we were both different people.*

'No, everything is fine. I'm pleased you are enjoying yourself. You've been working hard with Majeed.'

She smiled shyly at him before looking away. Was she so unused to praise? He stifled a deep sigh, acknowledging but not accepting he was not what she needed. There might be chemistry between them, but she needed more than that, much more. Something he couldn't give. Something he didn't want to give.

'When you are ready we will have our refreshment before returning to the palace. It's hotter than I'd anticipated.' The words were all but snapped from him as he tried to prevent the guilt he felt at letting Tabinah down from surfacing. Destiny didn't need to know all the sorry details of his last exchange of words with his sister, despite what she thought, because if she did she'd never see him the same way again.

'You're right,' Destiny said as she turned to look at some bright red silk, desperate to hide her disappointment at his withdrawal from her. She'd felt him retreat, felt the hot passionate man she'd glimpsed in the back of the car fade away. His eyes had grown hard and cold, his body had tensed as the totally-in-control ruler had returned. 'It's hot. I'm ready to return to the palace now, please.'

Moments later she was once again in the back of his car as it made its way out of the busy streets before heading back to the palace. Beside her, Zafir was a dark brooding presence.

'I have work to attend to now.' He kept his gaze focused ahead, as if he couldn't even bear to look at her. Had she misread the signals yet again?

The car stopped outside the palace and she knew she had to say something. 'Zafir?' She hated the question in her voice, but it caught his attention and he turned to look at her as his door was opened. She lost her nerve as his dark eyes locked with hers. 'Thank you for a nice afternoon.'

No, not that. In her mind she screamed the words as he appeared to digest what she'd said without a trace of emotion on his regal face.

'My pleasure,' he said sharply and left the confines of the car, speaking rapidly to his staff, his words fast and flowing.

Then her own door opened and she got out into the heat of the afternoon, glad to walk into the shade of the palace and even more pleased when she was finally alone in her room.

More bereft than she'd ever felt, although she missed her sister, as always, her thoughts went to her mother. What would she have suggested she do? Destiny dug her teeth into her bottom lip in a bid to stop the tears falling. She wouldn't let Zafir's sudden coldness shatter her into pieces. She was stronger than that. Life had made her stronger.

In an attempt to feel close to her mother, she opened her wardrobe and pulled out her bag, then the small box she kept her mother's diary in. Just as she always did, she smoothed her fingers over the top of the box, then opened it and touched the diary which lay within. It was the last true connection she had with who she really was and she'd been so glad she'd found it hidden away at the back of her mother's wardrobe.

She turned to the usual page she read and traced her finger over the flowing words.

I thought I'd found my forever love in the man I married and now I don't know what to do. We have a beautiful daughter who was my destiny and another child on the way, but his affection is growing cold and I feel now his love for me never existed.

Carefully, Destiny closed the diary and placed it back in the box and buried it in her bag once more. Her mother had wanted love but never really found it. Dwelling on the past wasn't going to help her now. Sleep, however, would, she decided, and lay on the bed, allowing its softness to cradle her, to soothe her as she closed her eyes.

When sleep came it was filled with images of the Sheikh she'd lost her heart to, the man she wanted above all others—the man she couldn't have.

It was dark when she woke, only a soft glow from a small lamp illuminating the room. Destiny sat up, feeling more emotionally drained than she had before she'd slept. On the table she noticed covered dishes and realised Mina must have been in with her meal and left her to sleep, but she wasn't hungry.

She felt trapped like an animal in a cage and had to get out of her room. She craved the warm night air on her skin as if it would salve her wounds after Zafir's aloofness this afternoon, which had been as good as rejection after her admission that she wanted him. She should never have said those words when they were riding in the desert. She should never have opened her heart, laying bare her emotions and needs for him to discard like yesterday's newspaper.

She wandered out into the peace of the palace garden, now almost in darkness except for the twinkle of small lights along the pathways. The night air was laden with scents from the strange and exotic flowers and above her the sky looked like velvet interspersed with sequins. It was magical and she stood looking up beyond the smooth cream walls of the palace at a night sky unlike any other she'd seen before.

A skitter of warmth ran down her spine and she was sure she could sense Zafir behind her. Did she want him that much? *Yes.* The unbidden answer came.

She could almost feel his touch on her shoulder, his hand lingering there, sending a frisson of heat to every part of her body, and she closed her eyes as his unmistakable scent enveloped her. Was he really here? Had he risked all protocol to come to her? Was this to be their night?

'Destiny.' His deep voice, so sexy, so seductive, proved she wasn't imagining anything.

She didn't dare speak, not wanting to break the spell by turning to him, almost afraid that if her imagination had conjured him up, as soon as she opened her eyes she would be alone. And she didn't want to be alone. She wanted to be with Zafir tonight. She wanted to be his, completely and totally, as the hours of darkness lay over the palace.

Then she felt him against her back, as he wrapped her in his arms, pulling her closer to him, his breath feathering her ear. 'I had to come.' His hoarse whisper broke the soft silence that enveloped them. 'I shouldn't want you, I can't want you, but I do.'

He kissed her neck and she leant her head back against him, allowing him more access. A shiver of anticipation darted around her body as his lips touched every bit of naked skin on her neck.

'Neither of us should want this, but we do.' Her words were a ragged whisper as her heart thudded in her chest. She wanted to turn to him, to press her lips against his, but at the same time couldn't break the tenuous contact they now shared. 'Let's just forget the rest of the world for a few hours, forget everything except what we feel now.'

His kisses stilled and she felt his chest expanding against her back with every deep breath he took. Had she said too much—again?

'I want to forget it all,' he said and pressed his lips into her hair, inhaling deeply as if taking in her scent. 'I want you in a way I've never wanted a woman before, but I can't be like other men. I have a duty to my country.'

'Just for these hours of darkness,' she whispered and opened her eyes to look once again at the stars. 'That's all we need, Zafir, just the one night.'

It was all she knew she could have and the fact that he asked nothing of her only made it easier for her. He expected nothing and therefore there wouldn't be any demands on her. She was safe, in control.

Her eyes widened as she heard the growled oath slip from him. Even though she didn't understand it, excitement raced through her as suddenly he spun her round to face him, his hands holding her arms firmly. She wanted this in a way she'd never wanted anything before and right now she was sure she was the one in control, not only of her emotions but him.

'You are like a witch. You've cast a spell on me and I'm powerless to resist you.'

'Then don't.'

Zafir's eyes were heavy and black with unconcealed passion. His face was as stern as it had ever been, as if he was wrestling with his conscience. Destiny felt desirable. No man had ever made her body ache so badly with need, so wantonly. Somewhere in the back of her mind a warning rang out but she wasn't in the mood to listen to anything other than the singing of her body as he looked at her. She didn't want to heed anything other than the pulse of desire coming from deep within her. She wanted to be his, she wanted tonight—regardless of what tomorrow would bring.

She reached up to stroke the hard angles of his jaw, desire coursing through her as her fingers touched that so perfect stubble. She wanted to give herself to him. A man who freely admitted he couldn't give her what she wanted. A man who represented everything she was trying to escape, one who sought complete and utter control.

With the speed of a falcon swooping on its prey, Zafir's lips claimed hers in a hard demanding kiss. His tongue plunged into her mouth, demanding and erotic. She couldn't believe the flirtatious groan she made, a sound like no other she'd heard before, but she wanted this—wanted him.

In answer his hand splayed on her back, pressing her into him, and she felt the hard ridge of his erection as her hips moved against his, forcing the flames of desire higher still. Her hands wound around his neck, determined that this time he wouldn't go, wouldn't leave her with that unquenched throb of need humming in her body. Her fingers delved into his thick hair, relishing its silky strength.

'This is too much…' His voice broke with huskiness before he kissed her once more, his hand sliding up her body, cupping the fullness of her breast as his tongue once again took up a frenzied dance with hers.

It was mind-blowing and she could hardly stand as the pleasure of his touch made her knees weak. She gasped into his mouth as his thumb caressed her tightened nipple, the silk of her *abaya* and the lace of her bra hardly any barrier at all. But still it wasn't enough, still she wanted more. So much more.

She forced herself to push away from him, finding it hard to catch her breath or even hear herself think above the pounding of her heart. Emotions and sensations she'd never known, never dared to hope to experience were in full control of her now. The inexperienced woman who'd left England was gone.

With a shy smile she slipped her hand into his and led the way to her suite of rooms. His fingers tightened around hers as he followed, giving her all the encouragement she needed.

Walking into the dimly lit room was startling after the near darkness of the garden and she felt him hesitate, draw back and stay on the threshold. He looked into her face, his expression questioning. Was he regretting coming to her?

'What is it?'

'This is all I can give, this night.' The warning there was clear, but so too was the sexy huskiness, giving her the confidence to be someone so different from the woman she'd always been. The last thing she wanted him to think was that she was an inexperienced lover and she definitely didn't want him to know she was a virgin.

'I know,' she said softly, meeting his gaze and tilting her chin up, emboldened by the desire in his eyes. 'I know.'

CHAPTER SIX

ZAFIR LOOKED AT her lovely face and felt as if an arrow had lodged in his chest. Destiny had turned his world upside down, making him take a long hard look at himself, at his life, but still it hadn't changed anything. He wanted her, wanted to be able to change everything so he could be with her for more than just a few snatched hours. But it could never be. Not when duty remained the most important thing in his life, the one thing he could not ignore.

Whatever happened between them, he was still the ruler of Kezoban, a ruler without a wife or heir because of his reluctance to commit. After Tabinah's death, that sense of duty was stronger than ever. He'd forced his sister into an arranged marriage and now he would do the same, but only after being with Destiny. Tonight would be theirs.

'It was by chance that our worlds collided, that we met in England—a chance that has given us this night.' He had to be sure she knew there could never be a repeat of this night and that nobody must know. 'Tomorrow…'

'I know, Zafir,' she whispered and moved closer to him, her eyes darkening to the colour of strong coffee.

'I know you have a new life to move on to, that nobody in the palace can know.'

'It is for your sake as much as mine.' He kept his voice firm, even as desire stirred ever higher. Did she have any idea how beguiling she looked, how seductive? But there was something else; despite the boldness of her actions, an underlying innocence shone through and he wondered just how practised at seduction she was.

She pressed her fingertip to his lips, jolting him with the intensity of that touch, chasing away such thoughts. 'Please don't say any more.'

He kissed her finger gently, then turned and closed the door to the garden before taking her hand and leading her across the vast expanse of marble that was her living room and through to the luxury of the bedroom.

He could smell her seductive scent, light and floral, making him think of England in the summertime, but also reminding him who she was and that making love to a woman in his palace was something he'd never done before. Did that mean she was different? He squashed that thought and focused his attention on the present, the moment he'd tried to avoid but had longed for so strongly for the last two weeks. Making Destiny his—for one night at least.

Destiny's gaze met his and she saw his doubt, his uncertainty briefly before the smouldering darkness of passion filled his eyes once more.

She wasn't sure who had moved, but suddenly she was in his arms, exactly where she wanted to be. She slid her hands down his back, loving the feel of his firm body as his lips kissed down her throat. His hands cradled her breasts, now achingly firm and sensitive as she arched herself towards him.

Anticipation sizzled between them as his mouth covered hers, teasing and light at first, then hot and demanding. She kissed him back, matching his hunger and deepening the kiss until she thought she would pass out.

He lifted his head up, taking his kiss out of reach, and she found herself looking at the dark skin of his throat, noticing the dusting of hairs. She'd been so consumed by need for him, she hadn't realised he was dressed casually in beige trousers and a white shirt made of the finest silk, embroidered with gold as befitting his status.

She smiled at the thought of seeing the man beneath his robes, as he was now and as she really wanted to see him. Had his chosen outfit been a way of coming to her as Zafir the man and not Zafir the Sheikh, the ruler of Kezoban? Right now she didn't care, didn't want to question. He was here and tonight she would be his.

'Something amuses you?' he questioned, his voice deep and regal as he held her away from him, watching her face intently.

'I was wondering if removing your robes would be as easy as what you're wearing now.' She stifled a nervous laugh, realising she'd never teased a man like this before, her experience of intimacy having been less than limited, more like non-existent. Unwilling to allow a man close, she'd given all her devotion to horses. Zafir was the only man who had breached the barrier she'd purposefully erected, made her want more, made her want to experience all the pleasure of making love—even if it was for just one night.

Her gaze slid down his body. Imagining him in his robes, she was aware that if tonight was all they had she'd never find out how to remove them. She pushed that thought to the back of her mind. Just being here, beneath his appreciative gaze, was so far removed from anything she'd done before. The heat of the desert must have changed her, made her a more wanton and passionate woman, one she'd had no idea she could be.

'It is as well that I can discard your *abaya* with ease,' he said and brushed a kiss on her lips, tasting them and sending heat racing through her body.

She tried not to think of how many times he might have done just that, tried to push aside all thoughts of the women who'd been in his life, desperately wanting to stay in the moment, to savour every touch, every sensation of being desired by him.

Instead she pressed her body against his, wanting more than just kisses. She felt again the burning hardness of his body, and heat unfurled deep within her. With a soft sigh, she gave herself up to instincts she'd never known she possessed, moving her hips against him.

Swiftly he pushed against her, giving her no choice but to move backwards towards the bed. His breathing was deep and ragged, echoing her own, as the back of her legs met the bed and she dropped back onto its softness.

Zafir covered her body with his as he took her mouth in a hard and wild kiss. She could feel the fierce intensity of his passion, his lips bruising hers, but she wanted more. Despite the clothing they still wore, she was in no doubt how much he wanted her and with each passing second she thought she might go up in flames.

She wanted him. It felt wrong yet so right. The only thing that was as clear as a star-filled night was that she needed him so very much. She wanted him to be the first man she made love to.

Her nails dug into his back as he kissed down her throat and she arched beneath him. His hand slid down her side, resting on her hip.

'Zafir...' She gasped his name as his tongue caressed her nipple through the silk of her *abaya*. It felt so good. 'I want you, Zafir.'

She reached down between their bodies, wanting to touch him. She fumbled with the fastening on his trousers, revelling in the guttural growl that escaped his lips as she touched him through the fabric, feeling the heat of him. She'd never undressed a man before, let alone touched one like this, but the fire in her veins emboldened her. She was acting on instinct that had lain dormant within her, waiting for him. Finally the fastening gave way and she felt the silk of his underwear, now barely able to conceal him.

He moved suddenly back away from her, bracing himself over her on the bed before lying beside her. All the while his gaze remained fixed firmly on hers, sending shivers of anticipation hurtling all over her. Her heart thumped a little harder when he pulled a foil packet from his pocket and she was shocked it was a consideration she hadn't given even a moment's thought to.

'Before we go any further...' His voice had become a deep husky growl which sent pleasure skittering down her spine and she watched in awe and even a little trepidation as he swiftly rolled on the condom.

His dark eyes held hers prisoner as his hand slid her

abaya up her thighs and he hooked his fingers into her lace panties. She shivered in anticipation and lifted herself up from the bed, enabling him to tug them down. His eyes were laden with desire as he smiled. It was a small smile that barely lifted the corners of his beautiful mouth, but one which sent molten heat coursing through her as he tossed the panties to the floor.

With his dark eyes fixed to hers he moved back between her legs, urgency in every movement, so much so that only the barriers of underwear had been removed. She panicked. Would he be disappointed? Would he know how little experience she'd had? She moved her hips up towards him, surrendering herself to the needs of her body. She felt him touch her, nudging insistently, before thrusting deep inside her.

She gasped as he filled her, and closed her eyes against the sudden pain. She couldn't stop another gasp from escaping, one mostly of satisfaction at having him inside her, of being possessed by him. Momentarily he paused and she felt his whole body shake as he looked down at her.

'Please, Zafir,' she said and wondered if that throaty sound had actually come from her, but already her desire was taking over as she lifted her hips, encouraging him.

In answer to her body's plea he moved within her, setting up a fast rhythm which threatened to sweep her far away. It felt so good, so right.

She clung to him, moving her hips faster and deepening every thrust into her he made. It was exquisite. She felt as if she were on the edge of a cliff, barely able to balance. She wanted to fall, wanted to give in to the pleasure of it, yet wanted to enjoy the moment of being with him for just a few seconds longer.

His arms shook as he balanced himself above her and she slid her hands inside his shirt, moving them across his back, desperate to feel his skin. Each move he made took her closer to the edge until she knew she had no choice. She couldn't hold on any longer. She had to go over. Her head fell back as she gasped in pleasure at the sensations rushing through her. He cried out, thrusting hard and deep into her, sending her over the edge until she no longer cared where she was, just as long as she was with Zafir.

Slowly her body floated down to earth, leaving the stars behind, and she opened her eyes, aware of the weight of Zafir's body on hers. His heart was pounding, echoed by hers, and his breathing was still fast and hard. It had been wonderful, more beautiful than she'd ever dreamt, but his words of warning came rushing back to her.

This is all I can give, this night.

'I'm sorry.' Zafir's voice was low and full of concern. 'It should not have been like that for you. I should have had more control, more thought for you.'

He stood up from the bed and disappeared into the bathroom. Her heart plummeted. How should it have been? What should she have done? Should she have told him she'd never had sex before?

She sat up, dragged her *abaya* down and clasped her knees to her chest. She closed her eyes against the rush of emotions engulfing her as she heard water running in the bathroom.

Was her night of passion over already? Well, if it was, she wasn't going to let him know how much it hurt.

* * *

Zafir stopped when he came back into the bedroom and watched as Destiny curled her knees up and dropped her face onto them. It was such an innocent movement, reinforcing what he now knew for sure. That despite her flirtatious teasing, her provocative words of desire, she was inexperienced and innocent.

She'd been a virgin and he'd taken her in a heaving rush, with scant regard for her pleasure. So intense had his need been he hadn't even removed his clothes. He hadn't seduced her as he'd planned, hadn't explored her glorious body while he lay naked next to her—he'd been nothing more than an eager youth demanding his own satisfaction.

He'd wanted to take things slowly, to seduce her and enjoy every moment of their short time together, but she'd been his undoing. Her kisses had inflamed a passion deep within him like no other he'd ever felt before. All sense of control had slipped away into the dark desert night.

He sat on the bed next to her and she looked up at him. Her brown eyes were wide and watchful. The forced smile on her lips twisted his heart and he touched her face softly. 'I'm sorry. I should have been gentler.'

'Why?' Her voice croaked with raw emotion and he ached to hold her, to ease the pain he'd caused. 'Because I'm inexperienced and it was my first time?'

Her stark words lanced through him but he couldn't look deeper into what they meant to him; he didn't want to acknowledge the tradition that as a ruler, a man of power, he should never take a woman's virginity, unless it was that of his wife. He pushed those thoughts away. Right now he had to make things right with Destiny.

He shook his head as he slid his palm across her cheek before pushing his fingers into her hair, holding her head, preventing her from looking away. 'Because you deserved more than that. I was like a teenager, eager, crass and totally selfish.'

She smiled at him, a real smile that reached her eyes, making them sparkle. 'No, not you.' She laughed softly, a sexy sound that made his pulse race all over again. 'You could never be that, not when you are the Sheikh.'

'And because I am the Sheikh, you should have told me you were a virgin,' he said, forcing his tone to remain soft as the guilt finally hit him.

'It's not exactly something a girl wants to admit, especially to a man like you. But isn't that why you came here tonight as the man I met in England, not the man who rules Kezoban? I expect nothing from you, Zafir. You made that very clear. We have only one night.'

He felt something tighten in his chest, as if he was being squeezed, and he knew she was right. He had come to her as Zafir, the man, in an attempt to shake off the guilt which just having her here in the palace was intensifying. Out of duty to his kingdom he'd forced Tabinah into a marriage she didn't want and yet in complete disregard for his duty he wanted to go to Destiny, a guest in his palace and a totally unsuitable woman.

Despite the war between duty and desire raging within him, he couldn't leave her yet. He might have behaved like a sex-starved youth, taking her so quickly, but now he wanted to hold her, to feel every part of her against his body and give her the pleasure and satisfaction she deserved. He wanted her more than ever and the hours of darkness were still around them. This was still their night. Tomorrow would come soon enough.

Slowly he leant towards her and brushed his lips over hers, whispering against their softness, 'Can you forgive me?'

Her hand caressed his cheek before she kissed him. It was a soft lingering kiss which set fire to his blood all over again. No woman had ever made him feel so hot. Never had he lost control like that so spectacularly. Yes, it had been a long time since he'd sought the pleasure of a woman's body, but that was no excuse for such animalistic behaviour.

'Only if you take me to bed,' she said shyly and looked into his eyes.

'I promised you a night of pleasure—' just thinking about her naked body made his voice turn hoarse '—and there are many hours before dawn in which I intend to make amends.'

'Promises, promises,' she teased, her fine brows rising suggestively, her innocent eyes darkening with desire.

'This time,' he said, standing up, taking her hands and pulling her up to stand before him, 'we'll take it slowly.'

The air around them sparked with sexual tension as he began to remove the silks from her body. She moved with him, lifting her arms until everything was just a crumpled heap on the floor. He watched as she slid her hands behind her back, undid her bra and dropped it to the floor, leaving her completely naked.

'You're so beautiful,' he said, not wanting to touch her yet, wanting to gaze at her pale skin, glowing in the lamplight. His gaze moved down to her breasts, watch-

ing them move slightly with each breath she took, her
nipples dark, hard and so tempting.

Slowly he undid his shirt, enjoying the hungry look
in her eyes as she watched him. He dropped his shirt
on top of her discarded *abaya* and feasted his eyes on
the thick curls nestled in the apex of her thighs, feeling himself harden with desire.

'And the rest,' she said, stepping closer to him, her
light floral scent weaving around him once more.

He pulled the remaining foil packets from his
pocket, tossed them onto the bed and removed the
rest of his clothes, leaving only his underwear. She
quirked her brows suggestively and he pulled the silk
down over his hips and moved towards her, taking her
naked body against his.

He kissed her, delving his tongue deeply into her
mouth, entwining with hers, as his hands moved over
her silky skin. She was so beautiful. Tonight she was
his and if he discarded his duty and guilt it felt completely right, as if they were meant for one another.

Destiny savoured the warmth of his bronzed skin
against hers. Her breasts were so sensitive that the
coarse hair of his chest against her nipples almost
sent her over the edge again. She smoothed her hands
down his back, over his buttocks, pressing him closer
against her.

'Zafir,' she gasped as his lips left hers. She felt as
if she was the one about to lose control as thoughts of
pushing him back onto the bed and sitting astride him
ran riot in her head. She'd never done anything like
this before, had no idea how to take the lead. But with

him it was different, as if her body knew his and knew exactly what to do.

Swiftly he swept her off her feet, cradling her against him as he walked over to the bed. She pressed her cheek against the firmness of his chest and inhaled his virile musky scent. In that moment her whole body burned with need and she bit her lip as he placed her on the bed.

Naked and aroused, he stood before her. She drank him in, from the wide shoulders to his firm chest muscles and the dark chest hair which arrowed down over his flat stomach. With hands that shook slightly she reached out and touched him, the heat of him arousing her further. He groaned in pleasure as she wrapped her fingers around him, exploring and pleasuring him.

Suddenly his hand grasped hers and he swore in his native tongue, his voice rasping. 'You're pushing me too far,' he growled as he lowered his body down next to her. 'When I go I'm taking you with me and I'm not ready to go there yet, my little desert minx.'

Destiny arched her back as his fingers slid down over her stomach and into her curls, teasing her until she squirmed against his hand. Then, slowly, his fingers slid inside her and she bucked against him, closing her eyes, trying to hold on to herself.

'Let go,' he whispered as he leant over her, his tongue twirling around her nipple.

'Zafir...' she gasped as his fingers went deeper and his teeth nipped at her. 'It's too much.'

'Let go, Destiny,' he said against her breast, his breath warm on her moist skin.

Suddenly everything splintered around her and her body floated away on the tide of passion, drifting endlessly on sensations she'd never felt before. She could feel him kissing down over her stomach, but was powerless to move as the ebb of desire carried her away.

Slowly she came back to reality and opened her eyes and looked directly into Zafir's handsome smiling face. She pulled him to her, wanting his lips on hers once more. His body covered hers as he kissed her with fevered passion, then suddenly he moved, pulling her with him until she sat astride him.

A blush crept over her cheeks. Had he known that was what she'd wanted to do?

She leant down and kissed him tenderly, her hair falling forward, creating a dark curtain around them. His hands moved over her back and down to her bottom, bringing her intimately close to him, and he moved upwards to her, sliding deep inside. She moved with him until reality hit her like a flash of lightning across the night sky.

'Zafir,' she gasped as she felt him insistently moving within her, as if he was on the brink of losing control, of claiming her as his once more. 'Protection—we need protection.'

'See what you do to me,' he rasped out as he withdrew and reached for the condoms he'd carelessly tossed on the rumpled bed earlier.

She smiled down at him, kissing him once more, this time eagerly welcoming him into her. It was like nothing else she'd ever experienced and throwing back her head she cried out as he took her over that edge once more, his own ragged groan letting her know he was with her.

For some time after she lay on him, feeling the thud of his heartbeat slow and inhaling his smell, knowing it would be burnt into her memory for ever. Trying not to think of what tomorrow meant, she moved off him until her body was curled against his. His fingers traced a slow pattern over her naked back, becoming lighter as sleep claimed him.

A tinge of sadness formed around them as she lay against his sleeping body. She was painfully aware of the hours ticking by. This was all she ever would have of him. He'd warned her, but still her silly heart wished for more. What woman wouldn't with the man she'd fallen in love with?

Zafir stirred, moving against her naked body, pulling her close against him. He mumbled something in his native tongue. She didn't have a hope of knowing what he meant, so kissed him gently, smiling when, through the haze of sleep, he responded.

In the dim light before dawn she could see his eyes were heavy with sleepy desire and the simmering heat inside her bloomed once more. His lips were soft and coaxing, the urgency of earlier now forgotten in a moment which seemed more loving than passionate.

Slowly and more gently than she'd ever imagined possible, she became his once more, knowing that the first tendrils of dawn would soon be slipping across the sky and this would be the last time she would ever be his.

For the first night in a year Zafir had slept without the intrusion of nightmares of Tabinah. He knew why. The reason smiled shyly at him as he opened his eyes. 'Good morning, beautiful,' he said softly and brushed his lips over hers.

Why couldn't every morning be like this? Why couldn't every night be like last night?

He felt his body tense as the answer hit him as if he'd woken to one of England's cold and frosty mornings. Nights and mornings could never be like this because he was the ruler of his kingdom and a man who *had* to put duty before his own needs.

'I really don't want to—' he moved to prop himself on his arm and look down on her; with dark hair spread across the pillow and passion-dazed eyes looking at him, he had to steel his body against the urge to make love to her one last time '—but it's time I left. I am already late for my morning ride and wish to avoid any speculation.'

'I know.' She smiled up at him and his chest constricted, making breathing difficult for a moment. 'We had one night. Now we must return to our own worlds.'

He blinked in shock, not having expected her to be so brutally honest. It dented his male pride to think she didn't want to cling. Already he knew it would make his need for her stronger, more intense, but he couldn't waver. He had to move forward in his life, do his duty, not just for his kingdom but the memory of Tabinah. It was time to select a bride from those who'd been chosen for him.

'Yes, Destiny, we must.'

He thought of the meetings planned for later that month, meetings that would procure him a bride— the woman with whom he would produce heirs for his country.

He clenched his jaw.

Duty again.

Always duty.

Duty had destroyed his relationship with Tabi-nah, forcing her to take such drastic actions. Those actions and his guilt now dictated that duty was his only choice.

CHAPTER SEVEN

LATER THAT DAY Destiny found concentrating on her work harder than ever, especially when Zafir arrived to watch her working with Majeed. She could barely function, just thinking of him and the hours they'd shared last night. Each image which came to her mind made her heart flutter and her pulse race. It certainly had been a night she would never forget, but it was over and time to move back to a professional relationship.

One quick glance at Zafir as he stood watching her, arms folded, his expression almost fierce, confirmed that. He would be expecting nothing but detached professionalism from her and that was what he'd get.

One night was all he'd been able to give. One night was all she'd wanted. One night to imagine what being loved would be like, but she hadn't anticipated it would be this hard the next day. She'd thought she was freeing herself, allowing herself to sample the pleasures of being with a man like Zafir without the complications of love, which for her mother had been the start of all her trouble.

Focus, she told herself as dust from Majeed's hooves in the sand rose around her. She was here to do a job. What had happened last night was not and never would be part of that arrangement. But, try as she might, she couldn't keep her mind from wandering and she certainly couldn't continue working with Majeed. Not with Zafir's brooding presence so close. She'd told him once she preferred to work without an audience, but perhaps it was time he was reminded of that, put herself back in control.

As if sensing her distraction, Majeed came to a halt and looked at her, his eyes watchful and his ears alert. She had at least gained the stallion's trust, but she knew that gaining Zafir's trust would never be possible. For whatever reason, he shut himself away and even last night, in the depth of passion as they first made love, he had guarded his soul. In the hours that followed, before dawn had lightened the room, she'd seen the real man and what being loved by Zafir could be like. It made her long for more, but she knew it was a futile dream.

'That's enough for today,' she said to Majeed and the stallion walked towards her and waited until she began to lead him back to his stable.

'You have made remarkable progress with him.' Zafir's words warmed her and not just because he was pleased, but because he was close—much too close.

She should have expected Zafir to join her. Of course he would want to know just how well his horse was responding to the hours she was spending each day with him. What she hadn't expected was the way her body heated, the way her skin tingled and the way her stomach somersaulted as he walked beside her or the way she yearned to have him close.

Thank goodness the stable boy was around to take Majeed from her. She was in grave danger of turning to Zafir in the hope he'd take her into his arms and kiss her as he had done last night. She knew they couldn't have any more so why was she grieving for something she'd never really had?

'I am confident that he will go beyond the palace walls before I leave.' Home was the last thing she wanted to think of. The idea of returning to England and leaving behind the man she'd given her virginity to was too much. How could she possibly turn her back on what they had?

But what did they have? He'd made it clear it was for one night only, that there could be no more than that.

'Walk with me back to the palace.' He didn't look at her and the superior tilt of his chin warned her it was far from a request. Unexpected anger zipped through her. He expected her to do just as he wanted, proving he was as controlling as her father. But didn't he have a right to be? He was her boss, even if temporarily, *and* he was a Sheikh, a ruler. Didn't that give him every right to want to be in control?

'We do not have an escort,' she pointed out, challenging him and his superiority.

He watched as the stable boy led Majeed away, then he turned to her, his eyes dark and his brows heavy. She couldn't help but look at his full lips and remember the kiss that had set fire to her so spectacularly. She could still feel the roughness of his trimmed beard on her skin.

'I don't give a damn. After last night things have changed.' The intensity in his voice shocked her.

'Nothing has changed, Zafir. I will return to England in a month and you will select your bride. Last night changed nothing. You made that very clear and I accepted it.' How could she be so bold, standing her ground so strongly when her whole body hungered for just one last caress, one final kiss?

He took her arm and led her casually away from the stables, but from the rigid line of his back she knew he was feeling far from casual. As they entered the cool arched walkways that ran the length of the palace, he stopped, forcing her to do the same. She turned to look up at him, noting the firm set of his jaw.

'Do you really expect me to forget last night so easily?' His voice deepened, the sensual tones sending an exotic shiver all over her.

'It is what you wanted.' She kept her words firm, not wanting him to know just how much she really wished he couldn't forget last night.

'Things have changed.'

'What things?'

'You gave me a precious gift and after such a gift I do not intend to turn my back on you yet.'

Destiny's mind fumbled for answers. What was he talking about? 'A gift?'

He stepped closer to her and she had to fight the urge to close her eyes against his scent. 'You gave me your virginity, Destiny. Have you any idea how potent that is? Or what it means to me?'

'I don't understand.' Was he saying he still wanted her, that what they'd shared was special?

'You are now mine.' His voice had softened, becoming so sensually seductive it was impossible to do anything other than look up at him, into the unfathomable darkness of his eyes. Her heart raced. Zafir didn't want to turn his back on her or the passion they'd shared, but his next fierce words shattered that illusion. 'I will come to your suite tonight.'

So it was all about possession—his possession of her.

Before she could say anything else, Zafir's aide came briskly towards them and she wondered how long he'd been near and if he'd seen them or, worse still, heard Zafir's words.

The thought of Zafir returning to her suite this evening sent ripples of excitement through her, despite his obvious domination. The tingles of excitement intensified as he looked across at her, the first sparks of desire in his eyes, and she could barely walk calmly beside the two men as they made their way along the maze of corridors.

Once again, Zafir stopped abruptly as they neared the guest suites. His aide thankfully walked ahead and then paused, but the suspicious frown on his face didn't disappear when Zafir moved close enough to her to whisper quietly, 'I will send your maid.'

'Mina? Why?'

'Doesn't every woman enjoy being pampered? Especially when she is expecting her lover.' His dark brows snapped together, but the polite cough of his aide prevented anything further and Destiny was left to watch him turn and stride away in a flurry of white cloth.

Was that what she now was? His lover?

Very soon, Zafir's intentions became clear when Mina all but forced her into a deep scented bath and began what Zafir had referred to as pampering. Did he ensure all his women were treated this way? Was she now one of his women? His latest mistress?

Zafir made his way through the palace gardens as night fell. All afternoon he'd thought of nothing else but Destiny, her soft pale skin, her silky hair and brown eyes which always held a hint of shyness. She was there in his mind with everything he did and had been since he'd first seen her that day at her home. Last night had only intensified that.

He thought again of the moment he'd realised she was a virgin. Had she any idea of the implications of allowing him to be the man who took that from her? She should have told him. It was something he'd needed to know, something he'd had no right to take. Deep down he was profoundly glad she hadn't said anything because, if she had, his conscience would never have allowed him to make love to her and he would never have known such completeness as he'd experienced last night. It had been so intense, as if they were destined to have come together.

His body hummed with anticipation as he entered the small private garden of her suite. He expected to find a contented and pampered Destiny waiting for his arrival, but she sat curled on the cushions in the living area of her suite, a cold and distant expression on her beautiful face as she looked up at him.

'Would you mind telling me what this is all about?' She held out her arms to show off the silk of her outfit, the kind worn by women all over his country, giving them modesty, but on Destiny it fuelled his ardour, making him want nothing more than to remove the bright coloured silk. The short tone of her words was the only thing holding him back from taking her in his arms and continuing what they had started last night.

'You did not enjoy the pampering?' He was so stunned he couldn't move and strangely found himself not in control of either his emotions or the situation.

'Any woman would enjoy all that has been lavished

on me this afternoon—if they were a woman of your harem.' The last words were spat at him, reminding him of the feral cats that roamed the old city's streets, hissing and spitting if anyone got too close.

Despite his earlier reassurances, she truly believed he had a harem—and that she was now one of his women! The idea was so absurd he laughed, which only irritated her further. With fury burning in her eyes she stood up, looking almost as lovely as she had when passion and desire had replaced her usual shyness last night.

'I do not have a harem. That is not my way. I am a man of honour and have been faithful to any woman I have had a relationship with, as I will to my future wife from the moment our marriage is announced.' A sliver of guilt sliced through him. He had honoured the rules his father had instilled in him as a teenager. He'd kept his affairs brief and far away from the palace—until last night. Honour was something he believed in as strongly as duty. Nothing would ever change that, not even a beautiful Western woman who'd sent spirals of turmoil through his life from the moment he'd first set eyes on her.

'So why this?' Again she held her arms wide, the silk of the gown she wore clinging to her curves in a way he'd never noticed on other women.

'I thought only of your comfort. You work hard. Hot dusty work. I thought you'd appreciate feeling more feminine.'

'Well, I certainly feel more feminine now.' She walked across the room away from him and sat at the farthest point she could, but he would not be deterred. His body still hungered for her, still wanted her, and he knew she was far from indifferent to him. Just as he had when he'd led the life of a single man, he was enjoying the chase, the challenge.

He poured a cool drink, passing her one, then purposefully walked towards her before taking a seat opposite her. He took a sip of the cool lemonade he'd learnt she was partial to and then placed his glass on a nearby table.

'That pleases me.' He held her gaze as a spark of attraction fizzed around them. 'And now I'd like to talk.'

'Talk?'

He might want to take her to bed and make her his once more, but after last night he needed to know more about her life, her reasons for making such a hard deal with him. Somehow she'd ensnared his interest, his passion and all he wanted was to know more—much more.

Her defensive attitude warned him he needed to use caution—that she could bolt as easily as an unbroken horse. He had no idea why, but he couldn't let her go now. Not yet.

'Yes, talk. Do you have an objection to that?'

'No.' She looked doubtful but her voice was much less defensive. 'What do you want to talk about?'

He knew he should address the concerns his aide had tentatively raised only hours after his aide had seen him leaving her room. He'd been warned she would be expecting more than he could give. The direct and unusually outspoken but trusted aide's voice was grating on his nerves. Were the palace walls so alive that his night with this woman had become common knowledge?

The thought angered him as much as the marriage

he must make for the good of his country. He was not ready for that commitment yet, but had no choice. He needed an heir.

Destiny's mind whirled. Zafir had sent Mina to pamper her until the whole suite was fragranced with new and exotic smells. She'd dressed her in gorgeous new silks and, although the maid had said nothing, Destiny was sure she'd known it was her ruler's intention to visit her at nightfall. He might not have a harem, but it appeared that spending the night in a woman's suite was accepted and maybe expected.

Now she sat alone, far from relaxed, and trying to put aside the hurt that he thought he could make her little better than his mistress while she'd given him her heart. Not that she'd ever let him know that.

The only sounds in the suite were those of the desert at night but, inside her head, her heart was thumping as she waited. Anger at his assumption she would go along with his demands and excitement at seeing him again, of having him to herself for a few short hours, mixed together in a swirl of confusion, making her light-headed. When he'd silently walked in from the inky blackness of the palace gardens he'd looked even more magnificent than he had last night. This time he wore his robes, their whiteness stark against the darkness behind him, and she had to fight the urge to go to him, to accept anything he was offering because this time he was Zafir, the Sheikh of Kezoban, a man to be obeyed.

'We need to talk, Zafir,' she said as firmly as she could manage, but the husky undertone to her voice didn't sound very convincing and she resisted the urge to add that she wanted to clarify that he expected nothing more of her because she didn't want to expose herself to the pain of love. She couldn't allow herself to feel anything for him and would have to guard her heart against it because she didn't want to be like her mother.

'Yes, we do.' He stood before her, as regal and handsome as he looked standing in his office as the ruler of Kezoban. 'I would like to know more about you, more of your time in England.'

His dark eyes never left her face and, even though distance separated them, she could feel him close to her. Her body was warm and content after last night, wanting more of those wonderful hours spent in his arms. She wanted to be his once more.

'Is this some sort of test to see if I am suitable mistress material for the supreme Sheikh of Kezoban?' She couldn't alter her defensive attitude. It was her wall of protection. Behind that wall she was safe, able to control whatever it was that had leapt to life between them last night as soon as his lips had touched hers, as if he'd branded her his.

'There is only one woman who can be suitable, as you know. The woman I select to be my wife, the mother of my heirs.' His tone had changed to icy-cold and she knew she was playing a dangerous game, but she needed to play it, needed to cruelly prove to herself there wasn't any future in wanting a man such as Zafir Al Asmari, Sheikh of Kezoban.

'So what are you doing here?' Her heart broke a little as the implications of his words sliced through her. She'd lost her virginity to him, given him her heart, yet she would never be anything else to him other than just another woman. She would never be suitable.

'It is my belief that our paths were destined to cross, as your name suggests. You were meant to be here, meant to heal Majeed. I see now that you have healed me, enabled me to move on to the next chapter of my life.' The firmness of his words left her in no doubt that he actually believed everything he'd just said, but what about the things he hadn't said? Did he believe it was his right to take her heart and break it, while she healed his?

Anger simmered dangerously close to the surface.

'And what is that next chapter? Your marriage?' Why did she feel so disillusioned? She'd known long before his scorching kiss that he was about to take a wife, that he needed a son. Even as she'd given herself to him, she'd known there would be nothing beyond that night. He'd made that perfectly clear and she'd thought she was in control. His presence here again tonight proved how wrong she'd been. He had been in control all along.

He stood and came towards her. Her heart fluttered at a ridiculous rate, making her light-headed.

'I want to know why.' He sat next to her, the exotic spices of his scent opening up memories of their night together, making images of their bodies entwined on the white sheets of her bed spring to mind.

'Why what?'

'You were a virgin, Destiny. Why me? Why last night?' He leant towards her, his dark eyes heavy with desire. Was he recalling their first night together as vividly as she was?

'I wanted to give myself to a man who wouldn't ask for more, a man who couldn't have any control over my feelings.' Heat rushed over her, colouring her cheeks and she lowered her lashes. How could he ask her that so boldly, so calmly, as if he had a right to know everything about her?

'What did you hope to gain, coming to Kezoban?'

'Gain?' Shock raced through her. He thought she'd slept with him for gain? Fury quickly doused all other emotions. 'I have only one thing to gain from being here in your country.'

'And that is?' His heavy brows rose, arching in total superiority. What had she been thinking, giving herself to this man, falling for him like a teenager? He was nothing if not in total control of everyone and everything. He was worse than her father.

'My freedom.'

Now it was his turn to be shocked and she enjoyed the moment of satisfaction that she'd been able to knock the wind from him. But it was short-lived. As ever, he was quickly back in control, quickly able to hide his emotions behind a stern and commanding expression.

'Explain.' The order was all but snarled at her.

He'd baited her long enough, see-sawing her emotions from extreme highs to lows at his whim and now she was angry.

'My father is exactly like you.'

He laughed, a bitter sound, his contempt clear. 'That is not possible.'

'Oh, but it is. He is cold, hard and equally as driven as you, but the trait you have in common is the need to control people, to dominate.' The tirade wouldn't stop and all her hurt from the past collided with her confusion about this man, making an explosive cocktail. 'I only agreed to be here so that, like my sister, I could escape his and my stepmother's rule. I need to finally begin my life now that I no longer have to look out for Milly.'

'Explain.' Again that one word snapped out in a furious command.

'My mother married my father when she realised she was expecting me. It was a marriage that would not have happened otherwise. She loved him but he did not love her. I wish I could have asked her more about it, but sadly she died giving birth to my sister. As Milly and I grew up, my father became harder and more controlling. I have helped Milly to set herself up in London and now I intend to do the same.'

'And that is why you drove such a hard bargain before agreeing to come to Kezoban?'

'Precisely. When I thought I was dealing with your aide—if you remember?'

'Then it is wealth you crave?'

'Why else would I be here? Why else would I have tried to seduce you?'

If he thought she was only sitting here with him, dressed like a woman from a sultan's harem, to get as much as possible financially from him, then so much the better. He wouldn't want to whisper tantalising sweet nothings as they made love and her heart would be safe. It would make creating distance between them so much easier.

'If it is only money you want, then I have a new deal to put to you.'

'What kind of deal?' Her head spun. He'd turned the tables yet again to his advantage. Once more he was in control.

'In less than three weeks I have to announce my marriage. Arranged marriages are not made for anything other than material gain. Therefore, I want to enjoy my remaining weeks as an unmarried man— with you.'

What was he trying to say? 'You mean you want to buy me? Pay me to be your mistress until you take a wife?'

Shock raced around her like lightning across a black sky. How could that one passion-filled night have come to this? He'd made it very clear that they would only have one night and now he was dangling more, much more, before her, tempting her, but would it be enough? Instinctively, she knew she had to be as cold and calculating as he was. She had to demand more from him, be the woman he obviously thought she was.

'I want only to make a deal that will give us both what we want.' He snapped the words out, his impatience as clear as a star-filled night.

'Very well. Double our original deal.' She kept her voice hard and her face set firmly as she looked at him, wishing with all her heart he was asking her to stay because he wanted her. How could she still want him, still hunger for anything he could give? Her childhood had taught her there was only one way to deal with such a man—to stay behind her protective barrier and be equally as cold.

Irritation and anger infused Zafir as Destiny made her demands, just as she'd done the day he'd first seen her. At least this time he knew her motives. His aide had been right, but that still didn't lessen the sexual chemistry which sizzled between them.

For the first time ever he didn't care about anything else. He wanted her—at whatever cost, emotional or financial, he didn't care. He had to spend every available minute with her before he entered into a contracted marriage, one that duty to his kingdom and guilt for the loss of his sister demanded he made.

'It doesn't have to be so businesslike,' he said softly and moved towards her, wanting to abandon himself once more to the ecstasy he'd found last night. Now she'd named her price and they'd struck a deal, he wanted to bring things back to how they'd been last night, when they had been nothing more than lovers coming together. A brief and passionate interlude in time.

She didn't move away from him and the parting of her lips told him all he needed to know. Despite her rigid posture as she sat among the cushions, she was as drawn to him as he was her. As compelled by desire as she had been last night. She was still his.

'But we have just made a deal. Doesn't that mean it is business?' Her voice was a whisper. Only hints of her earlier bravado lingered.

'We have just discussed the terms of our deal, yes, terms that will give us both what we want.' He stroked the back of his finger down the softness of her cheek, the quickly drawn in breath telling him all he needed to know. 'Now forget it. We need to explore the fire between us until it dwindles to cool embers.'

'What *is* between us, Zafir?' The earnestly asked question halted him and he looked into those soft brown eyes, now swirling with desire. How could he answer that when he didn't know himself? Damn it, he didn't even want anything to be between them. She could not be his destiny, his future, despite her name.

'Something that shouldn't be there, but is.' He

looked at her lips, so soft and inviting, wanting nothing more than to feel them beneath his. Whatever it was that had exploded to life between them that one night was now calling to him again. He was like a man possessed. All he wanted was her. 'And I cannot walk away from it—not yet, not until every last flame has been extinguished.'

'One night,' she whispered as her pupils enlarged, obliterating the soft brown of her eyes almost completely. 'That was all you said we could have. Just one night. So why more?'

'I have a duty to perform, Destiny. I must select a bride from a list chosen for me. Duty is the mantra by which I have lived my life and marriage is a duty I cannot avoid, but I am not yet married and, for a short while, I want to give us a chance to explore the attraction which exists between us. Can you deny it is there now, drawing us closer, despite everything?'

'But…'

He silenced her protest, pressing his lips to hers, kissing her like a man who'd been in the desert for many days. As he pulled her close, he relished the feel of her body against his and knew he didn't care about anything other than making her his once more. For two weeks he was free to be a different man, one not bound by duty and obligation to his kingdom.

For two weeks she would be his.

CHAPTER EIGHT

FOR TWO WEEKS Destiny had lost herself in the oblivion of being with Zafir and she had to force herself to remember it was nothing more than lust, that she was in Kezoban only to secure her future and her freedom from her father. It would be so easy to fall in love with Zafir and it was only the knowledge that she was just his latest mistress that kept her from doing so.

There had been times she'd wanted to call and confide in her sister, but the mere fact that she was having such a relationship with a man like Zafir would set the alarm bells ringing for Milly and she didn't want to worry her when they were so far apart. Neither did she want to admit that those alarm bells were also sounding in her own head.

Zafir represented everything she'd always wanted to avoid in a man. He was controlling, dominating and so handsome women would surely fall at his feet. And she'd done the same, as if drawn by forces she had no understanding of and little ability to resist.

As days had turned to weeks, she'd known he would announce it was over, that it was time for him to do his duty and select his bride. But how could she go back to her life in England and forget the passion, the desire they'd shared each and every night?

The first light of dawn crept in, tracing intricate patterns on the marble floor as it shone through the carvings around the archway and, as always, it signalled Zafir's return to his suite, to his duty as the Sheikh of Kezoban. But, just as last night had felt different, this morning was different too.

Instinctively, she knew exactly what was happening—their time together had come to an end. His insatiable need for her last night had been about goodbye, but she wished he'd warned her. Instead now she would have to pack up all the memories of being with Zafir and stand back whilst he chose his bride.

'I am leaving the palace today.' He turned onto his side, propping himself on his elbow and looked at her, but she couldn't meet his gaze, not when her mind was so full of wishful thinking. 'I shall be away for at least a week.'

She forced herself to be as strong as he was and sat up in bed, looking at him, but she didn't trust herself to say anything, not yet, not when her emotions were so dazed by something she'd known all along would happen.

Zafir sat up, pulling her close, kissing her with a passion which lingered from the night and she couldn't help herself. She moved closer against his naked body, the sheets of the bed only just allowing her some modesty.

'And when you return, you will be engaged.' It wasn't a question but a statement. She'd known all along that she could never be more than a passing affair for him, his final mistress before he married, but it still hurt, still cut deep.

He sighed as he moved, swinging his legs to sit on the edge of the bed, giving her a tantalising view of his strong bronzed back. She wanted to reach out and stroke her fingers over his skin, to feel his strength and power in every muscle, but he was no longer hers, even though she would always be his.

'It is my duty.' He stood up and, unashamedly naked, crossed the white marble floor to the robes he'd discarded last night with such haste. She drank him in, committing every last bit of him to memory. He pulled the white robes over his body and his dark gaze met hers across the expanse of her bedroom, the fire of passion now extinguished. Already he'd distanced himself. 'I am expected to produce heirs for my country.'

'I know,' she said firmly, determined not to cling to him or what they'd shared. She would show nothing but dignity and strength. 'My work with Majeed is almost complete and I will soon return to my life in England.'

She forced herself to think professionally, although her state of undress made that difficult, and clutched the sheet against her. She had to remember why she was here, why she'd even agreed to Zafir's demand that she work with his horse. She was in danger of falling in love with a man who could never love her, just as her mother had done. Replicating more of her mother's life story was her biggest fear.

The ever-present shadow of how her mother had died haunted her, making motherhood an almost impossible choice. So even if Zafir told her right now he wanted to make her his wife, she couldn't, not when children would be of paramount importance. She just couldn't risk leaving her child alone in the world, not when she and Milly knew only too well what it was like to lose their mother so young.

'You will come to my office before I leave—to discuss Majeed's progress.' The briskness of his tone told her he'd already switched from lover to Sheikh. What they'd shared was over.

'As you wish.' There was a crisp edge to her voice too, one born out of the need to survive. 'Once I have finished working Majeed, I will come directly to your office.'

He stopped and looked at her, his eyes as black as midnight, glittering in a way she'd never seen before. His heavy brows snapped together and she instinctively clutched the sheet tighter against her. This was not the way she'd envisaged their affair ending, not with such harshness on his handsome face.

He didn't say anything but held her gaze for a moment longer before striding out of the room and towards the doors which led to the palace gardens, as usual avoiding being seen by anyone in the palace. She knew he would now ride in the desert, then attend his duties before flying his hawk, a routine he'd kept to for the last two weeks. Had that been as cover for their secret nights together?

Pain rushed through her. Why had she allowed herself to become not only his mistress, but his secret mistress? A guilty pleasure he could never acknowledge. She'd barely even kissed a man before she'd arrived in Kezoban. So what had changed so drastically?

She was late. Zafir paced his office, waiting for Destiny to report on Majeed's progress, still irritated by her cool acceptance of his intended departure and now her inability to keep her word. He seriously considered marching down to the stables to see her. Had she been so pliant over the ending of their affair because she thought she had new power over him?

That would be a serious error of judgement. Nobody had power over him. He was the only son of the Sheikh of Kezoban—he'd been taught to be commanding even from a young age. Anything less would have been to let his father down, a man he'd admired and wanted to please. When his father had died he'd become the youngest ruler Kezoban had ever had at just twenty-four and now, six years later, the days of doing what he wanted were over. He had a duty to his people, his country—even Tabinah had failed to understand that.

He growled an oath, causing his aide to look suspiciously at him. For the first time in his life he wished he didn't have a duty to honour to his country. He wished he could be free to be the man Destiny wanted. The man she needed. He'd had affairs before, broken the ties many times, but never had it been as hard as this morning. As she'd looked at him, defiance shining in her eyes, he'd forced himself to remember that duty *had* to come first, which meant his feelings towards Destiny must be sacrificed. He'd made his father a promise just before he'd died, to always put his duty to Kezoban before anything and it was one promise he intended to keep.

As if conjured up by his thoughts, a servant entered, escorting Destiny to his office. This would be the last time he saw her before duty consumed him, taking him along the path of an arranged marriage. He had no real wish for marriage, but after Tabinah's death it was necessary, not only for the succession of his family as rulers of Kezoban, but for the promise he'd made to his father.

As Destiny walked in, he noticed her chin was just a little higher than usual and a spark of defiance glittered in those lovely eyes. Was this as hard for her as it was for him? Did she yearn for more nights like those they'd shared? He pushed the thought savagely aside. That was all in the past and it was time to do his duty and move forward.

'How is Majeed?' He kept the subject on the reason for her presence here in his kingdom, in his life. The reason she'd driven such a hard bargain. If he asked how she was, he would want more. He would want to hold her, to kiss her and make her his again, but he'd done that in the early hours for the last time and it couldn't happen again.

'His progress is good. He is responding well now and my work will very soon be complete.' She looked straight at him, her eyes hard, almost brittle. Beside him, he knew his aide was watching them. He could feel the other man's questions and suspicion, sense the scrutiny that was barely concealed. Anger simmered inside him. If it was so noticeable that there was something between him and Destiny then all his care to protect not only her reputation but his had been to no avail.

He'd never before so much as touched a woman in his palace. The life of a bachelor prince had been played out on foreign shores. The fact that Destiny had tempted him to even consider such an affair, right here in his palace, spoke volumes for the intensity of the attraction he had for her. But he could not act on it any longer.

Zafir turned on his aide, the harshness of his voice

unintended. 'Leave us,' he commanded in English so that Destiny would know what had been said.

'Sire?' the man questioned as he looked at him.

'Leave us.' The command in his voice reverberated around the white walls of his office and for a moment he thought he saw Destiny flinch, but when he looked at her properly she was as defiant as he'd ever seen her—and beautiful.

'I thought discretion was needed.' Her words slammed into him as the door of his office closed with a loud click behind his aide. 'If that little display doesn't alert suspicion it will be a miracle.'

'I am the Sheikh and I am about to leave the palace to meet with the families of potential brides. I insist on just a few moments alone with you.' The words fired out as he gave vent to his irritation.

Her gorgeous brown eyes, so full of emotion, sparked with fury as she glared back at him. Her lips were parted and he remembered how she'd kissed him as passion had engulfed her. She was beautiful, tantalising and almost everything he needed in a woman— but it could never be. He would be a fool to consider continuing with such a union. How could he when he'd forced Tabinah into an arranged marriage, making her so unhappy she'd fled the palace under the cover of darkness?

'We've had every night for the last two weeks, Zafir. Each and every one of them was more than "one night." It's time to move on with our own paths in life—different paths which should never have crossed.'

She stood firm and rigid. Was she so immune to him, so closed to the pain of saying goodbye that she could stand there like a regal princess who'd been trained since childhood to be so aloof? Such natural poise and decorum proved she could be a suitable bride.

Where had that thought come from? He'd never considered Destiny as anything other than a lover, even though she'd been a virgin. They were of different worlds, different cultures and beliefs, brought together only by their common interest in horses.

Zafir looked at her again, as if seeing her with new eyes. Sunlight streamed in around her from the archways and beyond her lay the desert and, dressed as she was, in clothing of his country, she looked as if she belonged, as if she'd been created especially for the role. Especially for him.

But being his wife was a role. The woman he married would need to be strong of mind and wilful in spirit. She would need to be someone the women of his country could look up to but at the same time she had to be prepared to be one of them. More importantly, she would need to provide him with healthy male heirs to continue his family's rule and enable him to fulfil the promise he'd made to his dying father.

Fury boiled up. How could he consider marriage for his own selfish reasons when he'd denied Tabinah exactly that?

'You shouldn't have dismissed him.' Destiny's sharp words snapped him back from the brink of thoughts of what could never be. When he looked at her everything in her stance seemed to confirm not only that she could be all the things he needed but that she was, as if fate was pulling them ever closer.

'You are right.' He turned and marched to the ornate arched window which looked out over the desert, the vastness as empty as his life now seemed, knowing Destiny would no longer be in it. But she was right. She had a life in England and he had duty to his family name, his country.

He refocused his thoughts. 'I should not have sent him away. It was remiss of me.'

As he turned to face her once more, he thought he saw disappointment on her face. He watched as she swallowed, and remembered kissing her neck, tasting the pale creamy skin as she'd lain beneath him, totally consumed by desire.

He shouldn't be having such thoughts. Passion and desire had never played a serious part in his life. Never had he been able to live far from the shadow cast by the role he'd been born into and yet, somehow, something was changing, shifting like the desert sands, making him long for something different, challenging the duty and honour which drove him.

'I will leave before you return from your trip.' The tone of her voice gave nothing away and he fought hard against the urge to go to her, to pull her into his arms and make her come back to life, make her want to be his again. This Destiny was cold. Too cold.

'As you wish.' He stood behind the gilt-trimmed desk, hoping to gain some strength from its solidness. He'd never been this emotionally weakened before, but then he'd never had two weeks of passion-filled nights with a woman who set every nerve on fire and stirred needs and desires he'd constantly pushed aside. 'I will make the arrangements. Mina will inform you when it is done.'

Destiny opened her eyes and, just as had happened for the last two mornings since Zafir had left, a heavy weight of despair settled over her, pressing her into the bed. It was still early and she tried to close her eyes and sleep, but the hurt caused by Zafir's lack of emotion or any hint of compassion as they'd talked in his office made her feel physically sick.

She turned restlessly in the bed to face the windows, watching as the daylight chased the darkness away, remembering Zafir leaving her bed, often reluctantly, to slip quietly through the gardens and back to his suite before resuming his usual routine.

That man had been a different man to the Sheikh she'd last faced, the one who was now able to switch off his emotions, making her doubt he'd ever had them. It hurt to acknowledge the last two weeks had all been about sex for him, his final act of recklessness before he settled down to do his duty—marriage for the good of his country.

It should have been as unimportant for her too. It was how she'd wanted it to be. She turned in bed again, trying to push back what she felt, deny its existence, but she couldn't.

She'd done the worst thing possible. She'd fallen in love with Zafir.

She closed her eyes against the pain of knowing he'd never love her and tried to ignore the nausea which claimed her, churning her stomach so severely she wanted to cry. She never cried. She was strong—she'd had to be and she always would be—but now she was so low, so heartbroken she couldn't even face dressing and going to the stables.

For the first time since she'd arrived in Kezoban there wasn't the smallest amount of pleasure or excitement in spending several hours working with such a magnificent stallion as Majeed. With a groan she buried her head beneath the pillow and begged for the oblivion of sleep.

When she woke again it was late and Mina had arrived with a breakfast tray. It was a treat she usually relished, but this morning, knowing she'd said goodbye to the man she'd given her heart to, breakfast, no matter how enticing, was the last thing she wanted.

Her stomach lurched and, without her usual greeting to Mina, she slipped quickly from the bed, dashing to the bathroom, where she splashed cold water on her face in an attempt to quell the heaviness which sat like lead inside her. She looked at the pale reflection of herself and closed her eyes against the washed-out image. How had she come to this? How had a man penetrated all her barriers and attacked her heart? She'd never wanted to be so vulnerable, always telling herself she would never love a man who didn't show her love. Yet she'd done just that when she'd fallen for Zafir.

Finally she returned to her room to find Mina had set out her breakfast on the table beside the open doors which led to the terrace and the gardens, but the idea of sitting and eating was the last thing she wanted to do. In fact just the thought brought the earlier nausea back with a vengeance.

'I have made a new tea for you,' Mina said in her accented and gentle voice, making her sound very motherly, which provoked a new urge to succumb to tears. 'It will help to put some colour back into your pale face.'

Destiny was too emotionally out of sorts to argue or be aggrieved at the comment and sat looking out at the garden and the path which wound its way through the exotic plants towards Zafir's private garden—the path he'd walked many times as he'd secretly visited her to spend the night in her bed. Nights that would never happen again.

Destiny took a sip of the warm tea, more to please Mina than to satisfy any need of her own for food or drink. The tea was fresh and reviving and settled the heartbroken queasiness of her stomach. Was this what it was like to be lovesick?

'This is good.' She smiled at Mina, who looked pleased. 'I guess I'm feeling a little homesick.'

'You do not like my country?' The older woman's smile had dropped and a worried frown creased her brow. Destiny realised she would miss Mina's kindness when she left.

'I love Kezoban. I'm really happy here, but my work with Majeed is almost over and it's time to think about going home. In fact can you arrange for me to leave earlier than planned?'

Once the words were said and she'd committed herself to leaving Kezoban, Destiny's sense of equilibrium returned. Today she would ride Majeed out of the palace. He was ready and had been for some time. She'd just put it off in order to stay in the dreamlike state she and Zafir had lived in for two weeks. But all that was over. Zafir had had enough of being the playboy Sheikh meeting his mistress in secret and wanted to return to being the duty-bound man his country believed him to be.

She had what she wanted—distance from her father's control—and, thanks to the deal she'd struck with Zafir, a means to start her new life in a flat near Milly. Thoughts of her sister crowded in on her and, not for the first time, she wished she could talk to her, but there would be time enough for that when she returned to England. Right now she had one more hurdle to cross with Majeed, then her job would be completed. She would be free to go, but she knew she'd never be entirely free of this desert land or its ruler. He would always be in her heart.

She dressed in her usual clothes for working with Majeed and Mina watched as she returned from the bedroom, an uncustomary look of concern on the older woman's face. She liked Mina, who was like the mother figure she'd lost when her mother had died so suddenly. Tears prickled at the back of her eyes as she thought of not having Mina around and inwardly she cursed the unfamiliar highly emotional state she'd slipped into.

She really must sort herself out. It was time to regain control of her life once more. Time to move on and admit her newly realised love was a lost cause. Zafir had made it clear when he'd bartered for more time with her that it could never be permanent or public. She only had herself to blame and now it was time to put it all behind her. She would finish her work with Majeed and leave.

Several hours later, she realised she'd had no idea of the time—she'd been so pleased with Majeed's progress, his trust in her—until the nausea had combined with tiredness and heat, forcing her to seek shade. She knew she shouldn't have stayed out so long. The sun scorched down on her and, despite the scarf which covered her hair, she felt as if she was on fire.

The shade of the large rocks at the foot of the mountains she'd ridden past with Zafir the morning of their ride would offer some respite from the heat and a chance for both her and Majeed to rest.

The stallion stood silently after she'd slipped to the ground to sit on a rock. She tried to push from her mind the story of Zafir's sister being bitten by a venomous snake, taking comfort in the fact that Majeed was calm, which meant he at least didn't sense any danger.

'Just a little while and then we will head back,' she said as much to herself as the horse. Suddenly Majeed's head lifted, his ears pricked forward. 'What is it?'

Destiny hoped it was someone and not something that the horse had heard, but when he whinnied she almost jumped and forced her weary limbs to move as she stood, gathering up the reins and trying to ignore the way her head spun. 'We'd better go.'

With more effort than she'd ever needed, she mounted Majeed and, as she pushed him out from the shade of the large rocks, he whinnied again. She glanced quickly around, anxiously scanning the ground for slithering forms, but the pounding of approaching hooves made her look up and out towards the desert sands.

Zafir.

What was he doing here?

Like a fantasy image, he was riding fast towards her, the long grey mane of the stallion flying out and his robes joining in the speed-induced dance. A cloud of dust billowed behind him and all she could think about was that he'd come for her, that he couldn't stay away, that wanted to be with her.

As he drew closer, Majeed shifted restlessly but that didn't alarm her nearly as much as the anger she saw etched in Zafir's face, anger which didn't fit with the thoughts she'd just been having. Once again she'd got it all wrong.

He pulled his grey stallion to a halt, dust spiralling from the ground, and Majeed spun round, anticipating some excitement after standing quietly in the shade with her. She tried to keep her gaze focused on Zafir but the effort made her dizzier than she cared to admit.

'What are you doing here?' she snapped at him, trying hard to control the thud of her heart at the image he created. He looked wild and untamed and the thud of desire leapt to life within her. As Majeed continued to prance excitedly her stomach lurched uncomfortably.

'I could ask the same of you. Have you taken leave of your senses?' His raised voice was hard, killing any last hope of him wanting her.

'I was doing my job. The one you contracted me for. To take Majeed out beyond the palace walls.' Majeed shifted restlessly beneath her and she forced every ounce of strength she had into her words. She would not be dominated by this powerful Sheikh. The attitude which radiated from him now was exactly what she wanted to escape.

'Come,' he demanded and turned the grey stallion around.

Before she had a chance to answer, he'd pushed the horse into a gallop, dust flying upwards in its wake, and Majeed reared up, waiting for her command to follow. Only the slightest pressure of her legs was enough to propel him forward and after his master. Majeed's fast pace jolted her, doing little for her unsettled stomach, and it took great effort to stay on board. Finally the palace was in sight and Destiny breathed a sigh of relief. Her head was spinning and her stomach lurched uncomfortably as the pace slowed to a trot and then thankfully a walk. All she wanted was to rest, to close her eyes and block everything out.

Zafir's blood fizzed in his veins as he marched ahead of Destiny, back towards her suite, sensing her following with every muscle in his body, but he was too angry to heed that now. What the hell had she been thinking to take Majeed out into the desert alone—in the heat of the day? The anger that had rushed over him as he'd learnt she'd brought forward her departure date had intensified as he'd ridden hard across the desert, knowing instinctively she'd be in the very place he'd taken her that morning they'd gone out, the same area that Tabinah had lost her life.

Guilt thrashed at him again and he gripped his hands into tight fists as he entered the suite, to find Mina waiting anxiously, the relief on her face at seeing Destiny behind him short-lived when she realised just how angry he was.

'You will rest.' He turned abruptly to Destiny, causing her to almost walk into him. The urge to reach out and steady her was intense, but he couldn't. Not yet. His emotions were running wild and he had to analyse them first, get himself completely back in control.

How had she managed to creep beneath every barrier he'd ever erected around his heart? How had she been able to make him feel, make him care for her? Worse still, how had that care changed to something much deeper, something he just wasn't able to accept, let alone act on?

'I have packing to do.' Her flippant reply tested him further, but the paleness of her face worried him and he recalled Mina saying she'd been unwell for the last two mornings.

He tempered his reply. 'First you rest, then you can prepare to leave. My plane will be at your disposal whenever you should choose to leave Kezoban.'

'My work is done now, Zafir. I want to leave— tomorrow.' He noticed the slightest rise of Mina's brow at Destiny's familiarity in addressing him, but he didn't care any more what anyone thought. Right at this moment he wanted Destiny to stay for a little while longer at least and give him the chance to deal with the way she made him feel. The fact that he now wanted to put her above his duty to his kingdom, even above the guilt he felt over Tabinah's accident, was alien to him. He couldn't think past it yet.

'I understand that, but I wish to hold a feast for you. A mark of my appreciation.'

'That is not necessary.' She walked across the room and pulled her scarf from her head, letting her hair tumble free, again heightening Mina's speculation as to what was going on between them. 'You have paid me to do the work.'

'It is tradition,' he impatiently tossed at her, wishing they were alone. But then perhaps it was for the best they were not. 'You may leave after the feast.'

Without waiting for her response he strode from the suite, marvelling at how a woman he found so attractive could be so infuriating. He was not used to his decisions being challenged—and she'd challenged every single one from the moment they'd met.

She'd also challenged his duty, the memory of his sister and the promise he'd made to his father.

CHAPTER NINE

THE NEXT MORNING, as the pink rays of dawn spread across her bedroom, Destiny felt the nausea return and she knew. She couldn't dress it up as homesickness any more. She had to face the truth. She was pregnant with Zafir's baby. Acknowledging that, even silently to herself, made everything not just terrifying but much more complicated.

Could it really be possible when Zafir had always been so careful? *Almost always.* There had been just that one time during their first night together when they'd been so consumed with need for each other that she'd had to remind him of the need for contraception. Was it possible that brief moment had been enough?

Fear speared through her as the nausea engulfed her, but it wasn't fear of facing Zafir—it was fear of being pregnant. What if she became ill like her mother? If only she'd had those tests done—tests that would re-assure her she wouldn't have to leave her baby alone in the world. A baby that wouldn't have an older sister to care for it, bring it up and protect it from the wrath of a dominating and controlling father.

She pressed her hands against her eyes, fighting nausea and fear as they battled for supremacy. If she had this baby she could die, but that wasn't what she feared most—it was the thought of leaving behind a baby.

So far she'd made every mistake her mother had made, from falling in love with a man who wanted nothing but to be in control to getting pregnant with his child. There was only one part of the pattern left to replicate.

Zafir certainly wouldn't want to discover she carried his child, not when he was about to make a marriage, one that would provide heirs for his kingdom. Legitimate heirs. She closed her eyes against the thought of how he would react to such news. She needed to see her doctor, the one who knew her mother's medical history. She dreaded what she might be advised to do about the pregnancy, but still there was no way she could tell Zafir yet.

All she needed to focus on was leaving Kezoban as soon as possible, but definitely before Zafir sought her out this afternoon.

As the room lightened she packed her few belongings and then took her mother's diary, holding the tattered box with suspicion. Had keeping such a thing, bringing it with her, been a bad omen, meaning she'd do exactly as her mother had done? She inhaled deeply against a fresh wave of nausea, then stuffed the box hard into her bag, trying not to think too much now.

She couldn't cope with such questions; she just needed to get home. But where was home? Her father would be furious about the deal she'd made with Zafir, but even more so when he discovered that she was returning pregnant—a fact she couldn't hide for long. There was only one place she could go and that was to Milly's.

With haste she dressed in her usual clothes, forgoing anything but the headscarf for modesty. She didn't want to arouse anyone's suspicion, especially Mina's. It would hurt to leave the friendly face she'd come to rely on without saying goodbye, but it was for the best. As far as she knew, the plane she'd asked for would be ready to take her away from the desert kingdom and the ruler she'd foolishly fallen in love with.

She put the final belongings into her bag and zipped it up. Mina could arrive at any time with breakfast. Just the thought of that made her even more nauseous than she could cope with, but she forced herself on, needing to be ready to leave as soon as possible.

She pulled her headscarf tighter, then picked up her bag and took one last look at her room, especially the bed where she'd discovered the joys of loving, the bed in which she'd given everything to Zafir and conceived his child. Thoughts of him brought tears to her eyes but she shut them tight. Crying was something she hardly ever succumbed to and now she knew why it was all she'd wanted to do lately, but tears were for later, not now.

With a sigh she turned and made her way to the door, only to see it open and Mina walk in carrying a breakfast tray, followed by a younger maid, carrying the most gorgeous deep purple and gold silk *abaya*. Mina directed the other maid to leave the *abaya* before retreating. As the door closed behind her, Mina frowned, glancing down at the bag she carried as she crossed the room to place the tray on the table by the open doors as usual. 'The Sheikh has requested your presence in his office as soon as you have eaten.'

The efficient tone of the maid gave nothing away but, even so, she would be sorry to leave her. 'Thank you. I will go there now—before I leave.'

'You are leaving? Now? What of the feast tomorrow? The Sheikh has sent a gift for you to wear.'

Destiny looked at Mina, not sure if the older woman would sympathise with her if she knew all the facts. What was she doing, thinking she could confide in a member of Zafir's staff? Pregnancy was really muddling her mind. Gift or no gift, she had to leave.

'Yes, now.'

'Are you well enough?' Mina's dark eyes met hers, unsettling and questioning. Destiny had the distinct impression that Mina knew she was pregnant with the Sheikh's baby. She thought back to the ginger tea she'd first prepared several days ago. Was it possible that Mina had known long before Destiny herself had acknowledged the sickness for what it was?

Dread raced through her. If Mina knew, had she told Zafir? Her loyalties would certainly be with her ruler. 'Of course I'm well enough. I just need to go home now my work with Majeed is done.'

Mina stepped towards her and took the bag from her, which she let go of without a fight. 'Eat some breakfast, then see the Sheikh before you make any more decisions.'

'There is nothing more to stay for,' she said quickly, panic at the thought that Mina might have informed Zafir making her legs weak and her head spin. She didn't want to inflict on herself, or her baby, a life empty of love because, although she loved Zafir, she knew he didn't and never could love her. Even if everything went right and she could go ahead with the pregnancy, she had no wish to raise her child in the shadows while he raised a family with his new wife.

Her mother's diary told the same story. It left her in no doubt that her mother had hoped for so much more when she'd become pregnant with her first child. She'd wanted love and the kind of happy-ever-after Destiny seriously doubted existed. Those longings had poured onto every page and she'd read the page which told her why she'd been named Destiny many times since.

Her mother had believed a baby would bring her closer to the man she loved, but her father was the same kind of controlling man as Zafir. He was as hungry for power and the unexpected birth of a child had not been what he'd wanted, but he'd done his duty and married her mother.

The horror of her mother's death, the blood disease she herself could have inherited, rushed at her. What if she had complications with the birth? What would happen to the baby if she too became a victim of that disease, as her mother had? It was why she'd been adamant she never wanted marriage or children.

'But there is time for breakfast,' Mina urged gently, so that those stupid tears threatened again and for a brief moment Destiny was tempted to confide in her. No. If Zafir didn't already know he most certainly would then. He had to be free to do what his position in life dictated. She didn't want to stop him doing what he needed to do, not when she might never be able to have the baby, a thought which was as devastating as the fear of following in her mother's footsteps.

The idea of putting off this last encounter with Zafir

suddenly became far more appealing. If she lingered at breakfast, maybe he would be busy with other work and unable to meet her. Much to Mina's delight, she sat at the table and tried to look delighted with the array of sweet pastries and fruit before her, but her stomach turned and it was almost impossible.

'I have made the ginger tea again—to help with the sickness.' Mina's words confirmed her suspicions. Of course the woman would know the signs of pregnancy. She'd probably served many women.

Destiny nodded. 'Thank you.' She couldn't say anything else. All she could do now was go and see Zafir and hope that he didn't know, then she could leave, allowing him to make his marriage deal. Only when she'd seen her family doctor could she decide how and when she would tell him.

Zafir stood by the desk as Destiny entered. She looked pale but a determined strength shone from her eyes. Had he got it all wrong? He was sure Mina's near insolence as he'd demanded to know where Destiny had taken Majeed had been an attempt to highlight not only Destiny's health but the reason for her current pallor.

He'd played that conversation over and over in his mind, convinced that it had a deeper relevance. It had been Mina's very insistent mention of sickness over recent mornings which had set alarm bells ringing.

'She is not well, sire.' He could still hear the worry in her voice as the words whirled in his head.

'Not well?' He'd swung round to face the maid, wanting an explanation.

'For the last two mornings, sire, she has been unwell.' Mina's usual subservience had been absent and she'd looked at him earnestly, but all he'd been able to think of was Destiny out on Majeed in the heat of the day, when she wasn't well. He hadn't wanted to hear anything else and had marched from the suite, but now he wished he'd demanded a full explanation instead of accepting hints that Destiny was suffering from morning sickness.

Just as when he'd galloped across the desert to find her, he knew that if Destiny had become pregnant from their union it would change everything. The child she carried was his child, his heir, and he had a duty towards that child greater than the duty to make an arranged marriage. In all probability, the child had been conceived the night he'd taken her innocence, which in itself tied him irrevocably to her.

He wanted to ask Destiny but, for a man who always guarded his emotions, he was overwhelmed with this unexpected news. He knew he wouldn't be able to put it into words without giving away his excitement at the prospect of being a father and what this turn of events meant for them—that his duty was now to her and their child…that they could be together.

He wanted to pull her to him, kiss her and tell her he'd do his duty, he'd look after her and the baby, but still she hadn't said anything and the underlying suspicion that he'd misinterpreted Mina's words, or that she herself was mistaken, was still a real possibility. He would have to allow Destiny time to break the news herself.

As soon as she did he knew exactly what he'd do. It wouldn't be the duty he'd always envisaged, of making an arranged marriage and producing heirs, but the duty to his unborn child. The duty of not a ruler, but a father.

Much to his annoyance, Destiny didn't say anything and he noticed for the first time her Western clothes and the obvious attempt to distance herself from him.

'You will not be able to leave today. A goodbye feast is organised for tomorrow and the next day my plane will be available to take you back to England.' He hoped she wouldn't need that plane but he saw panic in her eyes as she turned to him.

She was beautiful but distant. In her brown eyes was the same spark of suspicion and discontent he'd often seen in Tabinah's eyes during the months after her marriage had been announced. She had resented everything he'd done for her, all his attempts to make her life as comfortable as possible. He'd failed her, driven her to flee on the back of a horse she wasn't able to handle. He'd pushed her to it and he would feel guilty for that for ever. Had he pushed Destiny away too?

'A feast isn't necessary. I would rather leave today— now.'

'That will not be possible. It is tradition here in Kezoban to hold such a feast for a visitor. It will be done and you will attend. I have sent a new *abaya* for you to wear.' He couldn't tell her how significant that *abaya* was, that the colours were his and that by wearing it everyone would know even before he announced their marriage that he was claiming her as his wife.

'I need to leave now, Zafir. Today.'

'And offend my people? Offend me?'

Her eyes widened in surprise but otherwise she remained as calm and unruffled as a bird of paradise.

Would she really be so calm if she wanted to tell him she was expecting a baby? His baby. His heir. Yet still he trusted Mina's instincts.

'Can you assure me I will be free to leave after the feast?' The demand in her voice was clear and he wondered how he was ever going to turn the conversation towards her *illness*.

He walked towards her and she stood tall and firm. It was as if she wasn't carrying such a powerful secret, one that would change their lives beyond recognition. Overnight his duty had changed, become conflicted with all that he'd grown up knowing he had to do. He had as much duty to his child as he did to his country—if not more.

'You will be free to leave the day after the feast—if that is what you want.' He hesitated, strangely out of his depth, a sensation so new it unnerved him.

'It's what has to be done.' She looked at him, a fire in her eyes so completely opposite to the desire he'd seen smouldering within them that he couldn't help but step towards her.

'You're right,' he goaded. 'We both have our lives to lead, lives that should never have crossed, and now that you have completed your work with Majeed we must return to those lives.'

'Precisely,' she said and stepped away from him. 'Now I will leave you to your work.'

She hadn't said a thing about being unwell, hadn't hinted at anything to suggest she might be carrying his child. He couldn't let her leave Kezoban without knowing for sure. Anger rushed through him and he took a deep breath. He was not used to having information withheld from him, but letting his emotions rule, displaying how he felt, would not help the situation. Calm control was required.

'Destiny.'

She whirled round and looked at him. 'Yes?' Briefly he thought he heard a hint of hope in her voice. The small tremor in that one word pushed him on, that and the fact that he had to know. But he also had to hear it from her. She had to want to tell him. He had to exercise patience, the valuable lesson he'd learnt from the tragedy of losing Tabinah. That dreadful time had taught him that at least.

'Is there anything else?'

'No. Should there be?' Destiny's stomach turned over. The dark and brooding look in his eyes screamed suspicion. Did he know? Had Mina told him the secret she herself had only just discovered? She was more convinced than ever that the maid knew about the nights she'd spent with the Sheikh.

'I believe that there is.' He moved towards her and she stepped back as he came close, but breathed a sigh of relief when he walked past her to the large double doors of his office. That relief was short-lived when he turned the key in the lock.

Expectancy hung in the air as he looked at her. 'Are you going to tell me why you have been ill these past few days?'

'Heat, I guess.' The words slipped from her lips but she couldn't look up at him, couldn't look directly into the eyes of the man she loved and lie.

It's just until you are married, until you've kept your promise of duty to your father—and until I know if I can even have this baby.

She hated doing it, but she couldn't be the one who stood in the way of his duty. Her mother had paid the price of forcing a man into marriage because of pregnancy; it had all been written in her flowing handwriting. There was no way she was going to force Zafir into any kind of commitment.

He moved closer to her, his height towering over her, and she had no choice but to look up at him. She could see the dark stubble on his face, the glint of steel in his eyes and the clench of his jaw. Her head began to swim and the nausea she'd pushed successfully away returned with a vengeance.

Her body became like lead and the sensation of sliding to the floor overpowered everything. Then she felt the strength from Zafir's arms as he caught her, smelt his scent as she was pressed close against his hard chest and she closed her eyes, giving in to the need for oblivion—her need for him.

When Destiny opened her eyes she was in her room, on the softness of her bed, and Zafir, like a guard, was standing over her at the end of the bed. She glanced quickly around to see if Mina was there.

'We are alone.' He snapped the words out and she knew his mood had darkened. Alert to the prevailing sense of danger, she forced her weary limbs to sit up on the bed, the soft pillows behind her offering some comfort.

Still he wore that closed and cold expression and her heart sank. She knew she had to tell him not only that she was carrying his child, but that she would be leaving and would never want anything from him. What she couldn't put into words was her fear and the guilt she felt at not wanting his baby.

That fear was why she'd immersed herself in her love of horses, never looking for marriage and a family. All she'd ever thought of was that last entry in her mother's diary. She was scared that she too might have problems during childbirth which could take her life and leave her baby alone—and she knew what that was like.

'Zafir, what we shared was special, but it can never be. *We* can never be. Our lives are too different.'

He scowled at her, his eyes narrowing in suspicious anger. He reminded her of the hawks she'd seen him fly once when he had no idea she'd been watching. Just another image she would have to block from her mind, cast to the back of her memory.

'Sometimes changes happen and differences are brought closer, blending to become one.' His poetic words were sharp and the tone of his voice hard. If he'd said it softly, full of meaning, she would have had to stop herself from telling him that such a change had occurred. They would always be joined by the new life within her. A life she didn't even know she could give birth to safely because she'd stubbornly refused to be tested, preferring to hide behind the disguise of not wanting to be a mother.

But those poetic words hadn't been said with any trace of emotion, not even the smallest hint of the love she felt for him. She couldn't tell him, not yet. It would be better if he went ahead with the marriage he needed to make and she returned to England, where the payment for her work in Kezoban would enable her to seek the best medical help and, hopefully, reassurance that her fears were not founded in fact but the lasting pain of losing her mother. Only once she knew she could have the baby would she tell him—providing he'd done his duty and married, because she had no wish to repeat the example of her parents.

'I need to go home, Zafir. Back to England.'

'No.' That one word snapped out and she drew in a breath so sharp she almost couldn't breathe. Where had the gentle man who'd showed her the joy of love-making gone? What had happened to the man who'd kissed her so tenderly she'd wanted to cry? Why had this hard, cold and emotionless man replaced the man she'd fallen so deeply in love with?

'I *have* to go.' She leant forward, ignoring the swimming sensation in her head as she did so. The most important thing was to get away, as far away as possible before her heart broke completely.

'That is no longer an option.' He moved from the foot of the bed, his robes sighing softly and all she remembered was his body as she'd explored him for the first time, touching and kissing him. Heat suffused her cheeks when she finally met his icy gaze as he stood looking down at her, his eyes hard and unyielding. She had to push such crazy thoughts from her mind, had to focus on getting away, back to England.

'But,' she stammered trying to think through the fog in her mind, 'I have to go home.'

'You will not leave today.' His voice deepened and, if at all possible, the hardness in it became more pronounced. 'You are not well enough to travel that distance, not unless you see a physician.'

'Then I will rest and leave after the feast as planned. I'm just tired and a little exhausted by the heat.'

Through the hurt of losing the man she loved and the shock of discovering the very real possibility that she was carrying his baby, she conceded his last words were at least right. She wasn't up to going anywhere right now and she did need to see a doctor, but not until she was back in England.

'You will not leave this palace without my knowledge.'

She looked at him, amazed that the icy tone of his voice as he laid down conditions he had no right to make had become almost arctic. How could a man of the desert, a man so passionate, become so cold? She knew that the little colour her earlier thoughts had put in her cheeks was draining away rapidly as shock settled over her like an icy blanket. 'Not leave the palace?'

'You look very pale again. Perhaps I should send for my physician?'

'No,' she blurted out. That was the last thing she wanted. There was no way she wanted anyone knowing she might be carrying Zafir's child. It was bad enough that Mina suspected, but would a maid be in a position to divulge such a secret? She certainly hoped not. 'I'm fine. I will rest and leave tomorrow, as I said.'

'You will not be leaving tomorrow or the day after.' He looked at her, sparks of anger in his eyes, his jaw clenching beneath the finely trimmed beard, and in that moment she knew that her secret was not hers alone any more. He knew. Everything he'd said since she'd opened her eyes made sense now, from the need to rest, to the physician, to the changes that brought differences closer. He knew, but still she challenged him.

'Why not?'

He folded his arms across his broad chest as he

took in a deep breath and a sense of impending doom seemed to breathe from him, enveloping her completely. 'You will not leave Kezoban. Not when you are carrying my child.'

CHAPTER TEN

DESTINY COULDN'T SPEAK, couldn't even think. To hear Zafir say those words aloud sent a chill down her spine. He knew and, what was worse, he knew she'd kept it from him and that she'd had no intention of telling him. How did she now tell him she didn't want his child because she'd never been brave enough to have the blood test, even when Milly had? How did she say she might have inherited the same disease which had claimed her mother's life soon after Milly had been born?

Her past crowded in on her like a dark storm cloud, heightening the fear she'd been running from since she was a teenager and even more now that she was pregnant. Even though her pregnancy hadn't been confirmed, Mina's reaction to her morning sickness meant that clinging to any hope she'd got it wrong, that she wasn't pregnant with Zafir's child, was foolhardy.

'No, Zafir. I can't stay.' Finally she found her voice and it shocked her to hear the hardness within it. Whether it was in response to Zafir's cold detachment, a way of protecting her heart from further pain, or that she was still so numb with shock, she didn't know, but she sounded utterly heartless.

'Do not say that again, Destiny, not when the child

that grows within you is my heir.' The use of her name tricked her into looking into his eyes, their blackness deeper than space and so much colder. An icy chill slipped over her and she shivered, hugging her arms against her as she sat on the bed. Zafir no longer wanted her as he had during those illicit nights together. All he wanted was the child she carried.

'I am not staying. I *have* to go back to England.' She held his gaze, the frigid intensity of his almost turning her to ice. How could he be so cold, so unfeeling after all they'd shared? *Because he doesn't love you.*

He stepped nearer to the bed, closer to her. 'I will not permit it.'

'You can't keep me here, Zafir. I will not be your mistress, hidden away. I need to go home.' She couldn't tell him it was more than that. She was in love with him and she couldn't tell him the terrifying truth that she didn't even know if she could have the baby. If she went home right now and had the test it wouldn't stop the worst results coming back. And then what would she do?

'And you cannot deny me my child.' The harshness of each word as they were thrown at her made her eyes close against the pain of everything. When she opened them again he was still glaring at her, suspicion and mistrust in his eyes.

She swung her legs off the bed in such a sudden movement of determination that it not only made her dizzy, it forced Zafir to step back, taking with him that dominating presence and, thankfully, giving her room to think.

She stood up, trying hard not to grab on to the post at the corner of the bed for support. She couldn't let him know how weak she felt, how scared and confused she was. She didn't want to be commanded and controlled by him—or any man.

There wasn't any choice. No matter how hard it made her sound, she had to tell him. She swallowed down the bitter taste in her mouth and looked up at him.

'I cannot think about having this baby at the moment.' The words sounded strong and firm as they echoed around the room and she had the satisfaction of seeing his heavy brows furrow together.

'Cannot or will not?' The gritty anger in Zafir's voice only made her determination not to be pushed into something she couldn't do even stronger. Whatever he said, she had to go home and take the test. No matter how hard it was going to be.

'What I decide to do is not for you to worry about. You have my word I will be discreet, that this will not affect you in any way.'

'Not affect me?' The cold, barely controlled anger in his voice almost destroyed her confidence.

'You have your duty, your marriage to make and your life to lead.' She turned to walk away. She didn't know where, when his brooding presence filled her suite. If she could just walk away right now, she would. Fear spiked a fizzy kind of confidence into her, the kind she'd never had and she casually tossed her words over her shoulder. 'And I have mine.'

'Don't you dare walk away from me, Destiny.' Command rang in his voice, pushing her that bit further away, making her love for him seem unreal and totally impossible, as if she'd only dreamt it. But if she had truly dreamt about him, he would have loved her too. He would be with her as she faced possibly the worst moment of her life. If he loved her and was there to support her through it as she finally had the tests, could she do it then?

'You are mine and I am not about to let you go yet.' Each word destroyed that little ray of hope. Of course he didn't love her. She was just a possession. Those nights they had spent together had been about possession and now he wanted to rule her and the baby.

Adamant she was doing the right thing, she paid no heed to the warning in his voice, or the vibration of anger, and continued towards the doors which led out onto the terrace, to the very place she'd first thought he would kiss her. That night seemed to belong to another lifetime.

'Destiny.' Her name angrily rang out, frustration in every syllable. She couldn't blame him. She wanted to hide from him and the truth of the situation. She stood looking out over the exotic gardens, kept healthy and green by his innovative hydro schemes, something she couldn't help admire him for. Not that any of that mattered now. His voice rang out, clear and commanding, as he joined her outside. 'You cannot walk away from me.'

She wished with all her heart that she could, but instead turned to face him, every limb in her body rigid with anger. How had she ever thought he'd be different from her father? He was even more controlling and had been from the outset. Hadn't he hidden his identity to get exactly what he wanted?

'You cannot control me, Zafir. I will not be controlled by anyone. Not any more.'

'That is where you are wrong.' He stood immov-

able, anger coming off him in waves, the rise and fall
of his chest hinting at the battle going on inside him.
'You are carrying my child, Destiny.'

She dragged in a deep and heavy breath, desperate
to force oxygen into her body, anything that would
help her stand upright and face him. She felt so weak
she wanted to crumple to the floor but this was a battle
that had to be fought right now. She had to get back to
England, had to see her family doctor and face up to
having the tests done. Whatever came after that she'd
face, with Milly's help and support. She didn't want
Zafir involved and neither did she want him to do anything out of duty.

'It is your illegitimate child, one that will be nothing but a disgrace to you.' She flung the truth at him,
expecting him to recoil from it. He was the Sheikh of
Kezoban, the man who ruled the country and openly
admitted that duty and honour were the principles by
which he lived. He'd hidden their affair, so how could
he possibly want to acknowledge his child?

'How can you say that?' He moved quickly towards
her until he stood towering over her, reminding her
how it felt to be held by him.

Somewhere deep inside her a flare of recognition
leapt to life, her body swayed towards his and she
couldn't fight the urge to briefly close her eyes. When
she opened them and looked up at him, the sparks of
anger in his were subdued by desire. Could it be that
he too was resisting whatever it was that still hummed
dangerously between them? She couldn't deny it. There
was still something there, a connection which threatened to combust, dragging them back into its heated
core at any moment.

She couldn't give into it. Things had become so much more complicated. He wouldn't want to support her through this when he was about to make a marriage contract that would be so beneficial to his kingdom.

'We were never anything more than a passing affair.' She tried to make her words firm, to grind into them the kind of conviction that such a statement needed, but the hint of huskiness deflected that effort and she hoped he hadn't noticed it. Boldly, she continued, 'We are just two people who were in need of love and affection and who sought solace in each other's company.'

'Love and affection?' His brows lifted in that sexy way he always looked at her when they were alone, instantly disarming her, and as her pulse leapt she re-alised her error. This man didn't put any store in love, probably didn't believe in it; lust was all that had mat-tered to him. The two weeks she'd spent every night in his arms had been just a distraction for him, amuse-ment before he committed to marriage for the benefit of his kingdom. Hadn't their conversation the night she'd arrived in Kezoban proved that?

'Well, affection at least.' Her nerve began to falter, his closeness eroding all her bravado, taking her right back to the beginning, to that first time he'd kissed her after they'd ridden in the desert. 'Love can never be part of it. You have a marriage to make and I have a life to go back to in England.'

He nodded slowly and for a moment she thought she saw something resembling disappointment in his eyes before he looked quickly away into the suite as some-one knocked then tried to enter. He gave a command in his language, his voice steady and calm, and she was certain it wasn't an invitation to join them. When he looked back at her, his hard gaze meeting hers, all trace of disappointment had been extinguished; only a fierce intensity remained.

'Were you looking for love, Destiny?' The question threw her off guard almost as much as the sudden seductive tone of his voice. It was like silk over her skin and she stepped back from him, wanting to distance herself emotionally and physically.

'No.' Even to her own ears the denial sounded too fast, too vehement and she quickly backed it up. 'Never that.'

'So affection is all you desire?'

'Yes.' She tried not to think of the fact that she'd given herself so completely to him. She'd given her virginity and her heart exactly because she loved him, even if she hadn't recognised it until now. All she'd known was that being with him had felt right, so very right, and she almost stumbled over the untruth of her next words. 'Just affection.'

'Affection is a very good basis on which to build a marriage.' His voice had softened slightly, knocking her completely off balance. She didn't want to hear about his impending marriage, his affection for his chosen bride, not when she loved him so much.

'Yes, I suppose it is, but nothing has changed, not even with the possibility that I'm pregnant. I have to leave, Zafir. The last thing I want is to jeopardise your marriage.'

Did she want to leave because the thought of him with another woman, taking her as his wife, was too painful? Was it self-protection? Was that why she was so insistent on turning her back on the man she loved?

No. This wasn't about her any more—or Zafir. It

was about the baby they'd created. She had to know for sure if she had inherited her mother's antithrombin deficiency and the only way to do that was to go home to England and have the tests she'd refused, despite being urged by Milly not to. She could still hear herself telling her sister that there was no point, that she didn't want marriage and definitely not children.

'You won't.' He pulled her back to the present and closed the distance she'd created between them and she forced herself to stand still, to remain so close she could smell the desert on him and if she was brave enough to reach out, she would be able to touch him. But the fear she'd lived with, silently hanging over her, now demanded attention.

This was madness. She was in love with a man who didn't even know the concept of the word, a man who took control and power to the ultimate level and, more importantly, a man who was about to marry another woman.

To make matters worse, she was pregnant with his child—one she didn't even know if she could risk having. Her heart ripped in two. Memories of the night she'd been coldly informed she had a new sister but she didn't have a mother clashed painfully with the present.

There was no other option. She had to leave and if it meant putting up a fight then she'd do exactly that.

'There is nothing to discuss, Zafir. We are finished. I'm leaving. Today, tomorrow, I don't care, but I'm leaving.'

'You will not leave.' Zafir held his nerve despite the thud in his chest. He couldn't let her leave. She was carrying his child. The child was the heir he needed but it was more than that, much more. He needed Destiny. He had been hiding from that fact, running like a man scared ever since their first night together.

How could he want a woman so much when he'd denied his sister her chance at love and lost her because of it? Had he gone to Destiny that second night because he'd loved her? Or had it been because he'd wanted to make her his? Either way, he'd buried that emotion so deep beneath his need to do his duty he'd been unable to feel it.

What he felt for her was not just because of the fact that he was the only man to have made love to her. But by giving him her virginity she'd bound them ever tighter, tied them to each other emotionally in a way he'd never known possible and he didn't want to sever those ties. She was his and his alone.

It was that shocking revelation that had brought him back to the palace, forcing him to abandon any thought of an arranged marriage. He wanted only Destiny and as soon as he'd realised what Mina knew he was convinced fate had intervened, salving his conscience slightly. Whatever he'd thought his duty would be, it was clear that now his duty was to the new life they'd created. The heir of Kezoban. The idea of being permanently linked to Destiny, the woman he loved, was one he didn't in the least find unpleasant. Maybe in time she'd learn to love him. Plenty of arranged marriages started with strangers who later become lovers. But they weren't strangers. They had been lovers.

'I *have* to go, Zafir.' The pleading edge in her voice had become tinged with agitation. Was the idea of staying with him that unappealing?

'I will not allow you to leave.' The growl in his

voice made her look cautiously at him, but he had to make her see she couldn't leave. Not now she carried the heir of Kezoban. He intended to make their child legitimate and acknowledge it in every way possible.

'When does your chosen bride arrive?' she asked tartly, pulling his focus back to her face. Her obvious intention of riling him hit its mark. 'I'm sure she wouldn't want to find your mistress lingering here, especially when I'm shrouded in the speculation of pregnancy. I certainly wouldn't want to start a marriage with an illegitimate child in the background.'

'At least that is something we agree on.' He watched as she turned from him to look out over the gardens, dragging her long fingers through her hair in agitation. He wasn't being fair. She was expecting his child and had been unwell for several days. It wouldn't do to distress her further. It was time to make his intentions clear. 'My bride is already here.'

'All the more reason for me to leave right now.' She turned and looked up him and he thought he heard pain in her voice, felt the agony of saying goodbye, but as she began to walk away he knew he'd imagined it and he caught her arm, keeping her close.

His pulse, which still raced after she'd mentioned love and affection, thundered wildly in his head at the thought of what he needed to do. For one foolhardy moment he'd thought she loved him, thought that what they'd shared had been love, but she'd soon backtracked and he knew he couldn't tell her how he felt. Not now.

'You cannot leave, Destiny, not when *you* are my bride.'

She looked at him with wide eyes which never left his face and her teeth bit into her lower lip. The urge to stroke his finger over that spot, to soothe the pain, was so intense he had to let her go and step back or he would be in danger of displaying his true feelings and he hadn't yet begun to understand them.

He should be used to keeping his emotions under wraps, but telling her how he felt, that he couldn't imagine his life without her in it, was hard. He'd never loved anyone before, never experienced love. His mother had returned to her family home when his parents' marriage had broken down, any formal separation impossible, and she'd died a virtual stranger when he was only a teenager. No, he consoled himself, it was far better for Destiny to think he was doing his duty by his child if she herself denounced love so fiercely.

'No,' she said and stumbled back from him, each pace taking her farther away until she was against the wide archway over the large doors to the garden. 'I can't marry you.'

'You can and you will. Tomorrow's feast of thanks to you will now become our engagement. By nightfall the kingdom will know and before the moon rises full and bright over the desert, you will be my wife.'

'Are you mad?' she gasped out, her head shaking in denial. 'We can't possibly marry.'

'You are carrying my child, my heir, and I have never been saner in my life.'

CHAPTER ELEVEN

'No. I can't.' Destiny tried hard to stop her limbs trembling as she faced the man she'd fallen in love with, the man who was the father of the new life inside her—the man she *had* to leave. She had no option. The only thing she could do was return home and have the tests and for that she'd need Milly's support.

He moved towards her, fierce and powerful, every stride bringing her into contact with that powerful aura. 'The child you carry is my heir, Destiny, and you will not keep me from my duty as a father. Neither will you leave Kezoban.'

'You can't keep me here, not when I want nothing other than to go back to my life and leave you to do what you should do. You must make the marriage you'd planned on.' She knew her voice was trembling and that each word was barely a whisper.

'The child is my heir, Destiny.' His deep voice was more of a low guttural growl and she bit down hard on her lower lip again, trying to find even the smallest hint of inner strength. Nothing. Every drop of determination had left her, swept away as quickly as if a sandstorm had raged through the room.

'You need to marry for the good of your country and

I'm not that, Zafir. I never have been and never will be.'
She had to make him see how impossible his suggestion was. It tugged on her heartstrings to think that he
wanted her as his wife but she couldn't marry a Sheikh,
the ruler of a kingdom. She was not of his world and
didn't belong here but, worse than that, she wouldn't
marry him just because he felt duty-bound to do so.

Zafir glared at her. 'There is a greater honour at
stake now, a far more important duty to be done. One
that is much greater than my country. That duty is first
and foremost to my child.'

He moved closer and she pressed herself back
against the door, as if the heat of the fire had leapt out
at her. 'No.' She couldn't say any more, couldn't tell
him she didn't want him to feel any sense of obligation towards her or the baby. She didn't want him to be
forced to alter his life and certainly didn't want him to
be forced to marry her out of duty because of their baby.

Their baby.

She gulped back the raw emotion that rushed at her
from the past. She didn't know if she could do this, any
of it. Just by becoming pregnant and making a man
duty-bound to ask her to marry him she was repeating
so much of her mother's history. What if she repeated
the rest? What if she encountered the same problems
during the birth and left the baby alone in the world?
Would he be so keen to do his duty then? Her father
hadn't. He might have provided for her and Milly, but
every bit had been grudging and he'd ruled with an iron
rod of annoyance at being a single father. She couldn't
risk her child growing up like that.

These thoughts made her head spin, but she couldn't
give in. She had to convince Zafir he didn't have any

obligations towards her. The only reason she would ever have for marrying him was love—and that was something he scorned.

'Why did you keep your condition a secret?'

'Condition?' *How did he know?* 'What condition?'

'The baby. Why didn't you tell me?'

'I didn't want to say anything until I'd seen a doctor—until I knew it was certain.' His suspicion filled the air, the room heavy with it.

'You do not need to go back to England to do that. I will arrange all the medical care you need. As my wife you will have nothing but the best.'

Destiny's temper rose as she realised she'd jumped to conclusions. He didn't know she might be advised against having the baby but it did make everything he said even clearer. He was asking her to marry him out of a sense of duty. She retaliated, tapping into the strength she'd discovered when she'd struck her deal with him at home in England—anything was better than being forced into a marriage neither of them wanted, especially when she needed to go back home and try to find peace of mind.

'I didn't tell you because the deal we struck was for two weeks, not the rest of my life.'

Fury filled those dark eyes, making them narrow in anger. 'The deal we struck?' The incredulity in his voice was clear and it cut through her dying heart, but it was for the best. If he thought she was so mercenary that she'd use her pregnancy to barter with him, then he would send her from Kezoban faster than she could gather her packed bags.

As he looked at her, his eyes glittering and hard, fear prickled over her. What would he do next? Would he shout at her, march from the room after a torrent of heated abuse, just as she'd often seen her father do with her stepmother? Yet more proof that love needed to be the only reason for a marriage.

Instead he pulled out the chair from the table set in the shade of the terrace of her suite. With deliberate slowness he sat, leant back, placed his elbows on the arms of the chair and linked his tanned fingers together in front of his chest. The cold discipline was so unexpected she could only stare at him, unable to say anything.

'Sit.' The command was strong, his voice firm, the icy deliberateness of it a total contrast to the cooling heat of the sun as it began to sink lower over the desert beyond the palace walls, but still she ignored it, standing defiantly.

'We have much to discuss and I will not begin until you sit.' The aura of power shrouded him like a cloak and, even though she had nothing to discuss, she pulled out the other chair and sat opposite him, crossing her arms over her stomach, as if to protect the life within. He glanced down at her arms, a flicker of annoyance on his handsome face, then he looked back up at her, his eyes colder than she'd ever seen them.

'Nothing you can say will change my mind, Zafir.'

'If our time together has been about your financial gain, I will make a deal with you now that will ensure you live in luxury for the rest of your life, provided our child is raised as the legitimate heir to the kingdom of Kezoban.'

The coldness of his voice told her she'd been successful in touching that open nerve she'd uncovered. He was so furious, ice-cold, almost devoid of any trace of emotion. But she had one more blow to deliver, one that hurt her to think of it, let alone say it, but it was born of the fear from that last entry in her mother's diary.

'Even that generous offer will not change my mind, not when I do not want this baby.' By saying those words aloud it quelled all her fears, making her want to do anything to protect the tiny life inside her, even if it meant she had to ignore the love she had for this man.

As that callous admission left her lips she knew that, whatever she had to face, she would have this baby. Milly would be with her all the way and if the test results proved to be positive and she faced the worst, she would insist her sister brought up the baby. That way it would at least be loved, because Milly longed for marriage and children. That was why she'd bravely taken the test when she herself had shied away from it.

'I see.' His calm acceptance of the admission of her darkest fear was almost too much. 'So a deal which means you can leave Kezoban after the child is born would be mutually beneficial.'

'What?' She jumped up, sending her chair scraping across the marble floor of the terrace.

'I will pay you whatever amount you name to remain in Kezoban as my wife until the child is born.'

'I'm not leaving my baby here. What kind of woman do you think I am?' Did he really think she was that heartless? But wasn't that exactly what she'd wanted him to think? Now she wished she'd never said anything. She should have kept her fears to herself and just left.

'I believe you are the kind of woman who will want only the best for your child, and the best will be for him to be brought up here, in the palace, as a future ruler of his country.' Zafir still sat watching her, his hands remaining calmly linked before him, but the scrutiny in his eyes left her in no doubt that he was aware of every flicker of emotion she was trying to hide.

The ground beneath her feet seemed to move and her body swayed as if she had been aboard a ship for many days. She sat down quickly, not wanting him to guess her weakness. The only option she had right now was to agree to his outlandish terms in order to end this discussion. Tomorrow she would have to convince him that the only way forward was to allow her to return to England.

She swallowed hard. 'If the deal is right, then I will agree.'

'The deal will be right, make no mistake about that, and tomorrow at the feast our engagement will be announced.'

The next day Zafir was still mad with rage at how mercenary and calculated Destiny had been, bargaining with their child as if it was nothing more than an inconvenience she needed to be rid of. Just a few days ago, he'd thought he'd fallen in love with her, an emotion he had never experienced before, but how could he love someone so cold? All she'd done was string him along, lead him to believe there was something between them, when really she'd been working towards her ultimate goal of striking a deal that would set her up for life.

Whatever she did or said, there was no escaping the fact that now there was something between them, something he suspected she hadn't planned for. A child. His child—and he would do a deal with the devil himself if it meant he could keep his son or daughter in Kezoban and in his life. In just a few hours he would make the announcement that would seal that deal and tell his people that Destiny was to be his bride. He knew it would cause problems. She was different—but she was the mother of his heir, a fact which changed everything.

She was also the woman he'd fallen in love with and he'd come back to tell her that he wanted only her, but the realisation that she was carrying his child changed things. Emotions were no longer important. Love or hate didn't play any part in the deal he'd just struck with her. Duty was the driving force.

Zafir sat in his lavish banquet room, looking out over his people, but he was more distracted than he'd ever been. His attention kept flitting to the grand arched doors, waiting for Destiny's arrival. Still raw from her painful admission that she didn't want his child, he couldn't believe that he longed to see her, that more than anything he wanted to hold her and kiss her again.

He had to constantly remind himself that she was not who he'd thought she was. Her harsh admissions yesterday burned in his soul, dimming the love he had for her, but obviously it had not subdued the lust and desire. If she'd hoped to escape him she'd played it all wrong. Those admissions made him more determined to keep her in Kezoban and make her his wife.

Finally, as the great banquet room thronged with the elite of his kingdom, he saw her. The thump in his chest, as if he'd been hit by a weapon, caught him off guard. She looked pale, her dark eyes almost too big as she glanced around the room. Had she slept or had she tossed all night as he had?

Around the room the hum of conversation dipped to a curious whisper and he knew that was down to the lavish deep purple and gold silks she wore, exactly as he'd instructed Mina to ensure. They were his colours and marked her as his.

Across the room her gaze met his and, over the heads of his people, that spark which always sizzled when he saw her leapt to life once more. Nothing, it seemed, could dim that. He stood up on the raised platform and gestured her to be escorted to him. The guests parted as she made her way towards him, the whispers becoming more intense as a sense of expectancy filled the room.

She joined him on the platform and he took her hand, which alone spoke volumes to his people. He stood beside her and began to address everyone in Arabic, aware of her nervousness. Beside him she trembled but he continued to speak, putting out his arm to her in presentation as his announcement stunned those gathered before them into silence. For her benefit he repeated his words in English.

'Meet the woman I intend to marry, a woman from far away but whose very name, Destiny, suggests fate has sent her here to be at my side as my wife.'

As speculative whispers raced around the room he looked at Destiny. Her dark eyes, so soft and gentle, regarded him warily and he wished he could do more to allay her fears. He wanted to hold her close, kiss her beautiful face, but protocol needed to be followed. Their union had to be above question or reproach if his people were ever to accept it.

A cheer went up from the back of the room, followed by more, and relief flooded him. 'You are being received well.' He spoke in hushed tones, leaning close to her. 'My people like and approve of you.'

'When they discover the truth, they may not be so pleased with your decision to break with tradition and marry an outsider.' She spoke as softly as he had, keeping a smile on her face, an outward sign of happiness. Already she was performing the role of Kezoban royalty well.

'My people are happy. They see that you have made me happy, taken away the dark cloud which hung over us after Tabinah's accident. To them it is a love match.' He inhaled as he said those last words, catching the scent of her, filling his mind and his body with a rush of need, laced with guilt. He had no right to be happy, no right to feel the way he did for this woman, but it was an illusion he now had to live under—for the sake of his child.

'And what happens when they discover the truth about the baby?' Anger rushed forward, pushing aside guilt or need at her hard but whispered words. He had no idea what his people would say or do, when she followed through with their deal and left Kezoban, left him and their child after the birth. That was the only flaw in his plan, but he wouldn't worry over that now.

'All they need to know at present is that we shall be married within the week.'

'Within the week?' Destiny could hardly speak. When she'd made that deal with Zafir the day before, it had all been about ending the circles they were talking in, giving her time to be alone and think of what she really needed to do. But marriage within a week—that had not been part of the deal. She couldn't marry him, even if she knew the test would be clear; she couldn't link herself to this man for evermore. But hadn't that link already been created?

'We cannot talk here. I will come to you later.' A rush of activity heralded the beginning of the feast as music struck up and people settled down to eat, entertained by dancers. It was so far removed from anything she'd ever seen it was almost possible to think it was a dream, but it was very real. Somehow, she'd struck a deal with this man, one she secretly loved, to be his wife, but she'd never anticipated it would be so soon. She was trapped.

Mina approached them with a young woman at her side who offered her a single white flower. It was tall and elegant, its petals silky-soft as Destiny took it and smiled her thanks.

She almost jumped when Zafir's deep seductive voice whispered close to her ear, 'It is a symbol of fertility.'

She looked at him, wishing he wasn't so close, so dangerously attractive. 'She knows.'

Zafir smiled at her, the first genuine smile that made his eyes sparkle in a way she hadn't seen since the morning he'd left her bed for the last time. 'You have a friend and loyal servant in Mina.'

Destiny turned again to Mina, bowing her head slightly, and offered her thanks, wishing she'd had time to learn a few basic Arabic phrases, as 'thank you' in English didn't quite convey her full gratitude.

For the next two hours, Zafir stayed diligently at her side as more token gifts were bestowed on her. The feasting grew noisier as people enjoyed the excuse to celebrate but Destiny couldn't relax, not with Zafir's threat of seeking her out later in her mind. What did he want now? They had already agreed on how to proceed, or rather he had told her how it would be. He had taken control. How could she expect anything less from a man such as Zafir?

'Mina will escort you to your suite.' Zafir's words caught her attention as she watched the dancers, their exotic moves making her wish she could be as carefree as them. Maybe if she was, then she might have snared Zafir's heart. As she looked up at him, his next words sent her emotions and her pulse rate completely off balance. 'I will join you as soon as I can.'

Destiny knew this would be the final chance she had of settling things between them and, whatever he did, she would break off the engagement and leave. 'Should Mina stay, for propriety?'

She couldn't keep the challenge from her voice, couldn't help goading him, and the narrowing of his eyes told her she'd achieved her aim. She must not give him the chance to talk softly to her, in that sexy tone which made her forget all her worries. She couldn't let it happen. The only way she could see of leaving without any further implications was to antagonise him, push him so far he'd forget all about those hot nights when desire had claimed them both.

'Mina will guard your secret well, just as she has been doing since our first night together. She believes we are in love and will do anything to help bring us together in marriage.' The silky-soft tone of his voice was as challenging as her sharp words of moments ago.

'Then I see I have little choice.' Before he had a

chance to form a reply she turned and walked from him, following Mina, who had been waiting to escort her back to her suite. Why did everything he said and did become a hurdle to climb over? No wonder Tabinah had run away. His need to control was overpowering.

CHAPTER TWELVE

ZAFIR STOOD OUTSIDE Destiny's suite, bracing himself for the battle he knew he was about to face. Something was troubling her and he intended to find out exactly what it was, then remove that issue so that they could unite in marriage, enabling his child to be born in Kezoban and grow up as a future ruler within the bounds of a happy marriage. Maybe he did have to put his heart on the line, tell her how he felt. If he did, could she love him? The passion they'd shared made it plausible, but was it possible to force someone to love you?

He didn't knock but strode in to find her standing in the middle of the suite, arms folded tightly, still wearing the deep purple and gold silks he'd sent for her. He didn't even have the chance to close the door as her first words hurtled at him like a missile.

'I don't want to marry you.' Her defiance, if it wasn't so infuriating, would have been remarkable. She looked stunning, standing beneath the bright lights of the suite, her eyes flaming with anger and mistrust. But why? How had what they'd shared turned so sour?

'The marriage is arranged. The announcement has been made. It cannot be undone. Next week you will be my wife.' He clenched his hands in fury at the humiliation of being told he wasn't good enough for her, that *she* didn't want *him*. 'It is my duty to my child to marry you.'

'Duty?' She gasped the question out at him and for a second he reeled with shock. Nobody had ever addressed him so, but he should be more accustomed to it from this woman by now.

He strode over to her, intent on making her see that marriage was the only option, that he would not have his child born out of wedlock and, worse still, in a foreign land. His duty was to his kingdom and producing an heir was part of that duty. Now that he knew she carried his child, he would do all it took to protect that heir.

'Yes, duty. Something you are not at all familiar with.' He recalled the challenging look she'd given her stepmother the first time they'd met.

'How dare you?' she hurled at him in indignation.

'I dare because I will do anything for my child.' He matched her anger with cool reserve, knowing now more than ever he needed to remain in control. It wasn't right to upset her, not when she carried his child.

'A child I can't give you.' The quiver of desperation in her voice wasn't quite masked by her fury; if anything, it only revealed that there was much more to what she'd said than just those words.

'You are talking riddles. Speak plainly.' He narrowed his eyes, not sure what was coming next, but preparing to counteract it swiftly.

'Very well.' Her tone was flippant, her stance defiant and he resisted the urge to hold her arms and force her to look into his eyes in the hope that he could remind her of the passion and desire which had brought them together. He wanted to see that again, to know they could be like that once more. 'I cannot have your baby, Zafir, simply because I don't want to.'

A furious red rage fogged his mind. He'd thought they'd settled this. 'What are you saying?'

'That I cannot have the baby.'

An icy shard stabbed at his heart. Whatever the reason for such a bald and cold statement, he had to know it, had to find a way to fight it. 'I will not allow you to do anything to my child and, if necessary, I will not let you out of my sight until it is safely born.'

'It could cost me my life.' The pain-racked sob which broke from her froze him to the spot. The raw agony in her eyes made him hurt, as if an unknown force was squeezing his chest so tight he couldn't breathe. Memories of the night he'd lost Tabinah, of the guilt he'd carried ever since, mixed with the thought of losing Destiny. For the second time in as many days he faced the thought of life without her. He knew that life without the woman he loved would be impossible.

He couldn't lose her, not now he'd found her.

He lowered his voice to a gentle whisper, letting go of all the anger she'd provoked in him, sensing a genuine need, a real cry for help from within her. 'How do you know this?'

'My mother…' she swallowed down hard and when she continued her voice was a cracked whisper loaded with pain and fear '…she died soon after giving birth to my little sister—because of a hereditary disease.'

Why hadn't she confessed her fears from the outset? Now her unwillingness to tell him she'd become pregnant was finally beginning to make sense. Gently he took her hand and led her to the cushions of the seating area, urging her to sit. Then he too sat and, holding her hands in his, cautiously continued, 'What happened, Destiny?'

'It's a condition called antithrombin deficiency. She didn't even know she had it and each pregnancy increases the risk to the mother.' She looked up at him, tears shining in her eyes, and he fought hard against the need to hold her, to soothe her pain. This was something she needed to talk about first. His mind whirled. He had already alerted his physician to her pregnancy and he would know exactly what to do. He would give her nothing but the best medical care.

'She kept a diary but never made another entry after Milly was born.'

'And that is why you don't want our baby? You think you will be the same?' He fought against the need to hold her tight, to infuse her with all the love he had for her in his heart in an attempt to heal her pain. But she'd told him she'd never wanted love and if he confessed his true feelings it might be too much—for her and the baby. 'Can tests be performed to determine your health?'

'Yes.' She looked down at her hands, unable to maintain the contact they'd had over the last few minutes, and his heart felt crushed. She didn't trust him enough to share it with him. How could he ever make their marriage happy if she didn't trust him?

'Why have you not been tested?'

She looked back up at him and the pain in her eyes wrenched at him, tearing him to pieces. He just wanted to make it right for her. But could he?

'Milly had the test because she's always wanted to

get married and have children, but I've never been tested.'

His eyes narrowed. 'Because you didn't want children?'

'Or marriage.' The cracked whisper of her voice was more shocking than her admission. He was forcing her to do the very things she was trying to avoid and the fact that she was carrying his child was due to his mistake. He vividly remembered that first night when she'd had to remind him to use protection. All her pain now was his fault. He'd done this to her.

'I've done everything as my mother did. She fell in love with a man who didn't love her and then she was forced into marriage because of pregnancy.'

Her words dragged him back, but they were like a spear through his heart. She'd fallen in love with another man, one who didn't want her. Was that why she'd spent that first night with him, giving him something he didn't deserve? She'd been using him, using the powerful attraction between them to wipe away the memories of another man?

He couldn't focus on that revelation now; he had to keep in mind that the child she carried, the one she didn't want for fear of becoming ill like her mother, was his child, his heir.

'I will give you the best medical care in the world. You can have all the tests you need to ensure you and the baby will be healthy, but you will stay and become my wife. We can raise our child together, or you can leave after it's born, but it must be born within the bounds of wedlock if it is to be recognised as a true heir to the throne of Kezoban.'

'What if I can't keep the baby? What if the test is positive?' The fear in her voice was clear.

'Once you have the test we will know the situation.' His mind whirled with the implications of what she'd told him. He could lose his child but, far worse, he could lose the woman he loved and if he couldn't admit to her what he felt, he couldn't turn his back on her. He wanted to be with her as she found out. He wanted to help her through whatever came after—no matter what the results were. He wanted her because he loved her. Every second he looked into her eyes intensified that.

'I'm scared.' The hushed whisper held hints of shame and he fought against the urge to hold her, protect her from fear, but just by doing that he could scare her more.

'There is nothing to be scared of, Destiny. Not now. I'll be with you all the way. We'll deal with this together.'

'Why?' Confusion clouded her eyes and filled her voice.

'You are to be my wife, Destiny.'

'But I still couldn't marry you, don't you see?'

He shook his head, unable to comprehend what more she wanted.

'I know what it's like to grow up at the mercy of a man who never wanted to be a husband, much less a father.' She lowered her gaze and pulled her hand free of his, clutching hers tightly in her lap. 'I cannot do that to you, Zafir. I am not your destiny.'

All was becoming clear to him. While he'd been nursing his guilt about what had happened to Tabinah, she'd been running scared. Just as he'd lost Tabinah, he could have lost Destiny. The way he'd felt when he'd realised she'd taken Majeed into the desert rushed back at him, taking all the breath and strength from his body.

'I can't let you go, Destiny.' The truth of his emotions ripped from him, his words lacking any of his usual firm control, and she looked at him questioningly. Had he finally got through to her, finally made her see why he couldn't let her go?

'It doesn't change anything.' Sadness echoed in every word.

She took a small faltering step towards him but her next words destroyed any hope. He couldn't give up on her because he loved her.

'Even if you looked into the future and predicted I'd be in the best of health and give birth to a healthy baby, I still couldn't marry you.'

'Don't you see, Destiny, you gifted me your virginity and, even if that union hadn't resulted in a child, I am duty-bound by my honour to marry you? It is the way of my country.'

'But I was never a candidate to be your wife, I was just a passing affair, your last mistress before you married. You even went in search of a wife. Your honour didn't stop that. So what's changed?'

Zafir recalled how he'd felt as he'd met with the women who were presented to him. In each and every face he'd looked for Destiny. He'd longed for her as he'd lain alone in bed; she was all he could think about and because of that he'd halted his search. Even before he'd known she carried his child, he was sure she was the one, the woman he wanted to be his bride.

The very fact that he had chosen her and not let his

aides decide was an issue he couldn't get past initially. Was he right to seek marriage to the woman of his choice when he had forced Tabinah into an arranged marriage—making her so unhappy she had run away, losing her life in the process?

Now, to add to the confusion filling his mind and his heart, Destiny had admitted that she'd slept with him because she'd been spurned by the man she loved. Was the pain in his heart, the ache in his soul because he too had been rejected by the person he loved? Destiny couldn't love him because she loved another man.

He stood up, knowing he couldn't force her to love him, couldn't force her to stay. Her heart belonged to another man. He couldn't force his will on another woman. He'd done that to his sister and had learnt from it. He loved Destiny too much and he would do anything for her—even let her go.

'I have made you unhappy, just as I did to Tabinah. I will give anything you need, but please know that you are free to go, free to make your own choices. I will not force you to do anything.' The pain those words caused burned like fire in his throat, making them almost impossible to say.

'What of your duty to your country, your people?' Her face had paled and he worried he would upset her, make her ill.

'My duty is still to my country and my people, but it is also to the child we created out of love and affection.' He was testing, gauging her reaction to the mention of the emotions she'd already denied wanting from him. Now he knew why—because her heart belonged to another—but his heart belonged to her and if she left she'd take it with her.

* * *

Destiny's body, weary from the constant battle of wills, went rigid with anger. How could he say they'd shared love and affection? He'd already made it perfectly clear he didn't want anything to do with such feelings. He was just saying it now as a last-ditch attempt at keeping her in Kezoban.

'It wasn't love, Zafir, it was lust. Pure carnal lust.'

'Can you be so sure?' He came to stand before her, forcing her to look up at him and intensifying his domination, a tactic used often by her father. She stood quickly in an attempt to counteract it. 'Maybe it was lust that brought us together, but what if it is now something more? Can you turn your back on that?'

'Saying it isn't enough.' She hated that he was taunting her again.

'Then I will show you.'

Before she could do anything she was in his arms, her body responding as his lips met hers in a hard and demanding kiss. Fire leapt to life within her, scorching her heart and, try as she might, she couldn't stop her arms winding around his neck, keeping her close to his lean body. The need which rushed through her was so wild, so intense she could hardly breathe.

His hands cradled her head, keeping her in exactly the right place, enabling him to delve deeper with his kiss, pushing her further towards the edge. Sense suddenly prevailed and she pulled her arms from his neck, pushing hard against him.

Finally he let her go and she staggered backwards, her body pulsing with desire that would have to remain unquenched for evermore.

'That proves nothing but lust. It proves that I am

nothing more than a convenient mistress. I want more, Zafir, more than that.' She hated her ragged breathing as she fought for control and the heated flush of her cheeks.

Zafir too was breathing hard but his face wore an expression she'd never seen before. He looked vulnerable and exposed, as if he'd finally smashed down every barrier around him.

'What do you want?' The husky growl of his voice sent a tingle of awareness down her spine.

'I want a marriage made out of love.'

'Love will flourish if you let it—if you forget the man you claim to have given your love to and open your heart to one who does love you.'

Now she was confused. Was the passion he'd set free within her fogging her mind, mixing with the worry of the test she knew she had to face, making her imagine things? 'What man?'

'You said you'd done the same as your mother—fallen in love with a man who didn't love you.'

He took hold of her arms, pulling her closer to him, the fire of unsated desire sparking around them. *Open your heart to one who does love you.* Those words echoed in her mind but she was too scared to say anything. What if she'd got it wrong? It was bad enough he thought she loved someone else, but if she exposed her love for him, would he use it as a weapon to make her stay?

'Who is this man?' A hint of jealousy showed in his voice and she knew she had to be totally honest with him, risking her heart in the process if she'd got it wrong.

'He is a great leader, a very powerful man, exactly the kind of man I did not want to love.'

'Who is he, Destiny?'

'You.'

The silence which followed that one word was so tangible it was as if a mist had shrouded them, but the expression on his face rushed from disbelief to suspicion. He didn't believe her.

'Why?'

'Why what?' Did he mean why did she love him? Or why was he the wrong man for her?

'Why do you not want to love a man such as myself, to quote your words, a great leader, a very powerful man?'

'Because I have spent twenty-six years being ruled by a man who didn't have even the smallest amount of love inside him for me, his daughter. I have protected my sister, who is prone to speaking her mind, more times than I can remember from his wrath. He is only happy when he is controlling those around him. I came here because I cannot live any longer like that. The deal I made with you was my escape route.'

Zafir looked at Destiny, shocked not just by the admission that she loved him, but by the story of her childhood. No wonder she'd made that overzealous deal with him. She'd been desperate to get away from the man who was supposed to protect her. Her father.

'It is true I am a leader, but a leader of my people for the good of my country. I would never seek to dominate one person—not again.'

'Again?'

'Why do you think Tabinah left? Why did she ride

out on my horse, a beast that was far too strong for her to handle? Because I forced her into marriage, forced her away from a man she'd grown up with, one I've since discovered she wanted to marry. It was to him she was riding and planning to run away with. My need to control her made that happen.'

All the guilt poured out in those words. He should never have insisted Tabinah make that marriage. This was the twenty-first century and time for change. He should have seen that her heart was already taken. He'd lost her and he'd thought the same of Destiny when she'd said she'd given her heart to a man who couldn't love her and what he'd said afterwards had come from deep within his heart. He did love her.

Destiny's silence said it all. She was probably wishing she'd never admitted loving him.

'I see my words have proved you right. I am the all-controlling man you fear.' He let her arms go and turned from her, not wanting to see the accusation in her eyes. He had to leave, to walk away. He'd played it all wrong. Gambled and lost.

'Zafir.'

The softness of her voice stilled the thud of his heart and he turned to look at her, but remained silent.

'It wasn't your fault. Tabinah's accident.'

'How can you be so sure?'

'When love is involved, all sense or reason disappears. Whatever you'd have done, it wouldn't have been enough. Love can make you do crazy things, such as agreeing to marry a desert Sheikh and staying with him.'

He frowned and strode back to her. As she looked up into his face he saw love blazing from her eyes, so bright and vibrant he knew he'd found the one person who would always have his heart. His Destiny.

'You really mean that?'

'Yes, but what about the test? What happens if I have inherited the same condition which claimed my mother's life?'

'Together we can face anything, Destiny. I love you. Nothing else matters. I want you in my life as my wife for ever.'

'What if I can't have children? What of your duty to your country then?'

'Don't worry about that now. My physician will give you the very best care.'

'Then I can face anything if I have your love, because I love you, Zafir, so very much.'

He swept her from her feet, gathering her up in his arms, and made his way out of her suite, along the corridor of his palace, totally heedless of any servants.

'Where are we going?' The question held a hint of teasing and he looked down at her, his eyes devouring the softness of her face.

'To the Sheikh's suite.'

'What will people think? What about protocol?'

'They will think I'm madly in love with you—and they will be right.'

EPILOGUE

'I HAVE A gift for you.' Zafir's voice sent a shimmer of desire down Destiny's spine as he stood behind her, pulling her against his body.

She looked out over the palace gardens and to the desert beyond. So much had happened in the year she'd been here. Her life was so complete—married to the man she loved with a baby son who was the centre of their world. The fear of the tests was just a blurry memory now she knew she hadn't inherited anything from her mother other than the need to be loved.

In just a few hours, her sister would be arriving for what was fast becoming a regular monthly visit. How could she possibly need or want more?

'I don't need gifts, Zafir.' She turned in his arms to look up at him. 'I have more than I can ever want.'

He kissed her gently, his lips holding the promise of much more pleasure. 'This one I think you will want.'

He took her by the hand and led her from the suite, towards the stables.

'Why are we going this way? Have you bought another horse?'

His smile was full of love and it melted her heart all over again. 'You know me too well.'

Intent on pleasing Zafir, she walked with him, but when they entered the ornate stables she was astonished to see Milly.

'What are you doing here? I thought you weren't due to arrive until this evening.'

'Change of plan.' Her sister grinned as she opened a stable door. Destiny looked in and gasped. The bay mare contentedly eating hay was Ellie, the young horse her father had forced her to sell. She stroked the familiar silky coat and the mare responded, nuzzling against her in recognition.

'How did you find her?' She turned to Zafir, a strange urge to cry almost overwhelming her.

'With Milly's help.'

Destiny looked at her sister. 'How did you manage to keep it a secret?'

'With great difficulty.'

Zafir took her hands, pulling her to him, and she looked up into his eyes. 'Exactly a year ago, you arrived in Kezoban. You brought sunshine and the hope of a new beginning to my life and I wanted to celebrate that. What better gift than the horse you were forced to part with?'

Destiny smiled up at Zafir. 'I love you, Sheikh Zafir Al Asmari, so very much.'

'And I love you, my very own Destiny.'

* * * * *

ONE DANCE WITH THE SHEIKH

TESSA RADLEY

In Loving Memory of Sandra Hyatt
Wise Woman, Best Friend and Awesome Writer!

One

Who was she?

Dark red hair hung down her back, and as she shifted, the color changed like tongues of fire. Her tall, slender body was encased in a shimmering silvery grey gown that clung to her like moonlight on a dark night.

Rakin Whitcomb Abdellah had arrived at the giant white gazebo in the garden in front of the house where the guests were gathered in time to see the bride and groom link hands in front of the celebrant. It had surprised him that it had taken the usually responsible Eli only a matter of weeks to set aside the caution of a lifetime and to fall head over heels in love with his bride. But what had astonished Rakin more was the fact that Eli was marrying a Kincaid at all—since, less than a month ago, Kara's own sister had jilted Eli. Yet, once his gaze settled on the wedding group, it was the maid of honor with her glorious hair and eye-catching beauty who captured Rakin's attention as she moved forward to take the bouquet of red roses from the bride.

This could only be Laurel Kincaid, the woman who'd jilted his best friend Eli less than a month before their wedding day.

The woman who Eli had suggested could be the solution to all Rakin's problems.

A child, no more than three or four years old, strutted forward bearing a fat cushion. Rakin squinted and made out the two rings perched on top. Laurel stepped forward and held out a hand to guide him, but he tugged away, clearly reluctant to stand beside two flower girls. Instead he barreled his way between Eli and his bride Kara Kincaid, eliciting both chuckles and sighs as he stole hearts.

The maid of honor was scanning the guests.

Above the bouquet of red roses, her eyes were green. The brightest emerald Rakin had ever seen. Unexpectedly, her gaze landed on him. Time stopped. The murmurs around him, the sound of Kara saying her vows, the heady fragrance of the Southern blooms all faded from Rakin's consciousness. There was only…her.

Then she glanced away.

And the tension that had gripped him slowly eased.

Eli had warned him that his ex-fiancée was a beauty, yet Rakin hadn't been prepared for his body's reaction to her as their eyes had locked. Lust. Becoming romantically entangled with her was not an option. For starters, she was a Charleston Kincaid—not some nymphet with pleasure on her mind. And, if he took Eli's advice, the proposal he intended to put to her had everything to do with business, and nothing to do with pleasure.

Despite the gorgeous green-eyed, auburn-haired wrapping, Laurel Kincaid had *Do Not Touch* written all over her.

Yet even so, Rakin could scarcely wait for the ceremony to end, for the moment when he congratulated the newlyweds— and Eli introduced him to the maid of honor. Then he would decide whether she would fit in with his plans.

The rich scent of jasmine and gardenia announced that summer had arrived in the South.

Her sister's wedding was being held at the Kincaid family home, a two-and-a-half story elaborately embellished federal mansion where Laurel had grown up. The imposing facade flanked by decorative balconies, each with a pagoda roof, had always been home to Laurel and her siblings.

But at the moment she was less concerned with the details of the wedding venue than the identity of one tall dark and handsome stranger. Laurel had a pretty good idea of the identities of all the guests at her sister's wedding; after all, Kara had originally run all the guests' names past her when this was supposed to have been her own wedding.

And the stranger with the dark, exotic good looks hadn't been on it.

So where did Kara know him from? And why had her sister never mentioned him before?

If she didn't quit shooting surreptitious glances at the man her sisters would have her married off to him in an instant. And she wasn't interested in him; she simply wanted to know who he was.

Laurel averted her gaze and watched as Eli took Kara's hands in his, the gold of their newly donned wedding rings glinting in the late afternoon sun. Unexpectedly her throat tightened.

Oh, no. She wasn't going to cry!

She'd never been the type to gush tears at weddings…. She always smiled and said the right thing at the right time. So why was she suddenly feeling like this? This wedding was a joyous occasion, not a time to shed tears.

And heaven knew what interpretation people would put on it if she did start to cry. She scanned the enormous number of guests all dressed up and smiling. Laurel could think of at least one or two who would put the worst possible slant on it. Then the damage would be done, and rumors would be rife around the city that she was heartbroken about Kara marrying Eli—after she had broken off her own engagement to him.

Laurel was utterly delighted for them both. She was relieved she wasn't marrying Eli.

But no one would believe that if she started to weep.

Get a grip.

Her eyes fell onto her mother.

Now there was reason to cry. Elizabeth Kincaid was a legendary Southern beauty. Everyone said she'd have been crowned Miss South Carolina, if she'd ever entered—but soft-spoken, eternally elegant Elizabeth had too much class to enter beauty pageants. Instead, after her family had fallen on hard times, she'd married Reginald Kincaid and become one of the most accomplished hostesses in Charleston and brought cachet to the nouveau riche Kincaid name.

She was smiling as she watched Kara and Eli tie the knot.

Yet the mother of the bride almost hadn't made it to the wedding. She'd been arrested for killing her husband. The police had believed they'd had enough evidence to make a case. In the past months, in the very darkest moments, Laurel had worried that her mother might actually be convicted of her father's murder.

But her mother had been cleared.

And now suspicion for her father's death rested on the brooding half brother Laurel and her siblings had learned about at her father's funeral. Laurel would never forget that day—or the shock that her father had been living a secret double life for decades.

Now Jack Sinclair sat beside his mother, Angela Sinclair. Her father's mistress—and life-long love.

On Angela's other side sat her other son. The Sinclairs had been invited here today because Elizabeth Kincaid believed in always doing the Right Thing—even when it cost her dearly. The contrast between the half brothers was stark. Alan had none of Jack's dark moodiness. Blond and light, he was like the sun bursting through his half brother's dark thunder cloud.

Laurel decided she was becoming fanciful.

"You may kiss the bride," the celebrant was saying.

Eli bent forward, a head taller than his bride, and Laurel found herself looking away to give the couple a moment of privacy. Of course, she looked straight into a pair of dark eyes.

The generously proportioned bedrooms that Laurel, Kara and Lily had once occupied on the second floor of the historic federal mansion had been transformed into an impromptu bridal dressing-room wing for the wedding day. Pausing just inside the doorway of Kara's childhood room, Laurel took in the leftover feminine paraphernalia scattered around the room.

Open shoe boxes spilled tissue paper over the carpet. A posy abandoned by one of the flower girls lay on the bed. The fine lace veil that Kara had worn for the ceremony was already carefully draped over a chair back. On the dresser, between cut-glass perfume bottles, were four sparkling tulip glasses, and a bottle of champagne chilled in an ice bucket beside the dresser. A good way to calm the bride's nerves while she freshened up, Laurel decided.

Amidst the mayhem, Kara stood in front of a cheval mirror examining the hem of her wedding dress critically. "I haven't torn a hole in the hem, have I, Laurel?"

Moving forward, Laurel squinted at the delicately scalloped edge that Kara was holding up. "Not that I can see."

"Thank heavens." Relief filled her younger sister's voice as she let the beautiful white fabric drop. "I thought I might have put a heel through it when I came back down the aisle."

"Relax. It's all fine." Laurel scanned her sister's face. Kara's skin glowed, needing no added artifice. The shimmer of eye shadow accentuated her green eyes, but her lips had lost the gloss they'd worn before the ceremony. Laurel's mouth quirked up. "You make a beautiful bride, Mrs. Houghton—even without touching up the gloss that your groom kissed off."

It was true. Kara's radiance had given her the kind of beauty that came from inner happiness. Taking care not to crush the delicate wedding dress, Laurel gave her sister a tentative hug. But Kara had no such scruples and flung her arms around Laurel.

"Thank you, oh, thank you, for jilting Eli!"

Laurel looked into eyes almost the same green as her own, eyes they'd inherited from their mother. "Believe me, if I'd married your groom it would have been the biggest mistake of both our lives."

It had been one thing to drift into an engagement with Eli, but once the time to plan the wedding had arrived, Laurel had been distressed to discover her heart wasn't in it.

Instead of daydreaming about wedded bliss, she'd found herself dwelling on how static her life had become.

How predictable.

How boring.

And what it would take to get a life. To her discomfort, writing out lists of wedding guests who'd accepted their invitations to the big day had not even featured.

That was when Laurel had created the How to Get a Life List.

Jilt Eli. Item No. 1 on the List, as she'd started thinking of it, had looked so stark, so cruel when she'd stared at the two words topping the otherwise blank piece of paper, that she hadn't known if she was capable of breaking off her engagement to Eli.

His feelings would be hurt. Her family would be devastated. But writing it down had brought such a sense of catharsis that Laurel had known she'd had no other choice.

She and Eli were simply not meant to be.

To spare his feelings, she'd told him she couldn't marry him until the upheaval in her life—her father's murder, the shocking discovery of his other family and the anguish of her mother's arrest—had settled down. But the overwhelming relief in Eli's eyes brought home the knowledge that she wasn't the only one who wanted out.

Almost a month had passed since she'd jilted Eli. Today her ex-fiancé was celebrating the happiness he'd found—with her sister. Eli had gotten himself a life.

However, until putting on Item No. 2—red-lipstick—this morning during the final preparations, she had done nothing more about tackling the rest of the List. Breaking the strictures of a lifetime was proving to be daunting. Despite the List which she carried in her purse as a constant prod to action.

That had to change, she had to start living. Really living.

Like that electric moment during the ceremony when she'd met a pair of dark eyes and she'd been jolted by a surge of energy. That had been living.

Extricating herself from her sister's arms, Laurel lifted the bottle of champagne from the ice bucket and filled two of the flutes, then passed one to Kara.

She raised her glass in a toast. "Be happy."

"Oh, I am. Today is the happiest day of my life."

Her sister sparkled like a fairytale princess.

Laurel couldn't stop a stab of envy. She took a quick gulp of champagne before setting it down.

"Eli and I had always been such good friends, and I think we both hoped that would be enough—I know I did. But it wasn't. We lacked that special connection that you two have." They hadn't even shared the kind of physical attraction that had blasted through her after one lingering look from a stranger.

"It's love. Real love. He's my soul mate. I'm incredibly fortunate." Kara had gone all dreamy-eyed. Then her gaze sharpened. "How funny that you're the one Eli spent the most time with while we were growing up—"

"That's because we were the same age—in the same year at school and invited to the same social functions," Laurel pointed out.

"—But you've never met his other close friend."

"Rakin Abdellah?" Laurel had heard plenty about the grandson of a Middle-Eastern prince with whom Eli had become close friends at Harvard. "Such a pity he didn't make it to the wedding."

"He's here!" Kara put her glass down beside Laurel's, then slid onto the stool in front of the dresser. She picked up a wide-toothed comb. "Eli introduced us when he came up to congratulate us after the ceremony."

Laurel hesitated in the act of taking the comb from her sister. Was it possible…?

"Where was I?"

"It must've been when Flynn swatted the flower girls with the ring cushion and you went after him before he caused more chaos."

Waving the comb in the air, Laurel spread her hands. "How typical! I always miss the man. Every time Eli caught up with him when Rakin visited on business, I had something else going on. Maybe we're just never destined to meet." But she couldn't stop wondering whether the tall, lean man responsible for that shock of awareness during the ceremony could possibly be Eli's best friend.

"What was he wearing?" she asked Kara urgently.

"Who?"

"Rakin!" Laurel shook her head at her sister. "The man you were telling me about."

"I don't know—the only man whose clothes I'm focused on today is Eli."

Laurel laughed at her sister's goofy expression. Dismissing the hunk, she started to smooth Kara's hair where the veil had been fastened earlier. "Speaking of Eli, you'd better re-apply your lipstick," she told her sister.

Kara slanted her a wicked look via the mirror. "What's the point? It will only get kissed off again." Then her gaze narrowed. "Laurel, you're wearing red lipstick!"

Laurel shot her younger sister an indulgent look. "If you've only just noticed it can't be such a big deal."

"You've decided to go ahead with your plan to stop playing it safe!" Kara had stilled. "I know you told me you were going to spread your wings and work on being a bit more uninhibited, but I hadn't seen any more signs of it since I warned you to take care—and not to go too crazy."

"Can you see me, Miss Responsibility, going crazy?" asked Laurel with a light laugh.

"Okay, I shouldn't have told you to be careful—I've been wishing I never said anything. You should have some fun. What about getting Eli to introduce you to Rakin?"

"Don't you dare!" To stop her too observant sister from interfering, Laurel said, "Did you notice how protective Cutter's been of Mom today?"

"I think everyone did. He didn't leave her side."

"I think Cutter will be good for her—he seems to genuinely love her." Laurel patted the final wayward strands in place and stood back to admire Kara's hair. To make sure it held, she added the lightest spritz of hair spray. "And he risked a storm of scandal by coming forward to tell the police that Mom had spent the night of Dad's murder with him. That's what got her out on bail."

"I offered to plan a small wedding for Mom—elegant and discreet. But Mom was dead against it. She doesn't think they can get married until a decent time of mourning Dad has passed—"

"That's ridiculous." Just the idea that her mother was letting what people thought rule her life caused Laurel to see red. "Mom must do what makes her happy."

"I agree Mom deserves a little happiness after discovering the sordid details of Dad's secret life, and if marrying Cutter gives her that, I'll be his biggest fan." Kara swiveled around on the stool and examined Laurel. "And I didn't notice your lip color because I was too busy getting married." She clearly wasn't about to let Laurel off the hook. "But now I've noticed. I'm interested—I want to know what you're planning to do next."

Laurel could feel herself coloring. She wasn't even sure what she was going to do next herself. Confessing to the existence of the List, and worse, to imagining living out some mind-boggling fantasies—even to her sister—was way too much to bear.

"It's hardly world changing," she said off-handedly, thinking about her frivolous desire to eat ice cream in bed.

But that still left more....

Item No. 5, *Gamble all night.*

Item No. 6, *Travel to exotic lands.*

Okay, maybe they were a little world changing....

Tilting her head to one side, Kara said, "Hmm, you've never worn red lipstick—you always say it's too obvious—so that's already a pretty big change."

Red lips clashed with her auburn hair. It was trashy. And trashy was a sin. Leaning past Kara to avoid her sister's gaze, Laurel pretended to inspect her lips in the dresser mirror. There were no smudges—nor likely to be, unless she found someone to kiss.

Which brought her back to How to Get a Life.

Item No. 3 on the list was *Flirt with a stranger.* Her cheeks grew hot. Unlike most Southern women Laurel was a rookie in the art of flirting. Since entering her teens, she'd only had to look at a male to have him cross the room to meet her. Sometimes she'd hated the kind of attention her features brought. To deal with it, she'd cultivated a polite manner with no hint of flirtatiousness. The facade had served her equally well in her dealings as public relations director of the Kincaid Group. So why on earth was she adding an item like *Flirt with a stranger*?

Maybe she should've made that *Kiss a stranger*. The renegade thought startled her.

"You're blushing. Is it a man? Is that the reason for the red lips?" Kara's voice broke into Laurel's musings. "Is that the reason you won't let me ask Eli to introduce you to Rakin?"

"No man," Laurel denied, wishing that her complexion didn't color quite so dramatically. "The red lips are for me alone."

For one mad moment she was tempted to tell Kara all about the List. Then she cringed and the impulse passed.

Telling Kara would be insane. And Kara would start fretting again about Laurel exposing herself to danger—and the last thing Laurel wanted was to cause her sister to worry on her wedding day.

She drained the last of the champagne, then set her glass back down on the dresser. She caught another glimpse of her lips in the mirror above the dresser.

What would it be like to kiss the gorgeous dark-haired man from the church?

The shocking visual of crushed red lips sent a frisson of heat coursing through her.

Laurel came to her senses. What if he turned out to be Eli's friend? How trashy would that be? She'd always been the good eldest sister...the one to do as she was told. To study hard for excellent grades. To obey her curfew. She'd always set an example for her sisters to follow. No mini skirts. No ear studs and torn jeans. No shameless behavior with boys. No wild flings.

No trashy makeup...

She turned away from the mirror, intending to say something light and funny to her sister.

Only to find Kara had risen to her feet and was still watching her.

"I have to admit red suits you, Laurel. Makes you look like a movie star. Glamorous. Sexy. You always wear beiges and creams. I take back all my cautions, you should break out more often."

Laurel's heart lightened as she followed her sister to the door. "Careful! I might take that as permission to do something reckless."

Kara halted in the doorway, looked over her shoulder and smiled. "Why not? Start today. No time like the present."

Now? Tonight? Laurel's hands turned cold and clammy as Kara vanished out of sight with a whisper of French fabric.

It was one thing to talk about loosening up a little; it was another thing altogether to actually do it and let go. The sense of being poised on the edge of a precipice swept Laurel.

Should she take that first step into the unknown and walk on the wild side? Or should she stay in her safe world and risk never feeling quite satisfied?

The answer came quickly, so quickly it took her aback. She was tired of missing out. She wanted to feel more of that pulsing energy that she'd experienced earlier. That flutter of rebellion brought a surge of illicit pleasure.

Laurel drew a deep breath and felt her lungs fill, and resolve spread through her. Kara was right—there was no time like the present. She headed for the door.

Tonight, she'd flirt with a stranger.

Two

In the elegant, embellished salon downstairs, a twelve-piece jazz ensemble was playing blues, a smoky, elegant sound. Perfect for what had to be one of the high-society weddings of the year.

Laurel hummed and did a little dance step in Kara's wake and almost skipped into Alan Sinclair, who'd materialized in front of them, holding two glasses brimming with pale, bubbling gold wine. By some miracle he managed to keep the glasses upright, while Laurel apologized effusively.

"Major catastrophe averted," he joked.

All three of them laughed.

"These were intended for you, beautiful ladies." Alan held out the brimming glasses, his hazel eyes alight with good humor.

"Only a sip for me. I'm going to need my wits about me—I need to make sure I get all the guests' names right," said Kara with a gracious smile.

Laurel took the remaining glass. "Thank you."

"I didn't get a chance earlier to give you my very best wishes," Alan told Kara. "Eli is a lucky man."

"Why, thank you, Alan." Kara beamed at him. "I certainly hope you meet the woman of your dreams soon—maybe even tonight."

Alan laughed. "I can live in hope. But maybe we should wait a while—give you time for a honeymoon—before handing you another wedding to plan."

"I'd be thrilled to do another wedding. And, for once, that's not the businesswoman in me talking. I'm so happy, I'm ready to marry everyone off."

"He's a nice man," Laurel observed as they walked away, holding their glasses.

"Thoughtful, too," Kara agreed. "He'll make some lucky woman a good husband."

They'd reached the bridal table by now, and Eli leapt up to welcome his bride, his eyes warm and devoted as he seated her.

Feeling a bit like a third wheel, Laurel slipped into the vacant seat beside her mother and set her glass down on the white damask linen sprinkled with pink and crimson rose petals. A waiter appeared to fill it up.

"Where's Cutter?" Laurel asked her mother, aware that she was sitting in his seat. The whole world had paired up—even her mother.

Everyone except her.

A wave of loneliness swept her; then she shook it off. All the more reason to follow the List and find a stranger to flirt with—and where better than a wedding?

"He spotted Harold Parsons and Mr. Larrimore and went over to greet them." Elizabeth fluttered a hand in the direction of the bar. Following where her mother indicated, Laurel could see the white-haired lawyer talking to the head of Larrimore Industries, which had recently begun doing business with The Kincaid Group, making up a little of the losses TKG had suffered when several customers defected to Carolina Shipping. Why, only this week her brother Matthew, TKG's director of new business, had heard rumblings that Jack Sinclair was trying to outbid them on an important shipping contract through back-door channels.

Speak of the devil.

Jack Sinclair had pulled out a chair to seat himself at a table right on the edge of the dance floor. *How boldly arrogant.* He was behaving like he owned the Kincaid mansion. Laurel supposed inheriting forty-five percent of the stock in The Kincaid Group was responsible for some of that arrogance. She hadn't managed to get a handle on Jack yet. Dark, unsmiling and perpetually brooding, he made her a little uneasy. He'd certainly caused TKG enough headaches in the past few months to last a lifetime.

Then Laurel caught a sight of the smooth blond hair of his mother, Angela, seated beyond him. Something his mother said caused a ferocious scowl to mar Jack's features. Laurel shivered at the sight of his displeasure.

Why had her father's firstborn son bothered to come to the wedding, if he intended to sit there and glare? Was he only here today to fool the paparazzi into thinking he was an accepted part of the Kincaid family? Or were her siblings correct? Did Jack fear that by staying away he'd heighten the suspicion already surrounding him? Laurel didn't want to consider the possibility that her father had been shot in the head by his firstborn son.... It was too horrible.

She refused to allow Jack's presence to ruin the celebratory mood tonight. The pall that had hung over the family for months had finally lifted. Laurel intended to enjoy the occasion...and make sure her mom did, too.

Laurel caught Elizabeth's hand and gave it a squeeze. "I can't tell you how glad I am not only that you're here at the wedding but that you've been cleared of all those ridiculous charges. It's the best wedding gift Kara and Eli could ever have received."

"Today hasn't been easy," her mother confessed. "All the speculation. I'm sure there are people here this evening who still believe I killed your father. And everyone is so curious about Cutter—it's difficult for him, too."

Yet, in the way that was so typical of Southern society matriarchs, none of her mother's discomfort showed. Elizabeth's face was serene, her short, auburn hair with the elegant grey highlights was immaculate, the strain of the past four turbulent months carefully masked. Only the reserve in her green eyes hinted at the anguish she'd been through.

"You deserve some happiness." Laurel echoed Kara's words from earlier. Letting go of her mother's hand she reached for the glass Alan had given her. "And if Cutter makes you happy you shouldn't let what others think spoil that. Let's drink to happier tomorrows."

Elizabeth took a tiny sip, and then set her own glass down. "I do wish the police would hurry up and finalize the investigation. Not knowing who killed your father…" Her voice trailed away.

Her brothers RJ and Matt had some strong opinions about who might have killed her father. But now wasn't the right time to share them with her mother.

"I'll call Detective McDonough tomorrow to arrange a meeting for later in the week to find out if there has been any progress," promised Laurel. She shot the brooding interloper at the edge of the dance floor a surreptitious look. With luck, the police might finally have gathered enough evidence to toss Jack Sinclair in jail where her brothers said he belonged.

If her brothers were right, then Jack had been extremely devious—he'd made sure he had an airtight alibi, with several of his own employees vouching he'd been working late the night her father had died. Laurel didn't want to believe her half brother was capable of that kind of treachery. But as RJ had pointed out, Jack was a very wealthy man—made even richer by the forty-five percent stake he inherited in The Kincaid Group on her father's death. That kind of money could buy any alibi—particularly when the people supplying it already depended on him to earn their living. Laurel made a mental note to get an update from Nikki Thomas, the corporate security specialist the family had hired to investigate Jack Sinclair's efforts to sabotage The Kincaid Group. Laurel couldn't bear to see her mother so down, and Nikki might also have some thoughts about how to speed up the investigation—even though Laurel had once or twice suspected Nikki to be a little more emotionally invested in the ruthless man she was investigating than was wise.

Immersed in her thoughts, the touch on her arm startled her, and her head jerked around.

Eli stood there, wearing a broad grin. "Laurel, there's someone I'd like you to meet."

Glancing at the dark figure beside her former fiancé, Laurel found herself confronted by the handsome man she'd exchanged that sizzling eye-meet with during the wedding ceremony.

"Laurel, this is Rakin Whitcomb Abdellah." Eli presented him with a flourish. "Rakin, meet Laurel Kincaid, my brand new sister-in-law."

Honest to goodness, she was going to kill Kara!

Already she could feel a flush stealing up her throat.

"I've heard so much about you." Rakin held out his hand.

"Funny, that's exactly what I was about to say." Laurel set down her glass and took his hand. Her lashes swept down as she became conscious of the strength of the fingers against hers. "I'm surprised we've never encountered each other before."

"*In'shallah.*" Letting go of her fingers, he spread his own hands wide. "What more can I say? The time was not right."

Her gaze lifted and sharpened. "You believe in fate?"

"But of course. Everything happens for a reason. Today is the right time for us to meet."

Charmed, she started to smile. It looked like Eli's friend might be the perfect candidate for a flirtation with a stranger. "It is?"

"Yes." His black-velvet gaze was intent…and Laurel felt the primal power of the man.

To break the spell, she switched her attention to Eli and murmured, "You should be worried we might trade secrets—between us we probably know everything about you."

Eli chuckled. "I'm terrified."

"You're anything but terrified." Laurel glanced at Rakin, and found his dark eyes were bright with laughter

The band swung into the first bars of the first dance.

"Now there's something I am terrified about messing up. That's the bridal waltz," said Eli. "Let me go claim my bride."

Laurel couldn't help laughing as he hurried back to her sister. Conscious of Rakin's very male presence at her side as Eli led Kara out onto the floor, Laurel fell silent and concentrated on watching the dance—not an easy task with Rakin still looming over her.

A spotlight landed on the newlyweds. The guests sighed as they moved into the dance in perfect time, Kara's white dress fanning out to fill the ring the spotlight had created. They glided to the melody, and a few beats later, Laurel's sister Lily and her husband, Daniel, joined in, RJ and Brooke were next on the floor.

Laurel could see Alan smiling as he sat beside his mother at the table on the edge of the dance floor. Jack had disappeared. Laurel wished he could've practiced the same civility as the Kincaid family—at Elizabeth's request—were taking great care to show Angela and her sons tonight.

"Would you like to dance?"

Rakin's deep tone caused her to forget all about Jack's rudeness.

Silently she gave him her hand. The warm strength of his fingers closing around hers caused the return of that renegade fantasy of crushed, kissed lips, and Laurel abruptly lowered her eyelashes before he might read any of her dizzy imaginings. "Why, thank you, I'd like that."

He led her onto the dance floor and took her into his arms. The sudden intimacy came as a shock. The music swirled around them.

To break the seductive mood, Laurel said, "You met Eli at Harvard?"

"Yes, we shared some classes and sometimes went hiking together—we both like the outdoors."

"Yes. You were on the rowing team together, too, weren't you? I seem to remember hearing Eli talk about pre-dawn practices on the river."

He smiled. "Strange interest for someone from a desert country, hmm?"

"A little." She examined him. "Tell me about Diyafa."

"Ah, Eli has told you about my country?"

"Just the name. Diyafa." It rolled off her tongue. "It sounds so deliciously exotic."

"It is. The desert nights are warm and dry and the heavens above possess the brightest stars I have ever seen."

The whisper of his voice stoked her imagination. "How magical. I hate to confess this—but I've never been out of the United States."

"Never?"

She shook her head. "Never. I always intended to travel."

Item No. 6 on the List involved traveling to some far-flung exotic destination. She'd had a fleeting vision of herself standing in the center of St. Mark's Square in Venice or in front of the Sphinx in Egypt. Somewhere as different from Charleston as she could get.

She pulled a face. "Now I just have to turn that dream into reality. I even got myself a passport." Which she'd been carrying around in her purse, together with the List—and the letter from her father she'd received on that emotionally charged day when her father's will was read.

"Diyafa is a good place to visit."

Did he think she was trying to coax an invitation from him? Discomfort flooded her. "Oh, I couldn't take advantage of our acquaintance."

"Why not?"

Her lashes fluttered down. "We hardly know one another."

"I'm sure we can remedy that." He sounded amused.

Laurel's lashes lifted. Heavens, was she actually flirting with the man?

Then she examined her reaction.

So what?

Flirt with a stranger. It was on her list, and she was unlikely to ever encounter Rakin again. He might be Eli's other best friend, but before today she'd only ever heard about him. It would be at least another ten years before they met again; after all he was a busy man. Worth the risk?

Or was she going to chicken out? No. The time to act had arrived. Pursing her mouth into a moue, she gave what she hoped looked like a mysterious smile. "Maybe I will visit...one day."

An arrested expression settled in his eyes.

"You can let me know when you do." There was an intimate note in his voice.

He was flirting too!

Rakin was clearly a master at the art of flirtation. For once she was tempted to let herself go. To revel in the full power of her womanhood. This was a man she was facing, a real man with a wealth of experience with women.

"To be honest I'm more likely to visit Las Vegas—" she began with a teasing laugh.

"You like to gamble?"

Had his voice dropped? Laurel's heart beat a little faster. "I've never gambled seriously in my life. Certainly not in a casino."

Her mother didn't approve of gambling. A roguish uncle, the black sheep of the Winthrop family, had lost a fortune at poker, contributing to the dire straits the family found itself in before her mother's marriage into the Kincaid fortune. Gambling was seriously discouraged among the Kincaid children. No doubt that was why *Gamble all night* had made it onto the List....

"We'll have to change that—raise the stakes."

Yes, he was definitely flirting. If the intimate note in his voice hadn't made it clear, the gleam in his eyes confirmed it. Laurel gave herself up to the heady rush. "I wouldn't want to become addicted."

"That can only happen if the stakes are higher than you can afford."

"I'll remember that." She peeked at him through her lashes. "If I ever find myself in Vegas."

The song came to an end. She was hot and thirsty, yet Laurel found she didn't want the exchange to end. It was exhilarating. Fun. Yet risky. More than she'd ever banked on when she'd scrawled *Flirt with a stranger* on her list. The weight of Rakin's hand resting on her waist, the touch of his fingers against hers, the way his body had brushed against hers to the rhythm of the music was stealing over her senses.

"It's warm in here," she said, finally letting go of his hand and fanning her face. "I need a drink."

"There's a cool breeze outside," Rakin responded readily,

his hand sliding from where it rested at her waist to beneath he
elbow. As they skirted the dance floor he picked up two brim
ming tulip glasses from a passing waiter with his free hand
before leading her to the open doors.

Laurel hesitated on the threshold. Outside, the balcony ap
peared to be deserted.

Her heart leapt as his hand touched the sensitive skin unde
her elbow. Rakin's voice was deep and smooth as he said
"Come. It will be quiet and cool."

And she couldn't help wondering if she'd let herself in fo
more than she could handle as she stepped out into the South
ern night.

There was a slight breeze and the balmy night air was redo
lent with the sweet scent of magnolia and jasmine.

Rakin led Laurel to the shadows at the end of balcony wher
the sultry throb of the jazz band was fainter. Under the glow cas
by a wall sconce, he handed one of the long-stemmed glasses t
Laurel, then leant back against the wide balustrade. She tippe
the glass up to take a slow sip, and her gaze tangled with hi
over the rim.

Something—lust?—locked fast in the base of his stomach.

With her tall, slender figure wrapped in a column of moon
light silk, her magnolia skin, sparkling eyes and the crownin,
glory of her dark red hair, Laurel Kincaid was a very beautifu
woman. Any man would be aroused by having the full wattag
of her attention switched on to him. And, to his chagrin, Raki.
discovered he was no exception.

But he was interested in far more than the surge of attractio
between them. Holding her gaze, he drank from his glass, savor
ing the dry bubbles against his tongue. Despite the millions he'
added to the Al-Abdellah fortune, his grandfather was threat
ening to toss him out of the family business if he didn't marr
soon. So far, Rakin had resisted—love was not on his agenda
But the battle of wills being fought between himself and Princ
Ahmeer Al-Abdellah had now erupted into open war. Marriag
to the right woman might be the lesser of two evils. Eli's no

o-joking suggestion that Laurel might be the perfect bride to
et Rakin's grandfather off his back was worth serious consid-
ration.

And love would not be a factor…

One look at Laurel and his wily grandfather would ask no
urther questions. What man in his right mind would pass up the
hance to wed such a stunning creature? Her connection to the
Charleston Kincaids only served to make the deal even sweeter.
But first Rakin would have to sell the idea to Laurel—she was
Kincaid, there was no earthly reason for her to agree to help
im out.

Except business…

"So you'd like to gamble in Vegas?" he asked, swirling the
old liquid in his flute.

"Maybe."

He could hear the smile in her voice. Was she teasing him?
He couldn't read her expression. "You've really never been?"

"Only once—as a young child. But I don't remember it, so
. doesn't count."

"Such a lack is easy enough to remedy—but you shouldn't
o alone."

"I only discovered recently that I wanted to go at all. A few
months ago I could've invited Lily or Kara along with me. But
's too late for that—they're both married now. You may not
ave heard, Lily and Daniel decided to solemnize their union
a very private service just a couple of days ago—Lily didn't
want to overshadow Kara's wedding. They intend to have a
igger elaborate family affair in October after the baby is born."

She spoke in a matter-of-fact voice, yet Rakin thought he de-
ected a hint of loneliness in her voice. He was no stranger to
oneliness. An only child, he envied Laurel the bond she shared
ith her sisters and brothers. The closeness among the Kincaids
as evident in every look, every laugh.

The closest he'd come to that kind of relationship was the
iendship he shared with Eli—but neither of them talked much
oout family…or emotions. Sport, money and business were

their main lines of communication. "Marriage won't change th
fact that they will always be your sisters."

Laurel moved away from the light, to the end of the bal
cony. She raised her glass and sipped while she stared out int
the night. At last she spoke, "I know that. But now they hav
priorities of their own. Both of them have husbands…and Lil
is going to be a mother. The sisterhood will never be the sam
again." Her voice held an echo of sadness. Then he caught th
glint of startling white in the shadows as she turned her hea
and smiled. "Enough of that. I have plenty of friends with whor
I can visit Vegas."

Rakin didn't doubt that for a moment. She was vivacious an
breathtakingly beautiful. She'd have friends buzzing around he
like bees at a honey pot.

"How did you come to be friends with Eli?" he asked.

It had puzzled him when Eli had first spoken about Laur
Kincaid back at Harvard. Initially, Rakin had thought the tw
must share more than friendship. With his upbringing in th
traditional society of Diyafa followed by all-boys schoolin
envisaging a close friendship between a man and a woman ha
been foreign. But Eli had made it clear he and Laurel were not
ing more than friends—very close friends. When the news ha
come that they were engaged, Rakin had not been surprised. /
some point any friendship between a man and woman woul
have to cross into the sexual realm. Women and men were n
created to be simply friends.

Laurel's jilting of Eli, and Eli's ready acceptance of it—an
his wry joke that Rakin should marry her—had astonishe
Rakin. So, too, had the fact that Eli's heart had not even bee
the slightest bit battered after Laurel's desertion.

"Growing up, we were the same age—it seemed natural tha
we hung out together. Now, years later, with both of us sti
single and such good friends, we were invited everywhere to
gether. I guess we were linked in everyone else's minds as
couple long before the idea ever occurred to either of us." Sh
shrugged, and light glimmered on the pale slope of shoulde
left bare by her silver-gray dress. "The next step was marriag

But clearly we're better at being friends than lovers. There was no spark."

And that would explain Eli's philosophical acceptance of the breakup. Rakin put his glass down and took a step closer to Laurel; then he murmured, "You wanted spark?"

"Doesn't every woman?"

Something leapt between them. Before Rakin could consider his actions, he lifted a hand and brushed a strand of the dark fire from her cheek. Her dewy skin was softer than any he'd ever touched—and it left him hungry to stroke again. Abruptly, he dropped his hand before he could give into the moment's madness. "Everyone seeks that elusive flame—few are lucky enough to find it."

"You mean love?"

"I don't believe in love—I'm talking about what you called spark. A tangible force that connects two people in perfect harmony only a few times in a lifetime."

She tipped her head back and drained the last of her champagne. The elegant column of her neck gleamed in the lamplight. "Spark sounds...interesting. I used to think I wanted love more than anything else in the world."

"You don't think so anymore?"

"Nope." She giggled. "That should be 'No,' clearly and politely enunciated, of course."

Rakin found himself grinning at that absurdity. The revelation that she wasn't looking for some romantic notion of love eased his conscience. Business...and maybe some sparks...might be enough to persuade her to go along with his plan.

"Pardon my giggling." Laurel moved back into the pool of light beneath the wall sconce. "There hasn't been much to laugh about lately so this feels very good."

"It must be the joy of a wedding."

She raised her empty glass. "I suspect it may have something to do with the champagne, too."

The forthright observation startled Rakin. Had he at last found a woman capable of distinguishing between realism and romance? Quite possibly. She was, after all, a Kincaid, a busi-

nesswoman. It was starting to look like he'd struck twenty-four
karat gold. "Can I get you another?"

"Not yet. I've had enough. I think I might be a little tipsy.
I'm trying to remember how many glasses of champagne I've
had. Three maybe." She laughed again. "That's a first."

Straightening from where he leant, Rakin took the glass from
her and set it down on the balustrade behind them. "You've
never been tipsy?"

She shook her head and her hair swirled about her face.
"Never! My mother would be mortified, she would not approve."

At the mention of her mother, Rakin said, "I was sorry to
hear about your mother's arrest—it must have been a difficult
time for the whole family."

"It hasn't been easy." All humor drained from her face and
Rakin found himself missing the pleasure of it. "The police
are still no closer to finding a suspect. But thankfully Mom
has been cleared." Laurel shivered, and he knew it wasn't with
cold. "I keep replaying that last day through my mind. I was at
the offices until late in the afternoon. I even made Dad a cup of
coffee before I left. He glanced up when I set it down, I joked
that it was hot and strong just as he liked it. He laughed—Dad
didn't often laugh—and thanked me, then he went back to the
documents he was reading. That's the last image I have of him.
Daddy didn't even see me wave goodbye as I exited his office."

She broke off, and Rakin knew she was fighting back tears.

"But I keep thinking I should've have had some kind pre-
monition—noticed something," she said huskily. "I saw nothing
out of the ordinary. Several of the staff were still there when I
left—Brooke, RJ's assistant at the time, was the last to leave."

The memory was clearly upsetting Laurel. Rakin could make
out the gooseflesh rippling across the fine, smooth skin of her
arms.

Wrapping her arms around herself, she walked back to the
end of the balustrade. "I can't believe I never noticed anything."

"You weren't expecting anything to happen."

She fell silent. Finally she turned her head and a band of
moonlight fell across her face giving her skin the sheen of sil-

vered silk. "Out of all of us, Brooke blames herself most. In her statement to the police she mentioned while she was finishing up the filing backlog, Mom brought dinner to Dad that night. The police arrested Mom—she was the last person to see him alive and, until recently, she had no alibi. What makes Brooke feel even worse is the fact that she didn't even think to mention that earlier in the afternoon it was pouring rain and she had her arms full of blueprints when she ran for the office to avoid being drenched. A man in a hat and raincoat held the door open for her. No one has any idea who he was. Security didn't record his entry—they thought he was with Brooke. And, of course, she has no idea who he could've been. Detective McDonough thinks it's possible he hid in the building until after everyone—including Mom—left."

"And there's still no clue about who it was?"

Laurel shook her head, causing her hair to ripple over her shoulders. "Video security footage from an adjacent lot puts Jack Sinclair's vintage Aston Martin in the parking lot from late afternoon until around the time my father was shot—but he swears he was at his own office. Yet he never reported his car missing—or stolen."

The odd note in her voice made Rakin probe further, "But you think Sinclair might have murdered your father?"

"I keep hoping not. Dad obviously loved Angela—he wanted to marry her, but his parents wouldn't countenance it. Jack's clearly bitter about the situation. Fact is, he may be the firstborn son, but he's not a legitimate Kincaid. Dad tried to make it up to him—and to Angela. Yet despite the inheritance and power Dad gave him, he's behaving like he has a major grudge against the family—which makes it hard to view Jack in any kind of positive way."

"And you like to see the best in people?"

"I try." The eyes that met his held the kind of honesty he'd given up hoping to find. "But I don't always get it right. Let's talk about something else—I promised myself I wouldn't let Jack Sinclair ruin tonight. It's a celebration."

"I want to talk about you." With a sense of satisfaction, Rakin watched her do a double take. "Eli said you possess the kindest heart of anyone he knows."

It had crossed Rakin's mind in the past few minutes to throw himself at her mercy and ask her to help him out of a tight spot with his grandfather, but it went against the grain. Rakin never asked for favors. His pride would not allow it. All his decisions were based on considerations of mutual benefit—and hard profit.

She wrinkled her nose at him. "That makes me sound boring."

"Kindness isn't boring."

"Well, it's not very exciting either."

Rakin's eyebrows jerked up at that. "You want to be considered exciting?"

"I want a life." It burst from her. She looked taken aback at her own ferocity. "Goodness, that sounded much more melodramatic than I intended."

Maybe Laurel Kincaid didn't express her own wants often enough, mused Rakin. Taking two steps toward her, he asked carefully, "How do you intend to achieve the life you want?"

Her gaze shifted out to the night. For a long moment he thought she wasn't going to answer.

Then she turned her head, and her eyes glistened in the dappled shadows. "I'm going to do all the things I've never done. Things no one would expect of Laurel Kincaid, director of public relations of TKG, friend of the Library, patron of the Art Gallery—first person to join a committee for the next good cause."

Rakin couldn't suppress a smile at the self-deprecatory comment. "Like gamble in Vegas?"

"Exactly like gambling in Vegas." She lifted her chin a touch defensively. "It may not be meaningful, but it will be one brick broken out of the boundaries that are imprisoning me."

What was it about this woman that caused his heart to lighten and amusement to fill him? Leading him to feel as if he'd shed the burden accumulated over years?

Then it came to him. Under that ladylike exterior, Laurel Kincaid was a rebel. A real, genteel Southern rebel. Rakin had a feeling that she was about to throw off the constraints of a lifetime. The fates help them all. "You want to experience risk and adventure?"

"Oh, yes!"

Staring into her sparkling eyes, Rakin discovered he wanted to get to know this intriguing woman better.

Much better.

He desired her. More importantly, he liked her. It would be so easy to explain his predicament to her—he suspected she would listen. He could already visualize her head tilting to one side, her eyes fixed on his as he told her about his grandfather's threats to disenfranchise him from the company he'd worked so hard to expand. His predicament would arouse her sympathy—how could it not, given the parallels to Jack Sinclair's efforts to destroy The Kincaid Group?

Would her kind heart allow her to agree to a marriage of convenience?

Rakin suspected she just might even consider it. Eli had been right: Laurel would make him the perfect wife.

But he needed time to persuade her. Before he could check the impulse he found himself saying, "So come away with me to Vegas."

Three

"Come away with you to Las Vegas? Are you serious?"

Astonishment caused Laurel's mouth to drop open. So much for the certainty that her instilled equilibrium was unshakeable. Rakin's invitation had floored her. And, what's more, the rogue knew he'd surprised her—his eyes were twinkling.

"Absolutely serious." He'd closed the gap between them, and his broad shoulders blocked her view of the house. "You could have try your luck at the slot machines."

"I intend to do more than try my luck at the machines," she informed him. "My plan is to gamble all night—in the casino."

"That's a serious rebellion." His eyes crinkled as his grin broadened. "And I'm sure I can accommodate such a plan."

"Are you laughing at me?" she asked suspiciously, flicking her hair back over her shoulder.

"Why should I laugh at you?"

Because he considered her too staid, too much of a Goody Two-shoes to take him up on his offer? She took in his stance. His weight was perfectly balanced on both feet. In the shadows his white shirtfront was a startling contrast to his dark, hawkish features. The rash urge to surprise him rose before she could check it. Why shouldn't she take him up on his invitation to go gamble in Vegas?

Laurel drew a deep breath and said in a rush, "My mother was a Winthrop."

She paused expectantly.

When Rakin didn't react, she said, "I forget. To people not from the South, the name is meaningless. But in South Carolina the Winthrops have always been a force to be reckoned with." She gave him a quick smile. "Sounds terribly snobbish, I know. But in Charleston they're an old, well-established family who fell on hard times. A result of bad business decisions—although the decline had started way back. My Winthrop great-great uncle was infamous for his ability to gamble huge sums on property and poker—he lost at both."

"I'm sorry to hear that."

She shrugged. "It got worse. By the 1970s the family fortune had been exhausted, but the Winthrops were still determined to hang on to a lifestyle they could no longer afford. That meant a new injection of cash to maintain their social standing—cash that came from the Kincaid shipping and—ironically—real estate profits." Laurel gave him a wry smile. "The Kincaids must've been better at gambling on property—or, at least, more astute. As luck would have it, at the same time that the Winthrop family fortune was in decline, my Kincaid grandfather was trying to scale the old money bastions of Charleston, which—despite his rapidly growing nouveau riche wealth—had proved impenetrable up till that point. So he pressured my father into marrying my mother."

He stepped closer. "You sound cynical."

"Cynicism is not a usual characteristic of mine, believe it or not." Laurel shifted back until she could feel the hard balustrade against her hip through the delicate fabric of her dress. "But I don't think the way the older Winthrops or Kincaids behaved was particularly admirable—they brokered a marriage between my parents for their own gain."

"It is how things used to be done in powerful families." Rakin shrugged. "But your parents would have to bear part of the responsibility for agreeing to the arrangement."

"My mother fell in love with Reginald Kincaid." Laurel gave

him sad smile. "He was handsome, witty—what woman can
resist a man with a sense of humor?—and he had the means to
restore the family fortune. A veritable knight in shining armor.
She never stood a chance." She let out a shuddering breath.
"Why am I telling you this? We're here to celebrate Kara's wedding, not cry over the past."

"Don't let your parents' choices in the past color your future,"
he said softly. "Come to Vegas—I'll take you gambling if that's
what you want. Or we could just enjoy ourselves for a weekend."

Two…maybe three…days. What harm could come from a
few days of pure pleasure? There was something quite wildly
wicked in doing a deed that had always been frowned upon in
her family—her great uncle had a lot to answer for.

"You make it sound very tempting."

"But?"

So he'd detected her hesitation. "I don't know…."

"You are getting cold feet."

He was one hundred percent correct. Despite the warmth of
the balmy evening, she was most definitely getting cold feet.
She drew in a deep breath, conscious of the pungent scent of
jasmine on the night air. The sweet familiarity of the fragrance
made the conversation she was having with Rakin seem even
more surreal. "I shouldn't even be considering such a crazy invitation."

"Of course you should. It's what you want to do."

Right again.

Could he see inside her head?

Instantly all the reasons why she shouldn't go rolled through
her mind. Who would follow up with Detective McDonough?
With Nikki Thomas? Who would look after her mother? Her
sisters? For a moment she considered that her mother had Cutter
now, her sisters were both married. It would be liberating to
break free of everything for a couple of days.

Enjoy herself. Have some fun. Abandon the responsibilities
that were weighing her down.

Get a life.

Was it already too late? Had she forgotten how to live? Laure glanced up at the man who was offering her the biggest temptation of her life. His lips were still curved into a smile, the lower one full and passionate. Her gaze lingered there. *Kiss a stranger.* So much riskier than flirting. But oh so tempting…

She looked quickly away.

The sound of light footsteps on the balcony freed her from making a decision. Susannah, Matt's fiancée, was bearing down on them. Giving Rakin a curious glance, she said, "Laurel, your presence is required. Kara's about to throw her bouquet."

Laurel's shoulders sagged with relief. Tossing Rakin a small smile, she said, "I must go—duty summons."

"I'll be waiting for you."

He didn't need to say that he would expect an answer; that was implicit in his intent regard. Her smile turned sultry. Flirtatious, even. She was finally getting the hang of it. "I'll hold you to that."

A swarm of women had taken to the dance floor. Young and old—it appeared that every unmarried woman in Charleston wanted to catch the bouquet tonight.

Laurel's heart sank as she took in the spectacle. She came to a dead halt. "There are already enough desperate wannabe brides here, you don't need me to make up numbers."

"Kara specifically said she wanted you here," Susannah said sotto voce, shepherding Laurel forward.

As they reached the outskirts of the dance floor, Elizabeth joined them. "Hurry, Laurel. Kara's been waiting for you."

Laurel glanced from Susannah to her mother, and her tipsiness evaporated. "Do I detect a conspiracy?"

"Oh, no." Though both Susannah and her mother denied it, their eyes were stretched too wide.

Reluctantly, Laurel let her mother drag her into the center of the group.

Out of the corner of her eye she caught a glimpse of a tall, dark man in a beautifully tailored tuxedo. Rakin. Her head jerked about. He was standing beside her brother Matt—and she spotted RJ, and Daniel, Lily's husband, too. As she watched

Alan Sinclair joined them. All of them were grinning. But it was Rakin's dark gaze that brought tremors of excitement to Laurel's stomach.

I'll be waiting. The memory of his whispered words caused the excitement to rise another notch.

What answer was she going to give him?

"Laurel!"

At the sound of her mother's voice, her head whipped around guiltily.

"You need to go forward more—to the front. Kara is about to throw her bouquet."

Laurel balked. But the crowd around her had no such inhibitions. As Eli gallantly held out an arm to help Kara step elegantly onto the band's stage, Laurel was jostled forward.

From her vantage point on the stage, Kara scanned the crowd. Her gaze found Laurel, and her eyes lit up. Then she turned around.

Oh, no.

As Kara tossed the bouquet of red roses backward over her head, Laurel quickly ducked. Then she spun around to see who the lucky recipient had been of the bouquet obviously intended for her.

Elizabeth stood behind her clutching an armful of roses and wearing a bewildered expression.

"Well, congratulations, Mom, it looks like you're set to be the next bride." Taking pity on her mortified mother, Laurel placed a hand under her elbow and led her from the floor.

"Laurel, what are people going to think? Your father has only been dead for four months. Now I'm standing on a dance floor, a wedding bouquet in my arms. This is catastrophic."

Her mother needed a Get a Life list of her own, Laurel decided. She'd spent far too many years of doing the Right Thing. "Mom, stop worrying about what other people think. It's your life.... Live it. Let Kara arrange your wedding, invite your real friends to dance at it—and make Cutter a happy man. Marry him. Be happy."

"Be happy?" Elizabeth repeated. The lines around her mouth

lessened and her eyes brightened. "You're so right, darling. I will be happy. Thank you."

Laurel swallowed the lump in her throat. Was it really that easy?

Then Lily was there, too. "Great catch, Mom!"

"Oh, go on." Elizabeth's cheeks wore flags of scarlet. Yet she looked more vibrant than she had in years.

Kara arrived in a rustle of fine bridal fabric. She frowned at Laurel, who smiled back angelically.

"It was a mistake." Elizabeth shrugged apologetically to her middle daughter. "I know you intended for Laurel to catch it."

Laurel's smile broadened at the confirmation of the conspiracy she'd already suspected. Triumph at the success of her covert rebellion overtook her.

"Laurel needs a groom before she can have a wedding, so throwing her the bouquet was probably a little premature," Lily pointed out to Laurel's increasing amusement. But her relief was short-lived as Lily started scanning the men crowded around the dance floor. "Let me see. There must be someone we can introduce Laurel to. One of RJ's friends—or maybe Daniel knows someone suitable."

Again, her family was organizing her life.

"Hey—"

Kara overrode the objection Laurel was about to make. "Eli already introduced her to Rakin."

Laurel shifted uncomfortably as both her mother and Lily focused on her. "Rakin?"

"He's standing there—at the edge of the dance floor with RJ and Matt right now," offered Kara.

"Don't point." Laurel could have happily wrung her interfering sisters' necks as all eyes swung in his direction. With a touch of desperation, she begged, "And please don't stare."

"Why?" Lily was the first to turn back. "Are you interested in him?"

She flushed. "Not exactly. But nor do I want you causing the poor man any embarrassment. He's too nice for that."

"Nice? He's gorgeous!" Kara didn't mince words.

"Hey, that's the guy you were talking to so cozily on the terrace," Susannah chipped in.

"Ooh, you were on the terrace with him?" This time Brooke hounded her. "You've been holding out on us."

"I've only just met him!"

"But it sounds like you've gotten close pretty quickly." Lily raised an eyebrow.

Under the force of her family's combined interrogation, Laurel gave in. "Okay, he's invited me to go to Vegas."

"To Vegas?" It was a chorus.

"Hush, not so loud!"

"You're going, right?" That was Kara again.

"I don't know...."

"But you must."

"Or are you too busy at work?" asked Lily.

"Laurel can't use work as an excuse," piped Kara. "I know for a fact that her honeymoon was booked for the two weeks after her wedding, and I know she left those weeks open—even after the wedding was called off. There's nothing that can't be cleared from her calendar."

"I needed a break. It's been a busy few months." Laurel avoided Lily's keen eyes. She'd planned to take some time after the wedding to assess what she wanted from life. Now it looked like she was going to spend some of that time with Rakin. A dart of anticipation shafted through her. It would be fun. But what about her mother? "I promised Mom I would call Detective McDonough and arrange a meeting with him later in the wee—"

"I can do that, darling," her mother said quickly. "Don't let that stop you."

"No, I'll do it," said Brooke.

Laurel exchanged a long look with her future sister-in-law and saw the plea in her eyes. If it made Brooke feel like she was helping, that would be worth it. "That's a good idea, Brooke. Nikki Thomas might be able to help—you may want to give her a call, too."

Susannah put a hand on Laurel's arm and bowed her head

close to say softly, "I know you've been carrying a lot of the stress of the past few months, more than we probably realize. I remember it was you who called to let Matt know Elizabeth had been taken into custody."

"All of us have been under strain," Laurel responded in a low voice, so that her mother didn't hear. "I know that Matt has been incredibly worried about—generating new business to stanch the losses Jack Sinclair caused."

Susannah shrugged. "There are rumors of fresh defections all the time. But they can only be dealt with one at a time. Nothing you can do right now. You've done your bit. I know that like RJ, you've kept in close touch with the police and kept us all informed of developments. You need a break."

Then her mother was beside her. "I heard the end of that— and I agree with Susannah. Take some time off. It's your life.... Live it." Elizabeth directed a private smile to Laurel. "You deserve some fun."

"Ah, Mom." In gratitude of her mother's unexpected understanding, Laurel flung her arms around the older woman. Coming from the always correct Elizabeth, the words meant a great deal. "Thank you!"

At the back of her mind had been the thought that her mother would need her. With her other daughters now married, Laurel was the obvious choice to cosset her after her traumatic arrest for Reginald's murder. But her sisters—and Susannah and Brooke—had relieved her of the responsibility. The final—and most weighty—mental block had been removed. There was no reason for Laurel to decline Rakin's invitation.

"Now you have no excuse," Kara said with satisfaction—and Laurel didn't even try to stop the laughter that overflowed as her sister's words echoed her own thoughts.

Instead she said, "I should be mad at you. But how can I be? It's your wedding day—and you're matchmaking as many of us as you can."

Kara looked mystified at that. "What do you mean?"

"You can take all the credit—since you talked Eli into introducing Rakin to me."

But Kara was shaking her head. "Honestly, it wasn't me."
Her sister's reply left Laurel lost for words.

Laurel came toward him, her step light and buoyant, causing
the silver-gray fabric of her dress to swirl around her long legs.
Her lips were curved up and her face alight with what Rakin
could only describe as happiness. It gave her an inner glow, and
accentuated her beauty... and his heart missed a beat.

"Excuse me." Without a backward look to the group he'd
been conversing with about the state of the shipping industry,
he went to meet her. "Would you like to dance?"

She nodded.

A hand clapped his shoulder; then Matt's voice broke in.
"Rakin, we'll catch up again, I'd like to find out more about
some of those Diyafan market players."

For once, money and business were not at the forefront of
Rakin's mind. He said something to Matt that must have satisfied the other man, but he didn't take his eyes off Laurel.

He sensed he was walking a thin line.

Pleasure was threatening to overwhelm business. It would do
him well to take care and not to confuse his priorities. Then he
came to his senses. He was Rakin Whitcomb Abdellah. He controlled a billion-dollar business empire. His grandfather ruled
Diyafa. He'd never been the kind of man to let his heart rule his
head. Never.

Laurel Kincaid was business. He would not forget that.

"Let's dance," he said gruffly, and swept the most beautiful
woman he'd ever met into his arms.

The rhythm of the jazz was rich and deep, smoldering with
the passions of the South.

Laurel's body brushed against his, and involuntarily Rakin's
arms tightened. She was so soft and lush and incredibly feminine. A man could forget his resolve.

She stiffened, and he instantly eased his hold.

Business, he reminded himself.

"What's Flynn doing on the dance floor?"

She'd come to a standstill, and Rakin followed her gaze. He

might've been considering letting pleasure overwhelm him, but Laurel clearly had her feet firmly on the ground. The ring bearer from the wedding ceremony was weaving his way determinedly through the dancing guests. It hadn't been his close hold that had caused her to stiffen, Rakin realized with relief. It was the child. Wearing a pair of sky-blue summer pajamas with his dark hair slicked down, Rakin suspected the kid was supposed to be tucked up in bed.

"Hey!" Laurel slipped out of his arms in a whisper of silver satin, and caught the youngster's hand.

The boy's face lit up. "Aunt Laurel, you didn't catch the flowers Aunt Kara threw at you."

"You were watching?"

"When's Aunt Kara going to cut the cake? She said I could have some."

"This handsome rapscallion is Matt's son, my nephew, Flynn." Laurel told Rakin. Then she turned her attention back to the little boy. "I don't think they'll be cutting the cake for a while. Shouldn't you be in bed?"

He nodded, his blue eyes round with innocence. "Pamela told me a bedtime story."

"Mom's housekeeper," Laurel explained to Rakin. To Flynn, she said, "You should be asleep."

"I was excited…and I want some cake."

"So you escaped." Laurel grinned at him conspiratorially. "I tell you what, you can have one dance with us, then I'll take you back to bed. I promise I'll save you a ginormous piece of cake and give it to you in the morning. Deal?"

Flynn looked uncertain.

"Take it," Rakin advised. "You won't get a better offer tonight."

He held out a hand at a height Flynn could reach. Flynn's eyes lit up as he recognized the game. "High five," he crowed and slapped Rakin's hand.

"Deal," said Rakin.

Rakin watched with amusement as Flynn started to gyrate his limbs alongside them. He had the lack of inhibitions of the very young and threw his heart into every move. But, by the time the melody had faded, he looked exhausted.

A short, silver-haired woman hurried up to claim him.

"He gave me the slip," she told Laurel, after passing a lightning-swift glance over Rakin. "I'll put him back to bed."

As Flynn gave them a wave over his shoulder, the music struck up again. Rakin moved forward and gathered Laurel back into his arms. She didn't protest.

"Pamela, I take it?"

Laurel nodded. "Sorry, I should've introduced you, but I imagined she wanted to get Flynn off to bed before Susannah starts to worry about him."

The rapid once-over the housekeeper had given him had told Rakin that she was clearly an established part of the Kincaid family. It wasn't only Flynn and Susannah she was looking out for—there'd been a warning in that glance: *Be honorable, or have me to deal with.* Rakin smiled to himself. Pamela had nothing to fear....

Against his shoulder, Laurel murmured, "It's wonderful to see Flynn looking so much better, even though he's still thin."

Spinning her deftly around to avoid colliding with a couple who had come to a standstill in the midst of dancers, Rakin said, "He's been ill?"

"Very. For the past two months Matt and Susannah have had to be careful about allowing him out—to limit his exposure to germs. But he's had the green flag—he's well on his way to full recovery. Tonight is the biggest crowd he's been in since he got ill."

"No wonder he's excited. He's a great kid."

"I think so." Laurel laughed up at him. "We all do."

Her green eyes sparkled like precious gems. Emeralds. A sultan's prize. Rakin dismissed the fanciful notion. "Your nephew was right—you didn't catch the bridal bouquet."

He'd been amused how she'd lithely leapt out of the way of the bunch of flowers the bride had tossed at her. If he had any doubt about the veracity of her claim earlier that she wasn't looking for love, he certainly believed it now. She couldn't have chosen a more public place to make her lack of interest in romantic commitment clear. Laurel might as well have taken out an ad in the society pages to proclaim she wasn't interested in marriage.

"No, I didn't catch it."

Despite her polite smile, and the carefully enunciated "No," the dangerous glint he detected in her eyes told another story. The laugh started low in his belly. He did his best to contain it—to no avail. Her glint turned to a glare. Biting back his mirth, before they became the focus of attention of those other than her two sisters-in-law, who were trying to look as though they were not following their dance, he said, "I thought every maid of honor dreamed of being the next bride."

"Not me. I want—"

"Excitement...adventure."

That wrested a reluctant laugh from her. "You whipped the words right out of my mouth."

Rakin forgot all about her watching relatives. His gaze dropped down to her lips.

Why hadn't he noticed how perfectly they were shaped? The flowing curve of the top lip was a work of art, while the plump bottom one promised pure sin.

Instantly the mood changed, vibrating with suppressed tension. Her annoyance, his teasing, their laughter, all vanished. Rakin was no longer conscious of anyone in the room—except the woman in his arms.

Her lips parted, and she drew a quick breath.

"I'll do it," she told him in a rush. "I'll come with you to Vegas."

He hadn't expected a reply so soon.

He'd been summoning his powers of persuasion. Now there was no need. Tension Rakin hadn't even known existed eased. Had he really believed she would refuse? The way his muscles relaxed suggested he hadn't been as certain of Laurel as he would've liked.

His gaze lifted—and clashed with eyes alive with excitement. "This is only the start of the adventure," he promised her.

Triumph filled him. Laurel Kincaid was going to make the perfect trophy wife....

Four

Laurel's expression grew increasingly bemused as the limousine that had collected them from McCarran International Airport cruised along Las Vegas's famous Strip.

"There's no where else in the world like Vegas," Rakin told Laurel, watching as she tried to assimilate the staggering visual impact of the city.

"It's like a Hollywood set." She twisted around to look out of a small window. "I don't remember any of this from back when I was here as a child."

"Then I shall have to show you everything."

"I can't wait." Even under the tawdry neon lights of the limousine interior her eyes shone with excitement.

By the time the white limousine nosed into the forecourt of the luxury hotel he'd booked for them, Rakin half-regretted not reserving a suite in one of the more over-the-top resorts.

"There are more outrageous hotels." Rakin stood at the door as she emerged from the limousine. "But I thought you might appreciate somewhere more peaceful when a retreat from the madness becomes necessary."

Laurel clambered out to stand beside him. Dressed in a pair of white linen trousers and a taupe shell top she looked cool and comfortable. Pulling her sunglasses down from where they rested on the top of her head to shade her eyes, she said, "I can't imagine that 'peace' is a word one often associates with Vegas."

"Believe it or not, there are peaceful places to be found not far from here."

"Like where?"

"Eli and I came here a couple of times during vacations while we were at Harvard. The desert is vast and undisturbed. Beautiful. Sometimes we'd hike through Red Rock Canyon."

There was a long pause as she examined him.

"You were homesick," she said after a moment, a peculiar note in her voice. "You missed Diyafa…and your family."

Rakin didn't reply. But he was relieved he couldn't see her expression behind the dark, opaque veil of the sunglasses. He suspected it would be too kind for comfort. Pity was the very last thing he wanted from this woman he was determined to marry.

He certainly wasn't going to explain the complicated relationship he shared with his family. The overwhelming expectations of his grandfather that had started when he was barely out the cradle and set him forever at odds with his cousins. His father's fits of anger, which had caused his mother to weep inconsolably. His own growing resentment against his father that had increased after he'd been sent to boarding school in England. And the lingering guilt for abandoning his mother to deal with his father which had not been eased by the bravely stoic letters written in her perfect, flowing handwriting.

By his thirteenth birthday his parents had been dead—and by the time he and Eli had first hiked Red Rock Canyon they'd been buried for a decade.

So Laurel was wrong. The pilgrimages he and Eli had made to Vegas had nothing to do with missing Diyafa—or his family.

No need for her to know there were no nostalgic, happy memories for him to hanker after—or at least, not until he successfully talked her into marrying him to nullify Prince Ahmeer's latest round of threats. For now, he'd promised his Southern rebel fun and adventure—and he intended to ensure she experienced plenty of both.

Cupping her elbow, he ushered her in the porter's wake into the quiet, discreet luxury of the hotel lobby. A hostess rushed forward and offered them each a glass of champagne. Before Rakin could refuse, Laurel shook her head.

She flashed him a rueful glance. "I want a clear head—I'm not missing a moment of this."

Her humor caused his mood to lighten. "I like you tipsy," he said softly.

A flush swept along her cheekbones. "It's not gentlemanly of you to remind me."

Coming from his lady-turned-rebel, the statement caused him to chuckle. "I thought you were tired of social constraints?"

"Not so tired that I'll get tipsy again any time soon."

They'd reached the reservations desk. Laurel leaned forward to answer a question from the reservations clerk and Rakin was instantly all too aware of the taut, lean lines of her body. Her bare arms rested on the polished counter and she spread her hands drawing his attention to the rings that decorated her graceful fingers.

Her ring finger was bare. His gaze lingered on the band of pale skin that evidenced her broken engagement to Eli.

A light, summery scent floated to him. Rakin inhaled deeply. Could one get tipsy on perfume? he wondered, then shook off the absurd notion.

This was about business.

Not about Laurel's perfume. Not about the pleasure that her company brought. Hard to believe he'd only met her yesterday. It had been tough to convince her to come away today. Once she'd accepted his invitation, she'd immediately tried to buy time. She'd suggested the following weekend. Rakin couldn't risk her changing her mind. He'd pushed until she'd capitulated. He'd won. She agreed to two days. He had two days in which to convince her to marry him—and secure his position in Gifts of Gold, the company of which he'd been appointed CEO.

Two days…

He feared it wouldn't be enough. He'd have to tempt her to play longer.

50 ONE DANCE WITH THE SHEIKH

Once they'd completed the brief check-in formalities for the penthouse suite he'd reserved, Rakin wasted no time setting his plan of attack into action. Bending his head, he murmured, "I thought we might go exploring."

Laurel had taken her sunglasses off, and without the shielding screen her green eyes sparkled up at him. "Sounds great—I can't wait."

Some of her joyous enthusiasm appeared to be rubbing off on him because Rakin couldn't stop himself from smiling back at her. "Then there's no time to waste."

Laurel very soon discovered that Las Vegas did indeed have spectacular sights.

In fact, her mind was quite boggled by the end of the first hour. The interior of the Luxor hotel was concealed in an immense black glass pyramid guarded by a giant crouching sphinx. But inside, instead of the treasures of ancient Egypt, Laurel was amazed to find the reconstructed bow of the giant Titanic complete with a lifeboat. As she and Rakin wandered through the installations, Laurel was moved by the stories of the last hours of the crew and passengers on the ship's tragic maiden voyage.

The Liberace Museum, by contrast, with its collection of resplendent, unashamed kitsch, made her giggle. The glittering mirror-tiled piano and the rhinestone-covered grand were wonderfully over the top. On catching sight of Rakin's appalled expression as he inspected the famed red, white and blue hot-pants suit, a mischievous impulse overtook her.

She eyed the black jeans and dazzling white T-shirt he wore, then leaned close to whisper, "I think your wardrobe should include one of those outfits."

"It would cause quite a stir in Diyafa if I ever wore such a garment. A national disaster, in fact. There are still some conservative elements who would never recover from the sight of Prince Ahmeer Al-Abdellah's grandson sporting hot pants." Across the narrow space separating them, their eyes met, and for one charged moment a connection pulsed between them.... Then it passed and hilarity broke.

"Enough of museums," said Rakin, reaching for her hand when they'd sufficiently regained their composure. "I think we need a little more action."

A shock of surprise rushed through her as his hand closed around hers. The clasp was warm and firm. Rakin showed no sign that the gesture had affected him to the same extent—he was striding purposefully forward, seemingly unaware that they were holding hands like a pair of lovers.

She was making too much of it.

Rakin was treating her with the kind of warm friendship she craved. So why spoil it by imagining intimacies that didn't exist? She should take the gesture at face value and go with the flow. No need to overanalyze the camaraderie that was developing between them. That, too, was part of breaking free.

Easier said than done.

Laurel couldn't dampen her awareness of their linked hands, and she finally slid her hand out of his and came to a stop when a familiar skyline materialized ahead.

"New York?" The Statue of Liberty and the Empire State Building were interspersed with other landmark buildings. This was his idea of more action? But she had to admit the replica skyscrapers were impressive. "Oh, wow, there's the Brooklyn Bridge."

"The buildings are about a third of actual life size," Rakin informed her. "But it's not the sight of the buildings that will give you the adrenaline rush I promised."

"New York–New York? A rollercoaster?" she gasped moments later.

"Why not?" He shot her a taunting look. "Scared?"

Even if she had been, his all-too-male I-dare-you expression would have forced her to bite her lip. She'd told him that she craved adventure, so there was no way she was going to back down now.

She stuck up her chin. "Of course not. I love rides."

Love was a slight exaggeration. She hadn't been on a ride in years. A quick calculation left Laurel astonished by exactly how long it had been since she'd last experienced such a ride.

Where had the years gone? And, more to the point, where had her sense of fun gone? When had she let herself become so staid...so boring? When had she forgotten that there was a world out there beyond the confines of her family and the demands of public relations for The Kincaid Group?

"At least I did love them once upon a time," she added a little more dubiously, hoping that her youthful infatuation with roller coasters would return by the time they reached the start.

"The track twists between the skyscrapers—" Rakin jerked a thumb in the direction of the buildings "—rising to two hundred feet between the buildings."

"Thanks! That's very comforting to know."

"It reaches speeds of over sixty-five miles per hour—and there's a place where the train drops a hundred and forty-four feet."

The last snippet of information gave her pause. "Are you deliberately trying to frighten me?"

"I'd never do such a thing." But the twitch of his lips gave him away.

Humor rushed through her like champagne bubbles rising. "Of course you wouldn't."

"Any adventure needs a good case of butterflies to start it off—dread heightens anticipation."

That sealed it. "You are trying to scare me—wicked man!" She advanced on him, brandishing her purse.

Rakin grabbed her wrists before she could take a swing at him, his shoulders shaking with mirth. "Are you having fun?"

She stilled. Lowering her purse, she glanced quickly around. How quickly she'd forgotten to behave with the dignity that befitted the eldest Kincaid daughter. Embarrassment swept over her; then she banished it. Who amongst the hordes knew her? And who would even care? Freedom followed in a dizzying burst.

With wonder she said, "Yes, I'm having a fantastic time." She skipped into line beside Rakin.

"The trains look like yellow New York taxicabs—complete

with hoods and headlights." She thought they looked delightful, and not at all frightening.

"We're in luck, we're going to get front seats," said Rakin, as an attendant ushered them forward.

Once seated in the front row with the restraints securely fastened, Laurel's enthusiasm waned at the unobstructed view of the red track ahead. Luck? Maybe not. As the train started forward her heart rose into her throat. "Rakin, what recklessness possessed me to do this?"

"You're going to love it." Rakin's eyes gleamed with humor.

But Laurel was no longer so sure. Ahead of them the track climbed to the height of Everest. The train chugged up, and with each foot they progressed the butterflies that Rakin had stirred up broke free of their chrysalis in Laurel's stomach and started to flutter madly.

They crested the top of the rise.

Laurel caught a glimpse of the Las Vegas skyline laid out in front of them. In the distance, hills undulated in a long curve.

The train gathered momentum.

"Oh, my heavens!"

Rakin's hand closed around hers. Before she could catch her breath, they were hurtling down. Then they were rising…. The next plunge downward left Laurel's stomach somewhere in the sky above them. Air left her lungs in a silent scream. She could hear Rakin laughing beside her.

Ahead, high above, she glimpsed a complete loop of red track.

"Noooo…" she moaned.

She gripped Rakin's hand until her fingers hurt.

The train swooped into the upward curve of the loop. Tension, tight and terrifying, clawed at her body. Laurel could hear screams behind her. For a disconcerting instant the world turned over, hovered, blue sky flashing below them in a spinning blur; then everything righted itself. They sped down into a series of tight heart-hammering curves that pressed her thigh up against Rakin's.

A wild euphoria exploded inside her.

The Statue of Liberty flashed past, and Laurel found herself laughing. Moments later the train shot into womb-like darkness.

Rakin murmured something beside her, but the sound of her heart hammering in her head drowned it out. Her hand was still gripping his, and Laurel realized her nails must be digging into his palm. Hot, awkward embarrassment flooded her.

"Sorry," she muttered, letting go.

"It didn't worry me."

"I appreciated the loan," she said lightly, and Rakin chuckled in response.

Gradually her eyes adjusted until she was able to make out lights and shapes of an underground station. Noise surrounded her—the attendant's cheery greeting as he freed her from the safety restraint, the clatter of trains on the track.

When they emerged from the front seats Laurel's legs felt like Jell-O. But sheer exhilaration propelled her forward.

"You were right, I loved it!"

Laurel didn't care that she sounded breathless as she spun around to grin giddily at Rakin through the cloud of hair that had whipped around her face during the thrill ride. Right now she felt high on joy—prepared to take on the world. Anything he wanted to throw at her, she was game for. The surge of strength—the feeling that she could do whatever she wanted—was supremely empowering. Getting a life…

Yet Rakin wasn't even breathing hard. And, what's more, not even one dark hair had strayed out of place. A wicked urge to see him look a little rumpled stole through her.

"Again," she challenged. "I want to do it again."

It was evening, and the observation deck on the fiftieth floor of Paris Las Vegas's Eiffel Tower was deserted.

Rakin felt Laurel go still beneath the hand he'd placed across her back to usher her from the glass elevator.

"How beautiful," she breathed, and gestured to the warm, dusky light that turned the observation deck to burnished bronze. "It's like being in a capsule of gold."

He watched indulgently as she picked her way along the observation deck, her high heels tapping against the steel, to take in the dramatic view of the city stretching to the purpling mountains in the distance.

Laurel came to a stop and the fiery glow of the sinking rays lit the hair piled on top of her head, throwing the elegant black strapless dress she wore into sharp relief. Against the backdrop of the sunset she looked like a goddess waiting to be summoned back from earth.

"It has been the most extraordinary day," she said breaking the spell that held him entranced. "Recklessness drove me to accept your invitation."

His gaze fixed on her, he said, "Recklessness?"

"I gave in to the temptation to break the Winthrop ban on gambling." She spread her arms wide to embrace the view. "But I didn't expect this. I've no idea how you'll intend to keep the action—and the surprises—rolling tomorrow."

"Don't worry, there's plenty more to see," Rakin told her, and closed the gap between them. "Dolphins. Sharks. Lions. We haven't even started on the animal encounters."

The sideways glance she gave him held a very human glint of mischief. "Or we could try the thrill rides at the Stratosphere Tower."

Rakin groaned. "I've created a monster. Three rides on New York-New York, not to mention braving the Speed roller coaster at NASCAR Cafe this afternoon—and you still crave more?"

"I never realized what I was missing out on—I should've put *Ride a roller coaster* on my list."

"You made a list of things to do in Vegas?" Had he left anything out?

But before he could ask, Laurel colored and averted her gaze. A gust of wind blew a tendril of hair that had escaped across her cheek, and she brushed it back. "It's not exactly about Vegas."

"But you have a list?" he pressed.

Laurel gave a small nod.

Her reticence intrigued him. "So what's on it?"

"I can't remember," she mumbled and her flush turned a deep shade of crimson.

Laurel Kincaid was a terrible liar.

"Now you've woken my curiosity."

She muttered something. Then she pointed. "Look, isn't that pretty?"

Rakin allowed himself to be distracted. Far below, the Strip was starting to light up as Las Vegas prepared for the coming night like a showgirl dressing for an after-dark performance.

"Oh, and look there!"

Rakin's followed her finger. Three rings of fountains had leapt out from the lake in front of the Bellagio, the high plumes illuminated by bright light.

A glance at Laurel revealed that she was transfixed.

"We'll see the fountains from closer up during dinner." He'd booked a table at Picasso specifically so Laurel could enjoy the display.

"From up here it gives another perspective. This tower looks like every picture I've seen of the real Eiffel Tower. It's amazing."

Rakin hadn't moved his attention from her face. Her changing expressions revealed every emotion she experienced. Wonder. Excitement.

For one wild moment he considered what her features would look like taut with desire, her dark-red hair spread loose across his pillow....

He shut his eyes to block out the tantalizing vision.

"So have you ever visited Paris or Venice? I'd love to visit both."

To his relief her voice interrupted his torrid imaginings. "Not Venice," he said, his voice hoarser than normal. "But I've been to Paris often—my mother loved Paris. She attended the école Nationale Supérieure des Beaux-Arts on the Left Bank across from the Louvre."

"She's an artist?"

Rakin nodded. "She was—she died."

"I'm sorry. I didn't mean to reopen—"

The remorse on Laurel's face made him say quickly, "Don't worry. Talking about her doesn't upset me. She's been gone a long time. Most people avoid mentioning her—it makes them uncomfortable." It ran contrary to his own need to talk about his mother, to remember her as she'd been. Talented. Mercurial. Loving. "My father died, too."

"You must miss them both."

The memories of his father were much more ambivalent. But there was no need for Laurel to discover the undercurrents that lurked beneath the mask he carefully preserved. So he focused on the facts. "My parents met in Paris."

"How romantic."

It was the conclusion he'd expected—no, led—her to draw. His mother had also thought it romantic. His father had called it fate. Neither romance nor fate had been enough in the end.

The night they'd met, Laurel had asked him whether he believed in fate....

It was Rakin's turn to turn away. The sunset blazed along the skyline.

"It was spring time." The words forced themselves past the tightness in his throat.

"Even more romantic."

Without looking at Laurel, he continued to weave the tale that had become a legend of tabloid lies. "My parents returned to Diyafa for a lavish wedding, and I was born less than a year later." That had been the end of the romance and the beginning of his mother's harsh reality. As his father had the male heir he wanted, the sheik no longer needed to woo his wife. Duty, rather than desire, had kept his parents together until their deaths.

Rakin found he had a startlingly intense need to see Laurel's face. Forcing a smile, he swiveled on his heel. Her eyes held a soft, dreamy look. "I'd love to visit Paris in the spring."

"And walk along the Seine." Rakin knew all the clichés.

"How wonderful to fall in love in a city that celebrates lovers."

"That too." His parents' story had great spin, Rakin decided savagely. The lie still lived.

She tipped her head to one side and the last rays of the sun glinted off the diamond earrings that dangled against her neck. "And I'd like to visit Diyafa, too."

It was the cue he needed.

But instead of telling her about his grandfather's plan to oust him, Rakin glanced at his watch. "Our table booking is not far off. I'll tell you more about the country of my birth over dinner—and afterwards we'll do what everyone does in Vegas—gamble."

As he'd anticipated, the dreaminess evaporated, then she said, "The higher the stakes, the better. Don't forget I have every intention of gambling the night away."

The stakes were rising for him, too. So why had he not taken the opportunity that she'd offered? Why hadn't he told her what he needed? A wife to neutralize his grandfather's threats? A part of him recognized that he was being drawn into the fantasy he'd created for a woman he found liking more and more with every hour that passed.

A whole day had already passed. Too soon they would be leaving Vegas and the opportunity to negotiate her cooperation would be forever lost. He could no longer delay.

It was time to return to reality.

And get himself a wife.

Picasso at the Bellagio was one of Rakin's favorite restaurants.

"Bellagio is a village on the shores of Lake Como," Rakin told Laurel after their plates from the main course had been cleared away, and dessert menus left for them to leisurely peruse. He'd secured a table overlooking a balcony and the lake beyond so that Laurel would have a good view of the fountains dancing to the music.

"George Clooney has a villa at Lake Como, doesn't he?" Laurel's smile had an impish quality as she turned from the fountains back to him. "I'd better add that to the exotic places I want to visit."

"You're that keen to meet Clooney?" Rakin wasn't sure whether to laugh or be annoyed by her mischievous interest in the movie star—especially since before his grandfather's latest threats he'd been as eager as Clooney to avoid marriage and babies. And despite conceding to marriage, babies were forever off the agenda—not that his grandfather needed to know that.

She gave him an artless glance. "Isn't every woman?"

This time he did laugh. "You're a tease!"

The artlessness evaporated. Only to be replaced with a sincerity that he found infinitely more disturbing. "Not really," she confided, leaning forward and lowering her voice. "Only with you. I've never flirted in my life—yet with you it's easy."

Her candor was disarming. And the husky note in her voice thrummed through him, playing all his nerve endings to devastating effect. He didn't dare allow his eyes to stray lower in case her action had caused the provocative neckline to reveal even more tantalizing glimpses of skin. Instead, Rakin unfolded his napkin, placed it on his lap and said lightly, "I thought all Southern women were born flirts."

"Not me." She glanced down at the dessert menu in front of her.

He could've argued that she was learning fast. Yet Rakin suspected that she had little idea of the effect she was having on him. He was more interested in her than he'd been in any woman for a long, long time. At first, his interest had been piqued by Eli's comment that she'd make the perfect wife for the predicament he found himself in. Then he'd found himself really liking her. And now—

Well, now, his interest was growing in leaps and bounds.

Impossibly long lashes fluttered up as she glanced up from the menu. "I've been attempting to flirt with you because... I feel safe."

The naked honesty of her statement shook him. All attempts at maintaining the lighthearted banter deserted him.

"Aren't you going to order dessert?"

To his surprise, Rakin realized he'd set his menu down on the table. But he couldn't stop thinking about what Laurel had said.

"You find it easy to flirt with me?"

"It must be because you're Eli's friend." This time the smile she gave him was sweet rather than flirtatious. "I know you're trustworthy."

The brief flash of annoyance he felt surprised him. "Because Eli said so?"

"Well, he never actually said I could trust you. But he wouldn't be friends with you if he didn't trust you implicitly—Eli's not the kind of man to waste time on liars and frauds."

"So you accept Eli's endorsement—rather than your own instincts?"

Laurel hesitated.

"No, don't think too much." Placing his elbows on the edge of the table, he steepled his hands and gazed at her over the top. "I want an instinctual response—not one vetted for kindness."

"I do trust you."

The expression in her eyes told him she'd astonished herself. Keeping his attention fixed on her, he demanded, "Why?"

"I don't know." She said it slowly, her gaze flickering away, then back to him as though drawn by some power she could not resist.

"It surprises you." He made it a statement.

"Yes." Again, she hesitated. Then she said in a rush. "I've never made friends easily—my family has always been enough."

"And Eli."

"And Eli," she agreed. "But that was different."

The sharp blade of envy that pierced Rakin was unexpected, and he thrust it away before the feeling could fester and turn to poisonous jealousy. "In what way?"

"We were the same age. He lived nearby while we were growing up."

"You were being kind."

"Maybe. At first. But the friendship was between equals—I got every bit as much out of it as Eli did. Remember, I didn't have other close friends."

He nodded his head. "I can understand that."

"I suppose the reason I trust you is because I feel comfortable with you. I can't remember the last time I laughed so much."

Pulling a face, he said, "I must be a clown."

"No! You are anything but a clown."

He'd been joking, trying to make her smile again. But her rapid rise to his defense made him realize that Laurel was concerned she might have offended him. Too kind for her own good. She could have no idea that his emotions had been forged in a crucible guaranteed to produce solid steel. If she had, no doubt she would not be nearly as comfortable in his company.

Nor would she be contemplating visiting Diyafa. Her comment about adding Lake Como to the places she wanted to visit probably meant her list included the destinations to which she wanted to travel. Las Vegas might only have been the start of it. He'd work on convincing her that Diyafa should be next on her list.

"It is true," she was saying earnestly before he could question her about what other places were on her list. "I can't remember when last I felt as lighthearted and carefree as I have today."

"I will take that as a compliment."

Under the weight of his gaze, he watched the faint wash of color warm her cheeks.

Laurel dropped her gaze to the menu. "You know, I've no idea what to choose."

Rakin's mouth curved into a smile. "I'm going to have ice cream."

"Ice cream?"

"Something cool in this weather. But you can't go wrong with anything on the menu."

"My meal was fabulous."

"Every dish on the menu is inspired by places where Picasso lived in Spain and the South of France."

His comment prompted Laurel to gaze at a Picasso painting on the nearest wall. "What did your mother paint?"

"She created huge abstract canvases. Mostly inspired by the desert landscape." His father had hated them. The sheikh had wanted his wife to paint realistic portrayals of the Diyafan Desert. His mother had preferred broad sweeps of color that invited the viewer to put their own interpretation on the landscape.

"Do you paint, too?"

Rakin shook his head. "I studied business—although I will confess that I majored in classical studies in my undergraduate degree so I'm not a complete philistine." A smile tugged at his mouth.

"Philistine?" She smiled back at him. "I never thought that for a moment. Why classical studies?"

The curve of her lips promised him untold delights. Rakin forced himself to glance up. "You can't grow up in a place like Diyafa and not be aware of ancient history—but I also loved the old legends. Greek, Roman, Egyptian—Diyafa has some wonderful legends, too."

"Which is your favorite legend?"

There was only one answer he could give. "In present company, I'd have to say the story of Daphne and Apollo."

Laurel wrinkled her nose at him. "Why? Didn't she get turned into a tree?"

"A laurel tree."

Her eyes brightened with laughter. "You're making that up."

Rakin shook his head. "Apollo used the leaves to weave himself a wreath—and that's how a laurel wreath became a symbol of victory."

"Not much of a victory since the woman he loved had been turned into a tree."

"And even hollower, when you consider that she felt nothing for him—she was fleeing his pursuit."

"Poor Apollo." She glanced at him through her lashes.

Heat blasted through him. And Rakin resisted the impulse to tell him that if she was any more skilled a flirt, every man in the world would be in mortal danger.

"Have you decided what you want to order?" he asked instead.

"Chocolate—rich chocolate. I'll go with the restaurant's recommendation. And then I want to gamble."

Rakin couldn't help grinning at her reckless, single-minded determination.

"I haven't forgotten—we'll gamble all night long."

* * *

The hush that hung over the casino was broken from time to time by the clatter of chips and the muted exchange of voices as bets were placed. Silent waitresses glided past with trays of complimentary drinks. By invitation only, this was the domain of the rich, the famous…and the dedicated gamblers. And Laurel was growing to dread the sound of the chips being raked across the green baize.

Around the roulette table where she and Rakin had settled, several stacks of chips were growing to skyscraper heights. But, along with the thin man sitting opposite them and nursing a whisky with increasingly desperate eyes as his pile dwindled, Laurel was losing.

And her stomach had started to churn with disquiet. She'd lost at least five thousand dollars of Rakin's money in the first ten minutes, and a fair bit of her own after she'd absolutely refused to accept more chips from him. What damage would a whole night's gambling do to Rakin's fortune—and her own? "I'm starting to think Grandfather was right," she told Rakin in a low aside.

"Your Winthrop grandfather?"

Laurel nodded. "He considered gambling a curse."

"One you hoped to break tonight?"

"Hmm." She considered that. Had she believed that by winning on the tables she'd be proving that she could break the old taboo? Had she wanted to overturn—even by a small win—the curse of impoverishment that gambling, along with bad investments, had caused the Winthrops to suffer in the past? She wasn't sure. "I don't think my reasons were quite so inspired. I was probably more determined to try something that my family disapproved of—totally the wrong reason to do anything."

Rakin chuckled, attracting a glare from the gambler losing across the table.

Leaning closer to him, she whispered, "But I've already lost far more than I intended of the chips you gave me—and what I added." Laurel gestured to what remained of the stack beside her. "I'm seeing no evidence of any return."

"Spoken like a cool-headed businesswoman."

She slid him a searching glance. "I appear to share that trait with you, too—you haven't even placed one bet yet."

"I don't gamble."

"For religious reasons?"

"It's bad business. I don't like the odds—I prefer to put down money when I am confident of a healthy return."

"Now who's the cool-headed businessman?"

They exchanged smiles.

The croupier called for bets. Laurel hesitated, then shook her head.

Rakin touched her arm. "We're disturbing the players. Time for us to move on, I think."

At Rakin's whisper, Laurel slid off the stool she'd been perched on, and picked up her purse with some relief. "So much for my grand plan to gamble all night."

"You may discover your second wind after you've had a breather."

"I doubt it." She flicked him a wan smile. "What I have discovered is how fast one can lose money on the tables. I never understood how easy it is." And it had given her some sympathy for the black-sheep Winthrop.

Once out of the stilted silence of the exclusive casino, the bustling, busy vibe of Vegas was back with vengeance. Slot machines chimed all around them, their colorful displays flashing brightly. The sick sensation in Laurel's stomach started to subside.

They found an alcove in the lounge, and Laurel sank onto a plush seat. Rakin gave an order to a cocktail waitress, then joined her on the wide cushion.

"I think my grandfather would've approved of you."

"The same grandfather who brokered your mother's marriage to your father?"

Laurel nodded. "The very same."

"And why do you think he would have approved of me?"

"According to my mother, he did his very best to repair the

Winthrop family fortune in any way he could before he hit on
the idea of the marriage to a Kincaid. It was an absolute rule in
my grandfather's house that none of his children were allowed
to gamble. Mom said that he was furious when his eldest brother
lost Captain's Watch after betting on the horses."

"Captain's Watch?"

"The Winthrop family beach house." It had been in the family
since the eighteen hundreds. "Grandfather Winthrop paid Dad a
visit shortly after Mom and Dad were married—and Dad agreed
to do his best to buy it back. I believe it wasn't easy, and it cost
him a small fortune. But it was worth every cent." Laurel could
visualize the view from the wide windows of the beach house
out to the sea. When her father's will was read, Laurel discovered that her father had known exactly how much she loved the
beach house: he'd left it to her in his will. "We spent endless
summer vacations there. It's one of my favorite places."

"Then you must share it with me one day."

Before Laurel could respond, the waitress returned with a
glass of champagne and a frosted cola on a silver tray.

Laurel eyed the glass, then slid Rakin an amused glance.
"You're not intending to get me tipsy, are you?"

Rakin looked a little uncomfortable, and she instantly regretted teasing him.

"No, no," he denied as he signed for the drinks. "I wanted to
remind you that despite your losses on the roulette table, today
is all about fun—it's meant to be a time for new experiences. I
wouldn't deliberately set out to get you drunk."

Laurel touched his arm.

"Sorry, that was a joke. It was in very bad taste. Of course I
don't believe you're trying to get me tipsy. Why would you?"

Laurel's perception was chillingly acute, Rakin decided. He'd
hoped a couple of glasses of champagne would make her more
malleable.

She leaned forward, and the movement caused light to shimmer across the bare skin above the strapless black gown. It took
willpower not to let his eyes linger on the smooth flesh, the kind
of willpower he'd been practicing all night.

"Thank you so much for taking the time to come with me to Vegas," she was saying, and he was conscious of the feather-light caress of her fingers against his jacket. "I am having fun."

Ignoring the urge to stroke that pearlescent skin, Rakin reminded himself fiercely that this wasn't a date—it was a business meeting. And it was past time he put his proposal to her. "Las Vegas has met your expectations?"

She lifted her hand, and took a small sip of the bubbling wine, then set the glass down. She smiled warmly at him. "It's been much better! And that makes me appreciate your company all the more. I do realize you're a busy man—and you're getting nothing out of this."

He hesitated.

The pause stretched too long, and her smile froze.

"Actually there is something I want to ask of you," he murmured.

Wariness dulled the sparkle in her emerald eyes. "You want something from me."

Rakin hesitated, searching for the right words.

"Is it sex?"

He blinked. Sex? Had he betrayed himself moments ago?

"Is that why you invited me to Vegas? Was that all that today was about?" she accused scooting away along the seat. "Softening me up to get me into bed?"

He couldn't deny that he'd been purposely softening her up. Hell, he'd wanted her to be receptive. But not for…sex.

"I thought you were different."

Laurel was already on her feet, gathering up her purse. In a moment she was going to walk away and leave him sitting here like a fool. And the opportunity would be gone.

"Not sex," he said quickly.

But she didn't halt.

"Laurel…don't go!" He reached forward and caught her hand. Her fingers were stiff with outrage. Before she could yank her fingers free and storm away, he said, "Sex is not what I'm after. Sit down. Listen to my proposition—it has advantages for your family."

Her fingers stopped wriggling. "A business proposition?"

"Yes." Rakin knew it was now or never. "I want you to marry me."

"What?"

Laurel couldn't believe she'd heard Rakin right.

Shocked, she sank back onto the padded cushions in the recesses of the alcove and stared at the stark figure in the formal suit, his shirt pristine white and collar crisp and crease-free. A beautifully knotted narrow tie completed the picture.

He didn't look insane.

He looked dark, intense...and utterly gorgeous. Her heart skipped a beat. Scanning his face she took in the taut cheekbones, the lack of humor in his eyes. There were no signs of the fun companion who'd entertained her all day long.

"You're serious."

"Completely." Challenge glinted in that enigmatic gaze as he let her fingers go.

Giving a light, incredulous laugh, she spread her hands. "I can't marry a man I hardly know."

He tilted his head back against the high, padded back of the booth, and the gaze that locked with hers held raw intensity. "Laurel, there's nothing to fear. I am a businessman—utterly respectable and a little boring."

She didn't fear him. But to take a risk and marry a man she barely knew...the grandson of a Middle Eastern prince? Laurel wasn't so sure about the wisdom. "You're not boring," she said at last.

The warmth that seeped into the dark eyes caused a funny stir deep in her chest.

"Does that mean you will agree to marry me?" he asked softly.

Tipping her head to one side, Laurel tried to ignore the way her heart had rolled over and considered him. "You don't even mention love."

"So you want love? A proposal wrapped up in sweet words? Should I kneel on one knee before you?"

She shook her head slowly. "If I still dreamed of that kind of love I would've snatched the bouquet that Kara tossed at me."

Rakin gave her a slow, appreciative smile. "You're a realist. We haven't known each other long at all. . . and although I would like to think we've discovered much in common, I wouldn't insult your intelligence by talking of love so soon."

"Thank you—I think."

She was still trying to make sense of his bombshell proposal. He'd said that her family would benefit from the proposition. But what was in it for him? Her mind leapt from one scenario to the next. But none of them made any sense.

"You've asked me to marry you, but I still have no idea why."

The smile still lurked in his eyes. "You're a very beautiful woman, you must know that."

She could sense that he was prevaricating, even as she countered, "Beauty doesn't guarantee that a marriage will succeed—you only need to look at my mother's marriage to know that. You implied you were putting a business proposition to me—I didn't expect a marriage proposal."

"My marriage proposal *is* a business proposition."

Laurel started to laugh.

He sat forward, and his knee pressed against hers. "Believe me, it's not as crazy as it sounds. My grandfather has been threatening to change his will and disinherit me for years for not forming an alliance with the various women he has picked out for me—each time I have ignored his threats, because he is an irascible old man with plenty of life still left in him. He will cheat death for a while yet. But recently the threats have intensified. He no longer merely threatens to disinherit me on his death—now he has vowed he will force the board to vote me out as CEO. And, not satisfied with that, he will also transfer the controlling stocks he holds in the Abdellah business empire to my cousin. All this will be done if I am not married by my thirty-sixth birthday. It is no longer a matter of waiting until he dies to find out whether he has made good on his threats—he intends to disenfranchise me within the next year."

Rakin's face was a study in frustration.

"I have no intention of being robbed of the company. I have spent many hours of my life working to expand the Gifts of Gold division until it has become a first-class supplier of soft furnishings and luxury linens."

She knew from listening to Eli rave about his friend that every word Rakin spoke was true. He'd built up a network of clients across the finest hotel chains and resorts in the world, including Eli's.

"So I need a wife."

At that, Laurel couldn't help being conscious of the solid weight of his leg resting against hers. Even through his trousers and the sheer stockings that she wore, she could feel the warmth of his flesh. But she didn't shift away. "Will your grandfather really go through with such a pointless threat? Surely it would harm the family as much as you?"

"It's not pointless to him. He's a proud man—and he's accustomed to having things his way. Right now he doesn't care about profits. He wants me to marry, and this is the way he intends to bend me to his will."

"Who will run the company if he wrests control from you?"

"Ah, my grandfather already has that sorted out. The cousin to whom he is transferring the controlling stocks on my thirty-sixth birthday will be ushered in as the new CEO of Gifts of Gold. None of the board would dare act against my grandfather's orders."

"This cousin is married?"

"He is engaged—to a woman my grandfather handpicked for him." Rakin's lip curled up.

Understanding dawned. "You and your cousin don't see eye to eye?"

The sharp incline of his head confirmed her suspicion. "Zafar hates me. He would destroy me if he could, and I would die before I allowed Zafar to take this from me...so I will be married first."

"Wouldn't it be more advantageous for you also to marry a woman your grandfather had chosen for you?"

Rakin's eyebrows drew together, giving him a formidable air.

"That would give him too much power over me." The frown relaxed. "Besides, even if he scoured the whole earth, my grandfather could find no better candidate than you."

Laurel could feel her cheeks heating. "That is shameless flattery!"

"Not at all. You are beautiful and presentable. You are well connected…and incredibly gracious." Leaning farther forward he captured one of her hands. "And, to make sure you are equally happy, I will also make sure that our marriage will lead to benefits for The Kincaid Group."

Laurel jerked upright at his touch. "What kind of benefits?"

He had her.

Rakin was certain of it. She was going to agree to marry him—exactly as he'd hoped. He let her hand go and sat back. Not far away he could hear the chiming of a slot machine announcing a winner, the whoops of celebration that followed.

He focused on the woman beside him, the woman he was determined to have as his wife. "There are many exporters and importers in Diyafa—they rely on shipping containers to transport their products around the world. I will see to it that they are introduced to your family's business. I will do everything I can to expand the profile of The Kincaid Group within my circle."

"You wouldn't expect me to give up my role in the company?"

Laurel was even starting to speak as though their marriage was a fait accompli. Satisfaction spread through Rakin. "Our marriage would be temporary—such a drastic sacrifice would not be required."

"How temporary?"

Rakin shrugged, impatient with her insistence. "Once we are married, my grandfather will sign the stocks over to me, I will have control of the company…and you will be free to leave—to return to Charleston, and your family, for good."

She shifted to the edge of the seat, and the rogue tendril of hair fell forward. She brushed it back impatiently, and the pendant lights illuminating the alcove turned her diamond drop earrings to a cascade of sparkles. "But you would expect me to live in Diyafa, right?"

He nodded and crossed one leg over the other, keeping his pose deliberately casual, taking care not to spook her. A few minutes more…that was all it was going to take. "Otherwise my grandfather would not accept that our marriage was legitimate—and I cannot afford him to doubt the veracity of our union. But there would be compensations for living in Diyafa for part of the year. I travel a lot—and I'd expect you to be by my side. I make regular business trips to the United States, so you would see plenty of your family. You could continue doing public relations work for your family's business. I would never stop you. The technology in Diyafa is groundbreaking; you could work there with everything at your fingertips. I travel to many countries, too. Think about it, you would be able to work through that list of yours."

"What do you know about my List?" Laurel was staring at him, green eyes wide with shock.

He tried to keep the smugness out of his smile. It hadn't taken him long to fathom what was on her list. "It's obvious that you have a list of places you want to travel to. I know Vegas is on there for certain, you mentioned adding Lake Como—and you may even have considered Diyafa."

Rakin got the feeling she was debating something.

He certainly couldn't afford for her to have second thoughts now.

"Laurel, I will take you everywhere you wish to travel. We would visit the Taj Mahal, I would take you to the Tower of London. You could sip French champagne beside the Seine in the spring time. You will never regret the adventures you will experience."

The doubt vanished and her expression filled with yearning. "That's not fair. You're chipping away at my weakest point."

Of course, he knew that. For someone who had confessed to never having traveled much and always wanted to, he was offering the dream of a lifetime.

"It's not a weakness to have a dream."

There was an expression in her eyes that he did not recognize. "You're offering to fulfill my dream?"

He didn't need her romanticizing him. He was, after all, not the love of her life that his mother had thought his father to be. He wanted no misunderstandings. He was, after all, only a man. "It's not one-sided. Don't forget that I will get what I need, too."

"So this will be a win-win deal?"

She understood! He couldn't have chosen better if he'd spent the whole year searching for the perfect wife.

"Exactly," he purred. The dazzling smile Rakin directed at her was filled with triumph. "Why not accept my proposition?"

Proposition.

The word dragged Laurel back to what Rakin was offering: a business deal...not the dream of a lifetime.

Restlessness flooded her, and she leapt to her feet. "I think I've found my second wind. Let's see if I can break that Winthrop curse."

Rakin rose more slowly and blocked her escape. "You want to gamble more? Now?"

She shot him a look that could never be described as flirtatious. He was the cause of this...this turbulence that was turning her inside out. "You're asking me to take the gamble of a lifetime by marrying you—what difference is a few minutes going to make?"

He raised his hands in a gesture of surrender.

"Take all the time you need." The look he gave her was full of masculine confusion as he stepped away so that she could pass. "But it's hardly for a lifetime. It's not a permanent arrangement."

But Laurel didn't move past him. "I want a sign."

"A sign?" The confusion evaporated, leaving frustration clouding his eyes. "What kind of sign?"

"That marrying you is the right thing to do."

"And what would you consider a good sign?"

Laurel thought about it for a moment. "Winning back the money I lost on the roulette tables—losing it was very bad luck."

"But your family never wins." Rakin looked fit to burst.

A wave of amusement swept Laurel along as she headed for the gambling area. Now perhaps he felt as off-balance as she did. Over her shoulder, she tossed, "I'm going to stick to the slot machines this time. So chances are if I do win it would be an excellent omen."

Rakin made a peculiar sound.

Laurel turned, in time to see him produce a coin from his pocket.

"Heads or tails?" he demanded.

The absurdity of it struck her as she came to a stop. "You're asking me to make what might be one of the biggest decisions of my life on the flip of a coin?"

"You're about to risk it on a machine that pays pittances on pairs of cherries. I prefer these odds," he said grimly.

"I prefer the cherries."

He didn't even smile.

"You've got no intention of saying 'yes' to my proposal, have you?"

Laurel didn't answer at once. To be honest, she was confused—Rakin had turned her world upside down with his proposal. It was far more disorientating than the roller coasters they'd shared earlier. Or the flashing lights and loud chimes of the nearby slot machines.

Part of her wanted to leap in and say yes.

No doubt about it, marriage to Rakin would be an adventure. A chance to experience things she wouldn't otherwise. It certainly made good business sense. The Kincaid Group couldn't afford to turn away opportunities for new business—particularly not with Jack Sinclair still causing all kinds of mayhem.

But the more cautious side of her, the old carefully and conservatively raised Laurel Kincaid, warned that she didn't know Rakin terribly well, that this was an extremely risky proposition, one she should avoid at all costs.

All reason evaporated when he strode up to her and put his hands on her shoulders. "I should've asked you to marry me back on the balcony last night—I'm starting to think you might have been more likely to say yes back during the wedding."

His touch against her bare skin was…disturbing. Laurel struggled to think. At last she shook her head slowly. "You were a stranger then, I know you so much better now."

She realized it was true.

In the cocoon formed by his arms, for her benefit as much as his, she ticked off on her fingers what she'd learned. "One, you're fun to be with—I've never laughed so much in my life as I did today. Two, you're kind—you held my hand when you thought I might be scared that first time on the roller coaster. Three, you love the world around us—I discovered that at the top of the Eiffel Tower. Four, you're good with children—"

"You can't possibly know that!"

His hands dropped away from her shoulders, and her flesh felt cool where, an instant before, his fingers had rested.

"I do," she insisted. "You patiently humored Flynn at the wedding."

"Then marry me!"

His eyes drilled down into hers.

"Only if I win."

She swung away. From her purse she extracted a roll of coins. Tearing the wrapper with the casino logo from the coins, she fed them into the first slot machine she came to and hit the play button.

The patterns spun crazily.

When they came to rest, nothing lined up.

Not even a pair of cherries.

The same thing happened on the next play.

Laurel's heart felt hollow. It was ridiculous to feel so flat, like a loser, simply because she couldn't even hit the cherries.

Get a life. …

She hadn't felt this flatness earlier. She and Rakin had connected; they'd enjoyed each other's company. The day had been filled with joy. Her intuition told her they'd make a great temporary team—The Kincaid Group would benefit and so would Gifts of Gold.

It wouldn't be crazy to marry him—she liked him.

And the man didn't even gamble.

She stared at the rows lined with pictures and numbers. What was she doing? Rakin was right: she didn't need some arbitrary sign. This was a solid business decision. It made perfect, logical sense to accept his proposal.

She didn't need to prove that she could win.

Laurel knew she was going to say yes.

She hit the play button for the last time, and turned to give him the answer he was waiting for.

The cacophony of bells and electronic chimes rising in a hysterical crescendo caused her to whip around to stare at the slot machine.

In disbelief she read the flashing letters instructing her to call an attendant.

"The lights are flashing," she said, as numbness invaded her. "I've won."

Rakin was laughing.

"I've won," she said again.

But Rakin wasn't looking at the crazy, psychedelic fireworks above the slot machine. He was coming toward her his arms outstretched. "Looks like you've broken the Winthrop curse. You've hit the jackpot."

Her eyes lifted to the amount in white lights at the top: $22,222. It wasn't a fortune, but it more than covered her earlier losses. And it was definitely a jackpot. "Two must be my lucky number."

Then she was being swept off her feet into Rakin's arms. He spun her around as colors flashed crazily around her. By the time he set her down, the numbness was starting to recede as feeling returned…and with it, euphoria.

She grinned up at him. "I feel…" How best to describe it? "…lucky."

"We'll be lucky together." Rakin's gaze blazed into hers. "We will be married tomorrow."

Five

Today was her wedding day.

Laurel freed herself from the sheet that had twisted around her limbs while she slept. In one lithe movement, she swung her legs out of the bed and sat up. Hooking a finger under the narrow strap of her cream silk nightie that had slithered off her shoulder, she righted it.

On the bedside table the rose that Rakin had organized to be delivered with the check for her winnings rested in a glass of water.

Laurel's gaze fell onto the crumpled letter with the card tucked beneath that she'd placed on the nightstand beside the rose last night. The two documents that were dominating her life: her father's letter—and her Get a Life List.

She reached for the List first.

No. 1 Jilt Eli.

Laurel shut her eyes. No need to feel guilty, Eli was much happier married to Kara.

No. 2 Wear red lipstick. Check.

No. 3 Flirt with a stranger. Check. She'd done that with vengeance… and look where it had gotten her. Now she was marrying him. Even though she hadn't even kissed him yet.…

Laurel was smiling when she read the next item.

No. 4 Eat ice cream in bed. An absolute taboo in the Kincaid household. And last night when Rakin had ordered ice cream for dessert, she'd immediately thought of her list... and the visions that had flashed through her head had been dangerously X-rated. All too easy to imagine herself doing plenty of things she shouldn't even be considering with the dark stranger to whom she was growing curiously addicted.

Well, she certainly wouldn't be eating ice cream in bed with Rakin any time soon....

No. 5 Gamble all night.

Laurel read the entry again. Last night she'd proved—forever—that she had no need to gamble all night. It gave her a curious sense of peace. She was a winner in her own right.

No. 6 Travel to far-flung places.

Check. She would be going with Rakin to Diyafa. There would be more journeys beyond that. The passport she carried with her was about to be put to plenty of use.

Her face broke into a smile as she glanced down the remaining items.

She was well on track...even though the tasks grew tougher toward the end.

Laurel placed the list back on the nightstand. By contrast, the much-folded paper that her father's letter was written on had the texture of tissue paper between her fingertips. Laurel unfolded it, her eyes immediately drawn to the salutation and the first line.

My dearest Laurel,
If you are reading this, I am no longer with you.

Even though she knew the contents by heart, the words still had the power to clog her throat with emotion.

Her father had been gone for nearly five months, yet it was still hard to accept that she would never see him again. She read the letter through to the end, then set it down with a profound wish that they'd never discovered that her father possessed feet of clay. Discovering her father's secret life with Angela while he was still married to her mother had turned her belief in their happy marriage on its head. Had everything she believed about her parent's love simply been a lie?

Rakin might not be offering her love…but at least he was offering her honesty.

The benefits would be very real.

What he was offering would tick off the boxes of the shopping list of wants she'd scrawled before jilting Eli.

By marrying Rakin, she'd be actively fulfilling more of her dreams. At the same time, she'd also be able to source leads for new business to refer to her brother, Matt. That way she'd also be working actively on No. 9 on the List: *Help save TKG*. Rakin would be getting something he wanted—needed—out of the deal, too.

She had nothing to lose.

At the marriage license bureau it took only minutes of standing in the queue before Laurel found herself signing the application in the space beside the bold slash of Rakin's signature. She stared at the word printed in bold type below her signature: *BRIDE*.

Bride? For one wild second panic surged through her. A month ago she'd been engaged to her best friend. Someone she knew. Someone she was fond of. Someone she understood. She'd certainly never had any intention of marrying a man she'd only just met—and a sheikh at that.

Then her nerves steadied.

She liked Rakin. She trusted him. He needed a bride; the Kincaid Group needed more business. And he was going to help her become the woman she'd always wanted—secretly—to be.

Her pulse slowed down as the panic subsided. Behind the counter, the clerk handed Rakin a duplicate form.

"Cheapest place to get married is the Office of Civil Marriages. It's on Third Street, on the right-hand side, only a short walk away."

"We'll do a bit of research—but thank you for your help." Rakin flashed her an easy smile.

"Some of the hotels on the strip are mighty expensive." The clerk gave Rakin a once-over. Then she gave a wistful sigh. "But maybe that won't matter." The look she cast Laurel held a glint of envy. "Have a wonderful wedding...and good luck."

Laurel smiled back. "Thank you."

They exited through smoked glass doors.

Laurel caught sight of the signboards for lawyers and paused. It started her thoughts down a path not easily stopped. What would her family make of her impulsive wedding? Before she'd told Eli she couldn't marry him, she'd spent months talking to her family's attorneys negotiating a prenuptial agreement that the lawyers were confident protected both her and The Kincaid Group. Eli's lawyers had worked equally hard to ensure that the prenup was fair to him, too.

If her father were alive, he'd be having a stroke at the thought of any of his daughters marrying a man the family hadn't inspected, without a prenup, exposing The Kincaid Group to all manner of risks. No prenuptial agreement was a sin worse than unprotected sex—and that was calamity enough—in her father's opinion.

So she slid Rakin a sideways glance. What did she really know about him—beside the fact that he was Eli's friend? And she liked him. A lot. He could be a gold-digger—a gigolo—for all she knew. Quickly, she checked her thoughts. Told herself she was being ridiculous.

Rakin Abdellah was clearly a very rich man. Even the clerk had noticed the patina of wealth that glossed him, separating him from the average romantic swain who turned up in the marriage license bureau.

But the lessons of a lifetime caused her to say, "We should've signed a prenup. My family will kill me when they find out...." Her voice trailed away as Rakin took her elbow. "Where are we going?"

"To see if we can find a lawyer. I don't want you having any sense of guilt, or any reservations about this."

"I must sound like the biggest party pooper ever."

"Never." He was smiling down at her, and it eased the butterflies fluttering around in her stomach. "How could I think that? I admire you for being so clear-sighted—for thinking about protecting your family—and their livelihood."

In some childish, hidden corner of her heart, Laurel wished that he'd dismissed the caution she'd voiced, and swept her up in his arms, then charged into the Little Red House of Love to rush through their temporary vows.

At least, that way, she wouldn't be held accountable for what happened next.... That way she could blame him for whatever the outcome was.

And maybe the disturbing little niggle of doubt that had taken hold would've evaporated in a puff of smoke....

They caught the lawyer closing up his offices.

The slight, dark-suited man started to object, but one glance at Rakin's determined face convinced him to welcome them instead. A raised hand stayed the last-remaining paralegal who was about to slip out a side door.

With the recent negotiations with Eli so fresh in her mind, it didn't take Laurel long to explain what she needed. Rakin took even less time to get his requirements across. It reinforced what Laurel was starting to realize—under the handsome, charming facade lurked a tough negotiator.

A tiger, rather than a pussycat. With a tiger's feral instincts. Something she would do well to remember.

"You need to be aware that a prenuptial agreement entered so near in time to a wedding date can be held to be void for duress," the lawyer told them once they were seated around a conference table with plush, padded chairs in the privacy of his offices.

It was hardly the time for Laurel to confess that Rakin had proposed a temporary marriage—a mad adventure for her with some fringe benefits for her family's business thrown in—and a sane solution to Rakin's problems.

Laurel got the feeling that if the lawyer knew about the reasons for their marriage he'd consider them both a little mad—and advise them they were headed for trouble.

"Do you want to wait?" Rakin's murmur, loud enough fo

her ears only, broke into her speculative thoughts. She turned her head and looked into eyes that mesmerized her.

"Wait?" She raised her eyebrows.

"Take some more time to think it through." He gave her a tender smile that probably convinced the lawyer seated across the polished conference table that this was a love match.

Laurel almost grinned back. The misgivings that had settled over her began to lift. In their place, recklessness danced a wild waltz through her. She'd made her decision—she was ready for the adventure of a lifetime.

She was done being careful.

"No need to wait." Who was this stranger who had taken up possession inside her skin? With a defiant toss of her head, she spoke directly to the lawyer, "No one's forcing me to do anything I don't want."

"Laurel wants to make sure we both understand exactly where we stand—especially given that we both have family businesses to consider," said Rakin.

"Very wise." The lawyer pulled his yellow legal pad closer and uncapped his pen. "It may not seem like a very romantic thing to do, but it certainly shows you both agree on many basic things—very important for building the foundations of a lasting marriage."

When the lawyer suggested that each of them might want their own counsel, Laurel waved his concerns away. She'd been through all that once already with Eli. She knew what would be said, the cautions, the ifs and the buts that she'd considered so carefully the last time round. She knew the pitfalls, what safeguards were required.

It didn't take him long to make a note of what those concerns were. Or for the paralegal to reduce the terms to a draft both she and Rakin perused. Once the agreement was executed and the lawyer had arranged where to send the bill, the meeting was over.

"I wish you the long and happy marriage I am sure you will enjoy."

Laurel decided to leave their adviser with his illusions.

Clearly, he'd concluded this was a love match. A meeting of true minds. And who was she to disabuse him of that romantic notion?

Entering the hotel suite a short while later, Laurel kicked off her shoes and sank into the welcoming comfort of a plush L-shaped sofa with a breathy laugh. "Well, I'm glad that's done."

"Soon you will be Mrs. Abdellah."

Rakin extracted a bottle of champagne from the depths of the bar fridge.

"I'll help myself to a cola in a little while," Laurel said quickly. "Otherwise you might railroad me into more propositions."

He gave her a wry smile. "You're never going to let me live that down."

"Never is a long time." Lazily, she stretched her arms above her head. "I should take a shower."

"Relax for a few moments, there's still plenty of time to get dressed."

Dressed? Laurel gulped as her thoughts homed in on one overwhelmingly feminine worry. A dress. A wedding dress. She didn't have a dress. What was she to wear? With dismay she thought about the strapless black dress she'd worn to the casino last night. Black wouldn't do for a wedding. Even if it wasn't a marriage for love—there should still be some element of romance about the occasion.

"I don't have anything remotely suitable for a wedding," she confessed as Rakin closed the door of the bar fridge.

"Have no fear." He gave her a smug smile. "It's all been taken care of."

"All been taken care of?" Laurel echoed.

At his look at satisfaction, it fell into place.... Rakin had already bought her a wedding dress.

He'd clearly thought of everything—Kara would've been impressed.

The doubt devils returned. What if the gown didn't fit? Or

worse, what if she hated the design he'd chosen? How was she supposed to tell him that when he'd clearly been thinking of her?

If only Kara were here to help...

An image of the dress Kara had picked out for the-wedding-that-had-never-happened flashed into her mind. The perfect dress. An elegant fitted white lace bodice with a full skirt. She'd had more fittings than she'd wanted to get the fit just right.

But Kara wasn't here.

Besides the last dress Kara had picked out had suited the old Laurel. Perfectly. The Laurel who did exactly as everyone expected. Not the woman with an unquenchable thirst for adventure that she'd become.

Rakin had called her a rebel.

Suddenly she found herself looking forward to seeing what Rakin had chosen. Laurel found her lips creeping up into a smile as he settled on the sofa beside her. "You've bought me a wedding dress, haven't you?"

"Not quite."

Before Laurel could question what that meant his cell phone buzzed. Rakin reached for it. After a brief exchange, he killed the call. "Macy and her assistant have arrived."

"Macy?"

"She's a shopping consultant who came highly recommended, and she's picked out a few dresses you might like. But you'll need to make the final choice."

Laurel suppressed the ridiculous thrill of pleasure that gave her. He'd left the final decision down to her. For too many years she'd allowed other people to make decisions for her.

Rakin wasn't doing that.

A buzz signaling the arrival of the private elevator sounded, and seconds later the doors slid open. Macy turned out to be a tall, angular brunette with sharp eyes, and she was followed by a shorter woman who Laurel assumed must be her assistant. A bellhop brought up the rear, wheeling in a cart of boxes emblazoned with designer names.

"The wedding is tonight, right?" Macy radiated efficiency.

"Um...maybe," said Laurel thinking about how long all the

details for her wedding to Eli had taken to arrange. "But I'm not sure everything can be done in such a short time."

"No maybe about it," Rakin corrected. "Our wedding will definitely take place tonight—I will make sure of that." His wicked grin caused Laurel's heart unexpectedly to contract.

"Then we don't have any time to waste." Macy's clipped words broke the spell. "Katie, let's get those dresses out of the boxes." The assistant sprang to action and a swathe of fabric emerged in a shower of falling petals.

Laurel's breath caught. "Oh, my!"

"There are some things I need to take of." Rakin crossed the floor to tip the bellhop for his help, then made his way back to Laurel. "If you'll excuse me."

As he came closer Laurel found that her pulse had started to race. There was a glint in Rakin's dark eyes. Her heart slammed in her chest.

He was going to kiss her.

But when the kiss came, his lips brushed her cheek instead of her mouth. A perfunctory, too brief caress.

Then he was gone, the door to the suite's elevator sliding shut behind him.

Laurel slowly let out a breath.

"By the time he comes back you will look like the woman of his dreams," Macy said from behind her.

The woman of his dreams.

Being the woman of his dreams wasn't what this marriage was about. But Laurel didn't have the heart to smash the other woman's illusions. Laurel responded absently to the bellhop's goodbye when he and the cart departed, and then only she, Macy and Katie remained in the spacious suite.

But there was no question of any awkward silence as Macy conjured dresses out of their boxes along with accessories. The personal shopper's enthusiasm was contagious. Laurel glimpsed slips of lacy lingerie, gloves, stockings…and shoes with high, delicate heels.

But her gaze kept coming back to the dress Macy had unpacked first.

The fabric appeared to have been created from white rose petals. The design of the dress itself was deceptively simple, no flounces, no bows. It relied on the beauty of the fabric and the stark simplicity of the cut.

"Would you like to try it?" Macy was sizing her up with an air of an expert. "Your fiancé is a good judge of size—it should fit perfectly."

Laurel tossed caution aside. "I'd love to."

The dress slid over her head in a whisper of fine cloth. When Laurel opened her eyes she gasped...and blinked.

This was no conservative Southern lady that stared back at her from the mirrored cupboard doors. She looked sexy. So sexy. Yet still tasteful.

Laurel examined herself in the mirror.

"We'll leave your hair loose at the back, but these bits can be swept up." Macy was there, matching her actions to her words. "And perhaps a small spray of flowers here."

Laurel thought her eyes looked huge in her face. And her cheekbones were thrown into prominence.

"Katie's a magician with makeup. But not too much—you don't need it. A touch of eye-shadow and some mascara on those incredible lashes—this will not take long."

Laurel waited as the front strands of her hair were drawn up and pinned back.

"A ribbon, I think." Deft fingers wove the silk through her auburn hair. "Your complexion is so creamy."

By the time her hair had been arranged and her makeup applied in soft shades, Laurel felt like a siren. And when she finally heard Rakin's voice outside the bedroom door, her heart jumped into her throat. She swung around...and gasped.

Her groom stood framed in the doorway.

He was wearing a tuxedo that made him appear dark and formidable. And, in sharp contrast to his masculinity, a white rose was pinned to his lapel.

And, he was inspecting her with equal interest.

Laurel didn't even notice Macy and Katie file past him. All she was aware of was the touch of Rakin's eyes. On the V of skin between her breasts. On her mouth. Before his gaze swept up to meet hers. There was heat…and something more.

Suddenly it hurt to breathe.

This was crazy!

She shouldn't be feeling like this. Trembling. Like a teen on her first date.

She was a grown woman getting married to a man who'd turned her legs to water just by looking at her. This was supposed to be a business arrangement that would benefit both of them. It was a temporary fix. It certainly wasn't about this… this shaky, trembling sensation that she couldn't even name.

Whatever it was, it had made it hard to breathe. To hide what she was feeling, Laurel gave him her most charming smile.

He smiled back. She couldn't help noticing that he had a beautiful mouth. The upper lip had been formed by a master hand; the bottom lip was full, promising passion—

Get a grip.

Laurel searched for something appropriate to say. "You've changed already," she said finally. He'd showered, too. The smooth line of his jaw told her he'd shaved.

"You look exquisite." His voice was deep.

"Thank you." Laurel felt a blast of pleasure. All her life she'd been told she was beautiful: She'd been told in tones laden with envy, and she'd been told factually as if it were to be expected that Elizabeth Kincaid's eldest daughter should follow in her mother's footsteps. Yet never had she derived so much pleasure from hearing the words. Under the heat of his gaze, Rakin made her feel more like a woman than she'd ever felt in her life.

He was taking something from his pocket. "I brought you a gift."

"A gift?"

"A keepsake—to remember our wedding by."

He opened a slim, black velvet box to reveal the gold chain looped inside. As he hooked his index finger under the chain to extract it from the box, blue fire flashed in the light. A diamond pendant swung from the end of the chain, but Laurel lost sight of it as Rakin moved behind her. A moment later she felt the pendant drop into the valley between her breasts and then Rakin's fingertips brushed her nape, as he closed the clasp. A sensation of delicious delight thrilled through her.

Standing behind her, thankfully, Rakin wouldn't have noticed the electric surge of awareness. When his hands closed on her shoulders, Laurel stilled. But he was intent on steering her toward the mirror.

She breathed again.

"Do you like it?"

"It" was a flawless single diamond suspended in a simple gold setting to show off the glorious stone that nestled against her skin.

"I can't accept this!"

"Why not?"

"It's too…" Laurel groped around for the right word. Finally she settled on, "It's too much."

"You don't like it."

"No!" she sputtered. "I mean—of course I like it—it's beautiful."

"Then stop pouting and say a pretty thank you."

"I don't pout." Feeling awkward and horridly ungracious, she gathered her composure. "Thank you, it's truly lovely." A discomforting thought struck Laurel. "I didn't buy you a gift."

"I never expected one."

In the mirror, the reflection showed a sophisticated woman in a petal-strewn white dress with a dark, smiling man behind her. Her gaze homed in on where his hands still rested on her naked shoulders, the long fingers dark against her much paler skin. Laurel shivered. There was something so carnally sensual about the contrast of male and female, yin and yang, that it caused her latent awareness of him as an attractive man to rocket.

Her gaze lifted to his. In the mirror, their eyes met. After the beat of a charged second, Rakin let his hands fall from her shoulders. Laurel's breath hissed out.

"We should leave now," he said.

"Yes, of course." Laurel was only too grateful to bolt for the door—for, despite its size, the suite had become unexpectedly oppressive.

When next they returned to the hotel, they would be married.

Six

"The Venetian?"

Laurel flung her head back to read the name spelled in vertically arranged letters down the outside of the hotel's facade.

Her groom gave her a very white smile. "We're going to have photographs taken—we'll want something to remember the occasion by."

She'd been wondering which of the popular chapels Rakin had chosen for their wedding. Now Laurel flicked through the possibilities in her head. The Chapel of Bells or the Little White Chapel. Or even a wedding out at Red Rock Canyon—but then they'd hardly be coming to the Venetian for photos. Now she couldn't help thinking what others in the resort would make of the white petal-dress that pronounced romance—and bride.

Then she shrugged her self-consciousness aside. This was Las Vegas after all. Couples got married all the time. Most likely, no one would cast them a second glance.

That smile still played around Rakin's mouth. "You said you wanted to one day visit Venice."

Laurel smiled back.

But that turned to a gasp of awe as they entered the Venetian's lobby with its high, vaulted ceilings and ornate gold-framed painted frescoes that stretched across the vast space. "Oh, wow."

"A ride on a gondola perhaps? Would that be enough of an adventure?"

"A gondola?" A gurgle of laughter rose in her throat. "Yes, please! I can think of nothing more romantic to do on my wedding day." And Rakin had promised there'd be photos to remember the occasion by. Kara would be impressed!

"Good."

Laurel was even more astonished when they reached the waiting gondola. White and gold, it floated in a canal surrounded by buildings that looked like they'd been transported from Venice to be set along the cobblestone walkways beside the canal. Looking up she could see balconies with pillars and arches and intricate wrought iron, all capturing the detail of a far-away place.

A woman stepped forward offering a bouquet of white roses with sprigs of orange blossom.

"That's a bridal bouquet," said Laurel. Then she got it. "For the photographs?"

Rakin introduced her to Laurel as the hotel's wedding planner. The next surprise turned out not to be a photographer as she'd half expected, but a distinguished-looking wedding celebrant in a dark suit with a flowing robe over the top.

Laurel gasped as it all suddenly made sense. This wasn't just about wedding photos...

"We're getting married here?"

Everything was happening so fast.

The celebrant was already shaking Rakin's hand. Then Rakin placed his hand beneath Laurel's elbow and steered her to the waiting gondola. White petals drifted over them, filling the air with fragrance. As they landed on the pathway, Laurel trod carefully over them, loath to spoil such beauty.

Once they were seated the gondolier pushed off behind them, and the gondola glided along the glass-like water of the Grand Canal.

The space in the gondola was surprisingly intimate. In front of them was the celebrant, his robes giving him a majestic appearance. The limited space forced Rakin's thigh up against hers; and the taut pressure of the hard muscle caused a wave of warmth to spread through Laurel.

The celebrant began to speak. Laurel turned her head to find Rakin watching her with hooded eyes. Her heart thumped.

Excitement churned in her stomach.

When the celebrant started to recite the wedding vows, Laurel discovered that her voice shook a little as she repeated the words in the intimacy of the gondola. She was marrying Rakin Abdellah. Not for love...but for much more sound reasons.

When he took her fingers between his, she felt a little shock at his touch. Up until now this had been so businesslike, but his touch changed that...bringing a flare of heat.

The glint of gold gave her some warning as he slowly slid the plain, unadorned band onto her fourth finger. Her eyes leapt to his in surprise. She started to apologize for not getting him a ring, but the intense focus in his eyes silenced her. Her heartbeat quickened.

"You are now man and wife."

Man and wife.

Laurel swallowed, the daze of disbelief and disconcertment growing more acute.

A month ago she'd been contemplating marrying Eli; now she was married to a man she hadn't met until only a few days ago. A man who had promised her adventure and business opportunities—not love—and in exchange she would pretend to be the wife he needed to nullify his grandfather's threats. A man who had taken over her life...her thoughts...in a way she'd never anticipated.

Behind them the gondolier broke into song. The soulful strains of "O Sole Mio" wound their way around Laurel's heart and tugged tight. Her fingers convulsed beneath Rakin's. For an instant she wished this had been a real romance—the wedding of her heart.

But it wasn't.

It was a convenient arrangement—for both of them. Yet Laurel knew there was more than that to what was passing between them. Rakin had promised her experiences she'd never had…and he was delivering on that. Her world had shifted. And somewhere in the change, she hoped to find herself. Someone who didn't live to please others, someone who took joy in her own life: the Laurel Kincaid she'd never allowed herself to be.

"It is customary for the bridal couple to kiss beneath the bridges." The celebrant offered them an indulgent smile.

Before Laurel could graciously tell him that a kiss wasn't necessary, the gondola swept into the shadows under the bridge and Rakin's head swooped.

His mouth closed over hers and the bottom dropped out of her world.

Rakin's lips were firm—very male—brooking no resistance. She tensed under the unexpected arousal that spread through her like wildfire, and kept her lips firmly pressed together, telling herself Rakin was only doing this to indulge the celebrant. Yet he made no attempt to press further for a more intimate connection. Instead, after a pause, he brushed a row of flirty kisses along the seal of her lips.

With a final kiss on the side of her mouth, he whispered, "That dimple has been driving me crazy."

And then the bridge was behind them, and they were out in the light.

Laurel couldn't respond with a light laugh; instead she bit back a moan of feminine frustration as he lifted his head and put inches between them. But his eyes still held hers, radiating purpose. It took Laurel only a heartbeat of time to realize that his kiss had nothing to do with the watching celebrant, and everything to do with her.

He'd wanted to kiss her.

Flutters of apprehension stirred within her. Once again, her perceptions of their relationship had shifted.

Rakin bent his head toward hers. "Now the adventure starts for real."

A frisson of excitement feathered down Laurel's spine. Not

for the first time she realized that Rakin was a devastatingly attractive man.

To catch her breath, and gain time, she tipped her head back and closed her eyes. Yet still she left her fingers tangled with his, reluctant to break the remaining link between them. The rich serenade of the Neapolitan love song swirled around her, causing a flood of long-banked emotions to overflow.

This was supposed to have been a lark, mixed up with a bit of business. So how had it become the most romantic experience of her life? When she opened her eyes again, she found herself staring blindly at the stars overhead.

"They're not real," volunteered the celebrant. "If you watch carefully the sky keeps changing."

Of course they weren't real! Nothing about this crazy, wild ride with Rakin was real. It was an adventure. A fantasy. Her fantasy.

Yet in another way it was the most real thing that had ever happened to her. She was taking risks. Risks she would never have contemplated before she'd taken a leap into the unknown, out from the safe world of being one of the Charleston Kincaids, to do things that Laurel Kincaid was never expected to do.

Like marrying a sheikh she barely knew.

"The next bridge is coming up," the celebrant's warning broke into her thoughts.

Instantly every nerve ending sprang to alert. Laurel's heart was racing even before she met Rakin's gleaming dark eyes.

As the gondola glided into the shimmering shadows beneath the bridge, Laurel braced herself. Yet no amount of bracing could prepare her for the kiss that finally came. It knocked the breath out of her soul.

This time, Rakin took his time.

And this time the kiss was different.

Laurel gasped as Rakin tasted her, his tongue sweeping over her parted lips into the moistness beyond. Her senses leapt, and she found herself responding with wild ardor, kissing him back, linking her fingers around his neck.

Laurel forgot about the celebrant—forgot about the gondolier punting behind them—and gave herself up to the passion. Hot and fiery, it ignited and burned along her veins until her heartbeat thundered in her head. And all the time "O Sole Mio" washed over them. She'd been transported to another universe, an exotic world light years away from anything she'd ever known.

Nothing was ever going to be the same again.

Laurel had said very little since they'd alighted from the wedding gondola after exchanging vows.

Rakin was starting to wonder what was keeping her so preoccupied. When they'd returned to their penthouse suite a feast was waiting. But Laurel had only picked at bits of smoked salmon and some melon; she hadn't touched the sparkling wine Rakin had poured for her.

Now she blocked the open doorway leading out to the balcony that overlooked the acres of hotel gardens.

"You're very quiet," he said at last, coming up from behind her and placing a hand on her bare arm. "Don't you want something more to eat?"

She drew a deep breath, then said in a rush, "You promised this marriage wouldn't be about sex."

He did a double take. Had Laurel thought his concern for her was a come-on? "It isn't."

"Then why..." She cocked her head and dropped her eyes to rest pointedly where his hand lingered on her forearm "...that?"

His gaze followed hers. *Ah.*

"I like touching—I'm a very demonstrative man."

"Always?"

"Not always," he admitted.

"Then when?"

When he liked someone. When he was attracted to someone. And both applied to Laurel.

He made a sound that was half sigh, half laugh. "Busted. It seems that some sex might be involved after all."

But Laurel didn't laugh along with him. Instead, her gaze

lifted to his face. "Frankly, I've never known what the fuss is about."

She said it with innocent artlessness that was an affront to his prowess. Rakin was utterly certain he could change her mind. Arousal leapt through him at the very notion of teaching Laurel about the adventures of love. Huskily he said, "I could show you exactly what the fuss is about."

That evoked a startled look. The flush spread along her throat, down over the décolleté that her exquisite white wedding dress left exposed. She tried to laugh—it came out a strangled croak. "No, thanks."

But her eyes dropped to his bottom lip, lingered for a long moment, then leapt back to meet his before scuttling away. And in his trousers his erection grew rigid. Laurel was curious. And, forget killing the cat, her curiosity was going to be the death of him.

"Okay. No sex, only marriage," he promised, and wondered how the hell he was going to keep such a stupid vow.

Her tongue moistened her lower lip. "I wasn't even thinking about sex."

Who was she kidding? She'd brought the damn subject up! Lowering his gaze to her lush, red mouth, he said softly, "Of course you were. You're a very beautiful woman. You must fend off propositions all the time."

"I try to head them off before they happen," Laurel said with blunt honesty.

That brought his gaze back to her face and he searched to read what she was telling him. "You freeze them out?"

"Freeze sounds so…cold. I try to be a little kinder."

He gazed at her for a very long moment. The green eyes were more vulnerable than he'd ever seen them. They'd turned the soft, delicate shade of spring leaves dampened by rain. Rakin got the impression he was seeing a side of Laurel that few people ever did.

"What are you thinking?"

He shook his head, doubting Laurel would be comfortable with his observation. "Eli was right."

"About what?" she asked suspiciously.

"You really are a very nice woman."

Her lips curved up. "The feeling is mutual. I think you're a very nice man. So if it's not for sex, then why kiss me like that in the gondola?"

Rakin placed a hand on the doorframe on either side of her. "I could say to seal the terms of our agreement."

"It's a business agreement—it didn't need a kiss to conclude it, and it definitely didn't need two kisses."

He restrained himself from pointing out she hadn't rebuffed either kiss.

"I'm not going to lie," he settled for saying instead. "I would very much enjoy making love to you. It would be an intensely sensual and pleasurable experience for both of us. Another adventure—more for you to discover, I have no doubt about that. But if you wish sex to play no part in our arrangement, I will respect that."

But it would not be easy.

When she didn't respond, he grew more serious. "What are you waiting for? Do you believe there's someone out there in the world just for you? Someone who you won't want to freeze out?"

"Honestly? Love's been more than a little elusive. I'm not sure I really know what it is—even though I know there is a great deal more to it than sweet words. Kara and Eli have proved that to me." She shrugged. "Frankly, I'd settle for a marriage with the promise of adventure rather than love."

Relief filled Rakin, and the tension twisting his gut that all that talk about love and babies always brought drained out of him. "Adventure I can give you."

"Ah, but what's the catch? Are we still talking about sex?"

"No catch." Laurel raised her eyebrows so sharply that Rakin gave her an amused smile. "Not that kind, anyway. Not sex. At least, not if you don't want it, too." His smile became taunting. "Are you sure you want to close the door to the opportunity to explore something wonderful that might exist between you and me?"

Then he steeled himself for her rejection.

But instead of rejection, her eyes filled with curiosity. Her gaze touched his face, dropped lower, then came back. "Exploring anything between us? I just don't know...."

And her indecision left him in a worse, far more frustrating place than outright rejection.

"I'm going to take a shower," he said, his voice rough with frustration.

Talking about sex had made it hard to even think about sleep.

Laurel had showered in the luxurious bathroom off her room. She should've changed into the nightie that Kara, in her role as sister and wedding planner, had once upon a time chosen for Laurel's honeymoon. What on earth had possessed her to pack it? It seemed wrong to wear it now—because it had been picked out for her honeymoon with Eli.

And tonight was her wedding night...with Rakin.

So the sexy garment lay abandoned on the bed, and Laurel didn't feel like crawling into a comfortable T-shirt. She was far too wired.

Which was why she was sitting on the stool in front of the dresser in a one of the *HERS* monogrammed terry robes that the hotel supplied, thinking about her provocative brand-new husband. Because of him, the idea of a marriage in name only was proving to be a little disappointing.

Why not turn the relationship between herself and Rakin into a journey of exploration, too?

Laurel stretched sinuously. In the mirror above the dresser she caught sight of her neckline, which gaped open, revealing the rising curve of her breast. When she looked up, she caught sight of her eyes sparkling with interest and excitement.

Rakin promised to be an accomplished lover. Why shouldn't she take advantage of his suggestion?

Rakin came out the master bathroom toweling his hair, his body still damp from the shower he'd taken. He flung the wet towel onto the king bed.

He heard a gasp, and glanced up.

Laurel stood in the doorway to the master suite, her eyes wide at the sight of his nude body.

No point trying to cover up—it was far too late.

"What are you doing here?" he asked instead.

Her eyes gave her away. And instantly he was aroused.

He moved toward her. "You came for this."

She didn't protest as he took her into his arms. He kissed her, and her lips parted.

He paused, aware that once he started, he wouldn't stop. "Are you certain?"

Her nod was a quick, jerky movement. Rakin smoothed his hands along the front of her bathrobe, then slid them underneath. He caressed her arms, but the terry cloth hindered him. He pushed it back. It fell from her shoulders, then to the floor.

She, too, was now naked.

Rakin drew her down to the wide space of the bed, and came down beside her. He caressed her with long slow strokes, and she relaxed with a soft sigh. His thigh brushed hers apart, and he placed his mouth over hers.

This time the kiss was ravenous.

Rakin was breathing hard by the time it came to an end, and Laurel's eyes were wild.

Reaching out a hand, he stroked her belly; then he reached down farther…and touched her. A keening sound broke from her throat. Rakin stilled.

Laurel didn't move. Her eyes were closed and her teeth had bitten into the soft bottom lip that he'd kissed so thoroughly. She appeared to be waiting.

Gently Rakin stroked again. Her spine arched, and her harsh gasp broke the silence simmering between them. Her eyes popped open.

"Sorry."

Rakin took in the flood of pink on her cheeks.

"Relax," he urged. "Don't apologize."

"That moan…" Laurel looked uncomfortable. "It wasn't ladylike." She rolled over and buried her face in the pillow. "And describing it sounds much worse. Forget I said…whatever it was."

Rakin leaned forward and took her hands in his and gave a gentle tug. When she finally lifted her head, he said, "Listen to me. I don't need you to be the perfect lady. I want you to be yourself."

She gave him gentle smile. "Then there's one thing you need to understand: I am a perfect lady—I don't think I could be an imperfect lady."

He adored her sense of humor, the way she could laugh at herself…at the world…with him.

"Oh, I understand that."

"It's—" She broke off and her eyes slid away from his. She gave a breathless laugh. "I'm embarrassed."

He knew that too. And it was holding her back. Rakin threaded his fingers through her hair and tipped her head so that he could look down into her eyes. "Why?"

"Everything feels so much…more."

"More?"

"Stronger. More intense." She laughed again. "Do I sound crazy or do you have this effect on all women?"

Rakin didn't want to talk about other woman.

His bride was the only woman who interested him—and what she'd just revealed had pleased him. Maybe she wasn't holding back at all; maybe she was progressing in leaps and bounds.

Euphoria drowned him. "Then I'll have to prove there's still more to come," he growled throatily.

Her eyes glazed over in shock. "More? Is that possible?"

Laurel was a grown woman, but clearly she'd never encountered the right man to unleash her passion. Triumph swept him. He intended to change that. Lessons in seduction. She'd prove to be an eager student. He couldn't wait.

With a slow, deliberate smile he said, "I think there's more about adventure for me to share with you. But first I want a promise."

"A…promise?"

He nodded. "I want you to let yourself go. No restraint. No holding back."

Wariness shadowed her eyes. "What are you planning to do?"

The way she looked at him caused Rakin to give a crack of laughter. "Nothing too wild. All I want you to do is enjoy yourself."

"Enjoy myself? You mean…" She spread her hands helplessly. "What exactly do you mean?"

Rakin took pity on her and he lay back on the bed, propping himself up on one elbow. "Let yourself go a little…. Don't stress or feel awkward. Most of all I want you to forget all about being a Kincaid. You're you. Focus on being the woman you want to be. Above all, trust that every bit of pleasure you experience, I get to live it, too."

Laurel's eyes brightened. "I can do that."

"Now roll over—so that I can pleasure you."

She must be intoxicated, Laurel decided as she drew a deep, steadying breath. But this time not tipsy from the effects of too much wedding champagne as she'd been at Kara's wedding. Or even from the French champagne that Rakin had poured into slim crystal goblets when they'd walked into the suite. This time it was the impact of Rakin's closeness.

He filled her senses.

The rich warm gold of his skin, the way the light caught the high blades of his cheekbones, the dark velvet eyes that could be so forceful and compelling one moment, so kind and compassionate the next. And when his hand touched hers…sensations she'd never felt before prickled through her.

His lips whispered across the soft silk of her throat. Laurel arched her neck and he rewarded her with a row of kisses until his lips reached the hollow at the base of her throat. The lick of his tongue against the tender skin caused her to arch farther, her back coming off the bed.

The sound that broke from her suddenly dry throat was raw and without restraint—and definitely not what could be expected from a Southern lady—especially not a Kincaid. Laurel was trapped in the mindless web of pleasure where nothing existed.

Except Rakin.

And the shattering pleasure she was experiencing.

Twisting her head, she closed her eyes more tightly, her fingers twisting through his hair. Rakin covered her skin again with open-mouthed kisses that inflamed her further.

Her breath caught in the back of her throat as his lips closed over the tip of one sensitive breast. The sensation that forked through her was incredible. Hot. White. Spears of pleasure pierced her. Between her fingers his hair had the texture of rough, raw silk. When he broke off the caress, a sigh of denial shook her.

"Slow down," he murmured, before giving the other breast the same treatment, trailing a row of fresh kisses over the skin he'd uncovered.

How was she supposed to slow down when he was driving her mad?

Her hands dropped from his head and dug into the counterpane, and her back arched off the bed. She fought to keep her breathing even. Not to let it escape in the great gasping pants that instinctively seemed to want to happen.

Rakin, too, seemed to lose the race. His heart was pounding against her breasts, as he moved over her. Her legs parted, and she welcomed him, her arms closing around his back, reveling in the smooth satin of his skin against her palms.

It didn't take much more, before he came apart in her embrace.

Rakin rested his arms on the balustrade. The blackness of night enfolded him, while overhead the star-studded sky twinkled. In the master bedroom he'd silently sneaked from, Laurel slept.

He was restless.

The earth-shattering pleasure he had just experienced was not what he'd expected from his bride of convenience.

Foreboding rolled in the pit of his stomach as he stared out into the darkness.

Rakin was not accustomed to the unexpected. Despite what he'd told Laurel about letting go, every facet of his life was meticulously plotted, with careful consideration given to the outcome of each action he undertook. Being swept along by the force of the unknown was not part of his plan. It was Laurel who should be experiencing the thrall of adventure…not he.

He'd thought himself immune from the excitement of novelty. World-weary. Cynical. Not the kind of man to lose his head over a woman—not even one as beautiful as Laurel. After all, he didn't believe in love. He'd been immunized against that lethal condition from a very young age. Not that it stopped him from appreciating—or enjoying—women.

What he didn't do was go crazy over them or fall in love— that way led downhill to destruction.

And, even though he wouldn't call it going crazy, he was thinking way too much about his new bride.

The softness of her skin, the curve of her cheek…the sweet taste of her mouth. And that was before he got to the passion of—

Rakin censored his wayward thoughts. He didn't want her to stir again, not until morning.

For the rest of the night, he would let his bride sleep.

While he reminded himself why he'd married her. For business only.

Seven

Last night had been a mistake.

While Rakin had been courteous at breakfast this morning and unfailingly polite during the journey to the airport, Laurel detected a distance between them that she hadn't encountered before.

She wasn't imagining it.

Since they'd boarded the Learjet, she'd made a couple of light attempts to engage him in conversation, but he'd remained aloof and eventually he'd settled down on the sofa opposite and picked up the business section of the newspaper.

Her humorous, patient companion of the past few days had vanished without a trace.

And Laurel wanted to know why.

Pretending to be engrossed in a magazine, she flicked through stories about the latest celebrity scandals. But her brain couldn't stop buzzing. Had Rakin wanted a marriage in name only? Had he felt pressured to provide a sexual adventure for her benefit last night? Or was the passion they'd shared last night what he wanted? The notion was far too awkward to broach.

The lack of a clear answer left her feeling terribly unsure.

"Would you like a glass of champagne, madam?"

The attendant's voice jerked her out of her reverie. "No

thanks." Champagne was the last thing she needed. And with Rakin in this mood she couldn't even joke with him about trying to get her tipsy....

"Maybe orange juice?" suggested Rakin, looking up from his papers to her immense surprise.

"That would be nice." Laurel smiled her thanks as the attendant poured the juice and set the glass down on the coffee table.

"Don't hesitate to call for anything you need," the attendant offered before disappearing through a set of heavy curtains.

The touch of Rakin's eyes was distracting, especially with the silence that hung over them now that they were alone. Laurel swallowed. "Okay, so I know you have a grandfather who is a tyrant and a cousin. Tell me about the rest of your family."

"There's not much to tell. I'm an only child. My parents died in an airplane crash when I was twelve. My mother was American, my father was the eldest of two sons and four daughters all born and raised as part of the extended royal family in Diyafa. My grandfather is the youngest brother of the ruling prince." A glint appeared in his eyes as Laurel reacted in surprise. "But never fear, I am far enough removed from the throne for the internecine politics not to rule my life."

It was starkly delivered. The barest of information. Some of which he'd already told her. Heavens, she'd gleaned more color about him from what she'd heard from Eli over the years. Rakin had been enrolled in an English boarding school, where he'd remained in the traumatic aftermath of his parents' sudden death. Once his schooling was finished, his grandfather had sent him to university at Harvard—which had brought him in touch with Eli...and ultimately into her life.

Yet the bare recital of facts gave her little insight into the people she was about to meet, and no glimpse into the man behind the suddenly guarded facade.

"Tell me more," she insisted before he could retreat again. "I'll be meeting your grandparents. I want to make a good impression."

"You will meet them at a formal reception where it will be difficult to engage in intimate conversation, so it won't matter if you don't know all about my family. Try not to worry about making a good impression—just be yourself. They're going to love you."

Just being herself was easier said than done.

Laurel was starting to realize that she'd spent much of her life trying to be the person she thought other people wanted her to be. For her father she'd been the talented pianist, and later, the PR expert that The Kincaid Group needed. Her mother had brought out the responsible eldest daughter. With her sisters she'd been the role model. Only her childhood friendship with Eli had been free of all the posturing. Yet even that had changed once all their friends had started pairing up. . . and suddenly Laurel had again found herself playing to the expectations of others—that she and Eli should make a match of it.

It was curiously liberating to realize that with Rakin she could simply be herself.

He'd been completely honest about what he wanted from her: a wife who his grandfather would accept so that Rakin could gain control of the family business and stop it from being signed over to his cousin. Yet he was making it clear that he had no wish for her to pretend to be anyone other than the woman he'd promised to induct into a world of adventure.

She could still be herself.

And, the best thing about their deal, was that she'd had more adventure in the past few days than her somewhat staid, buttoned-up life had afforded her in the last three decades.

Raising his glass, he said, "Here's to new friends and new destinations."

It sounded hopeful as well as adventurous, and Laurel felt her enthusiasm rising. "I'll drink to that."

Their glasses filled with juice clinked together, and their eyes met over the rims in silent intimacy. The impact of it was profound. Laurel forced herself to glance away, not to reveal her sudden burst of confusion.

As the Learjet started its descent, Laurel caught her first glimpse of Rashad, the capital city of Diyafa from the air.

The city was built on a hilly outcrop and all around stretched an endless sea of sand as far as the eye could see. Shades of ochre and soft pinks with blocks of red clay dominated the city. Domed roofs and towering minarets gave the city a spicy exoticism. Yet interspersed between the traditional domes, Laurel could also see tall, modern structures of towering glass thrusting into the sky. A mix of ancient and modern.

Excitement surged. She swung around to Rakin, only to find he wasn't looking out the window but at her. The divide between them appeared to have been bridged. There was an expression in his midnight-black eyes that caused all her reservations about what had happened last night to evaporate, and her face broke into a wide smile.

"It looks like something from *Aladdin*—or rather, *Aladdin* meets the twenty-first century. I can't wait to see everything!"

The formal reception that Rakin had warned her about was held at a palace in the center of Rashad that resembled something out of *Arabian Nights*.

Laurel had never seen anything like it.

The floors in the immense reception room were made of colored marble arranged in intricate patterns. Gilded paneling carved by a master hand decked the walls, lit by sconces that cast a glow over the crowd. Around the edges of the immense room, large ancient urns added to the grandeur while lush arrangements of flowers gave the room extra bursts of color and a heady scent. The sheer luxury of the palace's interior took her breath away.

Its owner, Rakin's grandfather, was equally imposing.

Facing the man with his flowing robes and fierce visage, Laurel found herself unusually tongue-tied. Their meeting was brief, and Laurel felt as though the old man's sharp eyes were staring into her heart.

It was a far-from-comfortable experience.

Tula, Rakin's grandmother, was more approachable. Her wrinkled face bore the evidence of a lifetime spent smiling. And the hug she gave Laurel was as warm as her husband's greeting was suspicious.

"You have known my grandson long?" Prince Ahmeer Al-Abdellah demanded.

"Long enough for her to know she wanted to marry me," Rakin answered for her.

Determined not to be put on the defensive, Laurel smiled at Tula. "Your home is magnificent."

Tula nodded. "We have spent many happy years here."

"We should circulate among the guests. I have promised Laurel that I will introduce her to many people so that she can make friends," Rakin said, stretching the truth, "I will bring her to visit again when you are alone, perhaps tomorrow?"

"Rakin, I wish to talk to your bride!" scolded Tula. "You have made us wait for so many years. Now that you are finally married, you cannot drag your wife away from us so soon."

Laurel shot Rakin an I-told-you-so glance, which he ignored.

"Rakin tells me that your family is of some importance in America." Prince Ahmeer went straight to the heart of the matter.

Laurel nodded. "My mother's family has lived in Charleston for centuries."

Prince Ahmeer nodded in approval. "Your family has roots—like we have in Diyafa."

"Yes."

Before long, he was asking shrewd questions about the business interests of The Kincaid Group. His knowledge of container shipping was extensive, and Laurel was challenged to answer his questions. Within minutes, he was smiling and nodding, looking much more at ease.

Finally he clapped his hand on Rakin's shoulder, "I was concerned when you called to let me know you were married. But it appears that you have chosen well. I am satisfied. You may visit us tomorrow alone."

As the sheikh and his sheikha strolled away, Rakin murmured to Laurel, "My grandfather is not easily satisfied—you have worked a miracle." His mouth curved up. "But then I never doubted for a minute that you would."

And then there were the guests....

Men wore a mix of European-tailored suits, a sprinkling of tuxedos and dishdashas with white headdresses embellished with beautifully knotted cords. Most of the women wore Western fashions—only a handful in traditional dress. The women were beautiful, dressed in the finest designs that made Laurel feel almost dowdy. She'd played it safe in a black halter-neck gown, adorned only with the diamond pendant Rakin had given her to celebrate their wedding. She felt as wide-eyed as a child in this lavish gathering.

Half an hour later, Laurel found herself alone for the first time. She'd been fed delectable morsels of Diyafan food. And she'd been introduced to dozens of people—and her face hurt from smiling.

Rakin had been swept away by two men to meet a third whom he'd invited here tonight. He'd promised to return in minutes, and Laurel had urged him to go, assuring him she would be fine without him.

"You are Rakin's new wife."

She turned at the statement. A tall, dark-haired man clad in traditional robes was standing behind her. He stepped forward and smiled. "I am sheikh ibn-Ahmeer."

Laurel found herself smiling back.

"Yes, I am Rakin's wife."

"I had not heard about you before I was invited to welcome you—how did you meet Rakin?"

She should have foreseen this. She and Rakin had not agreed on the fiction that they would spread. Telling this man that they'd met for the first time, less than a week ago, would not do. Desperately she cast her gaze around the room searching for inspiration—or Rakin's return.

Rakin was no longer with the trio of men; instead he was talking to his grandfather, and it looked like the conversation had grown stormy. His grandfather was frowning, and Rakin's body language told her that he, too, was tense. That worried Laurel. She was getting the sense that he and his grandfather did not have an easy relationship...and that did not augur well for Rakin's plan to stop his grandfather from ousting him.

"So how did you meet?"

"Oh, I'm sorry, I didn't answer your question."

Laurel focused on him.

He was only a little shorter than Rakin with dark, liquid eyes that had a way of connecting to make her feel like the only woman in the room. After the way Rakin had ignored her and caused her to be a little hesitant, to be listened to, to feel interesting was a balm for wounds she hadn't even known she nursed.

She stuck as close as she could to the truth. "We have a friend in common." Let him believe that Eli had introduced them.

"So you have known Rakin for a while then?"

Help! How was she supposed to answer that? And, more to the point, what had Rakin led his grandparents to believe? Laurel did not want to contradict his version of their romance, but nor did she want to tell an outright lie, so she compromised by avoiding his question.

"It was at my sister's wedding that we finally realized we were fated to be together."

He gave her a searching glance. "Rakin is a fortunate man."

The expression on his face warned her that "fortunate" hadn't been his first response. Did this man suspect that her and Rakin's marriage was a sham?

Or was she being paranoid?

"Rakin and I have something special."

That was certainly true. No man had ever made her laugh, shown her what her life was lacking, in the same way as Rakin had. He appeared to accept her statement and their conversation became more general as she recounted her impressions of Diyafa.

Within minutes, they had discovered common ground. Her new friend had a sizeable property portfolio, and with her family's interests in developing the old container yards down on the battery, Laurel found herself telling him about the plans for the new development. A development that was currently stalled due to Jack Sinclair's interference which had resulted in a loss of investors.

"The returns will be good," she said enthusiastically. "The whole area is coming to life, being regenerated."

"You do know about the business."

She gave him a questioning look. "But of course. I'm the director of public relations for the company."

"Forgive me, I assumed it was a puppet position when you first told me what you do, a role without any real meaning."

For a moment she felt affronted; then it passed. "At least you are honest. No, I worked hard to get where I am today."

A flicker passed over his face, and Laurel wished she hadn't been so sharp in her retort. Then she shoved her regret aside. Wasn't this exactly what she was trying to get over? It was time to be her own woman, not to worry about what everyone else thought of her.

"Then I must certainly apologize for my rude assumption. You must be thinking I am a chauvinist."

It had crossed her mind, and Laurel held off politely denying his charge—as she might have in the past. Instead she said, "If you are interested in learning more about the project I can put you in touch with my brother, Matthew—there is money to be made."

"Yes, please do have him contact me." He fell silent for a moment as he studied her. "I think Rakin has chosen very well. You are going to be an asset to the Al-Abdellah family."

Where did he fit in to the family? But before she could ask, Laurel sensed Rakin's dark presence behind her.

When he spoke, his harsh tone jarred. "I see you have met my cousin."

"Your cousin?" She glanced between the two men with some confusion. "But I thought your surname was Ahmeer—not Abdellah."

"Zafar ibn Ahmeer is the name I go by within the family—in honor of my grandfather. But I am also Zafar Al-Abdellah."

This was the man who Rakin's grandfather had threatened to give control of the family business to if Rakin did not produce a wife? Zafar had been civil, pleasant even. He'd made her laugh—he was nothing like the ogre Laurel had expected. She cast her mind rapidly back over their discussion to check if she might have been indiscreet. Then she stiffened her spine.

Why was she worrying? There was no earthly reason why she shouldn't promote The Kincaid Group to anyone she met in Diyafa. Hadn't Rakin assured her that by marrying him she would gain access to his business contacts? And didn't she want to help her family protect TKG from any harm Jack Sinclair might do by gaining as many new clients as possible? Zafar's business interests dovetailed with that of The Kincaid Group. If he wanted to invest, his money would be welcome.

An aide appeared behind Zafar and murmured something to him in Arabic.

"I will ask that you excuse me, I have something to which I must attend." He dug into the voluminous dishdasha he wore. "Here are my contact details." He handed Laurel a card. "We will have plenty of time to talk again later, I am sure."

With an unsmiling nod in Rakin's direction, he followed the aide.

Rakin glared after his cousin, and it gave his features a harshness Laurel had not seen before.

Since their arrival in Diyafa, Rakin had changed.

At first Laurel had not been able put her finger on exactly how he'd changed; she'd only known that the difference was marked.

He was distant. He was aloof.

And it was not merely the tension between them as a result of the night they'd shared together in Vegas. This was different. It was complex. He'd lost that lightness of spirit that had captivated her, made her laugh, and assumed a mantle of authority and become increasingly remote.

Now, having met his autocratic grandfather, Laurel was starting to fathom what was happening.

Diyafa was his birthright. He was part of the ruling royal family. With his return, Rakin's persona had changed. He'd become more than a man; he'd become a sheikh.

* * *

The sight of his cousin staring into Laurel's eyes had goaded Rakin into returning to his bride's side. He'd cut his grandfather's complaints short, and hastened over to see what mischief Zafar was wreaking.

"What were you two talking about?" Rakin growled into Laurel's ear as he watched his cousin depart in a hurry. "Why did he give you his card to contact him?"

His wife's chin came up in a gesture he was starting to know too well.

"We were talking about real estate."

"That is all? Then why did he rush off as I arrived?"

"He didn't rush off, he was called away. You're seeing a conspiracy where there is none."

Her exasperation only made the knot that had started to form in his stomach pull tighter. "I have plenty of reason. You do not know Zafar like I do."

Her expression changed instantly. "He has done you harm?"

Rakin hesitated. Almost reluctantly, he said, "He has always been my foe."

He could see his response had surprised her. "Always?"

Wishing he'd kept silent, Rakin said with even greater reluctance, "From childhood we have been in conflict."

"You look like you are near in age."

"I am three months older." But he'd been sent away to England—while Zafar, his grandfather's favorite, had stayed.

"How sad! I would've have expected you to be friends."

"We were never encouraged to be friends." The brusque statement was not intended to illuminate the tensions that had existed between him and his cousin. Rakin waved a dismissive hand. "Talking about Zafar is of no interest. I came to find you because I want you to meet Ben Al-Sahr. He imports large quantities of cotton from the United States. Presently he ships mostly from other areas, but if the Kincaids can introduce him to a supplier in Charleston, that could change."

"Thank you, Rakin. I would certainly like to meet him—and I'm sure Matt would love to connect with him, too. I'll have to let him know to expect a call." She placed her fingers on his arm, and the smile she gave him was brilliant.

"Matt? It's Laurel." Across the world, her brother sounded half asleep. "What time is it? Did I wake you?"

"It's okay." His voice sharpened. "Laurel? Is something the matter?"

"No, no. Nothing's the matter." She crossed her fingers. "I got married."

She shut her eyes…and waited.

The eruption she'd anticipated wasn't long in coming. "You got married? When? To whom?"

"To Rakin. In Vegas." Before he could interrupt she added in a rush, "But we're in Diyafa now. Rakin wanted to introduce me to his family."

There was a long silence. Laurel found herself staring out of the window, over the planted garden outside the palace windows. The rosebushes were in bloom. Red. Yellow. Orange. All the fiery colors of a desert sunset.

"Does Mom know?" Matt spoke at last.

The pointed question caused a stab of guilt. "It happened so suddenly. You're the first to know."

"Oh." Matt fell silent.

"I'll call Mom next," she said quickly as the pause again expanded beyond what was comfortable. "Then I'll call Kara and Lily—and RJ."

"Kara and Eli have gone away for a few days."

"Oh." It highlighted how out of touch she was. It felt as if more than a few days had elapsed. Why should it surprise her? After all, more than the view out the window had changed—her whole life had changed.

"Why?"

This was the question she'd been dreading. Somewhere outside she could hear children laughing. "Because he's an attractive man?" she suggested tentatively. "Because—"

"Not why did you get married—why are you telling me first and not Mom or RJ?"

Relief filled her. At least the answer to that was easy. "Because Rakin introduced me to a business associate of his. He's a cotton importer and Rakin has convinced him he'd be better off buying in Charleston and using TKG for shipping. I wanted to warn you that he'd be calling soon."

"You get married and that's what you call to tell me? That your new husband may have sourced us new business?"

Matt sounded mad.

But why?

And why did men have to make it so difficult to understand them? She'd thought Matt would be thrilled—both at the news of her marriage and at the idea of the contacts she was making for TKG.

Finally Laurel settled for, "Yes."

"Since when did business become the most important thing in your life, Laurel?"

"What do you mean?" Bewilderment flooded her, quickly followed by a tide of sisterly annoyance. "For months all we've talked about is what's going to happen to The Kincaid Group. And sure, the position is a lot easier since Susannah's grandfather came on board with Larrimore Industries, but we're not out of the woods yet, Matt. The last thing I heard at the wedding before I left for Vegas with Rakin was that Jack Sinclair was causing trouble again—and that you were worried. I might not be there, but I can still do my best to help."

"Laurel, calm down."

"No, listen—"

"Calm down! No one is doubting that you do everything for this family—it's the reason everyone was so keen for you to take a break. You've been carrying a lot of stress—"

"So has everyone else!"

"I'm not arguing, but one of the things I realized when Flynn became ill, when I reconnected with Susannah is that there is more to life than business." His voice softened. "You've gotten married, so you've discovered that, too. The news of your marriage to a man you've fallen for is way more important than a new business contact."

Laurel couldn't come up with a single argument against what Matt was saying. Every word he spoke twisted deep in her chest. Her baby brother had become a romantic.

But what Matt didn't understand was that she and Rakin hadn't married for the same reasons as he and Susannah.

"Okay, I take your point," she said slowly. "But before I call Mom, RJ and Lily, you need to know that you might also get a call from Zafar ibn Ahmeer Al-Abdellah. He's interested in investing in the battery development. Look after him, he's Rakin's cousin."

"Family *always* comes first."

Laurel was still smiling when she set the phone down, Matt's words ringing in her ears.

Eight

The rest of the week passed in a haze of engagements.

Rakin kept his word. He'd introduced Laurel to a host of his business contacts. In return, she made sure that the fiction of their loving marriage was firmly in place whenever his family or the extended network of relations—was present.

There had been no repeat of that steamy night in Las Vegas.

And Laurel wasn't sure whether to be relieved or disappointed about it. Despite her inner tension about her increasing awareness of him, her respect and even affection for Rakin was growing in leaps and bounds. Yet there was still a part of him that she couldn't reach, a part that was closed away and tightly controlled.

They had been watching the sunset from one of the many balconies of the palace, when she took the plunge and asked Rakin, "Will we get a chance to see the desert any time soon?"

It was something she'd been hoping he would show her. In part, because the presence of the vast Diyafan Desert surrounded them in Rashad, but also because she had the strong sense that Rakin had been defined by the harsh beauty of the world beyond the city. It was part of his psyche. By understanding his relationship to the ancient desert, she hoped to learn more about what made him tick.

Understanding Rakin had become increasingly important to her. Laurel was beginning to realize that he would forever be more than a stranger who had introduced to her to a world beyond her imaginings. Yet she could not yet put a name to the complex emotions he roused. There was liking...and laughter... and desire.

And something more.

Something that hovered maddeningly out of reach, defying her need to capture it...contain it...name it. It was something that had crept into her soul by small degrees until it was part of her.

"We could go any time you want." Rakin rose from the carved olive wood chair where he'd been seated and, moving past her, he leaned against the stone balustrade, his back to the sunset. From this angle he formed a dark silhouette against the flaming sky. "You are eager to visit the desert?"

"Absolutely!" She nodded enthusiastically.

"Then we will go tomorrow."

"But only if it suits," she said quickly. "Only if your grand-father—"

The interruption was immediate. "I have done everything my grandfather could expect of me—and more." There was pent-up frustration in his voice.

He'd even married her for his grandfather.

Rakin might not have said that, but the truth of it lay between them, a silent divide.

She glanced away before he glimpsed her thoughts.

The palace gardens were cloaked in falling darkness. Only the distinctive outlines of palms stood out against the pale gold of the desert sky. The first star had appeared, and a longing to explore the world that lay beyond the city walls once more over-took Laurel.

"It will be my pleasure to show you our desert. I didn't offer to play tour guide back at your sister's wedding out of polite-ness." Humor filled his voice, and it warmed Laurel as he drew her gaze back to his dark shape. "I wish to see it through your eyes—it will be a fresh glimpse. My own personal retreat is near

Dahab, a settlement in the heart of the desert," he added. "We will go there."

"Another adventure!"

He inclined his head. "Of course. And I promise you it will be far more authentic than a black-glass pyramid fronted by a crouching sphinx."

She gave him an amused look. "You didn't find that exotic?"

Rakin shifted, and the sinking sun caught the movement as his mouth tugged into a smile. "Exotic maybe. Authentic, no."

Gratitude for the experiences that he had already offered flooded her. Laurel found herself on her feet, in front of him. And, before she could consider her actions, she was saying, "Thank you."

An eyebrow raised. "For what?"

"For giving me the opportunity to break free."

"If it was important enough, you would've done it anyway."

Laurel was shaking her head. "I'm not so sure I would ever have found the courage."

"Because your family needs you?"

She looked down and didn't answer.

Rakin could understand the pull of duty. It had dominated much of his life. "What about what you need?" he asked quietly, above her bowed head.

Her shoulders hunched up. "My needs…?"

"Yes. You have needs, too."

The words reverberated through his head, assuming a double-edged meaning Rakin had not intended. A wild, sensual glimpse of needs very different from those he'd been alluding to taunted him. The memory of her face alight with excitement after the roller coaster ride flashed through his mind. The wild sounds she'd made when they made love…

She'd been animated in a way he'd never seen her. Alive. Held in a thrall that turned her beauty into something far more primal and caused want to leap through him.

"My needs are not important." She spoke with a finality that told him she considered the topic closed.

Letting out the breath he'd unconsciously been holding,

Rakin placed a hand beneath her chin and tilted her head up. Her eyes were turbulent with emotion. He forced himself to ignore the want that flared, and concentrate on the yearning in her eyes. "Your needs are very important. It's time you start to put yourself first."

Her gaze clung to his. "What do you mean?"

"I think you know." The evening sun had turned her hair to a nimbus of auburn flame, and she looked breathtakingly lovely. But Rakin couldn't allow himself to be sidetracked. "Eli said kindness is one of your best traits, but it may also be one of your greatest shortcomings, too."

"That's contradictory."

Despite the dismissive words, all her attention remained fixed on him.

"No, it's not. You've always done what everyone else wanted—even when it wasn't best for you." He heard her breath catch. "You haven't been very kind to yourself."

"It would be selfish to think of my own needs at a time my family should come first."

"Only you can decide whether it would be selfish—because only you know what you really want. Staying in Charleston, going through the motions of a life that isn't what you dream of would've been condemning you to a half life." His fingers still rested against her chin, and her lips parted. He ached to capture the softness of that sweet mouth. He thrust his desire down. Relentlessly he pressed on. "You need to be true to yourself."

There was a pause. Finally she said in a low voice, "You're saying that by doing what's best for my family I've been dishonest."

"I think that all your life you've done what you think others want—rather than what you truly desire."

"I love my family—I love my job," she protested.

"I'm sure you do. I'm not saying that you don't," he said gently, his fingers straying along her jawline in a caress. He wondered if she'd realized yet that she'd allowed that love to become a trap that was draining her of her vitality and life force. "But what you've proved to me is that you feel a need to escape from everyone's perception of who Laurel Kincaid is. That can only be because you have a different vision of the real Laurel Kincaid. Don't forget it's your vision that matters." Rakin knew she was still defined in terms of the Kincaid name. He bit back the urge to tell her she was an Abdellah now. His wife. And that he placed no constraints on whomever she chose to be. "Your vision. Not your mother's. Not Eli's. Not mine. Only yours."

This time he watched her throat bob as she swallowed.

But what she said next startled him. "And you, Rakin? Are you loyal to the vision of what you most want?"

The helicopter descended to the desert below.

Rakin had wasted no time in putting the plan for them to visit Dahab into action. Through the bubble windows the gold expanse of the sand rose up to meet them. What from the air had appeared as a barren stretch of nothing, now rearranged itself into a myriad of colors. Rocky outcrops with bent tamarind trees nestling at the base. Ahead, stone battlements clawed their way up against the outcrop.

Laurel spoke into the microphone built into the headphones that had muffled the noise of their journey. "This is your retreat? Good heavens, it looks like a fortress."

"It was originally a fort."

The helicopter cleared the high walls surrounding the edifice and dropped onto a helipad. Minutes later, the pilot came around and opened the door, and Laurel clambered out, keeping her head down until she'd cleared the slowing rotor blades.

Outside, the desert heat was dry and dusty.

She gazed about with interest.

Closer to the house—fort, she amended—water cascaded over rocks into pools adorned with lush plantings.

"It looks like an oasis."

"It is an oasis. Come." Rakin placed his hand under her elbow. "It will be cooler inside."

"What's that?" Laurel pointed to a building jutting out in the distance.

"That's the stable block."

"Stables?" Laurel came to a standstill. The face that tilted up to him was radiant. "There are horses? Or are the stables empty?"

"There are horses. Not many—the royal stud is located closer to Rashad. But I like to ride when I am home so there are always horses."

"Can we ride?"

Rakin nodded.

Joy exploded in her eyes. "Tomorrow?" At his nod, she said, "Do you know how long it's been since I've ridden a horse?"

That startled him. "You can ride?"

"All Winthrops can ride—we were taken for our first lesson before we were five." Her beatific smile told him she'd clearly loved every moment.

"Then why stop?"

"So much else to do. My brothers carried on—they still play polo. But, as the eldest daughter, mother insisted I learn to play tennis and do ballet and piano so that my sisters would follow in my ballet slippers." She grinned, but Rakin detected a forced gaiety. "And Winthrops fish and shoot and hunt, too, so there was little time left for the demands of horse-riding lessons."

"You shoot and hunt?"

"I don't hunt myself, but I'm a crack shot."

Rakin knew he shouldn't have been surprised. Yet he couldn't help it. Laurel was so intensely feminine and ladylike he didn't expect the more physical side of her. Then he remembered what she was like in bed. More tiger than lady. Instantly desire stirred.

He overrode it.

"We will take the horses out tomorrow."

"I can't wait."

"Now, let me show you my home."

The ride surpassed everything Laurel had expected.

They rode out of the dark stable yard while it was still cool. It was the only way to escape the relentless heat of the day, Rakin told her, his stirrup chinking against hers as they rode abreast.

The mare she was riding, a gray with small pricked ears and the delicate dish face so characteristic of an Arabian horse, had an easy gait. By contrast, Rakin was mounted on Pasha, a strong stallion with a high-held tail and long mane.

For a while they rode in utter silence, the clip of the horses' hooves muffled by the desert sand. Laurel shifted in the saddle and inhaled the dry, already hot air. To the east, the first bright slivers of dawn had cracked the jet-black sky. All around them the desert was coming to life.

To Laurel's right a dark outcrop had taken shape, and now the first rays of the sun struck the rockface.

"What is that?"

"Jabal Al Tair. The mountain of the birds," Rakin translated. "We will make our way up as far as we can and watch the sun rise from a higher vantage point."

The stony path climbed steeply until they came to a place where the rise leveled out between two imposing rock faces.

Rakin dismounted first, then came to hold her mare's head as Laurel swung her leg over the back of the saddle and slid down to the ground. Handing the reins to Rakin, she watched as he tethered the two horses. Then she followed him along a winding, narrow path between the cliffs.

Once through the fissure, the path opened up into a broad rock platform.

"Oh, wow!"

They stood on the edge of the world.

In front of them the gold desert sands stretched to meet the rising sun.

"Dahab means gold. You can see where the name comes from."

"Yes." Laurel didn't even want to breathe to break the awe of the moment.

"Look," Rakin pointed.

She followed his arm. A hawk circled in wide swoops. "He's hunting."

"Yes," Rakin agreed, his eyes narrowed as he watched the

bird swoop down to the desert below. "See that blur of movement? That's a hare he's after."

The hawk rose, a silhouette against the rosy sky, the hare clutched between hooked talons. Ascending to the sheer walls above them, the big bird disappeared from sight.

Gesturing to the vista spread out in front of them, Laurel said, "It looks so empty, yet it's an entire ecosystem. It just took the sun coming up to reveal it." She shot Rakin a look that caused him to want to pull her into his arms and seal her smiling mouth with his. "Apollo driving his fiery chariot into the sky to meet the new day," she murmured.

Before he could turn thought to action, one of the horses whickered behind them. Laurel started to laugh. "You want to be up there, too?"

"It would be hard, hot work galloping that course every day," replied Rakin, leashing the rush of raw desire that she'd evoked. "Only an Arabian could keep up."

"Apollo himself would have to be pretty fit." Laurel let her gaze drift down Rakin's lean length. "A horseman with years of skill."

Rakin grew still.

"I want you," he said roughly. "Now."

"Now?" Laurel could feel herself flushing. "Here?"

"Yes."

The bald statement caused her to blink. Twice.

His cheekbones jutted out in hard angles from his rigid face.

"But it's morning." She heard herself, and shuddered. She sounded like a naive virgin. Both of them knew she was not that.

"It makes you shy to make love in the daylight?" he asked, and touched her. One finger trailed down her cheek. "Still? Despite what we shared that night in Las Vegas?"

Her heart contracted at his mention of love.

This marriage had never been about love…yet Laurel was starting to think increasingly about love. It wasn't something she had ever discovered. Her lashes sank hiding her eyes from his all-too-perceptive gaze. What she shared with Rakin had a depth and intensity beyond what she'd felt for men in the past.

This was different.

Could it be love?

She started as his hands closed on her shoulders.

"Laurel…?"

The husky sound of his voice caused her look up. Taut tension radiated from him. A rush of desire bolted through her veins. She knew he was going to kiss her…and she did nothing to stop him. Instead, she waited…and welcomed the surge of heat as his mouth opened over hers.

His tongue sank in. Hungry. Possessive. Laurel's hands came up to grasp his forearms and she held on tight, her response desperate with pent-up passion. At least she hoped it was passion. Not—

Or was this…hunger…this desperation…this powerful emotion possibly…love?

Fear of the answer finally made her break away.

Rakin's chest rose and fell as he sucked in a rasping breath—but he let her go.

After a beat he said, "So? You're certain you don't want to risk making love in the daylight?"

There was humor…and a dark passion that tempted her at the same time that it terrified her. "It's the idea of…" She swallowed, then carefully imitated the wording he had used ". . . of making love outside—where anyone might see us. What happened in Vegas was under the cover of darkness." Mostly.

He scanned their surroundings. "Who will see us? We are far above the desert. There is no one near." And he came closer.

So much for her thirst for adventure, her craving to break free.

"I know, I sound ridiculous. I can't explain it." She backed toward where the horses were tethered. And she damned all her inhibitions.

There was a glint in his eyes, as he murmured, "So my rebel is not such a rebel after all."

Laurel wished she had the gumption to pick up the gauntlet he had thrown down. "I'm not ready for such an adventure."

Nine

They were almost home when a boy came running toward them.

Rakin checked the stallion, and brought him to a halt beside the boy.

"Give me your hand." Leaning forward, he grabbed the boy's hand and scooped him up onto the stallion in front of him.

The horse started to stride out, neck arched and head held high.

"I am riding Pasha." The child's back was rigid with pride. "He's much better than Halva."

Rakin laughed out loud. "Don't let Halva hear that—her feelings will be hurt, and she might buck you off."

"Pah." It was a sound of disgust. "Halva is too old to buck."

Rakin shot Laurel a conspiratorial look. "Halva is kind with the sweetest nature in the horse kingdom. Nothing wrong with nice. And don't forget I learned to ride on Halva's mother."

They turned into the stable yard. An elderly man with a sun-beaten face came out of the nearest stable.

As Rakin reined the stallion to a halt, the boy muttered something and slid off the horse. By the time the stable manager had hobbled up, the boy had disappeared.

"That boy, he is a nuisance." But there was pride in the old man's eyes.

"Your grandson will be a fine rider one day—like his grandfather."

The pride grew brighter. "He does well at school. He learns more than his father or his grandfather ever did. English. Computers. All the villagers say we are blessed."

Rakin waved his thanks off. "It was time."

The more she learned of Rakin, the more complex he became. The news that he was responsible for educating the youngsters. His gentleness with the boy and his grandfather made Laurel forget the reserve that had distanced him from her. Instead, she found herself melting inside at his connection with the pair. The discovery of this softer side of her husband moved her more than she would've expected. Rakin's gentleness…his social conscience were more facets to admire about a man who was starting to occupy an awful amount of her life.

He would make a wonderful father one day…and a perfect husband.

One day…

When she was long gone. Looking away from the man who'd taken over so much of her life, Laurel reined the gray in and swung her leg over the back of the saddle to dismount. She slid to the ground, then walked to the horse's head, taking care not to glance in Rakin's direction.

Their marriage had not been forged for love or family. It was purely a temporary proposition. She was nothing more than a temporary wife.

And, despite the heat of the day, that reminder caused a chill to settle around Laurel's heart.

It was the final day of their getaway. Tomorrow they would be leaving as Rakin had a board meeting in the capital.

They'd retreated to Rakin's library after sharing a late dinner as they'd done each night. The past four days had been a time that Laurel knew she would treasure even after their marriage was over.

Today Rakin had taken her deeper into the desert to explore its magic. They'd explored towering rock formations where wadis—water paths that brought life to the desert—hid. He'd taken her to visit villages with markets that had delighted Laurel with their character.

She should've been exhausted.

Yet she was too wired to sit. Her mind was still whirring, stimulated by the color and excitement of the day. Instead of joining Rakin on the wide, overstuffed daybed, where heavily embroidered cushions added an exotic touch to the huge room, she made for the floor-to-ceiling bookshelves.

Every subject under the sun was covered.

Politics. History. Books about Diyafa; about deserts; about ancient cultures. In addition to the leather-covered books and coffee-table hard covers, there was a large selection of well-read paperback fiction. Modern literary novels and a selection of popular crime fiction. The collection revealed the breadth and scope of Rakin's interest.

"There's a large number of travel books both ancient and modern," Rakin said from the couch.

"I can see."

"Their journeys were fascinating—they were men driven by more than action, by a vision of what they wanted from life."

She was on her own odyssey, Laurel realized. And it was far from over. Blindly she stared at the shelf in front of her. Then her gaze fell on a shelf of smaller tomes. Poetry, she saw. One was a volume titled simply *Pleasures* in faded gold lettering on the burgundy leather spine.

Laurel drew it from the shelf, the calf binding soft against her fingers. As she opened it, the yellowed pages with a flower-printed border were revealed.

A verse caught her eye.

My love! Sun of my Dark Heart, brighten my Day,
Bring life to stone-dry Desert, warm me with your Fire;

As surely as Dawn follows the Star-scattered Night
And floods the Perfumed Garden of my Desire.

Love poetry. Oft read from the way the pages fell open.
Read by Rakin?
"What are you looking at?"
It was as if her thoughts had conjured up his voice.
"A collection of poetry."
She flipped the page over, and her eyes fell on an illustration. It caused her to gasp. A pair of lovers, entwined on a bed under a tree. The woman lush and voluptuous, her lover dark and powerful. Laurel stared down at the undoubted beauty of the naked flesh that the artist had painted.

Normally she would've felt awkward to be faced with such material. The man's head was flung back, a look of unrestrained passion on his face, while the woman looked utterly satisfied.

Heat balled in her stomach.

What would she give to see that look on Rakin's face?

She shut the book and slid it back into the empty space; then she crossed to where Rakin sat and dropped down on the wide sofa arm.

"Thank you for a wonderful day," her voice sounded hoarse. She couldn't look at him yet, in case she gave herself away.

His finger touched the tip of her chin, with a gentle pressure to turn her head. She resisted. His fingertip moved to touch her lip.

Then he said softly, "You must be tired—ready to go to bed?"

Was that a question in his voice? A suggestion? The heat in her stomach blazed through her veins. Her gaze dropped down to connect with his. And a spark leapt between them.

"Come here," he groaned.

Laurel couldn't have said who moved first, but she was in his lap, his mouth replacing his fingertip on her lips, and they were kissing fiercely. The fevered heat was soaring. Raging. Within a minute her control had shredded.

Their clothes came off in a hurry, and there was little time for preliminaries before Rakin pulled her astride him.

It was fast and furious.

With every pleasure-increasing stroke, she watched him. Every flicker of his eyes. The way his throat tightened as he swallowed and the moment his eyelids closed as a moan broke from deep in his throat.

There was something sinfully wonderful about having this much power over a man—especially one as strong and unyielding as Rakin. So far he'd called all the shots in this game of chess between them. Back in Las Vegas, he'd reduced her body to quivers, played it like a virtuoso until she'd learned hidden secrets about her psyche that she'd never imagined lurked behind her conventional ladylike exterior.

He'd unleashed passions she'd never suspected existed, awoken desires that she'd never considered would come to play across her mind every time he walked into a room.

But now it was her chance to turn the tables.

Rakin was every bit as hungry for her as she was for him.

When it came, the explosion of pleasure was sudden and satisfying.

And afterward Laurel dropped her head onto his chest, and the pounding of his heart told her that his composure was as stripped as hers.

He'd seriously miscalculated.

Rakin had left Laurel asleep, sprawled across the enormous bed in his bedchamber, and he'd come outside to the pool for a swim to calm the turbulence in his head.

Who was the fool who'd said business and pleasure didn't mix? Then broken the rule he'd created? Not once, but twice. Worse, Rakin suspected that it would soon be broken a third—even fourth—time and beyond.

He swam a length, then back, searching for the tranquility, the clear head, that cutting through the water had always brought.

But this time it didn't.

He stopped at the far end, grasped the rail and tipped his head back. The pool was lit up by the golden coin of the full moon.

Not even the beauty could capture him. Emotions churned inside him, too hard to separate—or even identify.

The click of the latch on the wooden gate set in the wall surrounding the pool, followed by the sound of a footfall caused him to turn his head and squint through the darkness toward the arch.

He caught a glimpse of something in the shadows; then the moonlight moved on white silk.

His wife.

At the edge of the pool Laurel stopped. She'd woken to find Rakin gone—and she'd come looking. She'd suspected she'd find him here in the pool garden behind the high walls. She made out his dark shape swimming toward her, his arms cutting through the water with quiet strokes.

He rose in the shallows, and the moonlight rippled across his wet shoulders. "Join me for a swim?"

"Oh, I intend to."

Laurel dropped her white silk robe. Beneath, she wore nothing. She stepped into the water.

Conscious of his eyes caressing her, she came down the steps, head high, shoulders back, proud of her nudity. The water was silken against her knees. Another step brought it swirling around her thighs and her fingers trailed over the calm surface. By the time she reached the bottom, Rakin was waiting for her. He rose from the dark pool, his hair slicked back, water streaming over his body. Her breath caught.

He was magnificent.

Pagan. Masculine. And too darn sexy for words.

Moonlight fell on his face, bringing his angled cheekbones into sharp relief, casting light on the fullness of his bottom lip. Her gaze dropped down…farther…skimming his broad shoulders, resting on the amulet that hung on his chest and back up to his mouth.

Desire twisted her in stomach.

She wanted him.

Again.

It should've shocked her. But it didn't. This feminine hunger for her mate was the most natural thing she'd ever experienced. Under the veil of the hot desert night, she'd shed her inhibitions. She reached out, stroked the side of his face. His chest rose in a groan, then fell as air rushed out. Her hand swept down... running along his jawline...and came finally to rest against the water-slickened skin at the side of his neck.

Against her fingertips, his pulse reverberated.

So he felt it too...this powerful hunger. Too strong to control.

Lifting her hand away, she reached out with one finger, touched the center of his lip as he had done to her hours earlier.

His lips rounded, and he sucked.

Laurel's nipples hardened, and a sweet pain contracted in her stomach with the erotic play. The liquid heat of arousal filled her.

"Yes," she murmured.

When he released her finger, she trailed it across his lower lip, leaving traces of moisture. Then, unable to resist, she stood on tiptoe and placed her mouth on that same spot.

His mouth became passionate, his tongue sinking past her lips, ravishing her. Promising her that what she'd started would be good.

The want twisting inside her leapt higher.

She shifted restlessly...and brushed against him. With a sense of shock she discovered he was naked...and already aroused. Her heart turned over at the discovery and her pulse started to hammer. His breathing had quickened, filling the silence of the night where only the soothing sound of the water trickling over rocks broke the dark spell.

"What do you want?" he whispered.

You. But she said nothing, only brushed herself up against him, in a language older than time. Her body telling him more clearly than words.

Embracing her, he dragged her through the water to him. Corded muscled met her feminine softness. A sigh whispered in the night.... It sounded as though it came from a long way off, not from her. The stroke of his hands down her back caused shudders to sweep her in torrents. When his strong, male hands closed over her buttocks, his fingers flexing into the rounded mounds…it was ecstasy.

Laurel arched against him, panting against his mouth, all too conscious of the rigidity of his erection. One rock-like thigh drove between her legs, forcing her stance to widen, giving him space to maneuver closer still.

She flung back her head, surrendering herself to the pleasure of his hands…his touch…gazing up into his face, that dark mask silvered by moonlight.

For a beat of time he looked like a stranger. His face taut with desire. No sign of the good-humored man she'd come to…like.

His hands speared through the tangle of her hair. He drew them through, fingers sensually combing the long strands. Her eyes closed. Was this how mermaids of old had felt? This primal passion for their all too human lovers? Caught up in the mood of the moment, Laurel leaned into him, inciting him…not caring that she was driving herself—him—crazy.

The shackles had been shaken off.

This last week, for the first time in her life, she'd been free. Free of restraints, free of all the expectations that came with the Kincaid name. It had taken action on her part to step from the existence that had been so familiar into the fear of the unknown. But the reward was infinite. She'd become someone… more.

Someone she no longer recognized.

The old Laurel would never have undressed and entered the pool, naked, with such abandon. Would never have pursued her wants…her needs…so blatantly. So wantonly. Even a few days ago it would've been too much.

Yet in her heart she knew what drove her tonight was more profound than raw passion. Their time together—this adventure—could not last.

It would come to an end too soon.

An emotion to which she had not yet put a name overwhelmed her. It was more than liking . . more than friendship…

or even respect…much more than all the other things she'd been telling herself she and Rakin shared.

She dared not use the word love…

Get a Life.

Under the water, the smooth friction of his leg against the sensitive skin of her inner thigh caused her to gasp. Her eyes shot open. The pressure increased, rubbing against her. Then his fingers were touching her, peeling back the petals to find the sensitive bud that bloomed within.

Heat roared in her head. She fought the shivers that threatened to break, to bring the escalating excitement to completion. She wanted to stretch this time…to savor it…to never let it end.

His blunt length replaced his fingers. The pressure increased. Then he was sliding into her with slow strokes. Laurel gripped his shoulders and squeezed her eyes shut, giving herself up to sensation.

It rolled over her, in hot, endless waves.

A final thrust and she felt the quivering tension take hold of Rakin. He froze. A harsh, rasping sound broke from his throat as his control shredded. It was what Laurel had been waiting for.

She let the tide sweep over her, allowed the shivers of satisfaction to take her. But she had a blinding insight that this was far from the end. This was only the beginning.

The power of the emotion that had been confounding her had to be love.

Joy bubbled up.

She was in love with her temporary husband.

Laurel shifted restlessly against him in the water, and Rakin tightened his embrace. The blood still thundered in his ears.

"Cold?" he asked, nuzzling her neck.

She shook her head.

But he lifted her up into his arms and headed up the steps to a lounger, where his towel waited. Once he was seated with Laurel on his lap, he drew the towel around her. Using a corner, he patted her face dry. She closed her eyes and didn't resist.

She hadn't said a word since that shattering experience in the pool.

To his surprise, Rakin discovered he wanted—needed—for her to say something.

Placing a finger beneath her chin, he raised her face. Her eyes remained stubbornly shut.

"Laurel?"

Finally her eyes opened. But these were not the sparkling gems he'd grown accustomed to; there were only shadows in the jeweled depths.

"What is it?" he asked. "What is the matter?"

"What could possibly be the matter?" Her lips curved into a smile. "I've just experienced possibly the best orgasm of my life."

"Good," he purred, and relaxed a little, relieved he'd been reading a problem where none existed. "It was pretty damn fantastic."

"Yes."

She was still smiling, but he couldn't shake off his concern that she was troubled. "Are you sure you're all right?" A nasty thought struck him. "I didn't hurt you?"

He'd been so hungry for her—and he'd been sure she'd been ready for him, despite the barrier of the water.

"Of course you didn't!" The smile had vanished, and she gave a little sigh. "I'm just tired."

Instantly he was contrite. "It was a long day...yesterday. I will take you back to bed."

"No, wait." Her words stayed him. "It's so beautiful here tonight. The moon—" she gestured "—the water. Let's stay a little while."

Rakin realized what must be troubling her. "It's our last night. We go back to Rashad tomorrow." It filled him with regret, too. The board meeting he'd been pushing for, for so long, now didn't necessarily seem so important. Giving in to the kind of impulse he seldom acted on, he said, "We could stay longer, if you wish."

She shook her head. "No, you'd miss your meeting—and your family is expecting you for dinner. We must go back."

"We will return here soon. Have no fear."

Yet even as his mouth swooped to claim hers, Rakin realized that in the shadows of her eyes there was something akin to fear.

Ten

Laurel had imagined that it would be a small, intimate dinner. But at least twenty places were set on the long table in a reception room with rich hand-painted friezes on the ceiling. Platters spread with kofta, parcels of rice and nuts wrapped in vine leaves, and mechwya—grilled vegetables dusted with paprika and ginger and speared on iron skewers—as well as an array of morsels with which Laurel was still unfamiliar had arrived on the large table. The dinner guests were beginning to gather around, with the exception of the men of the family, who were currently closeted in the royal salon discussing the future of Gifts of Gold.

Laurel's nerves were frayed with waiting to learn the outcome.

Had marrying her gotten Rakin the control of the Gifts of Gold as he'd wished? Would Prince Ahmeer permit Rakin to remain as CEO and pass the controlling stocks to him as promised? Or would the prince renege by giving Zafar control of the company—or even changing his will and making Zafar heir to those all-important stocks? Laurel didn't want to even contemplate what that would do to Rakin.

Her gaze kept straying anxiously to the huge double doors leading into the dining hall.

When the doors finally opened and a phalanx of men entered, her eyes went straight to Rakin. He carried himself with such authority it was easy to distinguish him from the crowd, but no sign of what had transpired showed in his inscrutable expression. Laurel knew she should not have been surprised.

Then his gaze found hers, and his expression softened.

He broke away from the others and came toward her. Conscious that they were not alone, she offered him a tentative smile. He settled down beside her.

Leaning toward her, her murmured in her ear, "Success. I am now the major stockholder in Gifts of Gold—the contract has just been signed. Now all that remains is for the shares to be physically transferred, which should happen in the next two days."

She couldn't restrain her joy. "That's wonderful."

He came closer. "Thank you."

This close he smelled of peppermint and aftershave, fresh and heady.

Then the significance of what he was telling her hit. Rakin no longer had any need to remain married. Had his grandfather only changed his will, he could've changed it back at any time. But a contract for the transfer of stocks provided far more certainty—no doubt that was why Rakin had pushed for a resolution.

It meant they could part ways sooner.

No need to wait. A couple of days and the transfer would be registered. Divorce proceedings would begin soon.

The joy that had filled her only moments earlier drained away, leaving her with an acute sense of loss.

It was a task to eat the beautifully prepared meal. Roast lamb accompanied by root vegetables fragrant with cumin and coriander. No doubt the tastes and textures were exotic and delicious—but it might as well have been straw. Laurel found herself wishing she and Rakin were still at Dahab, eating simple dishes out on one of the balconies overlooking the desert.

She loved her husband; she was not ready for this divorce.

Glancing at Rakin, she took in the dark business suit he wore

with a tie; his only concession to traditional dress was the headdress he wore. He caught her staring and gave her a warm smile
that lit up his face.

Caught by that warmth, she began furiously to hope.

Surely Rakin felt it too? They had so much in common. They
liked each other, they laughed together—and she knew that he
desired her. It was more than many couples had going for them.
There was no reason to get divorced—instead of a temporary
proposition their marriage could become real.

She touched his arm. "Rakin—"

An aide appeared on his other side. Murmuring an apology,
Rakin turned his attention to the aide who said something in
Arabic. Rakin's reply was brief. Pushing back his chair, he said
to Laurel, "I won't be long."

A hand touched her shoulder. Laurel pasted on a smile and
readied herself for the next round of civilities. She turned, and
found Rakin's grandmother beside her.

"You have eaten enough?" Tula slid into Rakin's chair and
rearranged her black flowing robe around her.

Laurel bowed her head. "Thank you. Everything was delicious."

The sheikha gave her a bright smile. "That is good. You must
look after yourself—we anxiously await your news."

Blinking at Tula, Laurel said, "News?"

The older woman leaned across and patted her stomach. "Of
a baby."

"A baby?"

Laurel knew she must sound ridiculously like a parrot. Yet
she couldn't help herself. It was strange to be holding such an intimate discussion with Rakin's grandmother—especially given
that she and Rakin had barely had time to get to know each
other, much less plan a baby. Yet she couldn't help remembering that she and Rakin had not practiced much caution…a baby
was not out of the question.

A shiver slid down her spine.

Unaware of the unease spreading through Laurel, the sheikha

made a sweeping gesture.. "You and my grandson will have beautiful babies."

How to respond to that?

Laurel laughed awkwardly.

"It is important for you to get pregnant."

Of course. This was about succession rather than beautiful babies. Feeling the heat rising in her cheeks at the deception she was about to weave, Laurel said, "We're taking a little time to get to know each other first."

The older woman shrugged. "You are married. Becoming acquainted with each other will come with time—you will have many years to do so. I, too, was once a new bride. I'd never met his grandfather before the ceremony. My husband always says he fell in love with me the day I delivered my first baby—Rakin's father." Tula beamed at the memory. "Rakin is very wealthy and now he has the responsibility of running Gifts of Gold. He will need a son to follow in his footsteps."

Staring at Rakin's grandmother in shock, Laurel knew there was no way she could expect the sheikha to understand that the marriage between her and Rakin was not about progeny.

Unless, of course, she could convince Rakin to make this marriage permanent.

Once again hoped surged. Rakin would want children, and why should she not be the woman to bear them? She loved him, they were married….

Laurel was starting to feel a whole lot better about persuading Rakin that it made no sense to get a divorce.

If only he loved her…

That would make it all perfect.

She could be patient. And there was the chance that perhaps he was already falling in love with her. The warmth in his eyes when he'd walked into the great reception room was a good start.

"It is not good to wait—you are not getting any younger," Tula was saying. "If you leave it too long you may become unable to bear children."

That was a reminder Laurel did not care to dwell on, and

it could ruin everything if, as she expected, Rakin wanted children.

In some secret compartment of her brain she'd been unconsciously clocking the march of time. It was one of the reasons why, when a procession of her school friends had trooped down the aisle, she'd been so eager to settle down with Eli. But it wasn't the reason she'd married Rakin.

A stab of regret pierced her.

The irony. Since her discovery that she loved him, she could envisage having children with no one but Rakin. He was the man she wanted to share her life with. He was the man she loved. He was the man she wanted to father her child—her children. He was the man she wanted beside her to watch them grow up.

She wanted more than a temporary arrangement driven by business and pleasure.

Even adventure was no longer enough. It tasted like ashes in her mouth. She wanted so much more.

"This subject is too difficult for you to address with your new groom? You are...shy?" The sheikha looked satisfied with what she clearly viewed as Laurel's modesty. "Then I will speak to Rakin's grandfather and he must tell Rakin he must do his duty."

"No!" Laurel couldn't bear the idea that the one area of their life where they shared intimacy might become riddled with conflict, or wrecked by expectations outlined by his grandparents. "That will not be necessary. I've taken note of your concerns and will discuss them with Rakin."

"My grandson has chosen well." The other woman's face was wreathed in smiles. "You are a sensible woman who understands what is important—your cooperation does not go unnoticed. You have brought great happiness to our family."

Little did Rakin's grandmother know that it had nothing to do with being sensible or cooperative and everything to do with her own eternal happiness.

"Rakin, your grandmother cornered me last night."

"Hmm?" They'd made love last night in their boudoir, after

the interminable evening finally drew to a close. Freshly show-ered, with the sun already rising for a new day, Rakin was ready to make love to his wife again, already eagerly admiring her scantily clad form.

He paused beside the bed where she lay and stroked her hip with meandering fingers, admiring the feminine curve, while trying to recall whether he'd already kissed the spot. What did it matter? He'd kiss it again before the sun was high to be cer-tain—he'd intended to leave no part of her uncherished.

"Rakin? Did you hear what I said?"

"My grandmother wanted to talk to you." He lifted his head and gave Laurel a slow, satisfied smile, already planning out how every bliss-filled minute of the next hour would be spent. He tugged the damp towel off and threw it onto the ground, leav-ing him naked. Then he sank down onto the bed, and reached for his wife. "Was she trying to persuade you to help organize her French film festival? It is her passion."

Laurel's eyes held a strange expression. Then she moved and the illusion vanished, forcing Rakin to decide he'd imagined it. "No, no—nothing like that. She only thought I should know that it was important for me to get pregnant as soon as possible. Ap-parently you are in dire need of an heir."

Had she expected him to laugh? If she had, she'd miscalcu-lated. Rakin rolled away from Laurel and sat up, raking his fin-gers through his hair before pulling the covers over his nudity.

A moment's silence followed in which he could hear his heart thudding in his chest. From behind him Laurel said tentatively, "Rakin?"

He turned his head.

"Is something wrong?" She'd come up on her knees in the bed. Her hair lay in long flags down her shoulders. Desire stirred. He suppressed it ruthlessly.

"I've never wanted children."

"You haven't?"

He shook his head.

"Then that's the one thing on which we differ. I've always known that one day I would have children. A family." She spread her hands. "Your grandmother spoke the truth—I am getting older. From her perspective, if we're going to have children we can't afford to delay too long. The sands of time will soon start to run out."

She offered him a pensive smile.

Her intransigence caused him to say more harshly than he intended, "I don't want a child—I never wanted a wife either. But I was given no choice. The charade of a temporary wife was my best solution."

A deep emotion flickered in her eyes; it was gone too fast for him to identify it.

Already she was turning away, reaching for the white silk peignoir at the foot of the bed and donning it. Rakin felt a piercing stab of regret. He let it pass. He'd never deceived her. Theirs had always been a marriage of convenience—and a temporary one at that. Laurel knew that. He'd never promised more than fun and adventure—and the added bonus of exposure to his business network There was no need to feel as though he'd let her down in some inexplicable way.

"Ours was never a union intended to produce children." He made his position clear with repetition.

Her shoulders straightened. "I know that."

She tossed her head and the dark auburn hair rippled like tongues of flame in the golden morning light.

But he couldn't let it go. There was a deep need to assuage the roar of guilt. "I promised you the adventure of a lifetime—not family bliss."

Her head twisted. "I'm well aware of that, and you've delivered on your promise. I'm not arguing that you didn't satisfy my need for every kind of adventure."

Surely, she couldn't mean what he thought she was implying?

Her gaze dropped down to where he'd drawn the sheet over his nakedness. Arousal blasted him. Heat rose in his face. "I am *not* a gigolo."

Her gaze touched the flat planes of his stomach, drifted over his bare chest, lingered on his lips. Finally she met his gaze and gave him a slow smile. "You could be. My own personal love slave. I rather like the idea."

"I was talking of other adventures," he bit out.

"Like bathing in the pool under the starlight?" There was a gleam in her eyes that he did not like. "Or sex in Las Vegas?"

He didn't like the bald way she referred to what had been a shattering experience simply as sex.

"Like bringing you to Diyafa, opening my home to you, showing you the desert, the ways of my forefathers," he bit out. "Like exploring places where few people have trodden. Like venturing forth on the horses…and bargaining with Bedouin. Adventures that few will ever experience."

He'd shared his soul with her.

"Ah, *those* adventures."

"Yes!" But he couldn't stop imagining the more erotic visions her wicked words had evoked. Rakin fought to keep his head cool and his voice level. "And I kept my part of the bargain about setting up business opportunities for The Kincaid Group. Already Ben Al-Sahr has been in touch with your brother Matt to find a cotton supplier in Charleston."

"Yes, I told Matt about that."

"Your brother has been in touch?"

She shook her head. "I called him. We've spoken several times."

"I knew you'd let your family know of our wedding. You did not tell me you were discussing business with your brother."

She gave a light laugh. "As you have made clear, this is very much a marriage of convenience only. We are hardly joined at the hip, Rakin."

She was smiling, but Rakin suspected underneath there lurked something else. Hurt?

"You are upset."

She tossed her head. "Why should I be upset because you choose not to have children? It's your decision, not mine."

That made him certain. She was most definitely upset. When a woman said things like that it left the matter in no doubt.

* * *

She had been such a fool!

Rakin had warned her from the start that theirs was nothing more than a temporary marriage of convenience. She'd known that. It had never been about love. It had never even been about sex—that had been an adventure he'd provided in addition to the rest.

Today Rakin had gotten what he wanted out of the deal—he still controlled the board of Gifts of Gold and soon his grandfather's majority stockholding would be signed into his name. He no longer needed her.

Scratch that. He'd never needed her.

He no longer needed a wife.

Any wife.

As far as her husband was concerned, the need for their temporary marriage was over. Yet, with her discovery that she loved him, from her point of view, their marriage had only just begun.

"You're heartless." The words burst from her before she could stop them. Instantly a sense of release swept her. It was true— he was heartless.

The skin had drawn tight across his cheeks.

"Not heartless—simply a realist."

Simply? Nothing about this relationship was simple anymore. Laurel couldn't believe she'd ever convinced herself that marriage to this man could be a lighthearted adventure. Fun. A carefree romp to break free from the drudgery that her life had become and help her complete her Get a Life List. It had all turned complicated—and come back to bite her in the ass. "I don't want to live my life in your reality."

He shrugged. "You don't need to. That's the advantage of our temporary marriage."

His attitude brought home how little he cared. About their marriage. About her. Rakin had what he wanted, and now he expected her to walk away from their marriage unscathed. Unchanged.

But she couldn't—because for her everything had changed.

The aftershock of the pain was devastating.

She loved Rakin.

He didn't love her. She had to face that, accept it and move on. This marriage was over. He'd just made it heart-wrenchingly clear he didn't even want to be married to her. Laurel couldn't fool herself that he was ever going to love her in the way she wanted—needed—to be loved.

"So what happens now? You clap three times, and our marriage is formally dissolved?"

"Do not be sarcastic," he said coldly. "It does not become you."

She drew herself away. "I need some fresh air—it's gotten a little claustrophobic in here."

He rolled away from her on the bed and closed his eyes. "I'm weary—I didn't get much sleep last night. We will finalize the matter later."

As the bedroom door closed softly behind his wife, Rakin's eyes opened.

There was no point storming after Laurel and bringing her back to heel with harsh words. He stared blindly ahead. It was better to let her cool down first—they could talk later.

Rakin had witnessed too many such confrontations between his parents as a young boy that had ended with shouting and slammed doors. He was proud that he had not allowed this confrontation to escalate in a similar manner. It had taken all his willpower not to tell her that she was being ridiculous. Their marriage would not be ended by a few claps.

If it was to happen it would be ended properly. Formally. Legally. Civilly.

They would remain business associates—even friends.

He didn't want to lose her friendship because of an outburst. And there was no reason for their liaison to end…even if their marriage did. The passion they shared was magnificent. He wasn't risking losing that. His preference was for their relationship to continue as it was…with no mention of children.

He would give her time to realize that what he spoke was nothing less than the truth.

Laurel was a mature woman. She would come round.

By the time lunch time came, she would have calmed down. Then he could comfort her—if that was what she really wanted. Or they could make love.

Right now he needed some rest. Shutting his eyes against the bright sunlight, Rakin drifted off to sleep satisfied that he had handled the problem in the best way possible.

Laurel let herself out a side door and stepped out into a walled garden she hadn't seen before.

It was an orchard. Even before she caught sight of the bright globes of fruit, the fragrance of orange blossom on the warm desert air confirmed it. The sweet scent evoked visions of her wedding to Rakin.

Their first kiss under the bridge in the gondola, the moment when her growing awareness of him as a man had crystallized into passion.

A passion that had culminated into the pain she felt now.

Well, she'd certainly made up for her reticence in the past. She'd had the fling of a lifetime. And now it was over.

It was time to come back down to earth and pick up the pieces of her life. Her real life. Not this romantic fantasy that she'd been playing out with Rakin. Laurel clenched her fists and moved into the dappled sunshine between the trees. Deep in her heart, under her anger at herself—at Rakin for disappointing her—pain splintered into sharp, piercing shards.

She ached. With disappointment. With loss. With loneliness at the idea of facing the future without Rakin.

The knowledge was growing that her escapade—her walk on the wild side—was over.

If there was one thing that had solidified in the past hour, it was the knowledge that Rakin did not love her, would never love her. But she'd fallen in love with him.

Big mistake.

His proposition had never contemplated that—nor had she

ever expected to fall head-over-heels in love with a charming
stranger. He'd made her laugh. He'd encouraged her to experience the adventure she'd craved and launch herself headfirst
from her safe existence.

She'd taken risks and been rewarded by joy. But now she was
also living through more pain than she'd experienced in her life.

If this was what love was like, she wasn't going to endure it.

One thing last night had proved to her was that she wasn't
the genteel Southern lady who could be trapped in a loveless relationship—even if she loved her husband. Uncurling her fists,
Laurel reached for a spray of blossoms from the closest tree.
Once she'd plucked it, she bent her head and inhaled scent of
the crushed sprig. She'd been Rakin's bride, but she would no
longer be his wife.

A pang shook her as she remembered laughing with him
in the Liberace Museum in Vegas. That moment when she'd
clutched his hand on the roller coaster and her stomach had
fallen away when the train had dropped into a void. Just as her
father had appeared so handsome and witty to her mother, Rakin
had appealed to everything she'd thought she needed with his
sense of humor, his readiness to lead her to the adventure she
craved.

But it was a mirage.

It could never be real—because he didn't love her.

Her pride would not let her stay. Beg for whatever he could
offer. She had to leave. Today. She would go back to the life she
knew, the life with her family and The Kincaid Group.

A life that was safe…

Laurel dismissed that fleeting rebellious thought that she was
running away. There was nothing for her to stay for. Rakin had
made that abundantly clear.

She would walk away with her head held high.

By the time Rakin came down for the midday meal Laurel
was gone.

"She told me it was a family emergency," his grandmother
explained as Rakin stood glaring at his grandparents in the great

anteroom in the palace. "You were still sleeping. I organized one of the royal drivers to take your wife to the airport. She was sure everything would be sorted out in a couple of days."

Sorted out in a couple of days? She'd been buying him time, so the transfer of his grandfather's stock into his name would go through and not be canceled.

Hands on hips, he fumed inwardly. "You didn't consider checking with me?"

"Family emergencies are women's work—not for you and your grandfather to trouble your heads about." His grandmother stared at him with bewildered eyes.

He wouldn't have wanted Laurel to face an emergency alone—if there truly had been one.

"Is something the matter, Rakin?" This time his grandmother's tone was laden with hesitation. "Is there something wrong other than a family emergency? Laurel appeared so happy last night."

Rakin let out his breath in an impatient sigh. "What could possibly be the matter?"

He swung around on his heel. His bride had been happy—until his meddling grandmother had started talking about heirs. Now she'd interfered again—and helped Laurel escape.

Maybe he was jumping to conclusions. Perhaps there was indeed a family emergency. The first step was to make sure that there was no family crisis, that she had indeed fled.

And that meant a call to Eli.

Which brought an unwelcome thought. She'd walked away without a backward glance from her engagement to Eli because she didn't love him. Rakin had been so certain he never wanted marriage…a wife. But now that his wife had run from him, making it clear that she felt nothing for him, he was surprised to discover he wanted her back.

There was no other woman he wanted more than his wife.

Eleven

Sunday afternoon Charleston welcomed Laurel back with warm, scented arms.

At the Kincaid mansion on Montagu Street, Pamela, the family housekeeper, opened the front door and greeted her with an enormous hug.

Instantly Laurel felt the pent-up tears pricking at the back of her eyes.

"Now, now my child. Why the tears?" Pamela drew her in and shut the door behind them.

"I've missed you all," Laurel said truthfully.

Halting at the foot of the white-carpeted, marble stairs that curved upward, Pamela told her, "Miss Elizabeth is upstairs. That nice detective just left."

"Detective McDonough?"

Pamela nodded. "That's the one."

"Has any progress been made with Dad's murder?" Laurel couldn't stop a flare of guilt. In the past two weeks she'd barely thought of her father's murderer.

"You'll need to ask your mother that." Pamela still hadn't started up the stairs. "What I can tell you is that we've made a start on packing up your father's clothes."

Her poor mother. Laurel exchanged a long look with the housekeeper. "How is she handling it?"

"Much better than I expected. How about I go and make a pot of coffee and let you see for yourself?"

Upstairs, Elizabeth was kneeling on the floor beside a pile of clothes and carefully placing a folded cable-knit sweater in a box. She stilled as Laurel came in. "Laurel! What are you doing here?"

"I've come home."

Elizabeth glanced past her to the doorway. "Where's Rakin?"

"I came alone. He's still in Diyafa."

"I'm surprised he let his new bride go off alone so soon."

Laurel sought for a way to break the news. Nothing could blunt the truth. Finally, she said baldly, "I've left him, Mom."

"Oh, my dear!"

Elizabeth was instantly on her feet. She folded Laurel into an embrace filled with warmth and the familiar scent of lavender.

Laurel closed her eyes, drawing comfort from her mother's arms. She felt like a little girl who'd rushed into the house to find her mother after roughhousing with RJ had led to scraped knees. In those days her aches had been fixed with a bandage and a mother's make-it-better kiss.

This time it was her heart that ached—and that couldn't be fixed so easily.

"Do you want to talk, my dear?"

The sympathy nearly undid her. Opening her eyes, she inhaled deeply and stared over her mother's shoulder. Did she want to talk? It came to her that there was probably no one who would understand what she was going through better than her mother.

After all, like Laurel's marriage to Rakin, her mother's marriage to her father had originally been brokered for business. Until Reginald had swept Elizabeth off her feet. Laurel shuddered. And, in a case of history repeating itself, she too had fallen for her convenient groom.

The major difference was that Reginald had convinced her mother he loved her. While Rakin made no such promises of

evotion. In fact, he'd made it brutally clear that he didn't want
wife…or a child.

"There's not a great deal to say," she told her mother. Laurel
nk down on the edge of the bed. "Come sit next to me and tell
e what you've been doing while I've been gone."

"That lovely Nikki Thomas has been to visit me—and she's
een talking to the police, too." Elizabeth gave a gentle sigh as
ne settled down on the bed beside Laurel. "In fact, the detec-
ve just left. His suspicion is firmly on Jack Sinclair. As you
now, the only problem is that Sinclair has an alibi—his office
aff say he was working late that night."

Laurel laced her fingers through her mom's. "But surely that
oesn't count? I mean, he could've bribed them to say that."
aurel couldn't believe the police were no further with the
atter than when she'd left for Las Vegas. Her mother had been
ght; it hadn't been necessary to stay. "And then there's also the
mall matter of his car parked in the lot near the TKG offices."

"But he denies parking his car there, too."

"How very strange." Laurel paused. "He must be lying. What
oes Nikki think?"

"She says she still wants to do more research—but she's de-
ermined to find the culprit."

Laurel had been too. She thought about the final item on the
ist. No. 10 : *Find Dad's Murderer*. The toughest task of all.
nd she'd made no headway on that. Laurel brushed her hair
ff her face with her free hand. Nikki would probably do a far
etter job solving the case than she ever could—so long as Nikki
idn't let her heart rule her head.

"If the police aren't getting anywhere, maybe Nikki's going
o be the best person to crack Jack's alibi." She gave Elizabeth's
and a squeeze. "The sooner he is arrested, the sooner you'll be
ble to get your life back together." And once Jack Sinclair was
rrested, any chance that he'd be elected President of TKG at the
une meeting would be scuttled for once and for all. Laurel knew
hat not only her mother, but she—and her siblings—would all
reathe a sigh of relief.

Her mother interrupted her thoughts. "I'm getting my life to-

gether now. I've asked Kara to help get my marriage to Cutt
planned. We'll probably be married in a month or two."

"Oh, Mom, that's such good news." Sadness touched Laure
She certainly hoped that her mother would have better luck wi
marriage than she'd had. Just thinking about her marriage—t
problems—was enough to make Laurel feel like sobbing h
eyes out on her mother's shoulder.

As dusk fell, Laurel stayed on at the Kincaid Mansion t
attend the weekly family gathering. Even though they were ve
surprised to see her, her family's support was immediate. Ma
was there with Susannah—Flynn had wandered off to discov
whether Pamela had any treats in store for him. RJ and Brook
were coming later.

Secure in the bosom of her family, amidst their concern, the
love warmed her.

Lily and Daniel had eyes only for each other.

Kara was utterly radiant, so beautiful, and exchanging secr
looks with Eli, the two of them clearly in their own worl
Laurel envied them the intimacy. That was the kind of ma
riage she wanted—and it was not the kind of experience Raki
would ever provide.

But one thing stood out as they were finishing the meal tha
Pamela had prepared for the family—the relationship betwee
herself and Eli had changed. He was her brother-in-law now.
no longer her best friend. The ability to talk to him with the ol
ease had gone forever.

And besides, how could she talk to him about Rakin? I
would be unfair. Rakin was his other best friend.

Yet Eli looked wretched, and she soon discovered why.

"Rakin called me," he told her from his position across th
table from her.

"Rakin called you?" Laurel stared at him. "When?" *Why?*

"He seemed to think we had some kind of family emergency
He wanted to make sure everyone was all right."

She glanced away, her face warming, and a twinge of guil

visted her heart. "I didn't think he'd care," she muttered. "I uppose that means his heart isn't a block of ice."

"Rakin has a heart," Eli told her.

"You think?" Her mouth twisted as she glanced at him. "I'm ot so sure."

It didn't need Eli's slanted look to know that she was being nfair. Despite her bitterness, Laurel knew he had a heart. After l, she'd seen glimpses of his kindness to children and the elerly. What Rakin didn't have was space in his heart for *her*. nd that would never change.

"This is my fault."

Laurel waved a dismissive hand. "Nonsense. Don't blame ourself for introducing us, Eli. We would've met sooner or ter."

"You don't understand."

Laurel's heart dropped like a stone at the haunted darkness his eyes. "What don't I understand?"

Eli looked around. Everyone else was engaged in conversaon. He lowered his voice. "I suggested to Rakin that he marry ou."

"*You* suggested?" Laurel fixed her gaze on the new brothera-law who had been such a close friend for most of her life and ho she had until not long ago thought she knew better than any ther man on earth. "When?"

"After you jilted me."

"Why would you do such a thing? Why?" It was a cry from e heart.

Along the table Lily stopped talking to Brooke and turned er head. Laurel quickly flashed her sister a reassuring smile. fter a moment Lily smiled back, and when Brooke spoke to er she turned away resume their conversation.

Laurel exhaled in relief. That had been a close call. The last ing she wanted was her sister's concern.

Shifting uncomfortably, Eli murmured, "Rakin had a probm. I told him you might be the solution."

"Just like that?" How typical. How very male. "And he agreed?"

Eli gave an awkward chuckle. "What man wouldn't? I to
him you were beautiful and smart and he couldn't go wrong.

Like a horse trader showing off her good points. Laurel spo
softly through gritted teeth. "Thanks, Eli!"

He looked as guilty as sin at the unfamiliar edge to her voic
"You're furious—in all the years I've known you I've never se
you furious, do you know that?"

What on earth was she supposed to say to that? Laurel did
even try answering.

As the seconds stretched into an uncomfortable silence, I
said hesitantly, "I could try to fix it."

"How?" she demanded.

"If I called him—"

"No!" She shook her head. "Absolutely not. I don't want y
trying to help."

"I'm sorry. I've hurt you. I never thought…" Eli shook h
head and let his voice trail away.

Laurel gave a most unladylike growl of frustration.

"That's the problem. Men just don't think about the problem
they cause!"

Lily had turned her head again. A frown creased her fore
head. Clearly she'd sensed discord. To allay her sister's su
picions, Laurel gave her sister the sweetest smile she coul
summon, and Lily's frown cleared.

"I can't be pregnant."

It was Monday morning, and the day was already to startin
to deteriorate.

The doctor glanced up from the results in front of her. "Yo
have not engaged in any sexual activity?" Concern glinte
behind her spectacles.

"I got married—and yes, we did make love." Despite La
rel's embarrassment, the doctor looked relieved. "But I neve
meant to get pregnant—we took precautions. Except once.
Laurel added, remembering the night in the pool.

"They are not always failsafe."

The urge to laugh hysterically rose. "I know that. Mothe

ad that talk with me when I was fifteen and went on my first
date with my best friend at the time's brother. What I meant is
this cannot be happening to me. I'm a grown-up. I'm sensible."
Even Rakin's grandmother had thought so. "I'm certainly not
the kind of woman who gets pregnant by accident."

The doctor grimaced. "Accidental pregnancies happen—
even to sensible, grown-up businesswomen. Treat it as a blessing. Because I have even more sensible grown-up patients who
would love to become pregnant by accident."

Those words struck home.

A lump formed in Laurel's throat.

She was not going to cry. Absolutely not. Instead, she said, "I
always planned to have a family. One day. Of course, I planned
to have a father for my children too—a traditional family."

The doctor looked confused. "I thought you said you got married."

Laurel shifted in her seat in front of the desk. "Yes, in
Vegas. But it's already over. I served my husband with separation papers this morning." Ignoring the other woman's startled
expression, Laurel thought about her mother betrayed and left
loveless. About her father murdered in the prime of his life. "But
we don't always get quite what we thought we wanted in life, do
we?"

At least her father had left her the beach house. She still had
that. Suddenly Laurel had an overwhelming need to be surrounded by the solace of the huge house.

As always, Captain's Watch, the great old house on the beach,
stood unchanged.

Built in the late eighteen hundreds when the great families
of the area had discovered the beach, it had stood for more than
a century watching the ebb and flow of the tides.

Opening the heavy weathered wooden shutters to let in the
May sun, Laurel felt a surge of renewed pleasure as she looked
out onto the strip of beach where she had spent so many hours
first as a child, and later as a teen with her dates and friends.
Her hand rested on her stomach.

"You'll have that too, my sweetie, I promise."

The great house and the acreage around it were hers. Her father had known how much she loved it here. Leaving the window, she made for the large hand-hewn timber table where the family had eaten countless meals and played board games on rainy days. In the center of the bleached wood lay the List— and the letter from her father.

Laurel knew she no longer needed the Get a Life list. She had a life. A life with a job, a family, and soon a baby, too. But she couldn't bring herself to throw the List away. Laurel poured the last bit of sparkling mineral water into her glass, and took a sip. The List had changed her life—or rather, it had caused her to re-evaluate what she wanted from life. She had grown, undertaken *experiences*—the word *adventures* reminded her too painfully of Rakin—and found a deeper understanding of who she was. She would never regret that.

Her gaze fell onto the empty water bottle.

Then she picked up the List. She read through it one last time. Only item No. 10, *Find My father's murderer*, remained incomplete.

And No. 4. But the idea of eating ice cream in bed seemed suddenly childish.

For now.

Maybe Nikki Thomas would have better luck than she in getting leads that would result in Jack Sinclair's arrest. She folded the card on which she'd scrawled the List in half, then in half again. Her left hand reached for the water bottle and closed around the smooth, cool glass. Laurel pressed the folded card into the narrow mouth of the bottle. It dropped into the belly with a plop. She let out a sigh.

The List had done its job.

Drawing out the letter that had been opened, read and re-folded so many times that it had the soft texture of crumpled tissue paper, she unfolded it and took in the words that her father had written.

My dearest Laurel,
If you are reading this, I am no longer with you.

But Captain's Watch is forever yours. For days your excitement before we arrived each summer at Captain's Watch would vibrate around the family, infecting everyone. You once told your mother that was because, even though the beach house never changed, no day was ever the same, that time spent at Captain's Watch was a summer-long adventure.

In the beach house there is a photo of you celebrating one such adventure. You are kneeling beside a sandcastle decorated with shells. I remember you persevering all day long after the other children had given up and moved on to other games. You stayed out there until, as the day was drawing to a close, I came to find you.

The sandcastle was finished and you were gazing at it with a look of such contentment on your face that I knew the time had been well spent. The following morning, you rushed out as soon as you awoke only to find that the tide had washed it away. You never cried. Instead you started building again, but this time you moved above the tide line.

I leave you Captain's Watch in the hope that it will bring you many more adventures through the course of your life. I know that your kind heart will open the doors to all the family who may want to join you at the beach each summer.

Happy family vacations always.

With my love,

Dad

Through the blur of tears, Laurel traced the flourish of her father's signature across the page with her fingertip.

The discovery that he had another family, other children, had been devastating to all of them—particularly to her mother.

But Rakin wasn't like her father in that way. He didn't already have another woman…or another child. To the contrary he'd told her he'd never wanted any children—or a wife.

Nothing changed the fact that he didn't love her.

But he needed to know that they'd created a child together. For the first time Laurel felt an inkling of empathy with Angela Sinclair. Angela had done the right thing. Laurel knew Jack's mother had tried to contact Reginald once, many years ago, to tell him she was pregnant—and failed in her quest.

The tears that had blurred Laurel's vision spilled over and tickled her cheeks as they trailed down. Holding the letter in her hand, she cupped her still-flat belly. Unlike Reginald, Rakin would have every chance to be part of her baby's early life.

Laurel could not even begin to think of how painful it must've been for her father to discover a decade later that Angela had borne him a son. A son who had grown into a bitter, brooding man, hating their father enough to one day kill him.

If only Jack could've known that his father had loved him enough to leave him forty-five percent in The Kincaid Group, Reginald's life work.

Perhaps if Jack had known that, it might have been enough to turn his hatred to hope.

But they would never know….

With gentle fingers Laurel folded the letter from her father and then placed it back into her purse. When she was finished, she reached for her cell phone.

After marshaling her thoughts, preparing what she was going to say to Rakin when he answered, she was almost disappointed when it diverted to his voice mail message. After a moment's hesitation, she killed the line.

She couldn't leave a message. This was something she needed to tell him herself.

In an hour she would call again—and if she couldn't reach him, then she'd just have to book a flight and go back to Diyafa.

Rakin needed to know they were going to have a baby.

Twelve

The sea sucked at her toes.

Laurel watched as the swirl of water disappeared when the tide sucked out again. The bottle with the Get a Life List bobbed on the surface about twenty yards out.

She knew she was procrastinating. Ever since putting the phone down earlier, butterflies had fluttered in her stomach. She'd been finding excuses not to call Rakin again. *Coward!*

This time she would leave a message for him to call her back. And if he didn't call back, she wouldn't leave it there, she would call again.

And again.

Until he knew.

Distracted by her thoughts, she didn't see the next wavelet until it washed over her feet. She yelped. The high tide was about to turn—and she didn't want to get the jeans she wore wet. Another wave came rushing in.

She backed up in a hurry—right into a hard body.

An apology ready on her lips, Laurel spun around.

Then froze when she saw who stood there.

Rakin.

"I called you just over an hour ago," she said, disbelief filling her. Had she conjured him up like a genie?

"I saw I'd missed a call from you—it must've come through not long after I landed. But I figured I'd show up instead of calling back."

"What are you doing here?"

His face darkened. "You can ask me that? After you arranged a legal separation?"

He must have flown from Diyafa the instant the papers were served. Her heart soared—that could only be good. Then crashed. Rakin didn't love her. There was nothing to hope for. He probably wanted to sign the paperwork off as quickly as possible. "There doesn't seem to be any point—"

"How can you renege on our marriage?"

The set of his face was frighteningly remote. A chill swept her. He looked more distant than he'd ever been. What would it take to reach him? Certainly not the news of her pregnancy.

"Rakin—"

"Nothing has changed. You knew the ground rules."

"It was temporary…that has not changed." But hope flared within her.

A dark eyebrow shot up. "Did I ever agree to end our marriage? Did you bother to ask before you took off while I was sleeping?"

Rakin was annoyed because she hadn't asked? The flicker of hope went out.

She loved him, and she couldn't carry on pretending that this was nothing more than a convenient arrangement.

She wanted more.

Much more.

"You don't need me anymore," she said. "You've gotten what you married me for—your inheritance. You even got it early."

Rakin gazed down into the pale face of the woman before him.

A shaft of afternoon sun fell across her skin, suffusing the fine creamy texture with a golden glow. Yet her eyes were dark and wary. A gust of breeze from the sea fingered strands of her dark red hair, spreading them across her cheek. Rakin reached forward to stroke the recalcitrant strands off her face, but she ducked away from his touch.

He dropped his hand to his side.

"You ran away." He had not expected the numbing emptiness that followed Laurel's departure. Suddenly the threats of disenfranchisement that his grandfather had been holding over his head for years hadn't seemed so important.

"I didn't run. I walked. One step at a time."

"You told my grandmother that you had a family emergency."

"A lie—I didn't want to tell her the truth: that I could no longer stay. Nor did I want to cost you your future by telling her the truth."

A cold fist gripped his heart. He wasn't reaching her. He was going to lose her....

Where was his warm, loving, sexy wife? Terror filled him. Was this how his mother had felt about his father? Was it this fear of life without him that had driven her to stay with a spouse who didn't love her?

Unrequited love was Rakin's idea of hell. He'd sworn never to repeat his mother's mistakes.

But living without Laurel would be infinitely worse....

He tried a business bribe. "You're going to have to come back to Diyafa. Ben Al-Sahr has a brother with another proposition for you."

Laurel shook her head. "No, I'm not. Matt can handle it. I'm going to stay here."

The terror doubled. She'd never refused an opportunity to benefit The Kincaid Group. She wasn't coming back to Diyafa. Ever.

The hollowness of the future faced him.

Unbidden, the legend of the laurel came back to him. Daphne had fled from Apollo, and when the sun god had caught up with her, embraced her, she'd turned into an inanimate laurel tree rather than stay with him.

It gave Rakin a terrible sense of déjà vu.

He had no taste for the hollow victory that lay in a laurel

wreath. The time had come to throw everything into it...renegotiate with whatever it took to get her back.

Drawing a deep breath, he played his ace. "We can try for a baby if that's what you want."

The shock in her eyes was unfeigned. "A baby? Of all the things in the world, why suggest that now?"

Her further withdrawal caused him confusion—panic even. He'd been so certain she wanted a child. Shaking his head to clear it, he said, "That's what you want, isn't it?"

Laurel didn't respond.

His panic and confusion grew. The reason she'd left was because he'd told her he'd never planned to have children, wasn't it? He'd been deeply shaken to find her gone. Devastated. But he would never tell her that. Exposing his heart in such a way was a risk he would never take.

Nevertheless he murmured huskily, "I'd like to father your child."

Instead of opening her arms to him, Laurel wrapped them across her chest and stared at him with accusing eyes. "This is a temporary marriage—based on sex and business. That's what you said. Remember?"

"I said many foolish things." He reached forward and stroked her arm, the satin skin soft beneath his touch. How he longed to touch the other, even softer places he'd discovered. "Men do that when they are afraid."

"What were you afraid of?"

Rakin dropped his hand.

Dear Allah...what did she want? Blood? *His* blood?

"You don't have to tell me if you don't want." She glanced away. Sunlight slanted off the sea, and Rakin caught the reflection of silvery tears in her eyes.

"Please don't cry." Reaching clumsily for her, he hesitated, then stuck his hands into the pockets of his jeans instead.

"I'm not crying." But tears spilled onto her cheeks as she turned back to face him, refuting her words. "At least, not really. Not sad tears. If you know what I mean."

No, she'd lost him. Rakin wondered whether he'd ever understand her. "Then why are you crying?"

She blinked, her eyelashes fluttering. "I'm relieved—thankful. I thought you didn't want children."

He'd never had much to do with children, and it was true he'd never wanted any of his own.

"Aren't you going to ask why I called you?"

Rakin wanted to hold her close, not worry about questions to which he didn't know the answers. But she was holding her breath, waiting for his reply. He sensed his response was important to her. "What were you calling to tell me?"

"That I'm pregnant."

"Pregnant?" Rakin felt the blood drain from his face.

She nodded, her eyes wide and expectant. What did she expect him to say? That he was thrilled?

Of course she did. Hadn't he just told her he'd like to give her a child? Hadn't she just told him of her fear that he didn't want children? Rakin closed his eyes, and tipped his head back. Trapped. In a noose of his own making. He swallowed and found his throat was thick. Now came the moment of truth.

"Rakin, are you all right?"

"I'm sorry." He opened his eyes. "It's a shock."

Her expression changed, became drawn. "You're not pleased. You didn't mean that about having a baby, did you? Not really."

She turned away from him, her shoulders slumping as she walked away with the tired gait of an old woman.

The pain of it made him call out, "Laurel, wait."

She froze, her shoulders drawn tight.

Coming up fast behind her, Rakin slid his arms around her, linking his hands below her breasts, over her belly where his child lay. Gently, ever so gently, he tugged her around to face him.

"Laurel…" The words dried up.

He stared at her. Frustrated. Hurting. Exposed.

Her shoulders sagged.

How could he say what she wanted to hear when the sentiments were nothing but lies? He wasn't pleased about the baby.

Not now. Not before they'd sorted their own relationship out. He didn't want her choosing to stay married to him because of the baby.

He wanted her to stay because—

Because he loved her.

This was like a terrible echo from the past. His mother had adored his father, but all his father had wanted had been an heir. History was repeating itself. Except this time, in a reversal of roles, he was the one who loved—and Laurel was the party who wanted a child. He loved her. It was unwelcome. It hurt like hell. He didn't need this.

All he could think was that, like his mother, he was not loved.

Pain tightened his chest.

He tore his gaze from her face. Rakin didn't even notice the wave that splashed around his feet, soaking his expensive sneakers as he stared blindly out to sea. The sunlight danced across the water glittering like diamonds. This must be how the sun god had felt pursuing Daphne after Cupid had wreaked his havoc. Unrequited love. His worst nightmare had come true.

Of course, in one of life's great ironies, his grandparents were going to be delighted.

Laurel was pregnant. He would have an heir. A successor for the business empire he was amassing would be assured.

Yet there was no joy. No stunning delight. Only endless dread.

He would be married to a woman who did not love him. Tied forever to Laurel with the strong, silken bonds of a child. Inescapable. He might has well have been imprisoned in the shape of a tree.

He couldn't let her go either.

Yet he knew he would never have the happiness he'd glimpsed too briefly in Dahab, the days and nights of pure joy. There would be duty and unfulfilled desire…and that would have to be enough.

He was trapped.

In'shallah. This was to be his fate.

* * *

Laurel didn't know what was wrong.

She only knew that Rakin had retreated. He'd been brooding ever since they'd come in from the beach half an hour ago. He'd given the interior of the beach house a cursory glance before heading for the comfortable leather chair her father had always occupied in front of the glass doors that looked over the beach.

At first she'd given him time to adjust to the revelation of her pregnancy. From her vantage point on the couch, where she was pretending to page through magazines, she kept sending him little sideways glances, but his mood had not relented.

He was thinking too much. It could not be good.

She'd known he would not be pleased about the baby given the sentiments he'd expressed back in Diyafa. But after he'd offered to give her a baby, she'd felt a lift of hope.

But his reaction had confounded her.

Was he hurting?

Laurel had had enough. She was hurting, too.

"Do you intend never to talk to me again?"

"What?" He gave her a blank look.

"Do you realize that's the first thing you've said to me since we came inside the house?"

"No." He shook himself and blinked rapidly. "I apologize, I have been rude."

"This isn't about good manners." She'd had enough of social expectations to last her a lifetime. It was ingrained in her family's genes. "This is about the fact that it hurts me when you wall yourself up behind that mask of self-control."

He stared at her.

This wasn't working. Laurel sighed. Perhaps she could shock him enough to drop that polite, urbane mask. "I'm going to need a pair of handcuffs."

"Handcuffs?"

"Yes. Handcuffs!" Her pent-up frustration was showing. "Sex seems to be the only way I can get you to lose your cool."

A flush darkened Rakin's cheeks. "There is no need for handcuffs to do that."

His murmur had caused her pulse to start to pound. "What do you mean?"

"It's not sex. It's you who makes me lose control."

The words were so soft she only just made them out. Her heart started to hammer. His honesty was more than she could ever have hoped for. Laurel went to sit beside him on the arm of the great chair. "Show me," she invited.

But the kiss was not raw with passion. Instead he brushed her lips gently with his.

Tender. What did this mean?

Finally he lifted his head and looked down at her. "I am terrified," he admitted softly.

It was true. There was fear in the depths of his onyx eyes.

"Why?" Then it came to her. This was about the baby. "You're worried for the baby? I know I'm an older mom, but lots of women wait until their thirties to have families now. I'll get the best medical care money can buy. It will be fine."

"No. Not that—my fears are much more selfish."

"What is it?" Now he was frightening her. "Tell me," she insisted when she'd had enough of empty, polite silences.

"Despite what I led you to believe, my parents' marriage was far from perfect. It wasn't the romance of a lifetime."

"Is that all?" Relief flooded her and she shifted closer to him. "Well, it turns out that my parents' marriage must've been far from perfect, too. But we're not our parents, Rakin. We don't need to repeat their mistakes."

His eyes locked with hers.

"My father never loved my mother," he said flatly.

Pain shot through her. He was telling her that he could never love her. He'd told her it was over between them. She'd already accepted that, so why was she letting the wound tear open again? Laurel squared her shoulders. "Even though my mother claims my father loved both her and Angela, I'm finding it very hard to reconcile my father's behavior in having a second family with any kind of meaningful love for my mother—it's certainly not the kind of love I want."

"But if he made your mother happy—"

"Exactly! And he was a great father. To all of us. And I can never forget that." With that off her chest, Laurel felt a lot easier. Now she had to come to an understanding with Rakin. One they could both live with. "After the divorce we can work at our relationship—and make sure the baby is well adjusted. We certainly don't need to keep each other miserable in an empty shell of a marriage. And we will both love the baby."

Rakin's gaze drilled into her. Then he said, "It wasn't only my mother that my father didn't love. He had high expectations of me. He was proud of me. But he never loved me."

Her heart melted. "Oh, Rakin—"

"What if I can never love this child?"

The terror was back in his eyes. Her heart ached. This was what he was afraid of?

"I've seen your patience with Flynn—"

"That's different." He waved her reassurance away.

Laurel persisted. "I saw you pull that boy onto Pasha—the way you gave him what he most dreamed of."

"Who wouldn't?"

"A person who didn't like children." Laurel wanted to throw her arms around him, hold the little boy in him close. "Believe me, if this is your fear, I assure you it is groundless."

He shot her a veiled look. "It is not my only fear."

"So what else do you fear?"

He shook his head.

"Rakin!" Laurel let a little of her exasperation through. "How can I help when you won't even let me know what you're thinking? Let go!"

"Letting go is the hardest thing you could ever ask of me." He drew a deep breath. "All my life I have been raised to be proud. To be restrained. To behave like a member of the royal family. To honor the Abdellah name."

Laurel couldn't help making the connection.

"Some men shouldn't be fathers. Yours may have been one of them." The uncertainty in Rakin's eyes caused her heart to contract. "Your treatment of Flynn at the wedding, of the boy who you put up on your horse is different from how your father would've responded. You are *not* your father."

Rakin shook his head. Laurel watched him rise to his feet and walk across the room to stare out the windows overlooking the sea. She sensed he was facing the most important challenge of his life.

And he was terrified.

"I love you."

The sound of the words was as soft as the whisper of a gull's wing on the wind. Yet it roared like a tornado through Rakin's brain. He wheeled around in disbelief.

"What?"

Despite the summery sunshine that streamed in through the windows, she stood with her arms folded protectively around herself, clearly steeling herself for his rejection.

Then she said it again. "I. Love. You." More slowly for sure, but still the same world-changing words. He hadn't misheard.

Rakin took a step forward. Then stopped.

Did she mean them?

Or was this obligation speaking…for the sake of their child? He despised himself for the moment of doubt as soon as he saw the sheen of emotion in her eyes. Relief buckled his knees; then strength and confidence flowed back through him.

She meant it.

Laurel loved him.

And this beautiful woman was so much braver than he. She'd risked all, baring her heart, risking his rejection.

He swallowed. Then demanded, "Say it again."

The green eyes he adored sparkled at him. "I love you."

Rakin didn't wait for a silence to follow. He gathered the strength that her words had given him and, taking a quick breath, he shut his eyes and forced out a whisper. "I love you too."

Then, needing to see her reaction, he opened his eyes. Moisture glimmered back at him.

"I'm not going to cry," she said determinedly.

"No, you're too happy to cry."

That wrung a laugh from her.

"I want to get married again," he said.

Joy blazed in her face. "Yes."

For a moment Rakin couldn't absorb it. "You agree?"

She launched herself into his arms. "Of course I agree."

"So where are we going to be married?" she asked a little worriedly her head resting against his shoulder. "I'd love to be married here with my family present. But it would be a little odd because we're already married. And wouldn't your grandparents expect us to be married in Diyafa?"

"I don't care where we get married—or who attends. The only person I want there is you." Rakin kissed the top of her soft, sweet scented hair.

"Like when we got married in Las Vegas."

Leaning back so that he could see her face, he said, "Except this time will be different. This time when we exchange vows I will know you love me. You will know I love you. That is what his marriage is about—celebrating our love for each other."

The wrinkle on Laurel's brow cleared. "We don't need anyone else there. As far as the world is concerned we're married already. This time is for us alone."

Rakin nodded.

"I feel free. I don't need to worry about what people think." Laurel mouth curved upward. "I loved the romance of our Vegas wedding."

"Then we will be married on the Grand Canal."

"We're going back to Las Vegas?"

Rakin gave her a smug smile. "I thought you might enjoy the real thing this time—a wedding in Venice."

She threw herself into his arms. "Oh, Rakin." Then she sniffed and laughed. "We're going to come back here every summer."

"Whatever you want." Rakin grinned, ready to agree to anything.

"I'm serious."

"So am I." His grin widened.

"You don't look very serious."

"I'm happy."

That got him another—more passionate—kiss. And for a few moments there was silence. When it was over, she said, "I want our child, our children—"

Rakin's eyes blazed. "Good. I'm glad we're in agreement. I do not want only one child."

"Yes!" Laurel knew what was bothering him. He had been an only child. "I want our child to have siblings. And every summer we'll come back here to the beach house. My brothers and sisters and their wives and husbands and children will be welcome, too." As her father had known they would be when he had left her Captain's Watch.

"That will keep you close to your family. But it's not like you'll be separate from them forever. We can jet over to visit them any time you like. And you'll still have your public relations work."

At that she flung her arms back around his neck. She'd half-expected him to demand that she give her work up. Relief filled her that it was a battle she didn't have to fight. "I love what I do."

"I know that."

"And as my wife you will have even more opportunities to gain connections. You may, in time, want to talk to your siblings about outsourcing the PR. That way you could set up your own consultancy, still work for The Kincaid Group, but you'd be able to source other clients as well."

"That's not a bad idea."

"I know," he said smugly. "I'm simply full of good ideas."

Laurel wrinkled her nose at him and laughed.

"I love it when you laugh. You hold nothing back. And you become more beautiful than ever."

"How can I help it? You make me happy."

Relief filled him. He was not his father. His wife would not become a miserable shadow of herself. She loved him...and he loved her.

Their children, too, would be loved.

Epilogue

The doorbell sounded.

Elizabeth Kincaid glanced around at the family who'd already gathered in the salon for pre-dinner drinks. "That should be Laurel and Rakin."

"I'll let them in." Pamela disappeared to open the front door.

When Laurel appeared in the doorway to the salon with her tan, dark husband behind her, Elizabeth immediately saw that her eldest daughter was not the sad character who had visited only a few days ago—she glowed. Rakin's arm was settled possessively around her waist, his lean length complementing her fiery beauty.

After they'd all exchanged hugs and greetings, Laurel announced from the circle of her husband's arms. "We've got news for you all."

Silence fell over the room.

"We're expecting a baby!"

Excitement erupted. Kara squealed. Lily, blossoming from her own pregnancy, was the first to leap to her feet and give Laurel a hug. Susannah wiped away the tears of joy that had sprung to her eyes.

And Brooke rushed to give Laurel a kiss. "RJ and I aren't

having a baby just yet. But this is almost as exciting as bein,
pregnant myself."

Laurel hugged her sister-in-law. "Don't take too long—it wil
be fun for our children to have cousins the same age."

Elizabeth swallowed as Brooke gazed across at RJ. "I don'
think it will be long."

Everyone started talking at once.

His arm around Kara, Eli edged them both forward to stan
beside Laurel. Then he said, "I take it this means I'm forgiven?"

Laurel took his hand in hers, and Elizabeth's heart swelle
at the sight of the gratitude on her eldest daughter's face. "If
hadn't been for you, Rakin would probably never have proposec
so I owe you a thank-you from the bottom of my heart."

Kara retorted, "There's a certain déjà vu feeling about this
I seem to remember my gratitude to you for jilting Eli."

Her middle daughter's forthrightness made Elizabeth gas;
But everyone else laughed. Soon Elizabeth was laughing, too
It brightened her face and she caught a tender look from Cutte

He was her rock. She had a second chance at happiness an
love. The future was already brighter than it had been for a lon
time. If only the questions surrounding Reginald's death coul
be settled, everything would be perfect.

She spared a thought for Angela Sinclair. It couldn't be eas
knowing that the police had your son under suspicion for hi
father's murder. Elizabeth looked around the room at her son
RJ was shaking hands with Rakin. Matt had pulled Flynn ont
his knee and was stroking his son's dark hair while he talked t
Lily and her fiancé Daniel.

She had her family. They were safe and happy. It was Ar
gela's world that was about to turn upside down—

Pamela's voice interrupted her thoughts. "Ten minutes unt
dinner will be served. Flynn, come wash your hands."

Crossing to the bookshelves, Elizabeth drew out a fat leathe
bound family album. Baby pictures. It seemed appropriate give
Laurel's news and Lily's pregnancy. One day, not too far awa
by the sounds of it, Brooke and Matt would join them, too.

Then she crossed to sit on the elegantly carved sofa besid

Cutter. Placing the album on her knees, she gave Cutter a secret little smile. Then she said, "Before Pamela serves dinner, gather around—I want to show you all how beautiful Kincaid babies are."

No one needed second urging, and within minutes she was surrounded by the family she loved.

* * * * *

JOIN US ON SOCIAL MEDIA!

Stay up to date with our latest releases, author news and gossip, special offers and discounts, and all the behind-the-scenes action from Mills & Boon...

 millsandboon

 millsandboonuk

millsandboon

night just be true love...

LET'S TALK

Romance

For exclusive extracts, competitions
and special offers, find us online:

 facebook.com/millsandboon

🐦 @MillsandBoon

📷 @MillsandBoonUK

Get in touch on 01413 063232

For all the latest titles coming soon, visit
millsandboon.co.uk/nextmonth